Praise for *The Dead Lands*

'Part *The Stand*, part *Station 11, The Dead Lands is bro...ling, dark and brilliant'

Ja...   ...rer

'With its fluid integration of ...   ...nd freedoms into a near-future so...   ...with the contemporary zeitgeist, this novel is a reminder that the best speculative fiction speaks to the concerns and issues of its time'

Publishers Weekly

'Written in sharp, jagged prose that's just as strong evoking landscapes as it is tackling the vivid action sequences . . . fascinating, weird and extremely well-written'

SFX

'*The Dead Lands* is an ingenious thriller, relentlessly driven by Benjamin Percy's powerful writing'

Jess Walter, author of *Beautiful Ruin*

'Finely crafted and relentlessly inventive. Percy writes with a strong line, his rhythms incantatory and musical. The book crackles with action and adventure, and his descriptions of the wonders and disasters along the trail are as vivid as any accounts from the Corps of Discovery journals . . . Like the journals, *The Dead Lands* will often take your breath away'

Washington Post

'This post-apocalyptic reimagining of the Lewis and Clark passage is a thrill ride through a nightmare America. *The Dead Lands* is gorgeous and haunting and full of heart, like some wonderful offspring of *The Hobbit, The Road,* and Stephen King's Dark Tower series'

James Frey, author of *Bright Shiny Morning*

ALSO BY BENJAMIN PERCY

Red Moon
The Wilding
Refresh, Refresh
The Language of Elk

THE DEAD LANDS

BENJAMIN PERCY

HODDER

First published in Great Britain in 2015 by Hodder & Stoughton
An Hachette UK company

First published in paperback in 2015

1

A CIP catalogue record for this title is
available from the British Library

ISBN 978 1 444 77005 6

Printed and bound by Clays Ltd, St Ives plc

Hodder & Stoughton policy is to use papers that
are natural, renewable and recyclable products and made from
wood grown in sustainable forests. The logging and manufacturing
processes are expected to conform to the environmental
regulations of the country of origin.

Hodder & Stoughton Ltd
Carmelite House
50 Victoria Embankment
London EC4Y 0DZ

www.hodder.co.uk

For Lisa

PART I

All stories are in conversation with other stories.
—Neil Gaiman

PROLOGUE

S HE KNOWS THERE IS something wrong with the baby. She has known from the very beginning. First there was the nausea that left her bedridden for weeks, dizzy and barely able to eat, chewing on cucumbers, filling up on springwater. Then the surges in temper, the blackening headaches. And finally a stillness inside her when there should have been movement—a fluttering, like the tail of a trout; that's what her friends told her—so that she would twist her body and prod her belly until the child readjusted itself, assuring her it was there, it was alive.

They live in a windowless cabin high in the mountains. Others live not far away, some near a spring-fed stream, others cut back in the woods. Together they form a village of sorts, happily isolated, wary of outsiders and change, fearful of the stories told by their elders, stories of an illness that causes a bloody cough and blistering fevers, stories of missiles raining from the sky and cratering the earth, stories of scavengers with meaty breath and teeth filed into points.

Outside the snow is knee-deep. Before long it will be taller than her husband, taller than the cabin, and every day they will need to shovel a wide passage from their door in case they should be trapped, shrouded.

Sometimes she dreams the child is not a child. It is a grub, fat and white and segmented, with black eyes. It is a beast with tiny yellow fangs and tiny yellow claws, its body covered in fur as sleek as an otter's. Or maybe it is a nothing, a dark spirit, a possessed vapor, and her body the house it haunts.

So she is relieved when she gives the final push and feels a tear, a gush, an emptying—and then the midwife smiles and coos and says, "There now." She cuts the cord with a knife. She carries the child to the table and wipes it clean with a rag.

3

Juliana bunches towels between her legs and watches the child through heavy-lidded eyes. Everything is fine. Everything will turn out all right after all. She is, as her mother always said, a worrier.

Then she notices something. The absence of something. The baby is not crying. The baby has not made a sound. The midwife stands over it, the red rag in her hand like a crushed rose.

"What's the matter? Is it alive? It's alive, isn't it?"

The midwife nods.

"Is it all right?"

The midwife looks at her, looks at the baby, with a mouth that quivers with words she cannot express.

"What is it? A boy?"

"A girl."

"What's wrong?"

Her voice comes out a choked whisper when she says, "Her eyes." She drapes a blanket around the child and hurries to the bed in a rush to be rid of it.

Juliana accepts the child and tears away the wrappings. Her face—splotchy and wrinkled and coned from birth—looks like any baby's face. But her eyes—they are wide open, seemingly lidless, with no whiteness to them, all pupil, no iris, as if splashed full of ink.

The midwife says they will worry about it later. For now the child must eat. The midwife thumbs down the baby's chin and plays its mouth along her nipple, while Juliana massages her breast and brings from it a thick, yellowish bead of colostrum. The baby nods toward the taste but will not latch on. She keeps pulling away to stare at Juliana. It may be a trick of the light—the cabin so dim—but the baby's large eyes appear somehow sorrowful. Juliana struggles to hold the baby's head in place. She does not believe the baby should be strong enough to do so, but she is, arching her back and twisting her head to study Juliana's face.

Robert cannot take the sound of her screams. Or the sight of his wife writhing naked in pain. He tries to help at first, packing snowballs to rub along her wrists and ankles and forehead, but he cannot stop staring at her belly, which seems somehow separate from her, the skin so tight it appears ready to split, almost purple in color, with a white line running down its middle. He thinks he sees shapes in it, what look like hands, a face pressing against the skin, the baby trying to claw or chew its way out.

So he pulls on his boots and doeskin jacket and escapes outside. Snow falls and accumulates on his shoulders when he paces. He is a simple man who pleasures in small things, the song of a nuthatch, the last flare of sunlight on the horizon before night rushes in, the taste of rare lamb and oak-aged whiskey. His wife confuses him. She is a woman of many moods, rarely steady in her feeling, weeping when she says she loves him and draws him into a hug, weeping when she laments him and hurls a dish at the wall. He has learned, when her anger spikes, not to say anything. Not saying anything is the best medicine for their marriage. And making himself scarce. After one of her spells—that's what she calls them, as if they were dark magic—he might chop wood or weed their garden or wander around the bend to his nearest neighbor, Colson, for a game of cards or dice.

He hears another cry from inside—the loudest yet and the worst sound imaginable, like an animal dying, falling from a cliff or rent in half by an ax—and he can only hope that the baby is here, that this is the end.

The snow is thick—and his mind distracted—so he does not look east, where through the falling snow he might notice a faint orange glow, his neighbor's cabin burning. And when he paces, the snow creaks beneath his boots, so he does not hear the hushed passage of the two men clambering up the hill toward him.

They appear as beasts, robed in bearskins, the hollowed heads of which rest atop their own, the snouts like toothed visors that throw a shadow over their faces.

They run a few paces, their boots splashing up snow, and then crouch down. Run and then crouch. In this way they progress up the hillside, threading through trees, trampling icy bushes, plunging over frosted logs. Then they duck down and scuttle close and lift their heads slowly over a lip of snow to observe him pacing and muttering—and then, with a white, sparkling explosion, they rush forward.

At first, they try to wrestle him down, shoving him, trying to kick out his legs, but he puts up enough of a fight that they stop trying and jab a knife into his stomach and then drag it across his neck. They hold him down in the snow until he bleeds out into a red slushy puddle, until his body stops struggling.

———·———

When the door first crashes inward, Juliana is fatigued enough by the labor and distracted enough by the child that she does not scream. She only thinks, How strange, a bear. Hurrying out of the night and into the cabin. Shaggy and caked with snow and thudding across the floorboards.

It pauses near the fire, the snow melting in the heat, steaming off its fur—and only then does she see the bearded man beneath the skins, the light brightening his eyes into orange coals. In one hand he grips a knife. Its metal is bloodied—a red patina with ice crystals flowering from it.

The midwife edges her way along the far wall and tries to dart past him, and he lets her—but just before she reaches the doorway, another bear-suited man steps through and seizes her and drags her into the night, her screams muffled by the snow.

The first man starts toward Juliana. She is naked. She is physically ruined. She is beyond exhausted after eight hours of contractions, two hours of hard labor. But still, she tries to fight him. She nestles the baby into a blanket on the bed, then lurches her body to the edge of the mattress, reaching for the rifle her husband keeps there.

The man dulls her with a fist to the temple. A momentary hush falls over the world, and her vision narrows. She notices the lantern flickering on her night table. She notices a knot, like an eye, peering down from one of the ceiling's crossbeams. She notices the skis and poles hanging from the wall, the wedding afghan her *oma* knitted draped over a rocking chair. Then the world widens and comes crashing into motion again and she realizes she is no longer in her bed. The man is dragging her across the floor, toward the door, his hand a crushing manacle around her wrist.

She cannot walk, though she tries. Her legs stumble and collapse beneath her. Her knees thud the grooves; her feet needle with splinters. Her belly feels carved out by a hot spoon, but the anger boiling inside her gives her strength. She cries out and throws back her body, battling his grip.

He strikes her again, knocking the last bit of willfulness from her body, and then mummies her in a blanket and hefts her over his shoulder.

She does not scream, My baby, though she knows she ought to. She only looks back to the bed, where the child lies in a nest of blankets stained with her blood and embryonic fluid, watching her curiously with eyes as black as the night that soon envelops her.

CHAPTER I

THE WALL IS A constant in Simon's life, everywhere he looks, impossible to miss. Yet it is as common as dust, as heat, as the sun's blazing path across the sky, and it is easy to go days, weeks, without noticing it. It is of uneven height but at its tallest point reaches a hundred feet from the ground. In some places it is made from plaster and mortared stone, and in others, heaps of metal, the many-colored cars of another time, crushed and welded together into massive bricks that bleed rust when it rains.

There are those who guard the wall, who every day climb ropes and rebar ladders to position themselves as sentries upon its flat top, wide enough for ten men to walk abreast. They carry knives at their sides and bows on their backs. They wear wide-rimmed brown hats. Their skin is sunburned and sand scoured and their eyes pale and pocketed from the dark-glassed goggles they wear while staring into the wastes surrounding them. From the ground, they appear specks, no bigger than birds.

There is life inside the wall. There is death outside the wall. That is what they, the citizens of the Sanctuary, have been told over the 150 years since it was erected. Here, in what was once downtown St. Louis, they have laws, elections, currency, farms, wells, markets, a hospital, a prison, even a museum that offers the vestiges of the lost world. But outside—in the Dead Lands—in the sun-washed sandy reaches of the desert, among the dried wigs of sagebrush, the pines that twist upward like tormented souls, the sunken grocery stores and corroded gas pumps and crumbling weed-choked subdivisions, there are nightmares. And now someone is on the way to face the nightmares alone.

He can hear the drumbeats of the death parade echoing through the Sanctuary. A few minutes ago the sun sank below the wall.

Twilight is approaching, the end of the day and the end of a life, the traditional time for the police to escort their worst offenders to the execution site—through the gates, beyond the wall, to the altar.

Shadows drape the streets, but the last light still flames the tops of the highest buildings. The Dome—the home of the mayor, once the capitol building—glows like a half-moon against the paling sky.

Simon hurries to the gates. Not because he cares who has been sentenced to die, and not because he wants to witness the spectacle of the parade, but because others do. The roads and pathways there will be full of people. Distracted people. Distracted people who won't notice a hand slipping into their purse or pocket.

He crosses a wooden bridge that spans a sewage canal. He zigzags through a garden of agave, its serrated leaves biting at his ankles. Sotol and prickly pear and date palms and even a few gnarled cherry trees. He pauses briefly to pluck a handful of fruit and pop them into his mouth before starting on his way again. The cherries are shrunken and bitter and he sucks on them while darting down an alley busy with trash and rats and lean-tos and a VW minibus that has been converted to a shelter. This leads him to the central avenue, a wide, cobblestoned thoroughfare jammed with people. Some wear burlap and cotton and wool stitched from fresh materials. Some wear the leftovers of the world before—hoodies, jerseys, jeans, sneakers, boots—decayed polyester and threadbare denim patched with leather or plastic squares. Some paint their lips and their eyelids. Some wear necklaces that rattle with teeth and keys and bottle caps. Many are deformed, with shrunken arms or six-fingered hands or ears that look like babies' fists or slitted noses or blind white eyes. Many are tumored and blotched with burns and cancers from the sun. Many of the men have beards and many of the women long braids with feathers nested in them. Aside from the occasional bright flare of orange or red or yellow, most of what they wear is the color of stone and sand, shades of gray and brown. They all wear hats. And all of their mouths are raw and chapped from lack of water.

Simon spits out the cherries' stones and joins them. He is short and slender for his age, so he is able to slip through the crush of bodies. He is good at this, sneaking his way through things—his body through buildings, his hands into pockets and drawers. His mousy hair and narrow face make him unnoticeable, forgettable, which suits him perfectly.

A jingle cart rolls by, dragged by a man with a mossy beard that reaches his waist. Dust rises in a cloud behind him, the dust that is everywhere. The cart—a welded collection of rusted license plates anchored to two different-size wheels—is covered with tiny bells that chime at every rut in the road. The man calls out his wares, medicines and candies, medicines and candies. No one pays him any attention. All eyes are on the procession worming its way down the avenue.

The deputies are dressed in black—broad-rimmed black hats, black shirts with a star on the breast tucked into black jeans tucked into black boots with sharp silver tips—their standard uniform. They wear holsters—for machetes, not for guns, since all firearms were long ago outlawed in the Sanctuary.

The first man carries a drum, a yellow hide stretched across a broad round frame. A skull is painted across its face and he slams a mallet against it. He walks in rhythm to the beat, every other step intoned by a deep, hollow bong. He is followed by two women with torches, the smoke trailing behind them, threading together in a black cloud that hangs over their prisoner. He is obscured by the smoke and by the crowd. He hunches over, his hair masking his face, his wrists and ankles bound by chains that rattle with his every trudging step. He is followed by two more deputies, who shove him along whenever he slows.

This is early summer. The day was as hot as an oven and twilight has brought little relief. Simon tries to breathe through his mouth. The odor of so many unwashed bodies unsettles his stomach. He jostles, trips, tickles, blows in an ear, making people move, and when they move, he takes advantage of their momentum and distraction and filches coins from pockets. Everyone's clothes are coated with dust, so that when they move little puffs rise off them. A girl watches him sneak a loose ring off a woman's pinky. She is clutching a naked plastic doll with no eyes and half a head of hair. He smiles at her and brings a finger to his lips and she smiles back and hides behind her father's leg.

Everyone peers over each other's shoulders, trying to glimpse the prisoner. The drum sounds—again and again—and over its tolling a voice calls out loudly for them to move aside, move along. The crowd does as the man says, separating and then converging around the deputies once they pass by.

The voice belongs to Rickett Slade, their sheriff. He wears the same uniform as his officers. He is a massive man, thickset, with broad shoulders, a head like a pocked boulder, and hands the size and texture of rough pine planks. His eyes are too close together and lost beneath baggy folds of flesh. What little hair he has ringing his head is as pale and downy as corn silk. "Make way," he says. "Make way for the dead man who walks."

Simon slips a bracelet off a wrist, unclasps a necklace, some made of gold, some made of plastic, all worth something, even if only a trade at the bazaar, a brick of cheese, a loaf of bread. His pockets are nearly full and he has pushed his way to the front of the crowd when he looks up and sees the prisoner, really notices him for the first time. The jowly cheeks. The nose and cheeks brightly filamented with capillaries. The same mousy brown hair as his own. It is a face he recognizes. It is a face others in the crowd recognize, several of them whispering his name, Samuel.

His father.

Simon is familiar with death. It is impossible not to be in the Sanctuary. He has witnessed the lashings at the whipping posts. He has dodged the knives that flash in the streets and bars. He has seen his pale-skinned, rib-slatted mother laid out on a slab of stone with her breasts scarred over, both removed, though not in time to stop the tumors bulging like toads from the glands beneath her neck. But that doesn't stop him from feeling a dagger jab of dread. His father is being marched to his death.

His father is a drunk, and when he is drunk he makes loud pronouncements about everything from the unfairness of the rations to the foolishness of their new mayor. He often spirals into dark moods that round his hands into fists, sharpen his words into blades. For this reason, the two of them haven't spoken much over the past year, ever since Simon took to the streets.

There was a time when they used to get along—when his father would wrestle with him or tell scary stories or play Billy Joel and Beatles songs on his guitar, when they would work together on the small garden that grew in their windowsill boxes. That was before Simon's mother died, before his father tried to purify his grief with gallons and gallons of tequila. On more than one occasion, after getting slapped across the face, knocked to the ground, or shoved in a closet, Simon wished him dead. Now the wish will come true and he wishes he could take it back.

Beyond the wall, hairless sand wolves roam with eyes as yellow as candle flame. There are giant spiders, with trapdoors netted over and dusted with sand. Snakes longer and wider than any man's arm, with fangs that can pierce leather. Big cats with claws that can shred metal like paper. Some say the flu—the cough and fever that brought about the ruin of the world—still hides in the throats of caves, in the closets of old buildings, riding the breeze like the spores of some black flower that will take root in your lungs, though most believe it perished alongside everything else.

A ranger once told Simon about a dead deer, found in the outlying forest, that looked as though it had been peeled open and turned inside out. The same fate he met a few weeks later, his head torn off and his belly emptied and his limbs gnashed down to bones. Beyond the wall, wildness took over, things with big claws and sacs of poison lay in wait. This—Simon can hear in the voices that tremble with fear and sadistic anticipation—is what awaits his father.

People begin to cry out and pull back, mobbing away from the gates, knowing they'll soon open, afraid of what might come hurrying out of the twilight. The sharp, reedy call of a bone whistle precedes the steel arm being lifted from its hangers. The double doors—made from logs reinforced with metal—are heaved open and the deputies continue into the gloom. They will take his father to the altar in the woods, a stone platform to which he will be chained.

Some people linger with ghoulish fascination, while others disperse, off to pursue whatever business remains for them this evening. The farmers in the stables milking heifers, butchering pigs. The tailors shearing sheep and spinning wool into yarn or treating the hides of animals with chemicals that bleach their hands a cancerous yellow. The tattooists inking designs onto arms and necks and faces. The whores spreading their legs on flea-specked mattresses. The bartenders filling tumblers full of eye-watering, throat-burning liquor. The jingle carts and pharmacists hawking snake poison and medicinal jellies and pills for coughs, kidney stones, genital infections. The vendors in the old warehouse selling clothes, pottery, tools, fruit, charred meat on a stick, whatever scraps the rangers bring back from their excursions beyond the wall: cracked and faded Happy Meal toys, dented espresso machines, football helmets with rotted-out padding, shattered tablets, laptops with sand spilling out of their keyboards. They are eager to return to normalcy—opening a window, tying a shoe—while his father will be torn to pieces.

Simon remains fixed in place. His eyes are on the wall. As if it has betrayed him. Betrayed his father. There are those whose jobs concern mending and fortifying the wall. That was his father's trade. His arms were crosshatched with cuts and his hands colored with bruises and caked with cement. He broke his leg once, after a fall from the upper reaches of the wall, and he healed oddly so that he seemed to drag himself about more than walk. And now the man who spent his life repairing and making fast the thing that holds the danger outside is now the man thrust from its safety.

The bird perches on the wall. It observes the prisoner hauled away, the crowd scattering, and then, with a creaking snap of its wings, it takes flight. It appears to be an owl, though not like any other in the world, made of metal and only a little larger than a man's fist.

Torches flare up all around the Sanctuary to fight the intruding night, and the owl's bronze feathers catch the light brightly when it flies from the wall, then over the gardens, the stables, the ropes of smoke that rise from chimneys and forges and ovens, the twisting streets busy with carts and dogs and bodies that stumble out of doorways. The wind blows cinders and dried bits of grass up into dust devils, and the owl blasts through them.

The skyscrapers and high-rises needle upward from the center of the Sanctuary—Old Town, they call it—and the mechanical owl darts between the canyons of them now. Some of them still have windows, but most are open-air, so that they appear like a vast and rotting honeycomb inside which people crouch like brown grubs.

The owl's wings whirr. Gears snap and tick beneath its breast. Within its glass eyes, an aperture contracts or expands depending on whether the owl casts its gaze at light or shadow.

The remains of downtown St. Louis have been built over and repurposed to the degree that someone who stepped across the centuries would not recognize one for the other, everything sunken and leaning and crumbling and patched together in a way that appears accidental, the city covered with a dusty skin and seeming in this way and many others a dying thing, its windows and archways hollowed eyes, its streets curving yellowed arteries, its buildings haggard bones, with its footsteps and hammer strokes and slammed doors like the beating of an arrhythmic heart and the many swarming bodies like black mites feeding on whatever might be scrapped, salvaged.

Turbines spike the tops of many buildings. They are made from rescued metal and they creak and groan and spin rustily in the wind that never stops blowing. They feed into unreliable wiring that snakes through some of the buildings so that lights sputter on and off and empty sockets burn red and sometimes flare into fires. And the lives of the people here are energized in a similar manner—frayed and sizzling, capable at any given moment of burning out.

The signs are still there—Supercuts, Subway, McDonald's, Curves, Chili's, Chipotle, LensCrafters—though they are hard to spot, their colored plastic fractured and lichen spotted and dulled to the yellowy shade of an old man's teeth.

What was once a sandwich shop is now a blacksmith and welding studio. From its doorway steps a man who holds a clamp that grips a red-hot square of metal—maybe a door hinge or hoe blade—and he dunks it into a bucket of horse piss and follows the steam trailing upward and through it sees the owl blur overhead like a comet.

What was once a salon is now a dentist's office. In the corner a dryer chair sits like a dead astronaut. The studs grimace through the places where the drywall has rotted away. Near the open window, a dentist peers into a mouth of butter-colored teeth, one of them black, and, just when he secures it with his pliers, the owl flashes past his shop and he startles backward with the tooth uprooted and his patient screaming in his chair.

On a balcony an old woman lounges in a threadbare lawn chair that nearly sinks her bottom to the ground. She wears stockings that are wrinkled at the knees and rotted through to reveal her bony ankles. Her feet are stuffed into an ancient pair of laceless Nikes, the soles as hard as concrete. She drinks foul tea from a dented thermos. Above her hangs a wind chime of old cell phones that clatter in the breeze. When the owl buzzes by her, she shrieks and the thermos falls thirty feet before clanging and splattering the street below.

She knows whom the owl belongs to. They all do. And they fear it as they fear him.

The museum—once city hall—is one of the grandest buildings in the Sanctuary, six stories high, with a vaulted red-slate roof and marble floors and walls made of sandstone. It has the dark-windowed, stained-stone grandeur of a haunted mansion. Swallows squawk and scatter where they appear as scratches against the purple-black expanse of sky. The owl skitters to a stop on one of the upper windowsills. It approaches the glass pane and taps its beak.

In the street below, a few people pause to point at and whisper about the owl. "Magic," some say. "Freak," others say.

———•———

A richly patterned threadbare rug covers the floor. The walls are hidden behind bookshelves weighed down with leather tomes and yellowed maps carrying the geographies of unexplored worlds and an ancient US flag that bears seventeen stars, its red stripes faded to brown, its blues to black. The ceiling is angled with exposed timbers. Despite the heat of the day, a log flames in the fireplace, flanked by two stone horses made from onyx. The man seated at the desk is always cold. He wears an oversize gray wool cardigan. His hand now gathers the fabric tighter around his neck.

This is Lewis Meriwether, the curator. He is clean-shaven, unlike so many men, his milk-pale skin offset by the black hair sprouting stiffly from his head. He looks older than his thirty-three years, his posture slouched from all his time at his desk, his face long, with flattened cheekbones and a nose as sharp as the quill he keeps next to his inkpot. His eyes are blue but red rimmed. They bulge from all his time spent reading. He has been here all day and was here all of last night. He rarely sleeps, prefers night to day. The sun gives him headaches and burns his fair skin and drags all the people from their beds. He has never been fond of people. And they have never been fond of him. They whisper about him when they pass through the museum, startle from him when he makes a rare appearance, the wizard in the tower, the hermit in the cave.

Lanterns are lit throughout the room. The logs smolder in the fireplace like dying suns. His desk is a lacquered red, its sides and legs carved into so many dragons twisting into each other. A map is unrolled before him, weighed down with a teacup, a yellow agate, a chipped plate carrying a black heel of bread, a candle burned down to a blistered nub. Every now and then he stirs a spoon through a bowl of cold corn mash. Otherwise he studies the map with a bone-handled magnifying glass that roams a ring of light across the brittle, yellowed paper. Here are snowcapped mountains, lush forests, rivers as thick and blue as a lizard's tongue—a landscape alien to the one he knows, what lies beyond the wall. His whole life he has spent dreaming of distant worlds. They call to him. And though he might imagine himself elsewhere, he feels safest and most comfortable here, at his desk, a voyeur.

His focus is so deep that he does not hear the owl tapping repeatedly at the glass. Nor does he hear the door open, the footsteps thudding across the floor. They belong to a muscular girl with short hair, square bangs. This is Ella, his aide. At the edge of his desk she stacks a tall armful of papers, brittle and torn and tied with twine, mismatched in size and font, some the computer printouts of another time, others the remains of books that have lost their binding. When Lewis does not address her, she says, "What you asked for. From the archives."

He lifts a hand to acknowledge or dismiss her.

She makes no move to leave. Her mouth tightens into a bud.

He sighs through his nose and sets down the magnifying glass with a click and looks at her with his eyebrows raised in a question he doesn't bother asking.

"My hands are paper cut. And blistered from the lantern I've been carrying." She holds them up as evidence. "It took two hours to find what you wanted. I've been gone *two hours*. For two hours' worth of work, you'd think I deserved a thank-you. Wouldn't you think that?"

His fingers are as long as knitting needles. They lift the magnifying glass again, but before he peers through it, his eyes settle on the window, where the owl waits. "You may leave now." He spits out his words like chips of ice.

She nods at his plate, his bowl. "You haven't eaten."

"I said you may leave. Now. Thank you."

When the door clicks closed behind her, he rises from his desk and approaches the window. He lifts the latch and holds out his arm for the owl to climb upon. He can hear the ticking of its cogged wheels, the creaking twist of its knobs and gears, beneath which he detects a grinding that might be dust, the dust that creeps into everything. Later, he will have to unscrew the owl, brush it out, wipe clean and oil its guts.

But first he draws the curtains. The room falls into deeper shadow. He holds up his arm, as if to send the owl into flight. Instead it goes rigid. Something clicks and snaps inside it. Its eyes glow, circles of light. A milky projection spills quaveringly across the wall. Without expression he studies the march of the death parade, the crowd of people surrounding it, until the owl's eyes dim and the projection sputters off and leaves him in darkness.

———

Simon hates what his father has become, but he doesn't hate him. They share good memories. They share a complicated love. They share the same blood. And this is what compels him to do what he does next.

He brags that he knows his way around any door and into any room in the Sanctuary. Their new mayor talks often about how everyone needs to do their part, now more than ever, contribute to the common good, specialize in a trade, and Simon likes to think that this is his role: he is a thief, the very best of thieves. Light-fingered and considerate. He doesn't hurt anyone, not like some brute in an alleyway. And he never leaves behind a mess—splintering a door, upending a drawer—never takes more than needs to be taken, redistributing wealth.

But what he never brags about—what he never tells anyone—is

that not only can he sneak his way into any corner of the Sanctuary; he can also sneak out.

His father is the one who told him about the sewers, the many tunnels that run beneath the ground, all of the entries cemented over. For safety, it was said. So that nothing could get in. "And so that no one, not a one of us, can get out of this reeking pit," his father said. He was always saying things like this, calling the Sanctuary a prison, the politicians its wardens.

It was in the museum that Simon found the passage. He liked to go there sometimes—after hours, when no one could follow him around and yell at him for getting too close, for touching the artwork and artifacts. He liked to touch. But he never stole from the one place that belonged to everyone. Late at night he would crawl through a window and wander the many long, high-ceilinged rooms and put his face right up to the paintings, run his fingers along the brushstrokes. He would duck under the ropes to an exhibit—petting the scaled spine of an alligator, clacking his fingers across the keyboard of a dead-eyed computer, climbing into the Toyota on display to twist its many knobs and wrap his hands around the steering wheel. One time he fell asleep inside a covered wagon exhibit.

People said Lewis—the thin, strange man Simon saw sometimes at a distance—kept company with the devil. They said he studied black magic. They said he knew everything that ever happened and would happen. They said nothing escaped his notice in the Sanctuary. The owl was one of many spies, the rats and bats and cockroaches also in his service. Simon did not believe them enough to stay away from the museum, but he believed them enough to stay away from his quarters on the upper level. He looked often over his shoulder and one time startled at the sight of a lantern floating down the staircase, a figure descending and speaking softly, maybe talking to himself or maybe uttering some incantation.

Simon ran then, bolted down to the basement, a vast storage area filled with wooden boxes, draped paintings, dust-cloaked specimens. He hid there for hours. A faint dripping caught his attention and he found in the floor a grate—and beyond the grate, a metal ladder that descended into darkness.

It was several weeks before he gained the courage to return and wander the tunnels below—and several weeks more before he discovered another grate with moonlight coursing through it. He climbed up to find himself outside the Sanctuary, along some ruined street where houses and storefronts had collapsed upon themselves and trees rose through blisters in the asphalt. He outsourced his thieving then. As if he was a ranger. From buildings and cars he pirated metals, plastics, leathers, to then pawn to vendors at the bazaar. If anyone ever asked where he came upon such a thing— a toaster, a phone, a trumpet, DVDs, a plastic tote full of eyeliner and brick-hard foundation, things that often had no value outside of curiosity—he would say he found it. That's all. He found it.

Just as he now finds his father. Chained and kneeling at the altar. Simon has been here before, what he believes to be some sort of town square, the altar at its center once a fountain, with the crumbled faces of children as spouts. The stone is painted with the blood of those chained here before his father.

At first Simon thinks it is too late. His father's skin appears gray and waxen in the moonlight. His head hangs low. Then Simon sees his chest rise and fall, hears a wheeze. He is sleeping or weeping. Weeping, Simon discovers when he climbs the altar and his father raises his head and widens his damp eyes and says, "Simon? No. No. What are you doing?"

"What does it look like? I'm here to save you."

"You shouldn't. You can't." There is no venom in his voice, none of the nastiness that made Simon leave him, just exhaustion, sadness, worry.

His father continues to protest as Simon examines his wrists, assessing the locks that hold him in place so tightly that his fingers are cold and lifeless. Simon keeps a thin knife with a hooked tip at his belt. He uses it now to pick at one of the keyholes at his father's wrist, prodding and twisting, feeling for the lever, listening for the click. He is well practiced at this, but it still takes a long three minutes before the one hand, his right hand, falls free.

His father's wrist is bloodied and he cries out briefly at the cramps wracking him. Then he throws an arm around his son. Simon struggles against him, but his father has always been a big man and has put on even more weight from his drinking. Simon heaves but his father clings to him—not fighting him, the boy comes to realize, but hugging him.

"Dad! Quit it. There's no time for this."

"Shh. It's too late, son."

"What do you mean?"

"Can't you hear?" Both their bodies still for a moment. Then his father leans in, his mouth at Simon's ear, so that the whisper sounds like a shout, "Do you hear it?"

Simon listens. The adrenaline coursing through him creates a barely traceable hum at the edge of his hearing. At first that is the only sound. He studies the black buildings and the black trees and the blacker shadows between them. The wind rises and falls, as if the night is breathing. The branches murmur. Then comes a snap, a stick underfoot. Gravel crunches.

Something is coming. No, not one thing, but many, he realizes, as more sounds crackle and whisper and thud out in the darkness. Simon brings the knife to his father's other wrist and hurriedly stabs at the lock.

His father knocks away the knife. "You need to go," he says—and then, "Please, son." The desperate kindness in his voice is impossible to ignore. "Please. *Go*. Now."

Simon wants to stay. He wants to fight. But his father pushes him and he stumbles away from the altar just as something humpbacked and four legged creeps into the square. The moon has sunk from sight, the night now lit by stars alone, and he cannot make out anything more than that: a hunched darkness, as if the night has congealed into a figure.

"Go!" his father says, and Simon finally listens, hurrying away as a second and then third creature join the first.

"Here I am!" his father is yelling. "Over here!" Rattling the chains and whooping, making as much noise as possible to distract from Simon's escape.

The yelling soon gives way to screaming. Simon runs. He cannot stop the tears that make the spaces between stars blur and the sky appear to gloss over with a phantasm.

CHAPTER 2

THIS MORNING, as the sun rises and reddens the world so that it appears it might catch flame, Clark stands at her sentry post atop the wall. Around it reaches a burn zone of some seventy yards. Beyond this grows a forest with many broken buildings rising from it, black-windowed, leaning messes of skeletal steel and shattered stone. The remains of the St. Louis Arch, collapsed in the middle, appear like a ragged set of mandibles rising out of the earth. In the near distance, where once the Mississippi flowed, stretches a blond wash of sand.

Somewhere out there, hidden from view, hide yammering sand wolves, cat-size spiders, droves of javelinas with tusks longer than her fingers. These are the dangers that find those chained to the altar. Twenty minutes ago, the deputies departed the Sanctuary—and they return now with a stretcher bearing the body of a man. The man from last night's death parade. His face is unrecognizable, hidden beneath a seething mask of flies. His body is shredded or chewed to bone in most places. His belly is split open and his entrails dangle from him like red ropes.

For as long as she can remember, this has been the punishment doled out to those who committed rape or murder. But now they have a new mayor. And with a new mayor come new policies. He has made it treason to complain about the rations, to so much as speak ill of his administration. He wants them to know his ears are always listening, his eyes always watching. Now this body, this so-called traitor, will be paraded through the streets, an example for everyone. These are difficult times, with their water running dry, and difficult times call for unforgiving measures. Everyone has a job, the mayor says. That job is to serve the Sanctuary. They are all part of the same organism, and if anyone does anything to threaten

24

it, they will be excised like the melanomas that stain the skin of so many.

The gates open and close behind the deputies. Clark walks to the edge of the wall and balances precipitously there. She imagines what it would feel like to slip, to fall, the wind roaring in her ears, the ground rushing toward her face. Join the fate of the man. He, after all, believed what she believes. He said aloud the same things she keeps caged inside her. For her to call this place home—to feel not sheltered but imprisoned—and do nothing? It's too much.

That's why last night, after the death parade, she drank herself into oblivion. She tried to hurry past the bar. Then she heard the laughter spilling out of it, and she paused in the wedge of lamplight that fell from its doorway into the street. She could see, through the rib-cage doors, beyond the swell of bodies, a man onstage plucking a guitar and stomping his foot and singing "Paint It Black"—and she gave in to the excuse that she would stop in for *one* good song, *one* strong drink. She had promised she wouldn't, but her mood was foul and the night was hot and she was so thirsty.

Her name is Wilhelmina, a family name, a name she despises, a weak, perfumed, lacy thing she can tolerate only if shortened to Mina. But mostly she goes by her last name, Clark. Depending on the light, her hair appears red or blond, same as the sand. With a knotted strip of leather she keeps it tied back into a short tail. Her face is hawkish, her eyes always narrowed and her mouth always tightened as if tied at the corners by knots.

Though the bars serve other liquor—gin, vodka, whatever else is in the well, some hooch that goes down like snake venom—people drink mostly whiskey and mescal and sotol and tequila, and that was what she was drinking last night, tequila. The liquor was distilled in better times, when water ran more freely, aged now to potency and costing too much coin. The floor was wood shavings, the stools were old tires, and the ceiling scrap metal welded carelessly so that through its many holes she could see the stars spinning above like the ringworms in her glass.

People hurled feathered darts. They huddled together in card games with mismatched decks. They played pool with leather-tipped steel rods and rocks ground and polished into balls. The warmth of the liquor raced to her fingertips, pulsed at her temples, and before long she was burning inside like the cigarillo pinched between her lips, burning like the candle she held her elbow over too long on a bet, burning like the pain in her hand when she broke the nose of the bartender who asked her to leave, told her she had had enough.

She had had enough all right. This morning she can feel her heartbeat in her forehead, like a door slammed over and over again. She wears a wide-rimmed hat and shaded goggles, but still the sun seems too bright when she stares off into the ruined wilderness that reaches to the horizon, where sometimes she believes mountains are visible, though no one else will say so. They claim she is seeing what she wants to see. They claim it is a mirage, a trembling image brought on by the heat, like some hellish counterpart to her wall, spiny and manned by the spirits of dead giants.

She takes a pull of her canteen to try to fight the cottonmouth, but her body barely lets her swallow. The wind gusts. It sighs. It whistles through the many hollows of the wall in which swallows and wasps nest. It carries sand in it that stings skin and eats holes in cloth and dulls the edge of a blade. It nearly knocks her from the edge, and she wobbles back onto the landing.

The Sanctuary reaches across a mile in some places, a half mile in others. The wall is not a circle or a square—it is shapeless, an improvisation that became a permanent corral. She is a sentinel. She rotates in her duties, either scavenging outside the wall as a ranger or patrolling its perimeter on sentry. Every sentry is assigned a two-hundred-yard section of the wall marked by iron braziers filled with wood with torches lit beside them. If any threat emerges from the forest, whether man or beast, they are to hurl the torch upon the brazier as a flaming alarm.

Her uniform is not the night black of the deputies, but gray and brown, as though mended from stone and wood. Her job is to stare out at a fractal landscape of umber and dust and ruins, guarding against whatever awaits them in the Dead Lands. She does not answer to the sheriff. She does not serve as an enforcer. She does not hurt others, only protects. But still, her job feels like a betrayal of conscience, since she patrols the very wall she believes they need to escape, no matter the risk. Better to seek out life than wait for death in this dried-out fishbowl. She used to loudly debate this with others at the bars; these days, sharing such an opinion will only get her killed. But she is right. She knows she is right.

There were eight wells in the Sanctuary, all of them broad-mouthed pipes with metal ladders built down their throats. Three of them have collapsed, their casing pinched off and deemed impossible to repair due to some shifting beneath the earth. Another has gone dry. The remaining four are guarded by deputies who regulate the long lines, the people who come dragging jugs for their daily ration. A wind turbine lifts the water and shoots it from a spigot. The motor sits directly over the well, grinding away and dusting the water with rust and turning the impellers that reach deep into the aquifer beneath them.

The water used to come in a minerally gush. These days the spigots dribble and sputter. The mayor says he is meeting with workmen who might worm their way down and extend the pipes, dig deeper, find the cold, good water that must be waiting to be tapped beneath their feet.

People are worried. Buckets and barrels and leather bags hang from every corner of the city to capture any rainwater—and a network of canals funnel water and sewage to their meager crops—but the clouds have not gathered and burst in more than three months, the standard of the past few years, the stretches between downpours longer and longer. People boil their urine for drinking water. They sleep below tarps that gather moisture from their breathing and channel it into a pot. They ration out the stores they keep in buckets and barrels. They drink the blood of bats and rats and birds. This is not a sustainable existence—the Sanctuary slowly knuckling in on itself like a dried date.

Below, Clark can hear the sentinels gathering into a ranging party. The stamping and snorting of horses, the creaking of leather, the clinking of spurs, the shifting of arrows in their quivers.

The sun rises high enough to crest the wall, and in a rush last night's shadows retreat and the windows flash and the canals brighten into many diamond points. The sun, the cruel orange eye that cooks the sweat from their skin and the water from the ground and the clouds from the sky. The temperature in the Sanctuary immediately spikes fifteen degrees. The space beneath the gates, though, remains a pocket of shadow, and it is here that the riders gather.

The bone whistle sounds, the gates groan open, and the rangers ride out two horses abreast. They all wear hats to battle the sun and neckerchiefs to battle the dust. At their lead is Reed, the chief of the sentinels. Even from here she can see the long black braid twisting down his back like a shorn noose. She wills him to turn in his saddle and look for her, but he does not. She imagines she can feel his disappointment radiating off him. Earlier, when she stumbled out of her quarters and reported to the stables, he took her face in his hands and shook his head and told her to climb the wall. She was in no shape to ride, still drunk from the night before.

A great wing of dust rises behind them—and the wind carries it toward her, the grit pattering her clothes, biting her face when she watches them depart. It will be another week, she's guessing, before he allows her to rotate back from sentry to ranger. He disapproves of her drinking not only because of the hazard to her body, the interference with her duties, but because he cannot risk her speaking loosely to others. The risk is too great—given their plans. She doesn't know when they will leave, where they will go, or how they will get there, but she will not die here. She will escape.

She understands why Reed punishes her, but she hates him for it. Because she hates the wall. She prefers to move, to escape. Ride at a gallop with the reins wrapped around her fist and the wind knocking her hair. Fire a whistling arrow into a buck's breast. Collect jackrabbits and coyotes from her many traps. Fill satchels with juniper berries for the distilleries. Salvage steel and copper from buildings as dark as tombs. Kick through the skeletons that lie everywhere and rip the drawers out of dressers, pull open cabinets, upend toolboxes, dig through closets. By comparison the wall is stillness...the wall is control...the wall is imprisonment—that she finds maddening.

There is much she finds maddening. As a child she bit her grandfather when he wouldn't give her another one of the salted nuts they ate for dessert. After being teased and tripped by a group of boys, she picked up a fist-sized stone and knocked the teeth from one of them. She kicked the leg of a table and sent supper crashing to the floor. She dropped a beetle in her baby brother York's mouth when, as an infant, he wouldn't stop crying. Not much has changed. Her whole life she has been told this is her greatest weakness, her inability to control herself. She tries. But whenever she is provoked, like a bees' nest disturbed, something swarms out of her, something out of her control, making her capable of anything. Of escaping this place.

An hour later she remains so deadened by her hangover, so caught up in her thoughts, she does not notice the panicked voices or the smoke billowing from a torchlit brazier until it has risen so high that it occludes the sun.

People wear hoods or hats with squared tops and crisp round rims, but Lewis has never paid any attention to what might be fashionable. His keeps the sun out of his eyes—that's all that matters. Its rim is floppy and its peak high and its color a speckled gray. He wears a long duster of the same color. Its many pockets hold many things. It billows around him and makes him appear like a wraith.

People make way for him and turn to watch him in his passing. He knows their nicknames for him: the gray man, the freak, the magician. He hears them whispering now, just as he hears them whispering in the museum. They say he once turned a crying baby into a croaking toad. They say his heart is made of cogs and wheels and his veins run black with oil, the same as his mechanical owl. They say he creeps around the Sanctuary at night, crawling through windows and approaching bedsides and experimenting on people when they are sleeping, dosing them up with potions, cutting them open and sewing them back up with invisible thread. Sometimes parents say, to naughty children, you better be good or the gray man will steal you away and stuff you full of sawdust and make you into an exhibit in his museum.

He walks among them now, and they startle away from his figure. "Look," they say. "There he is." Horses snort. Carts rattle. Men shout. Forges glow. Swallows twitter. Meat sizzles over cooking stoves. Dust flurries like snow. He shades his eyes with his hand and looks up only briefly at the smoke rising from the wall. A black cloud of it roils, as threatening as a thunderhead, backlit by the sun.

Then he pulls his hat brim low, his gaze once again downcast as he approaches a narrow concrete building tucked into a street of narrow concrete buildings. The sign over the door reads YIN'S DRY CLEANING, but it has been splashed with black paint and a hand-carved wooden sign next to it reads APOTHECARY.

Apothecaries, tinkers, blacksmiths, seers. Old words, old ways. So much about the world has reverted, so that it is not so much the future people once imagined, but a history that already happened, this time like a time long ago. Lewis read a story once about the birth of a baby who looked like an old man, with silver hair and wrinkled skin and eyes fogged by cataracts. As the years passed, his appearance grew younger, and by the end of his life he was a drooling infant barely able to care for himself. In this way Lewis sometimes feels they have as a society cycled back without the hope of moving forward again.

A bell jangles when he walks inside. The shop is dimly lit with candles and the linoleum floor has been worn down to pitted concrete. The man behind the counter has skin as brown as bark. His shoulders are thin and bony and from them rise a head topped by a thinning crown of gray woolly hair. This is Oman. He does not fear Lewis, not like the others. They deal with each other regularly and have developed not a rapport, but a comfortable business relationship. Behind Oman rises a wall full of cubbies and shelving units. A snake is curled up in a jar full of foggy green liquid. In another bottle float black eggs. In another, hairless mice. There are hundreds of baskets, brightly colored vials, bottles. Spiders spin webs in glass cages. Herbs hang from the ceiling like roots from the roof of a cave.

Oman has the habit of chewing the leaves of a smoke bush. They have stained his teeth a tarry black. "How is she?" he asks.

"She is the same."

The counter is made of Formica curled up at the edges. Oman sets a mortar and pestle upon it and grinds up a combination of herbs. Then he removes a blue bottle from a shelf and takes a dropper to it and squirts out several ounces of the medicine and stirs the herbs into a paste that he stores in a small yellow vial once meant for pills, the remains of some prescription still smeared across it.

"And how are you?"

If Lewis was the type to share, the type who offloaded all his aches and worries and displeasures onto others, then he might complain about the dreams that bother him nightly. In them he sees a man. An old man. His veins are as stiff and pronounced as roots. He is so ancient he cannot walk without the help of a cane made from a twisted length of wood, cannot eat unless his food has been mashed up. His face is never clear, always blurred or hidden by the long white hair that rings his bald, spotted head. Sometimes he sees the man waiting by a window. Sometimes he sees the man sitting in a library. Last night, the man stood by a river, all his attention focused on an eddy, the sort of deep black pool where a fat fish might surface. Lewis feared the man might fall when he waded into the water up to his knees. With his cane he stirred the eddy until a whirlpool formed. In the dark funnel the man saw a familiar face and whispered a name, *Lewisssss*.

But he says nothing to Oman. He only takes the vial on the

counter and secrets it up his sleeve—then in its place sets a square silver canister.

"More?"

"Yes."

"You look tired."

"Double the order for this week." He clatters out a pile of coins, nickels worn down to silver discs that bear the faintest ghost of Jefferson's profile. Pennies, nickels, dimes, quarters, the occasional half or silver dollar, all smoothed like stones in a river. This is their currency.

"Double it?" Oman collects the coins and pulls down a wide-mouthed bottle full of white powder. He pulls off the lid and scoops four generous spoonfuls into the silver canister. "You are tired."

"Not tired enough. Do you have anything for sleep?"

"I've some opiates that—"

"No. No dreams. No hallucinations. I just want to put my head down and for there to be nothing."

"Of course."

Lewis keeps one of his fingernails long, his pinky. He digs it into the pile of powder and lifts it to his nose. Snorts. A shudder goes through his body. His eyes tremble closed—then snap open a second later when the door jangles and a blade of sunlight falls across the floor.

A woman with a shaved head and black uniform clomps into the shop. A deputy. She has heavy-lidded eyes and a nose with a raised worm of a scar at its bridge. "Lewis Meriwether," she says.

Lewis sniffs, wipes his nostril clean with a knuckle. "What?"

"The mayor wishes to see you."

Lewis stares at her for a long few seconds. "But I do not wish to see the mayor."

She hesitates, takes a step back. "He said you'd say that."

"Tell him I haven't made any progress."

"He said you'd say that, too."

"Good. Then we're both clear."

"I'm afraid." She swallows hard. "I'm afraid that's not possible."

I'm afraid, she says. Yes, she is. She is afraid. Lewis can tell from the muscles bulging in her jaw, the twitching of her eyes. She is afraid and so must fight the fear with bluster. A machete hangs from her belt and she rests a palm on its handle. "You'll have to follow me," she says.

———

Clark might hear hoofbeats. Or maybe it is just the slamming of her pulse. She stares down the road that leads from the Sanctuary. It extends a quarter mile before petering into many avenues of broken asphalt and trampled earth. This place, where the road ends and the ruined wilderness begins, is marked by a massive tree. The Witness Tree, Clark calls it, as it has been there longer than any person, longer than the Sanctuary itself, a spectator to the rise and fall of humankind. It carries no needles or leaves, its branches as bare as bones. But so many crows roost in it this morning that it appears laden with some dark, poisonous fruit. They shift their wings and scrape their claws and mutter among themselves—until the rider appears. The horse screeches out a whinny and clomps its hooves, and the crows take to the air in a swarm, *caw-caw-cawing*.

The rider is at first mistaken for a ranger, one of their own. Then the sentries glass her and see her horse is unarmored, plainly saddled, its tack unlike the jeweled black leather guards that run along the muzzles and flanks of their stable. Her body is caked with dust the same dun color as her doeskin leggings. She is small, her feet barely reaching the stirrups, but confident in her posture so that the horse seems a rocking extension of her. She slows to a trot at the clearing that surrounds the Sanctuary, just outside the gates, where the ground is raked of weeds and scorched black.

It is then that one of the sentries hurls down his torch. The wood in the iron brazier crackles to life. The blaze that signals alarm, the blaze that will draw every eye in the Sanctuary to the wall with wonder and fear.

No one has been seen outside the Sanctuary for decades. Its citizens have long been told that they are the last human survivors, that the rest of the world has perished. Something Clark has never wanted to believe. Years ago, she remembers touring through the museum and pausing to study an exhibition on space. There was a faded, wall-size photograph of the moon's surface and a man standing upon it in a thick white suit with a glass-visored helmet. Lewis appeared beside her. They'd known each other growing up, never friends. For years, in fact, she made games out of teasing and torturing the thin, sickly boy—one time hog-tying him and hanging him from a balcony, another time pegging him in the ear with a stone fired from a slingshot so that to this day its tip is torn. But that was fifteen years ago, and though she has never apologized, that has not stopped Lewis from nodding to her in the streets, standing beside her quietly that day at the museum. So many people feared him, but she saw him only as a wiser, longer version of that same sickly boy.

"Why did they do it?" she asked him.

"For the same reason humans always explore. To satisfy their curiosity. And to see what they might exploit." He pointed to a squat metal device with insectile legs and a broad dish wrapped in gold foil. He explained it was a transmitter, a way of yelling into space. "They hoped there was something else alive out there."

"Did they ever find it?"

"No."

"Do you think they would have?"

His voice was cold and clean, each word delivered as if printed on tin. "In the sky spin trillions of galaxies. In each of those galaxies spin trillions of stars. Orbiting these stars are trillions of planets. It is impossibly stupid and self-absorbed, within that mathematical construct, to believe that life could exist in only one case, on our tiny rock of a planet."

There was a time, Clark knows, a time long before she was born, when her great-great-great-grandparents were children, when mobs of people would appear regularly before the gates, sometimes begging and sometimes trying to battle their way in. Some of these strangers gave up and wandered away. Many remained stubbornly in place or tried to scale the wall until downed by a rifle, which in those days the sentries still carried. And a few, so the stories go, built catapults and tried to hurl the dead into the Sanctuary— poisoned, bloated bodies that split open when they impacted the wall but never crested it. But that was a long time ago, and over the years survivors appeared less and less frequently, finally trickling away, vanishing altogether, the last one spotted sixty years ago.

Now a rider has come. At first the girl seems at a loss, much like the sentries. Her horse snorts and stamps its hooves and spins in circles, while she twists in her saddle, staring up at the wall, trying to make sense of it, its height and expanse and jumbled design a bewildering sight. She wears a broad-rimmed hat and pulls it off now to set on her saddle horn. This reveals a pale line across her forehead—and the dirtied face of a teenager beneath it, maybe sixteen, eighteen. Her hair is dark and cut shoulder length, a wild tangle of burrs and twigs. And though her eyes appear sunken with shadow, they are not. They are black. Totally black. Outer-space black even on the brightest day.

The fire in the brazier crackles and smoke continues to billow upward like the rain-laden cloud they have all been praying for. Clark can almost hear the whispers and gasps and mutters come fluttering up from the Sanctuary as everyone wonders what is the matter, what has been seen. Several sentries have gathered over the gates. One of them has his bow drawn and Clark puts a hand to the arrow and lowers it now. "No," she says. "Don't you dare."

The girl does not call out to them and they do not call out to her. Clark is mute with wonder. They all are. This is not a moment they have prepared for. The girl is the equivalent of a ghost wandering a cemetery, something to fear as well as celebrate, because finally there is proof—that's what this is, *proof*—that there is something else out there.

Then comes the thunder of many horses, the rangers returning. A storm of dust accompanies them.

The girl's horse startles one way, then the other, uncertain where to turn—and the girl, too, whips her face back and forth between the wall and the fast-approaching rangers. She tightens her body and seems ready at one point to jab her heels and fly for the forest, but she remains.

The rangers slow as they approach her and then split their column and surround her in a half ring. Several draw and notch arrows. Behind the girl is the wall and before her their mounts. Whether it is her black-eyed gaze or her spectral emergence from the Dead Lands, several of the men are disturbed enough to mutter the word *witch*.

Reed drags off his hat and neckerchief. He has what Clark has always thought of as a fox face—sharp, cunning, the corner of his mouth often hiked up in amusement. So different than he appears now, his expression slack-jawed, fearful. Not the leader he needs to be in a moment like this, with the other rangers shivering their arrows in panic.

"Hands up," Reed says. "I said, hands up!"

Slowly the girl lifts her arms.

"Where have you come from? Who are you?"

She opens her mouth to speak, but his voice barrels over hers in his panic. "What's—what's wrong with your eyes? Are you diseased? Where did you come from? What do you want?" The questions come so rapid-fire that he doesn't seem to want an answer.

This is when Clark begins to run. She pounds along the walkway until she reaches a ladder, rebar welded and mortared into place. She swings her legs over the edge and lets gravity take her down, snatching and kicking at the rungs as she descends. People are always telling her to remember her place. "You're not the boss," they say. "Quit meddling," they say. "Shut your mouth," they say. She does not care what they say. She thinks with her guts. And her guts are telling her Reed is about to lose control.

Clark loses her grip, barely catching herself, then continues down, down, down, leaping the final ten feet and landing with a roll and popping up into a sprint and yelling, "Open the gates!"

A crowd has gathered. Their eyes are on the smoke in the sky and on her as she approaches. The guard stationed at the gates shakes his head and crosses his arms and says, "Not on your orders."

She pushes past him and slams a palm against the barred double doors and tries to yell through them. "Reed! Reed, stand down! Please! Let me talk to her!"

The guard grabs her by the elbow and she twists around and chops his larynx with her hand. He doubles over, trying to catch his breath. With a kick, she sweeps out his legs. The keys rattle at his belt. She swipes them, jams them into the deadbolt, twists it open. A two-hundred-pound beam hangs across the doors, and she gets her shoulder beneath it, grunting it off on one side, then the other. It lands with a clang.

By the time she pushes open the doors, it is too late.

She can hear their voices—Reed is yelling, the men are yelling.

"Get away from here! Now!"

"You need to leave!"

"What's wrong with your eyes, witch?"

The girl is cantering one way, then another, reaching into a leather saddlebag and saying, "I came here to—"

Her words are cut short by an arrow to the hand, another to the shoulder, her body quilled. She hunches forward with a garbled scream. And then another arrow catches her in the throat and the scream is silenced.

In the chaos that follows—when her horse, driven mad by the smell of blood, bucks and hurls her to the ground and races in a circle and pounds off for the woods, when the rangers surround her and wrench her arms behind her back and bind them, when Clark asks Reed what the hell is wrong with him and he tells her to shut up—no one notices the letter.

The letter the girl had been producing from her saddlebag. A square the color of an eggshell, folded and sealed with a red circle of wax. It has been flung and stamped and blown aside, nearly lost at the edge of the clearing.

It lies there, like a scrap of bark, until a bronze owl drops from the sky and collects it between its talons and takes off with its wings creaking and gears twittering.

This morning Simon wakes in the lean-to he calls home. It is built against an alley wall, made of stucco and corrugated metal, tall enough at its peak for him to stand upright. The wall is plastered with salvaged images. A man with a stubbled jaw and a cowboy hat mending a barbed-wire fence with a pack of Marlboros rising out of his breast pocket. A sleek red car blasting along an open highway. A woman in a yellow bikini kicking her way out of the ocean. The torn covers of a few old books by Stephen King, Louis L'Amour, J.R.R. Tolkien. They are all brittle, faded, tattered. He doesn't understand them, not completely, but they pull him in some way, give off a charge. These are the only treasures he keeps here—the rest stashed on rooftops throughout the Sanctuary—his lean-to merely a place to sleep.

He feels nauseous—his stomach an acidic coil—but cannot stop himself from filching a rat kabob from a market booth. He takes a few rubbery bites before tossing it aside. He makes his way to the morgue, in the basement of the hospital, a pillared marble building that shares a block with the museum. Here he worms his way through the ventilation pipes—navigating his way left, left, right, shimmying down one level, then right, right, right again, trying not to sneeze at the dust he stirs up, trying not to clank his knees and elbows against the metal—to see his father one last time before he is processed. Another hour and his body will be rendered into fat for candles, bile for ink, ligaments for stitching, bones for tools, meat for the pigs, every part of him translated into something useful.

The morgue is one of the few cool places in the city. He has been here before, to steal medicines and instruments—and to view his mother's body after the cancer ate its way through her. He stares through the ventilation grate, not expecting to get any closer than this, watching the morgue attendants deconstruct the dozen or so bodies cooling on their slabs.

Then a white-jacketed nurse pushes through the door and says the sentry fires have been lit, that something is happening outside the wall. Everyone departs the room in a hurry. Simon slides aside the grate. Dust spills out and he drops to the floor. He approaches the slab upon which his father has been laid.

Lamps glow and pulse and their shifting yellow light makes the bodies appear to tremble in their sleep. A bucket and a tray of instruments sit next to his father. Simon breathes through his mouth to try to fight the smell, the nausea that makes the floor feel unsteady. His father's skin is gray-green where it isn't red. He is slashed and chewed in so many places, his stomach torn open completely, a tangled pile of yarn Simon tries not to look at, studying instead his father's face, the remaining half of which appears serene, transfixed by a pleasant dream, as if death were the only way to find peace in this place.

His father prized above all else a guitar strung with rusty baling wire. He kept the fingernails long on his right hand for plucking. Simon takes that hand now—the hand that made music, the good hand, the best part of his father—and kisses it and makes a silent vow to one day revenge him.

———

Lewis has known the mayor, Thomas Lancer, longer and better than anyone else in his life, though they can't be called friends. Not anymore. There was a time, so long ago, when they were children, when they would thumb marbles beneath the table while their parents dined or ride bucking sheep for sport or play prey/predator in the gardens, one sneaking up on the other with his hands made into claws.

Lewis remembers especially loving the drum game. One of them would race off with a handheld drum while the other tied a blindfold around his eyes and waited for the thumping to sound. Thomas always preferred that Lewis pursue him—beating the drum sometimes softly, sometimes loudly—leading him through the Sanctuary, down alleys, through stables, over bridges, into and out of buildings, until finally Lewis crabbed out a hand and caught him.

The game has not changed so much. Thomas beckons him now with a deputy instead of a drum.

The Dome is gold leaf and during the day shines like a second sun. Its halls are made of marble interrupted by grooved pillars and oil paintings and frescoes and sculptures and staircases that spiral into many dark-wooded chambers where the lights sizzle on and off depending on how hard the wind blows.

Lewis needs no escort. When the deputy guides him by the shoulder, around a corner or down a hall, Lewis shrugs her off and says, "I know." He grew up here, after all, sliding down the staircases, reading books in the library, exploring the crypt, his father the longtime mayor. Then came his death, and Thomas's election.

One hundred and fifty years ago—when the world began to fall apart, when the flu mutated and millions began to die, their lungs hitching until they coughed up blood—several businessmen and politicians and National Guard units fortified downtown St. Louis with the improvised panic of people scrambling for cover against a sudden storm. There was no time for committees, for debate, for a show of hands. There was not even enough time to collect toothbrushes, rifles, photo albums, to call upon family members to join them. They had to make the immediate decision to live or die. The flu was airborne. It was burning brains with fevers, choking lungs with blood. And it was coming. So the wall rose around them, like a swift buckling of the earth.

A constitution followed a year later. They did not call themselves a country. They were a sovereign city, a temporary haven awaiting reincorporation. The United States would rise again, and in the meantime, they would uphold as many democratic principles as they could while maintaining strict control. They elected their mayor and city council to two-year terms. All firearms were abolished, all currency collected and redistributed.

Lewis's father was elected and reelected for more than thirty years. When he died, Thomas, a member of the city council, announced he would run for mayor. He had such an easy way with people, always smiling, looking deeply into eyes, taking a hand with both of his and not letting go. His campaign slogan, *Evolve*, asked that people reconsider the Sanctuary. Previous administrations insisted that the world was not lost, that the Sanctuary was a temporary haven, that one day the country would reunite. Thomas argued for an end to the lies. He wanted everyone to recognize that they were on their own, that they needed to change, to progress. The Sanctuary was more than an old city—it was the new world. He designed a flag—what would become the flag of the Sanctuary—red, white, and blue, but carrying a single star.

Several approached Lewis and begged him to put in a bid. They said people liked familiarity. His name, Meriwether, carried currency, had history. People would vote for him because he would make them feel safe.

Lewis said they were fools. People detested him. He was not familiar, despite his last name, but the very definition of unfamiliar. Different. Weird. Unsettling. If his father walked through a crowd, they swarmed him; if Lewis walked through a crowd, they scrambled to escape him. And he had no interest in politics. He only wanted to retain his stewardship of the museum, the place he served as an aide throughout his childhood, the only education available in the Sanctuary after children left school to work at the age of ten.

A few put in bids against Thomas, but he dominated the ticket. People believed in his platform. They wanted to evolve. They were ready for change—and they got it.

A heavy oaken door swings open and tendrils of steam escape it. Water splashes. Someone titters. Lewis enters the bath, the marble floor rising into a rectangular tub bigger than a bed. Three square windows are cut into the wall and they flood the room with light that swirls with steam through which Lewis observes Thomas.

He sits in the middle of the tub, joined by a long, lean boy who couldn't be more than twenty. Lewis seems to recall his name as Vincent. It is hard to remember them all. Some are male, some female, all young. Thomas once told Lewis he would screw anything, as long as it had skin and yielded to him. His wife, he claimed, was made of bone. So he found other ways to entertain himself. Vincent must be special—he has lasted longer than the others. The boy licks his sponge across Thomas's back and shoulders, his neck and belly. His face is a foaming mess of soap, costuming him with the beard he cannot grow. His eyes appear glazed—perhaps from sex, the heat, the glass of brown liquor resting at the edge of the tub.

Lewis clears his throat and says, in the pause that follows, "You demanded my audience."

Thomas blearily observes him, then startles to attention. "Lewis." Waves of water slosh when he lifts his arms in greeting. "I'm so glad to see you, so glad you could come."

"I didn't have a choice."

Thomas dunks his head and works the soap from his hair and then rises sputtering. His face appears to sulk even when he smiles. A trail of gold hair drops from his belly button to his groin—otherwise his skin is as bare as an infant's, maybe shaved. "Yes, well, you know how you are."

"Reluctant."

"Always busy. Always working. You never have time for old friends." He turns to Vincent, who smiles at him curiously, his sponge oozing soap down his thigh. "Go away. Though I may call for you later."

Vincent climbs from the bath and wraps himself in a robe and splashes through the puddles on the floor on his way out. Thomas watches him go before eeling his way to the head of the tub, hooking one arm over the edge. On the ledge rests a tray piled high with baked grubs. He snatches one, pops it in his mouth.

"There is no life without water, Thomas. That is the immutable law of the universe."

Thomas suckles the grub. "What are you getting at?"

"Do you know how upset people would be if they knew you were taking baths?"

Thomas makes a dismissive gesture, then lets the beak of the grub slip from his lips. It drops to the tray with a *tick*. "We recycle the water. Everything here will be bucketed into the gardens."

"How generous of you."

His eyes narrow and his voice drops to a whisper. "So have you done it?"

"No."

"Have you even tried?"

"Yes."

"That's a lie. If you can build an owl, you can build a gun. You can build me whatever I ask for."

Thomas is right. Lewis is lying. He has not tried and he will not try. Three months ago, when someone began painting protest slogans across buildings, when a brick crashed through one of the Dome's windows, when an effigy of the mayor was found floating in the sewage canal, Thomas approached Lewis about the possibility of black powder, of guns. Their forebears had thought it unwise, in such a contained community, to make it any easier to kill what few people remained in the world. And in the second amendment to their constitution, all rifles and pistols were destroyed. When Lewis reminded him of this, Thomas raised an open hand. "I know. I know what they said. But times are different. They had *water*. I need to be able to better control my people."

Thomas has never appeared physically threatening, but his mind has a shrewd capability for violence. Even when they were children, he knew how to hurt, placing a hand to the chests of those who wanted to be with him most, saying, "You may not play with me." Now Lewis sees a similar sharpness in his expression, a barely controlled fury that twitches the corners of his mouth. "You wouldn't want to see your precious museum closed, would you? Then all the knowledge would be left to those who know what to do with it. Men like us. The less people know, the better off they are."

"The better off you are, you mean." Knowledge is a threat. Lewis is a threat. It isn't the first time Thomas has mentioned closing the museum. There was even a motion to do so last month during a city council meeting—so that the space might be occupied, its many treasures repurposed—but it was struck down.

Thomas says, "You are deeply unpleasant, you know that?"

"Closing the museum is an empty threat. People would riot. It's one of their only pleasures."

"It's a shadowy junk pile, a haunted house. You're the only one who takes pleasure in it." Thomas is smiling, but he clenches his jaw as if to keep himself from swallowing something bitter. "What about your mother?"

"What about her?"

"I would hate it if something had to happen to your mother."

"Be quiet."

"Death might actually be a favor. It's not as if she knows whether—"

"I said, shut up!" With that Lewis kicks the tray and it splashes into the bath and the grubs dirty the water and a small wave rolls into Thomas.

The two men stare at each other for a long moment, and then Thomas's severe expression breaks and a bright laughter overtakes him. The water ripples around him. "You know what I love about you? I can always count on you to speak your mind. That's what I love about you." He climbs out of the bath and water trails off his body and makes a silvery path on the stone floor. He pulls a towel off a shelf and wipes himself dry. He is a short man, the top of his head coming to Lewis's shoulder. Though he is lean, he is also soft, cushioned, not a bone on his body visible. "You've heard about the rider?"

"I have."

"A girl. Amazing. They say her eyes are as black as night."

"So they say."

"She's a mutant. She's poison. And when everyone hears about her—when they begin to dream about other worlds and doubt the wall—what then?"

"It has nothing to do with *doubting the wall*. This is what we've been waiting for. This is why the Sanctuary has survived. Hope."

"You're wrong. The Sanctuary has survived by keeping people afraid."

"You're worried they'll leave. Maybe they will. Shouldn't that be their choice?"

"We're talking about the survival of the human race. Forty thousand people. I am responsible for them."

"The rider proves there are others. Maybe your responsibility isn't so great after all."

Thomas throws the towel over his shoulder and goes to a window and looks out it and heaves a sigh. Lewis joins him there. From this high vantage, in the center of the Sanctuary, so much of the city can be seen, the topography of streets and buildings arranged around the Dome as if they have begun to orbit around a drain.

Thomas lays a damp hand on Lewis's shoulder and says, "Something bad has been coming for a long time, old friend, and I'm worried it's finally here."

CHAPTER 3

OUTSIDE THE HOSPITAL a crowd gathers. Their low muttering is like the thrum of a hundred wasps' wings. Their hats shadow their faces and their expressions twist through a range of emotions—dread, hope, disbelief, curiosity—refusing to settle on a single one. They want to know if the rumors are true. They want to know if a rider has come out of the Dead Lands.

"Is she sick? What if she's sick? They shouldn't have let her in."

"Someone said her eyes were black. Like a doll's eyes."

"They shouldn't have let her in."

"You know what this means, of course? This means there are others out there. We're not alone after all."

"Wherever she came from, it must be worse off than here. Otherwise, why would she leave it? Maybe she's the first of many. People looking for help when we don't have help to give. This is the beginning of some trouble; I can feel it. They shouldn't have let her in."

Far from all these voices, deep within the hospital, in a stone room with no windows, she sits in a wooden chair. A lantern hangs from a chain and presses the shadows into the corners. Her face is hard-edged, sunbaked. She wears a doeskin vest and leggings, but no shoes, her feet as thick and gray soled as hooves. Her skin is deeply tanned, filthy except where her wounds have been dressed, the dirt and sweat and blood wiped away from her shoulder, her hand, her stomach, wrapped with cotton bandages. Her wrists remain bound. What looks like a white scarf is tied around her throat. A rose of blood blooms from it.

There is a scarred metal table before her. On it Clark sets a bowl of salted sunflower seeds and a mug filled with water murky and warm, but the girl doesn't seem to mind as she rushes it to her mouth and guzzles it down. Then she sputters and doubles over and brings her hands to her throat, to the place where the arrow pierced her. She does not emit a sound, gritting her jaw through the pain before righting herself and staring at Clark where she leans against the wall and then at Reed, who sits opposite her.

Clark demanded to be here. She berated Reed, calling him a fool, calling him reckless, calling him a failure. To allow *this* to happen. The arrival of this girl might be the most important thing that has ever happened to the Sanctuary, and he stands by with his mouth hanging open as his men pincushion her with arrows. Clark said she would speak to the girl and he conceded to her then just as he conceded to her in bed, letting her take the lead, telling him where to put what and how fast or slow to move.

Clark will take care of the questions. She will ask them kindly. She will try to make the girl forget about her injuries, and she will try to distract her from thinking about the fate that awaits her. Clark has no doubt that the mayor will isolate the girl, pervert the situation, use her to his advantage. There isn't much time.

The girl's eyes, black and empty, seem to look through them. Many in the Sanctuary are born with deformities—cleft lips, stunted legs, misshapen skulls—blamed on the radiation, the same as the cancer that afflicts so many. But Clark has never seen anything like this. The girl appears insectile, as if she were less than or more than human.

"She's not sick?" Reed says.

Clark says, "Of course she's not sick. No one's sick anymore. That's all in the past. You know damn well that's just a ghost story meant to keep people afraid."

"Maybe so, but still, I'm asking. You're not sick, are you?" He asks this with the half-joking, half-worried tone of someone who says, "You're not going to kill me, are you?"

The girl shakes her head, *no*. She cannot speak. Her injured throat makes even breathing difficult.

They lay a sheet of paper and pen before her. She makes no move to pick it up. "Please," Clark says. "I'm sorry about what happened to you. I'm sorry you're hurt. Not everyone here is a friend. But I am. And if I'm going to help you, I need to understand why you're here."

There is a long pause—punctuated by another *please* from Clark—and then the girl slowly and clumsily picks up the pen. She can write. Not very well and not very fast, maybe because her dominant hand is injured or maybe because she is unpracticed. Literacy is never a given in this time. Her writing looks like a bird's scratching, and her eyelashes, bleached from the sun, like little feathers.

Clark asks for her name and she writes, *Gawea.* Clark asks how far she has come and she writes, *Far.* Clark asks where she has come from and she writes, *Oshen.*

Reed says, "Impossible."

Clark shushes him and then asks the girl where, what part of the ocean, and she writes, *Oregon.*

Reed shifts in his chair, wanting to say something but holding back.

Clark speaks, with hopefulness rounding her voice, "Describe it."

Her pen scratches paper. *Fish. Lots of rane. Grene gras. Apals. Blakbary. Mowntins.*

This is enough to silence them for a long time, the thought of a place where clouds share the sky with the sun, where rain falls every week and fills rivers and lakes darting with trout. The trees weighed down with apples red, green, and gold. Corncobs growing to the size of a man's forearm. The woods tangled with blackberries, their juices and your blood oozing together as you fill a bucket and gladly risk the threat of thorns.

The girl's eyes might be alien and remote, but her face is earnest and pleading. She *believes* in what she is telling them, and that makes Clark want to believe too. It is as if, like some seer, the girl has sketched to life a dream she thought was hers alone.

Help me, she writes.

Reed has not washed up or changed out of his ranging gear. His hat is in his lap and his face looks like the cracked remains of a mud puddle. When he leans forward, laying his hands flat on the table, his leather vest creaks. Normally his posture is straight, but this afternoon his body appears bowed, the shape of a question mark. At moments like this Clark can't help but consider him weak. He should be taking orders; *she* should be in charge. His voice is hushed when he says, "How can we help you? Why are you here?"

Sent.

"By whom?"

Burr.

Reed says, "Who is Burr?" at the same moment Clark says, "Why were you sent here?"

The girl's attention flits between them, then settles on Clark. *Brot letter. Letter tels yu.*

"Letter?" Reed says over the top of Clark saying, "What letter? We searched your horse—there was no letter."

Letter for—

At that moment the door crashes open and the sheriff, Rickett Slade, fills the doorway, and then the room, the space seeming smaller. He moves swiftly for such a big man. He does not pause to acknowledge any of them but stalks directly to the girl and pouches a hand behind her head and slams her face into the table and knocks her unconscious.

Slade breathes fiercely through his nose. Clark can never tell where his eyes are looking, pocketed as they are into his face, but he seems to regard them both at once. "I will take it from here," he says. "You are excused."

"On whose authority?" Clark says.

Slade says, "Your girl has a mouth on her, doesn't she?"

Before Reed can respond, Clark says, "I said, on whose authority?"

"As always, I speak for the mayor."

Heavy brown curtains choke away all but a cool white line of moonlight running down their middle. There are no paintings on the walls, no decorations on the bureau except for a single short candle sputtering on an iron tray, illuminating this room in the upper stories of the museum. There are, in abundance, books. Some yawning open. Some closed with a ribbon or feather marking his place. Stacked along the walls, piled and tiered across the floor, like their own kind of furniture.

Lewis stands between the room's two narrow beds, his own empty, the other occupied by a woman. Her body is so slight it barely dents the blanket that covers her, tucked all the way to her chin. Her downy white hair twists across her pillow like the silk from a split milkweed pod, and Lewis runs a comb through it now. His movements are delicate, with first the comb, then his fingers, as he untangles the snarls, neatens her hair into a white halo that surrounds her ruined face.

His mother suffered a stroke three years ago, and since then, he has cared for her as she once cared for him. He was so often sick as a child—wracked by fevers that sweated into his mattress the imprint of his body—and many of his memories are of her hovering over him in the dark, laying a cool washcloth on his forehead, humming lullabies.

Now the left side of her face appears melted. She sometimes yammers at him, as if reciting some foreign alphabet, but mostly she remains still and silent, propped up in a chair, curled up in bed, sleeping with one eye closed, the other half-shuttered.

He sets down the comb on the night table between their beds and picks up the vial from Oman and uses a dropper to squirt some of the tincture into her mouth. It is meant to increase brain activity, speed recovery. Whether it works, he does not know and does not particularly care, as long as he is doing something for her. She smacks her mouth at its bitterness and regards him with her one good eye. He gives her a pained smile.

The owl, too, sits on the bedside table like a little brass clock. When Lewis sets down the dropper, he notices beside it a letter. It is sealed with a red circle of wax that bears the imprint of what looks like an eye.

"What's this?" he says and tears open the letter. He holds it before a candle whose flame trembles like his hand as he reads.

The entry to the museum is a fanned set of stone stairs. Lewis rushes down them with the letter in his hand and then secreted up his sleeve. He pauses for a moment on the sidewalk, listening to the small sounds of the city at night, the groaning of the wind turbines, before hurrying in the direction of the prison—where he knows the rider is being held—and where he does not plan to sign in with the guards or request permission to speak with their prisoner. In his gray duster he appears yet another shadow sliding along the street, and he has ways of making himself unseen, of distracting and then sliding past whoever might block his way.

He does not know what hour it is—he has trouble keeping track of time—but guesses it late, the streets empty. There are no lamps lit. The buildings are stark and silver-gray. Beyond them the black mass of the wall rises into the less-black sky, and above it hangs a half-moon, the shadowed side of it visible, but barely.

He has so many questions. He tries to keep them straight in his head, but they crawl all over each other and merge into a swarming mess like so many fire ants. It is because of his distracted state of mind that he does not notice the two men charging out of an alleyway until they are upon him.

The last thing he sees, before they drag a bag over his head and carry him bodily away, are the black sacks that shroud their faces.

It takes a moment for his eyes to adjust. At first he can see only blackness interrupted by the four torches flaring around the room—as if he is floating through some region of outer space lit by many competing suns—and then the room begins to take shape.

He knows he is underground, from the staircase they dragged him down, the steadily cooling air, and its sulfuric, mushroomy smell. The floor is crumbling concrete. Square stone pillars are staggered throughout the space, the basement of some store that must have once sold children's toys. There are heaps of rusted bicycles and baby strollers, a life-size clown with hair made of red yarn, moldy stuffed bears, shelving units full of video game consoles.

Among the stone columns stand a dozen or so bodies—whether men or women, he doesn't know. They surround him, he discovers when he spins in a circle, all of them wearing black sacks over their faces.

"Go ahead. What do you want?"

When one of them speaks, he can tell the voice is a put-on, roughened to sound deeper than it is. "What do you know about Oregon?"

He checks his sleeve to make sure the letter is still there. "Oregon." Until now, he has never said the word aloud, though he has read it countless times on maps, in books, and only minutes before in the letter. He feels as if someone has reached into his head and stolen what preoccupies him. He tries to keep his voice as calm as possible, but still it quivers. "Why do you want to know about Oregon?"

"Do you know the way there?"

"I don't know," he says. "I know maps. I know paper. But that's not the same as—"

"You want to leave this place, don't you, Meriwether?"

That voice. Husked over, but familiar. He stares at the black sack. Holes have been cut into it for the mouth and eyes. He wonders if he can recognize someone by the eyes alone. The figure retreats a step.

Lewis says, "What do you know about—"

"You want to. Who wouldn't want to? You've always dreamed about leaving this place. That's why you bury your face in books and maps. You like to imagine that there might be more to life than this. You aren't alone. We feel the same. We want you to take us beyond the wall. We want you to help us find the way to Oregon."

"Absolutely not."

"We need your help."

"I am needed here."

"We need you."

"I am needed here."

"By your mayor or your mother?"

"I am needed here." He feels something rising inside him—boiling, spilling over. If it was a taste, it would be bile. If it had a color, it would be red. "Don't make me upset. I'm getting upset."

The ceiling seems to lower and the stone pillars to crowd around him like bars. The masked figures sneak closer, knot around him. His breath is whistling through his bared teeth. He is blinking back tears. He imagines that beneath their clothes are bones, that they are a horde of skeletons beckoning him into an open grave.

"Or what?" the voice says. "You'll call for help? No one can hear you. We are asking you nicely. But we don't have to ask you at all. We can make you—"

He tries not to let happen what happens next, but he cannot stop himself. His hands rise, unbidden, as if separate from him. Something takes form on his mouth, not words but sounds no one else would recognize, long vowels and flat, hard consonants uttered with speed and volume unlike him.

He feels a *woof* inside him, as fire makes when it finds a pocket of oxygen, and he can feel a heat in his hands. He hurls it—he does not know a better way to describe it than this, as if the heat were a heavy ball—at the figure across from him. The room brightens. The figure flies backward, as if dragged by an invisible wire, until stopped by a stone pillar. He cannot be sure over the thunder of his own voice, but he believes he hears a woman screaming.

She—yes, it is a she—writhes against the column and cries out, tells him to stop, calls him by name. "No, Lewis! Stop!" But he does not. He is outside himself, taken over by some current he only moderately understands. When he breathes, it is with a concussion of heat, and when he sees, it is through a scrim of hot, floating sparks, as if he is burning up inside. Her feet rise off the ground—she is suspended in the air—her arms lashing as if she might cast off whatever grips her. Her mask peels away from her face, and he sees then the copper-colored hair, sees the face twisted in pain. Clark.

He goes silent and drops his hands, and in doing so releases her. She falls heavily to the floor, a knot of limbs. She coughs and gasps for air.

Lewis feels a sudden exhaustion, as if all the energy in his body is spiraling down some pipe, and he knows he must escape this place before he collapses himself.

He looks at the masked figures around him to see if they will test him. But they are retreating, clutching and tripping over each other, falling back onto the bikes, bringing down a shelf of stuffed animals, and so he brushes past them contemptuously.

CHAPTER 4

THERE HAS ALWAYS been something different about Lewis.

When they were children, playing the drum game, Thomas could not understand how Lewis so expertly pursued him, despite his blindfold, always stepping around holes or over piles of excrement, climbing ladders, navigating alleyways, so that sometimes he was accused of cheating, peeking. But he wasn't. He just had a way, if he concentrated deeply, of seeing without his eyes.

There were other things, too. The way he occasionally dreamed things before they happened—a conversation, a dropped dish, an illness. The way he sometimes saw colors around people, like wind-blown shawls, green, red, purple, the occasional black. When he told his mother this, she would silence him, put a finger to his lips, telling him the fevers were to blame, telling him not to say anything to anyone else. Especially his father.

His father did not have time for him, but when he did—when his eyes seemed by accident to settle on him—they inevitably narrowed. If crying, Lewis needed to toughen up. If struggling with a stuck door, he needed to thicken out. If reading books, he needed to get outside and express interest in the things other boys his age cared about—fistfights, slingshots, hunting rats, chasing girls, building things. Lewis wasn't leadership material, his father said. He wasn't someone others wished to be.

Lewis could endure his teasing and scolding, but not the hate, not the biting spittle-flecked words when his father discovered what he was capable of. There was the time, when he was seven, he could turn the pages of a book or nudge a bird off a high ledge or roll a ball by merely sweeping his hand through the air, for which his father kept him locked in his room for days. There was the time, when he was nine, he built a mechanical beetle that helicoptered its wings and flew a fifteen-foot circle before returning to his hand, after which his father crushed it beneath his heel. There was the time, when he was twelve, that he told his father not to ride in a parade because something bad would happen; and then something bad did happen when an assassin's arrow took him in the shoulder: his father came home not to thank Lewis but to slap him so hard he left a red and then purple and then yellow slash across his face.

Lewis spent so much of his time in the Dome's library, climbing ladders, pulling books off shelves to study. He loved novels like *Peter Pan*, *Lord of the Flies*, *The Wizard of Oz*, stories about escape, about worlds within worlds. And he loved histories as well, pretending himself back in time, learning the mechanics of how people and their countries had risen and fallen so many times before. But he favored science, especially physics, the motion and energy of the world.

He likes things that are quantifiable, that can be labeled and understood logically. This is why he was drawn to a book called *The Evolutionary Ladder*. He found it in the Dome's library and it concerned the next big step, what might happen to humans in the coming centuries. It spoke at length about a film and comic book character named Tony Stark, who developed a robotic suit that made him into the hero Iron Man. The suit was the equivalent of an exoskeleton, something that offered a shell of defense while also enhancing strength and speed, allowing Stark to hurl cars or punch through walls or blast through the sky with rocket boosters. For years, the army had been chasing something similar, an enhancing armor. Though their version—at the time only a prototype in a lab—did not make a soldier *super*. It made him more efficient, able to do better the things he already did, like carry gear weighing more than one hundred pounds and decrease musculoskeletal injuries. It wasn't about rocket boosters. It was about basic augmentation. As if hurrying along evolution to suit the soldiers' tasks. There were other examples. Such as a hundred-thousand-dollar battery-powered exoskeleton that helped a man, paralyzed below the waist, walk again—and even finish a marathon, though it took him twenty hours. And a technology—called electroencephalography, built into a pair of goggles—that could sense signals in the brain associated with the unconscious recognition of danger, a threat-warning system that would blend mind with machine to enhance defensive response.

"You don't need much of an imagination," the author wrote, "to see that humans will continue to adapt to these technologies by developing ever-more sophisticated means of neurological control. The day will then inevitably come when some people have the ability to control such machinery with only their thoughts. The mind becomes a muscle, able to wirelessly interface with objects separate from the body. This is our next leap as humans," the book concluded, "so that several centuries from now the seeming magic of telekinetics will be reality."

Sometimes that made a kind of sense to him. When he felt a headache coming on and a crack reached suddenly across a window. When he took a breath and a candle across the room snuffed out. When he snapped his fingers and a pencil rolled off a desk. Maybe his mind was like the world: sometimes certain things came together by chance and by fate—like the sparking of electrons, the merging of species, the mutation of a virus—and modified the rules.

The thought frightens more than excites him. One day, when he was a teenager, after a group of boys teased him, shoved him around, he came home with a split lip and a pouched blue-black eye and a poisonous sense of self-loathing. One of his cats happened to rub between his legs and then hissed and backed into a corner and curled up on itself and died. He did not understand then what he was capable of. He still isn't sure.

Anger—or any heightened emotion—seems to key a lock, help him into a hallway full of dark happenings. So he tries to keep his temper muted. He tries to keep his emotions as gray and blank as stone. He tries to focus his energies on more practical matters, managing the museum, studying history, tinkering with his inventions. But he has been having dreams lately—dreams about an old man with long white hair and a warm whispering voice, dreams about pressing his hand to sand and green grass growing in the shape of it, dreams about blowing fire from his lungs like a dragon, dreams about splitting open trees and even mountains by concentrating hard enough, dreams about, no other word for it, *magic*. The old man spoke to him in his dreams. He wanted Lewis to stop hiding from himself, embrace the strengths he kept contained. And while these dreams at first made him uneasy, he has come to find them weirdly comforting, as if someone out there regarded him with a paternal kindness, wished him well.

Ever since his hands burned and he hurled Clark—the room brightening with the expended energy—his body has felt achy, his mind slow, as if hungover. He wishes it was all a dream, but he knows better. He still feels in a dream now, as he stands in the museum's Sun Room, the largest of its galleries, a high-ceilinged space with tall, rounded windows running the length of it. He is holding the rib of a stegosaurus in his hand, the long, sharp curve of it like a yellowed scimitar. He rotates the exhibits every month. *The Rise of Egypt. The Fall of Rome. The Space Race. The Great American West.* For the past two days—with the help of Ella, his aide—he has been building dioramas, bolting together bones, hanging posters, readying one of their most popular displays, *When Dinosaurs Ruled*.

Whenever people walk through the museum to study their enormous skulls, their spiked teeth, their rib cages like baskets big enough for several men to fit inside, they seem in disbelief that something so fierce and powerful could be wiped out so easily. From there, he knows, it doesn't take much imagination to recognize that at any moment something can come blazing out of the sky and change everything.

He hears a voice, Ella's. She is saying his name as if it were a curse. She stands on a stool and wrenches a bolt into place that will secure a section of vertebrae. "You aren't listening to me?"

"Apparently not."

"I've asked three times whether this stage will be labeled Cretaceous or Jurassic."

He rubs a hand across his face. "I'm not myself."

"If you would simply sleep, like a normal person would, like I tell you to regularly, maybe this wouldn't be an issue." When she speaks, she punctuates her sentences with the wrench, jabbing it in the air as if to knock him about with it.

"You're right."

"Eight hours. That's what I get. And I feel great." She brings the wrench to her temple. "My mind is sharp. My body is healthy. Unlike yours."

"Yes. I'll try that. Eight hours."

The museum is a sacred space, a cathedral sought out in dark times. People hush their voices and remove their hats when they walk through it. They close their eyes and lower their heads before the exhibits. Lewis knows he makes people uncomfortable, just as people make him uncomfortable, so he remains hidden away in his study during their open hours. Ella has become the public face of the museum. She watches over it, answers any questions people might have when they retreat here. The space is shadowy and cool, orderly and manicured, full of polished treasures. It is everything the Sanctuary is not. Its celebration of the long, difficult novel of humanity, the individual stories that make up the larger story of civilization, gives people hope, purpose. Others have endured and so will they.

But today it is empty, because everyone is at the stadium.

Lewis told Thomas not to do it, begged him not to sentence the girl to a public death, and on what grounds? Terrorism. That was what Thomas told everyone. Two decades ago two rangers had gone missing, believed dead, though in fact they had abandoned the Sanctuary. Somehow, all this time, they managed to survive on their own. This girl, their daughter, had come hoping to lure others out, to breach the wall and risk all their lives. It was an act of terrorism. She was a terrorist.

Lewis said, "Everyone will recognize that as a lie."

"Fear beats logic every time," Thomas said. "You'll see. Everyone will be screaming for her blood."

"She's a child."

"What's the average life-span around here? Thirty? Forty? She's practically middle-aged."

This was yesterday in the Dome, where they met in a first-floor sitting room. Thomas lounged in a wingback chair while Lewis stood. He refused the offer of a seat, refused a plate of spiced grasshoppers, refused even a smoke. "Let me speak to her. Please."

Thomas wore snakeskin boots and fondled a thin wooden pipe. He tamped a pinch of tobacco and sparked a match and brought the flame to the bowl and puffed until it glowed orange and smoke tusked from his nose. "How does this have anything to do with you?"

"If there are indeed outlying communities, we need to reach out to them."

Thomas made an encompassing gesture with the pipe. "Do you know what has kept people alive all these years? They believe. They believe in the wall." His voice was quiet, but Lewis knew this was how he yelled. Smoke swirled like a storm taking form. "What you're talking about would threaten everything we've built here."

"Their faith has already evaporated like all the water in the world."

"The rains will come. They always do."

They always had—this was true. But it had been so long, months now, that rain felt like a barely remembered dream, the same as his election promises. More than a year ago, when he took office, he promised he would rebuild the crumbling sections of the city. He would rid crime from the Fourth Ward. He would expand the gardens. He would drill a new well and repair those broken. He would make every citizen live up to their potential, live their best life, evolve, whatever that meant, and so on, none of it true. And with the wells failing and the storage tanks emptying, the weather felt like a punishment, like a reprimand for his election, the round reaches of the sky a magnifying lens that sharpened the sun that would crisp them to death.

For a moment Lewis considered telling Thomas about the letter, sharing its secrets, but only for a moment. In case Clark should actually make good on her promise and depart the Sanctuary, Thomas should know as little as possible about where she is headed. "I would like to speak to her. Before you do what you're planning to do."

"No, I don't think so." He sucked at the pipe and it sizzled with his breath. "*But*. If you give me what I've been asking for, if you give me my guns, I'll *consider* letting you speak to her."

"No."

Thomas rose from his chair then. Even in his boots, he was a head shorter than Lewis. But somehow he made himself seem bigger, in the way of a petulant child, his pale face growing red as he approached Lewis. He held out his pipe like a weapon and Lewis backed away until he could retreat no farther. Thomas leaned in so that his smoking breath made a hot wind on Lewis's face and he choked on the taste. "Do you know what I can do to you? I can do anything I want to you."

"You're threatening me again?"

"I'm telling you the way things are, old friend."

———•———

The streets are empty except for dogs lounging in shadows, dust devils that die as they take shape. The wind carries the creak of the turbines and the distant cheers and whistles from the stadium. In an alleyway a figure appears—a woman dressed in the black uniform of the deputies—surveying the street before darting across it like the shadow of a crow. It takes only a moment for her—her face obscured by a black hat and neckerchief—to scale the wall of the museum and slip through an open window.

She pauses in the half-light, her eyes adjusting, taking in her surroundings, an interactive exhibit featuring the games of another era. There are chess- and checkerboards, tables strewn with playing cards and a jigsaw puzzle that comes together into a pot of gold at the end of a rainbow, bins full of balls and bats and racquets and mallets, game consoles with slits in their sides and wires tentacling out of them.

She slips out of the room and into a hallway festooned with suits of armor from various ages and regions, some clad in reeds, others in metal, before climbing the stairs, fast but not so fast as to clomp her boots or whine a floorboard, every step a whisper. She glances over her shoulder often and sticks to the shadows.

Here, at the center of the museum, the building rises into a square tower, its highest story consisting of Lewis's office and living quarters. She pauses on the landing with her head cocked—and then peers over the railing, back the way she came. Voices swirl faintly upward, Lewis and his aide, their voices sharp and bullying—but distant.

She seems confident she is alone now as she starts down the hall and knobs open the door to a room that remains as dim as twilight. The floor is a mess of books. The windows are curtained off, and the sheets of one bed are tidily made, squared and tucked beneath their mattress. The sheets of the other hold down an old woman who smells of lavender and rot and urine, who observes the approaching black-clad figure with one bulging eye. When the figure hovers over her a second before gently pressing a pillow to her face, she does not struggle except to lift a hand, let it shiver and fall.

The owl observes all of this from the night table, its glass eyes trained on the figure who remains hunched over the bed for a long time, long enough for her arms to quake, for her legs to collapse so that she kneels beside the bed as if overcome by a terrible prayer.

A lamp on the wall sputters and emits a dim, brown glow. Before it can brighten fully, she wobbles upright and stumbles from the room and in doing so trips over a stack of books and knocks into the bureau, and then the door, as if lost in some dark place, uncertain where she is.

Lewis and Ella are struggling up the stairs with a femur the size of a log. They have rested several times on their way up from the basement, and he has stumbled twice and nearly lost his grip. She is cursing him all the way, asking why they cannot wait, why this has to happen now. Normally they seek help from one of their custodians or guards, but the museum is closed and everyone is away, no one wanting to miss the execution.

Lewis lives most often in a state of poised stillness—seated at his desk, bent over a book. He has never been interested in any sort of exercise. But these past few days, ever since he hurled Clark against the pillar, he has felt a restlessness that needs some outlet. He doesn't know if it is the lingering sense of power—the humming at his fingertips, as if they were orange-hot blades struck on an anvil—or the possibility of escape, stealing past the wall, exploring landscapes that he previously believed would exist for him only on paper and in dreams. But he cannot sit still. He cannot stop pacing, tidying. He desires movement.

He and Ella rest again when they reach the landing, setting down the femur with a thump. She wears the outfit of a boy: short pants, short-sleeve shirt with a leather vest. Her hair is damp with sweat, plastered to her forehead. "I'm sitting on this thing, whether you like it or not," she says and collapses onto the bone, a yellow-brown bench with hairline fissures running through it. The cracks in it are like the cracks in everything—cracks in concrete, cracks in rubber and asphalt and glass, cracks in faces ruined by the sun. Nothing is new.

Above them rises the bowl of a rotunda, one of two in the museum, each bearing a fresco—the sky by day, the sky by night. Theirs is the night, star-spangled and moonlit.

Lewis would love to reach for the silver canister inside his pocket, shove his nose into it, snort his way into a numb, pleasant dream. But he has heard enough scolding from Ella this afternoon. He pushes his fists into the small of his back and stares upward. He breathes heavily and says between breaths, "I would love to walk on the moon."

Before he finishes the sentence, he hears his echo, the ghost of his voice whispering back.

Ella glances up as if she might spot another version of Lewis hovering above them. Then she looks at him, smiles until dimples pocket her cheeks.

"Say something," he says. "See if it comes back to you."

She leans back her head, her mouth open and ready to call out, when—from somewhere upstairs—comes a distant sound, a slam and groan, like something heavy shoved across the floor. Then the patter of footsteps.

The two of them look at each other, startled, before pursuing the sound's source, taking the stairs two at a time.

CHAPTER 5

THE SANCTUARY'S founders deliberately signed their constitution on July Fourth. They hoped to at once borrow and revise the sentiment of nationhood. They were America. A miniature version—living off hope, waiting for help—but America nonetheless. For a long time this worked. On what came to be known as Resurrection Day, people painted black circles beneath their eyes the night before, to indicate sickness, and washed them away the next morning, to signify health. Gifts were exchanged. A costume parade—full of dancing skeletons—marched through the city, ending at the stadium, where so many years ago men pulled on padded armor and crashed into each other while chasing a football, where the faded murals of the St. Louis Rams still adorn the pocked concrete tunnels and walls that surround the field, and where the citizens of the Sanctuary drank and feasted and danced.

The mayor always rode at the back of the parade—as Thomas does now—wearing a bone crown on a bone chair atop a horse-drawn wagon decorated with clattering bones. He waves at the people who fill the sidewalks, but no one waves back. They watch him with what can only be fear and distaste. His waving slows, then stops altogether, along with his smile, and he tells the driver to hurry up, hurry up already. His eyes dart about, as if he is worried something might be hurled at him.

Today, before the Resurrection Day feast, the rider will be killed. Many, including Lewis, including the city council, have asked Thomas not to do so. He would spoil the fun, they said. Ruin the holiday mood. People need something to celebrate. If he insisted on killing the girl, why not drag her out the gates and chain her to the altar, like everyone else? Because she comes from

65

out there, Thomas said, so she must be punished in here. Here, too, he has a captive audience. He wants to put an end to the graffiti, to the effigies, to the underground mutterings of whatever faction is out to ruin his time in office. At the stadium he will force people to see what he wants them to see, a demonstration of his power.

The synthetic dome that once covered the stadium was long ago torn away and salvaged, so the sun beats down this July Fourth on the many seated now in the lower deck, more than twenty thousand bodies, all shading their eyes and squinting painfully. Everyone studies the four black-mouthed tunnels at the corners of the field. Their voices begin as a hesitant mutter that rises into a charged hum the longer they wait. Energy emanates from them like waves of heat, some combination of loathing and confusion and excitement for what they are about to witness. Afterward, there will be music and food. There is that at least. Not like the feasts of the old days, but something.

All around the stadium hang flags—Thomas's flag—with the single star burning brightly at the center. There is a spattering of applause when the mayor and his wife take their place high among them, along with several deputies, servants, and members of the city council—at midfield, in a boxed-off suite with an open window from which they wave.

Her name is Danica. She looks like a piece of jewelry, she knows. Another ornament for the mayor. If he is deserving of her attention, he is deserving of theirs, the logic goes. Her hair is so blond it appears white. From a distance people find her beautiful, but up close there is something unnerving about her appearance. Her many sharp angles—her collarbone, her thin lips, her chiseled jaw, her sharp fingers—make her appear like something that can cut through its own clothes, shred its own skin. And though she keeps them hidden in her shoes, her toes are strangely extended, good for gripping. Pants are all anyone seems to wear anymore, but she never appears in public without a dress, this one white linen and already brown along the hem from the dust she cannot escape. She wears a gold chain around her neck that matches her gold belt, her waist as wide around as her husband's thigh. Sometimes he calls her his lovely bone.

Thomas drops into a seat and brushes the powdery dust from its armrests. A servant brings him a plate stacked high with dates wrinkled like ugly little heads. "Oh," he says, "this is just what I wanted."

She prefers to stand and shakes her head stiffly when offered a seat beside him.

———

The day before, Clark sought out her brother, York. He was easy to find, a street performer who tumbled and juggled and blew fire and swallowed swords. He could send cards in a riffling arc from one hand to the other. He could lose a coin from his palm and find it in the mouth of another. He could sing a thousand songs and tell a thousand stories. She needed only to look for a crowd, a flurry of applause, and there he was, entertaining the long line of people waiting to fill their jug at the well.

Clark's father died, like so many died, of cancer. A purple blotch swelled on his nose, then spilled across his cheek, a melanoma the doctors cut away, leaving a hole in his face, too late. He lost weight suddenly, lost his balance regularly, and soon began to lose his mind when the tumors took seed in his brain. Her mother did not marry again but a decade later became pregnant with York. He was Clark's half brother but felt more like a son, as her mother died not much later, so blotched with melanomas she appeared splattered with some foul wine. The sun would kill them all, it sometimes seemed.

From a distance, for a few minutes, she watched him perform. He dipped daggers in linseed oil and set them on fire and tossed them in flaming ellipses. He was bareheaded so that people could see his face and so that he could see his daggers. His arms were a blur. His forehead was beaded with sweat. His smile so wide it reached his ears. His hands were too square and meaty for his arms, and his lean neck bunched into a fist of an Adam's apple. She had tried to enlist him as a sentinel, but he resisted. "I don't want another boss," he said, "when I've already got you."

She couldn't lay off him. She tried, really tried, but couldn't resist swatting the back of his head, bullying him with her words, every time he made a foolish decision. They shared the same blood. He was hers—that's how she felt—like a hand or tooth. By taking care of him she was taking care of herself. He wanted to make people smile, give them some small escape, always goofing, whereas she was always serious. These days, most everyone is some shade of brown, but people still smile when the two of them stand beside each other as siblings, with his nut-colored skin and her fiery hair and freckled face.

She waited for him to catch the daggers—one, two, three—and extinguish them each in his mouth, waited for the applause and the coins people tossed his way, before approaching him and tugging his sleeve and saying they needed to talk.

"About?" He had a gap between his teeth he showed often in a smile.

"About the kind of thing that can get us killed."

He packed his bag and swung it over his shoulder and blew kisses to three young girls before following Clark from the square.

She said, "You're performing at Resurrection Day?"

"Yeah, but they want something different now. Not just for the feast, but before, too. Warm up the crowd before the execution."

"Even better."

"What's going on?" He nudged her with his elbow. "Are we making a move? Is this it?"

They entered an alley, and its tight walls clapped away the sun. In shadow they walked and she whispered, "Consider this your final performance."

In the stadium, hundreds of tables have been arranged into four squares, with two wide corridors splitting the space between them in the shape of a cross. At the center of the cross rises a freshly constructed gallows with a noose dangling from it that casts an eyelet shadow. The body will dangle there through the meal to follow, when people file from the bleachers to their seats and a band strikes up a merry tune.

York races out of a tunnel and along one of these corridors. A ripple of applause works its way through the crowd. He cartwheels and tumbles and finally pounds his way up the gallows and swings from its noose and then spins in a circle to survey his audience.

From his pants pocket he withdraws what looks like a black rope that he keeps pulling and pulling and pulling and pulling and then snaps like a whip. It unfurls then, ripples in the wind, opens up into a massive silk scarf, maybe twenty feet long and half as wide. He begins to manipulate its form, bunching it first into a storm cloud that dots the ground with rain. Then his hands slash and twist when he knots it into the shape of a giant raven. It caws and pecks at his hand before taking flight and fluttering one way and then another. His lips seem not to move when it calls out in its croaking way. Then he snaps the scarf and it unrolls to its full length, and he twists it into a rope, what appears to be a snake curling along the stage, before coiling up at his feet.

Again he reaches for his pocket. This time he produces a red stone, a blue stone, an orange stone. He transfers the stones one by one to his opposite hand until they fill his palm like a cluster of fruit. He shoots them into the air, spinning them upward in a colored blur. The stones rise higher and higher, ridiculously high, until they might scrape the sky. He adds to their rotation an apple he takes intermittent bites of, and the crowd erupts, crying out with pleasure, crashing their hands together in applause.

York can't seem to help it—he smiles so widely his eyes vanish into folds—and then the smile vanishes and the apple core falls to the ground and the stones fall and clatter into his pocket, blue, orange, red, when the girl is escorted onto the field.

No one screams or boos or stomps their feet. Instead the stadium plunges into silence.

Her wrists are bound and she is led by two deputies who hold her by the elbows. Her face is puffed with bruises. She wears a scarf of bandages. Whether she is limping or resisting the deputies, it is unclear, but they drag and support her.

From her midfield suite, high above the rest of the crowd, the silence is such that Danica can hear the scraping echoes of their footsteps. A trail of dust rises behind them and ghosts away with the wind.

When the girl arrives at midfield, some of the people in the stands begin to yell, their voices swelling, some pitched high, some low, the many layers of sound eventually merging into one sustained note that seems to shake the air. Whether they are calling out questions or calling for mercy or calling for blood, it is hard to tell.

The girl appears so thin, like a piece of wood somebody whittled and gave up on. Though there remains something strangely vibrant about her. Her skin has an earthen richness. Her hair is the same black as the vultures that spin in the sky. Her posture is unyielding despite her circumstances. Danica watches her with grim curiosity when the deputies lead her up the steps of the gallows to the platform.

The people in the stands watch too—whether hopefully, judgmentally, Danica doesn't know—but when the girl turns in a slow circle and tries to meet their gaze, they drop their faces and go silent, as if frightened her dark eyes alone might carry some contagion.

Vultures tornado the sky and she stands among the black, swirling color of their shadows. She looks as if she might say something, but the injury to her throat prevents it.

Then the deputies fit the noose around her neck, and Thomas stands up to cheer and clap his hands. He swings his arms so wildly that he knocks an elbow into Danica and she staggers a few steps. As she does, she looks to the doorway behind her, where Reed stands. He nods at her.

She runs her hands along her dress, straightening out the wrinkles. She leans in to her husband and tells him she feels ill, she will see him later.

"What?" he says, then, "Oh. Fine." Not even bothering to look at her, his eyes on the field, his hands still clapping sharply together.

———

She follows Reed at a distance, down a staircase, along a concrete corridor with rusted pipes veining its ceiling. He slips through a door and she is not far behind him. Light streams from a single window. The air smells of metal and leather and oil. The deputies use these rooms for storage. Bows hang from hooks on the walls; knives and bats and arrows lie strewn across a table that runs the length of the room.

Just as she enters, Reed shuts the door behind her and presses her against it. What they are doing is kissing, though it looks much like eating. Their mouths opening and closing hungrily, their teeth biting down on lips, cheeks. When they pull apart, their faces are a splotchy red and he is bleeding from the corner of his mouth.

"What have you learned?" she says.

"They're going to do it. They're going to leave. They're making every preparation."

"They, they, they. Don't try to separate yourself from them."

"We, then. We're going to do it."

"Are you?"

"You can come. You should."

"Hmm."

"You must."

"Are you still fucking that woman?"

He gapes at her, his hesitation all the answer she needs.

71

"I thought so," she says.

"I don't feel about her the same way I do you."

"Is that right? She's just someone to fuck?"

"I love *you*. I do. And I want you to come with me."

"That's nice of you."

"We've been waiting for the right moment. It's here. We've been talking about this for a long time. Now is the time."

"We've been *talking*, yes. Doing is something else entirely."

"We're trying to get Lewis Meriwether to join us."

She snorts through a smile. "Why do you keep bringing him up? What use is he?"

"He knows more about the outside world than anyone else. He knows more about *every*thing than anyone else."

"He knows paper. He doesn't know blood or dirt or sweat. Besides that, he has the fortitude of a sick child."

"I wouldn't be so sure of that. There are things about him that would surprise you."

"*Please*. You're not fool enough to believe in what people say about him. Lewis, the eater of children, the binder of spells, the freak in the dark tower."

"I might be."

She runs a hand along his beard, then pinches a whisker and rips it out. He flinches and she shoves him aside and walks to the table at the center of the room. "So you're suggesting that we uproot, say good-bye to all we have built here, on the word of one girl?"

"If it's true—if what she says is true—the country there is rich."

"*If* it's true."

"Is there any future here? Really?" Her back is to him, but she can hear him slide closer to her, can feel his breath at her neck. "What does your husband say?"

"Do we really need to talk about him?" She picks up a dagger— black handle, black blade—and runs her finger along its edge. "He says it's not true. Of course he says that. And he says—even if any of it is true—no good can come of it and we must put it behind

72

us. The more people know, the less sure they will be of everything. That's what he says."

"Look at it this way. Even if we stay here, this is a chance to trade, to open lines of communication. To unite. Maybe even make a kind of country?"

"How patriotic of you." She turns around and prods his belt with the knife. "The other possibility is that this is all a pipe dream."

"I'd like to think it's true. We've got to believe in something."

She drops the dagger on the table and reaches her hands around his neck, massages him until his head lolls with her fingertips. "Relax," she whispers. "Relax."

His eyes shutter closed with her rubbing. "This could be a chance for us to start over too."

Her tongue darts from her mouth and wets her lips. "Enough talking." She releases him and turns around and lifts up her dress until it bunches around her waist and leans over the table stacked with steel. "Hurry up and take me."

———

The black-clad figure races the streets, cutting through alleys, breathing in panicked gulps, before finally collapsing in a shadowed alley. The neckerchief peels away to reveal a face—Clark's—just in time for her to vomit freely.

She throws her hat aside. Her hair has come loose from her ponytail. Her stomach clenches and empties. With a line of spit hanging from her lips, she cries out with inarticulate shame and fury. Out of the cracks come several scuttling beetles, joined by a black-winged butterfly, to drink from the mess she has left for them.

She roughs her mouth across her wrist. There was a time when she found herself often in this position, hunched over, her throat surging, yesterday's meal flecking her lips and a bottleful of tequila puddling the ground between her feet. She couldn't stop herself.

One drink always became ten drinks—and she would end every night swinging a fist or falling into bed with someone she couldn't remember in the morning. She didn't have any sort of excuse. Drinking was a way to antidote the boredom, the sense of purposelessness. Drinking was a way to numb the anger she always felt coiling inside her. Maybe. But in the end she believed it came down to the sort of person she was—a woman of great appetites.

Soon she will leave this place. And when she leaves, she will have escaped her old self, the old Clark. She will be able—they all will be able—to begin again. Lewis's mother is dead, but she was *already* dead, a ruined vessel no different from the city presently rotting around her. Clark was doing her a favor; she was doing Lewis a favor. I am trying, she thinks. I am trying to make things better, trying to help. But she knows that the murder—no, the *death*; that's a better way to think of it—the death of the old woman will weigh on her chest like a cold stone.

For the moment, though, she need only worry about Lewis. More than once in her life she has witnessed the unexplainable. A storm of dead crows raining from the sky. A plant, like a long green finger, that came twisting out of the ground when she spilled water from her canteen. The man with the parasite that grew so massive inside him that his belly distended and shifted as if from some alien pregnancy. The seers in the market who could read your past and future in your palm, in tea leaves, in the squiggly purple guts of rats. But never anything like the other night.

People have always spoken of Lewis as if he were and were not human. He has always struck her as a kind of weak phantom, a shade of a man, but it was not until he hurled her back against the pillar, not until she suffered against what felt like a giant, fiery pair of hands, that she understood what he was capable of and why they needed him on their side more than ever.

She knows—everyone knows—of his difficult history with the mayor. She knows about Thomas badgering him for guns and black powder. She came to the museum costumed as a deputy and made certain the owl observed her clearly. She is counting on his mutiny. But if Lewis discovers it was her—and who knows what he can see—then she knows her guilt over smothering an old woman will be the least of her troubles.

She rises to her feet and spits and takes a deep, calming breath. Over the years she has found ways to keep her temper in check. To breathe in through her nose, out through her mouth. To sketch out words on her palm with a fingernail: *hate*, *mad*, *fuck*, *die*. This helps settle her now—to loosen her coiled sense of confusion and loathing—as she races through the maze of streets.

She needs to hurry. If everything has gone according to plan, if her brother has done as she asked him to do, then they won't have much time.

When York first climbs the gallows and swings from its noose, he uses a razor tucked in his palm to thin the rope to a few threads. Then the deputies march across the field, dragging the girl between them, and York descends the steps and momentarily loses his focus. In part it is her eyes, like polished balls of obsidian, but more than that it is her. The oval cut of her face, the regal way she holds her head. In her own way, she is beautiful. He stares at her dumbly until they march her up the thirteen steps of the gallows. Then he shakes off his trance and positions himself below, waiting for the trapdoor to open.

In his head he has rehearsed their escape so many times that it already seems a reality. There are four tunnels in the stadium, each as black as a skull's sockets. Down one of them waits the mass of caterers and musicians who will take to the field following the execution. Down another tunnel huddle a few deputies, though most of them patrol the bleachers. The other two tunnels are unoccupied, the corridors to the south side of the stadium strewn with sand and half-collapsed. York has scouted them, picked the lock of a side door, stowed weapons and clothes in a nearby alley. The streets will be empty when he and the girl race to meet Clark.

But that's not what happens.

The deputies fit the noose around her neck, and she looks to the sky as if in prayer. Her black eyes reflect the white-blue expanse swarming with vultures. Her body goes rigid, and York hears something then, though he cannot place the sound so much as he can feel the attendant shiver, the air like struck tin.

Vultures always swoop over the Sanctuary, but they come together now by the hundreds, more and more of them drawn from rooftops and thermals, coalescing into a spinning black funnel with the gallows as its axis. The crowd follows her gaze upward. They murmur and shrink in their seats as if they can sense what's coming. And then it comes.

The cyclone collapses and all at once the vultures fall on the stadium. They are a terrible rain, but not the one everyone has been praying for. Big balls of air come rolling off their long-fingered wings, making a wind strong enough to raise dust devils all over the field. People squint their eyes and throw up their hands and cry out in voices that match the scratchy timbre of the vultures. Some of the birds land on shoulders and some of them swing by as if on wires. Their claws slash; their bald red heads dart in for a bite.

Four of them dive the gallows. Their wings are as wide as a man is tall, and so black that the sunlit air seems striped by midnight. The deputies do not have time to reach for their machetes. They barely have time to hold up their hands. One of the men reels back and falls from the ten-foot platform. The ground meets his back with a meaty thud that knocks the air from his lungs and leaves him momentarily paralyzed, too stunned to lift his arms and ward off the vulture that swoops onto his chest.

The other deputy—with a vulture pinned to his shoulder, his face cowled by its wings—falls onto the lever that opens the trapdoor. By this time, York has ducked beneath the platform, out of the sun, into shadow, away from the birds that sweep and dagger the air. So when the trapdoor swings open, when a square of light appears above him, when a body tumbles through it, when the noose catches and snaps, he throws out his arms and snatches her from the air.

They don't have time to pause, but for a moment his body stiffens, arrested by the sight of her in his arms. Her expression is flat and her eyes give him nothing back, not hate or gratitude or fear, so he feels compelled to say something. "Hi." And then, "I'm here to help."

Something softens in her face and he feels relieved, as if from the pressure of a knife. She might fit easily into his arms, but she could hurt him if she wanted to. Impossible as it may seem, she is responsible for the vultures. He doesn't know how he knows this, but he does, and he accepts it with the awe of a child who watches a magician spit fire and spring bouquets from ears.

The crowd is still screaming and the vultures are still plunging when he puts her down and she slips the noose off her neck and grabs his hand and runs for the south tunnel. He finds himself hurrying after her, even though he is the one who should be yelling, *Follow me!*

CHAPTER 6

M OST OF THE sentinels live in a stucco building with shuttered windows next to the stables. There is a kitchen and latrine and common room on the ground floor, apartments on the upper three levels. Clark keys open her door and can barely shove her way inside, the floor so cluttered with rank piles of clothes and the named and unnamed objects she has salvaged from the Dead Lands. A broken blue mug. A golf club. A faded red can of Coca-Cola. A typewriter with rows of gleaming yellow teeth. A snow globe with a white-bearded, red-suited Santa inside it.

As soon as she closes the door behind her, she begins to strip, tearing off the deputy's uniform and stuffing it beneath her bed. On the wall hangs a cracked mirror, mossy and veined with age, and she studies her reflection in it, her body pale, her face and hands rough and sunburned.

Then she picks up some clothes from the floor and smells them before pulling them on.

Her brother is safe, the girl is safe—for now. Deputies will gather. They will march the streets and knock on doors and overturn closets and pantries and basements and attics, and they will make black Xs on a map for the places they have already visited. Not only will the mayor appear a fool for losing the girl; he will appear a cruel god for upending every drawer in the Sanctuary in pursuit of her. Clark will be questioned once—within the next hour or so, she guesses—and Reed will vouch for her and her loyal service as a sentinel. A few days later, when the deputies seek her out again, she won't be around for them to find.

Her mind vibrates; her guts feel feathery. She makes her hands into fists and presses them to her eyes. She could use a drink. Terribly. A few weeks ago, she promised Reed she would stop. Just like that. Like a door had closed, bolted. She relapsed once, the other day, after the death parade. She does get quivery when she passes a bar, when she sees people drinking or smells liquor on their breath, but the real trouble comes at night.

She dreams of drinking. Glass after glass. Gallons of whatever is being poured. Bathing herself in it. And when she drinks in her dreams, her knees do not wobble. Her words do not slur. Instead she is happy, unafraid. This feeling—a good feeling, warm and expansive—carries over when she wakes, feeling drunken, the world slippery around the edges, and sometimes it is an hour and two cups of tea later before she can shake it.

Now, as she lies back on her bunk, staring at the ceiling, her mind is drifting, her hand is reaching for a bottle that isn't there.

When the door opens and Reed steps through it, she rushes out of bed and takes the back of his head and shoves her face against his and drinks deeply of him until he pushes her back with a confused laugh. "Okay," he says, "okay. I assume this means everything worked out? They're safe?"

"They're safe." She still holds him by the head, his braid wrapped in her fist. "You smell funny."

"And you taste like bile. Want to trade more love poems?"

"You do. You smell." Her eyes sparkle angrily. "You smell like some flower."

"Forget about it. I sat next to some reeking woman at the stadium."

"What woman? *Her?* You said you were done with—"

"I said forget about it." He pushes her hair back from her forehead and kisses it. "What happened with Lewis?"

She releases him then and falls back into bed and forces her head into the pillow as if to suffocate the words, "It's done. She's dead."

———

Lewis is not the only body in his bedchamber, but he is very much alone. He kneels over his mother in much the same posture as the one who murdered her. Her face is a ghastly rictus of pain. He draws back the sheet to reveal the slim length of her, like a bundle of sticks. He does not cry—he cannot remember the last time he cried; he doesn't know if he is capable of it—but he embraces her, drawing her body toward him so that it arches, her head lolling painfully back. He holds her like this for a long time. And while he holds her, the night gathers outside and deputies shout in the streets and the room flickers with light as the owl projects over and over again the grainy image of the deputy smothering her.

As expected, the deputies come for Clark. They ask about her brother and she says, "Half brother." They ask if she has seen him, and she says, "I throw him some coin if I see him performing, but we don't talk much, not anymore." She denies any knowledge of his whereabouts, expresses her disgust and astonishment, and says she will be the first to let them know if he comes crawling to her. Then she excuses herself. "I have to work."

She paces the wall all through the night as a sentry and now it is dawn and her eyes buzz with exhaustion and with the competing thoughts that bump around inside her head like bees in a jar: the possibility that she may escape, the possibility that she may not, that she may spend the rest of her life caught in this globe, like the one she salvaged from the Dead Lands, with sand instead of snow churning through it.

She tries to concentrate on her hands and feet, finding a good grip on the ladder, the strips of rebar cemented into the wall, but even now her mind wanders, her hands curling around metal in much the same way they curled around the corners of the pillow pressed down on the old woman's gaping face.

The sky is pinkening, the first bell ringing, the Sanctuary coming alive around her when she drops onto the roof of an ancient school bus, then its hood, then the ground. A halo of dust rises around her. The faded, sandblasted black letters of ST. LOUIS PUB-

LIC SCHOOLS still reach the bus's length, but it has no wheels, the undercarriage sunken into the dirt like a wallowing beast. Its occupants stir awake. They tear aside the rags hanging in the windows and curse her for waking them. In response, she fights a yawn.

There are many farms in the Sanctuary, all of them guarded and gated off, and though she isn't supposed to, she cuts through one of them now, climbing and jumping the iron-spiked fence, hurrying her way home. One of the sewage canals is diverted through the quarter acre, its many small channels oozing and buzzing with flies. She tromps past a raised box of sweet potatoes, another clustered with beans, another spiked with corn, others with barley, wheat. The dirt is dusted with bone meal and moistened with sewage, some cocktail of nitrogen and phosphate to increase yields.

Several gardeners wander around, irrigating and harvesting. One of them asks if she thinks she can do whatever she wants and she says, "Pretty much," before climbing the fence and dropping down on the other side.

She walks down a tight, shadowy street, so tired that at first she isn't sure she hears what she thinks she hears—a whisper— her name. But when she turns, she sees the man standing twenty yards behind her. The wind tunnels through this cement corridor and knocks his gray duster back to reveal the thinness of his figure. Lewis.

He is far enough away, and the wind gusting enough, that she cannot be certain how his whisper carried so far, as if he tossed his voice like a ball through the air. "Come."

She feels her face redden with a rush of blood, her guilt announcing itself. She cannot find her voice at first but manages to strangle out a question, "What do you want?"

He says nothing, only stares at her with those cold blue eyes, before turning, his duster snapping grayly behind him like a spectral hand beckoning her.

She follows him, not knowing what he knows, not wanting to know. Everything hangs in the balance, as if poised at the edge of a great chasm, and she feels at once ebullient and fearful. She does not notice the street unscrolling beneath her feet—until she finds herself in Old Town and climbing the steps of the museum. They seem to shake, but it is she; she is shaking.

He does not hold the door for her and he does not pause once they enter, but continues forward without looking back, gliding through the entry with the golden compass emblazoned on the floor and continuing to a circular stone staircase that from the landing seems to wind down into tighter and tighter circles, like the inside of a shell.

"Where is the girl?" he says.

"Safe."

"There are only so many places to hide."

"They won't find her. I can promise you that."

"People are saying she called the birds down from the sky."

"That's what they're saying."

"I need to talk to her."

"Only one way that's happening."

They descend three stories. At every landing, there is a doorway, and beside every doorway a lantern. By the time they enter the basement, shadow overpopulates light. Lewis tries a switch, but the bulb above them explodes with a spray of sparks. So he unhooks the entryway lantern and holds it ahead of him as he walks. She follows in her own private darkness while ahead he seems to float in a sputtering orange light that reveals the half-seen shapes of their surroundings—hallways that elbow into rooms full of shrouded paintings, glass-cased moths with eyes patterned on their wings, a harp with cobwebbed strings, a dust-clotted tiger with a raised paw and a snarl frozen on its face—stacked high all around them, sometimes with only a narrow corridor between. She rams her knee into a crate and six cockroaches come scuttling out from beneath it.

Lewis continues to creep along before her, his back hunched and bony. There is a smothering, airless feeling down here, and it is easy to imagine the light extinguished, the darkness collapsing all around her. It is easy to imagine Lewis pinning her to a velvet board, like one of his moths, making her a part of this vast, rotting collection.

Then he is standing before a giant American flag—a real one, not the mayor's single-starred version—its stars and stripes stained and faded and untwining along the edges. He tears it away from the wall. They both cough at the dust that swarms the air and sleeves their throats, and when she calms her breathing, she notices the wooden door with the iron ring Lewis takes in his hand.

The wood has warped and the door has not been opened in many years, so Lewis must heave three times to expose even a thin black gap. He sets the lantern on the floor and takes the ring now with two hands—and at last the door opens with a groaning complaint.

The faint tang of oil breathes from the closet. Lewis holds the lantern into the space to battle back the shadows, and it takes Clark a moment to understand what she is looking at.

She recognizes them from books, from paintings and photographs. An arsenal of pistols and rifles, black barreled, with wooden and plastic grips, dozens of them neatly stacked on floor-to-ceiling shelves. "Are those—"

"Yes." He clears his throat. "I'm not sure what else you have in the way of supplies, but we'll need stores of water especially and—"

"What does this mean?" She is trying to read something in his face, doubting what he has shown her, doubting him. He does not appear excited or afraid, his expression resigned to a hard frown.

"It means I'll go." His face tightens and untightens. He speaks so quietly, as if he barely believes the words: "I'll go."

She is not the type to cry, but right then she feels a tear slip from her eye and down her cheek.

"But first, there's one more thing you need to know." With that said, he reaches up his sleeve and pulls from it a letter. "It concerns the girl."

CHAPTER 7

N O ONE KNOWS where the flu came from. Some say a long black car pulled up to a gas station and from it stepped a black-haired man in a black suit, who coughed once into his fist and gripped the pump and muddied it with his phlegm. Others say that late one night—for a few minutes, all over the town of Ames, Iowa—the faucets ran yellow, as yellow and as thick as melted wax, polluted by a terrorist or maybe some parasite loosed from deep beneath the earth. And still others say a featherless crow the size of a child tumbled down a chimney and onto a fire that charred it into a black pile of bones and sent a diseased cloud into the air all over town, one that people breathed into the pink pit of their lungs, where a burning sensation gave rise to a cough.

That was how the sickness began, with a cough, a needling itch at the back of your throat that grew steadily worse until it felt like your chest was clogged with burrowing ants that you must—you simply must—expel, barking raggedly into your hands until they were spotted with blood. Accompanying this was a fever so powerful that a wet washcloth steamed when placed on your forehead. Your brain cooked. Your vision went red, with twirling black flies along its edges. And all this time you were coughing, coughing, until it felt as though your guts might uproot and push out your throat.

One day, it was simply there, among the people of Ames, the virus rooting in their lungs like red-tipped mushrooms. The USDA labs were located there, level-four security clearance and host to every animal-borne pathogen in the world, from anthrax to bird flu to Ebola, and many speculated that it came from there, from an unwashed hand or an open laboratory window or a pricked finger. The deadliest viruses must meet three criteria. They must spread swiftly, by a cough, a kiss, a sneeze, a hand testing a melon at the supermarket or gripping a pole in a subway car. They must be unfamiliar to humans, so that antibodies cannot defend against them. And they must kill the infected. This virus met all three.

On average it took people five days to die. During that time, their chests collapsed inward with every hitching cough. Their throats rasped. Their lips bruised like wilting lilies. The blood vessels in their eyes burst and they wept blood and because they were propped up on their pillows the blood raked down their cheeks.

This was October and the leaves turned a shimmering gold and came loose from their branches and revealed the patterns of the wind, twisting and swirling along the streets, lawns, ballparks, making a clattering music. And when the wind kicked up and the leaves rushed past and clung to the leg of someone's jeans, like a starfish, damp and splayed, they would hurriedly wipe it away, as if anything the air carried might cause harm.

When parents said, "You'll catch your death," they meant it, grabbing their children as they raced out the door to hand them a jacket, yes, but also a surgical mask. "Stay in the yard," they said. *Don't breathe*, they wanted to say.

It was unsettling, not trusting the air, lungs filling up like dark closets that might hide ghosts. Everyone bought masks. Not just surgical masks—because the stores emptied of them almost immediately—but carpenters' masks, gas masks, even Halloween masks. Anything, no matter how ineffective, to make them believe they were choking away the germs.

Doctors prescribed medicine, but medicine did not help. Scientists gave the virus a name, H3L1—also known as Hell. It wasn't long before the hospitals were full, before the schools closed, before the sidewalks in Ames crowded with reporters. Three people died. And then, in one night, three hundred. Everyone rushed to the grocery stores and pulled from the shelves cereals, pasta, granola bars, canned fruits and vegetables, bottled water, whatever would last even after the electricity snapped off. "The worst is happening," they said. "The worst is here."

In Ames, a Budweiser delivery truck pulled up to a Hy-Vee and an hour later pulled away. A Greyhound grumbled back and forth to Minneapolis, its tailpipe coughing along with its gray-faced passengers. A charter plane. A Japanese hatchback. A bicyclist stopping through on his way across the state. And all those letters licked closed. The sickness spread.

The infected rose from a hundred to a thousand to a million in a matter of days. There wasn't time for quarantine. There was barely enough time to utter the word *pandemic*.

For a few days, everyone blamed Ames, so that the town felt like the eye of a black whirlpool with sunken lungs and broken ribs swirling through it. But then the sickness fingered its way across Iowa and into Minnesota, Wisconsin, Illinois, Missouri—spreading outward from the heartland—the country, the continent, the world. There was no one to blame anymore. And there was no difference between good and bad, young and old, or at least not that the sickness recognized. Everyone was eligible for death.

At a time when everyone should have stayed home—that's what the television said, before the channels gave way to static, *stay home*—people instead went to church. At St. Cecilia's in Grand Forks and at Trinity Lutheran in Chicago and at the United Methodist in Memphis, people wandered in and out throughout the day. The services and vigils were ongoing. The candles burned down to bubbling pools of wax. Everyone wore their masks, but the masks didn't always help. They breathed each other's breath and they tasted wafers and wine and they brought their hands together in prayer and they sang, how sweet the sound, until the coughing overwhelmed them and they hunched over and fell to their knees in awful genuflection.

The power went out. One minute refrigerators were humming, radios playing, lamps glowing, and the next, their mechanical brains went dark and silent. Those who were still alive brought matches to Sternos and sparked on their propane grills to cook. The police spray-painted black Xs across doors, the hieroglyphs of the infected, most of whom were already dead. All the windows of all the stores were gaping mouths broken by the bricks of looters, and in the evening the glass caught the last of the dying sunlight so that the streets of the towns and cities seemed to sparkle.

Then the horizon flashed, the air trembled, as if beset by constant thunderstorms. These were nuclear warheads. China was the first to fire. Then Russia. The United States responded in turn. And soon Britain and India joined them. The missiles scorched the sky, made blackened craters out of cities. When New York and then Boston vanished in a fiery pulse, the Atlantic Ocean poured into their smoldering craters and the steam of millions of ghosts blurred the sky. The nukes were meant as a last-ditch inoculation, to cease the spread of the virus, but they only hurried along the death of the world.

Nuclear power plants, one by one, after losing their power and their employees, after emptying their emergency backup generators, descended into a state of meltdown. Their containment caps cracked and the cracks glowed as red as magma and from them seeped a heated, poisonous breath.

In the nineteenth century, the sun had bulged and erupted and lashed the earth with billions of tons of protons and electrons, a geomagnetic storm unlike any other. The sky had whirled with auroras of colored light. Telegrams had vanished midtransmission. Telegraphs had smoked and erupted in flame, along with anything else plugged into the now sizzling circuits. Many believed the gates of heaven or hell had opened.

The effect was much the same when thousands of missiles shocked the ground and mushroomed the sky, when hundreds of power plants cracked open and disgorged their core. Those electrical grids still functioning now sparked and fried. Satellite and GPS signals scrambled. The energy released by the flares and explosions, caught in the earth's magnetic field, splattered and raped the world. The wind rose and the clouds swirled in and took on a purplish red color and the air smelled like ozone. Radiation spiked. Rain blistered skin and yellowed grass.

For millions and millions of years, the biosphere was a contained environment. Nothing came from above, save for the occasional meteor, and nothing came from below, except for lava spewed from volcanoes. This changed when people began burning fuel, choking the seas and skies with CO_2, cranking up the temperature decade after decade. But there were more than four hundred nuclear power plants around the world, and the colossal radioactive energy released by them and by the missile strikes resulted in a supercharged global warming, the equivalent of a million volcanoes erupting at once.

The Gulf Stream, the northward current that followed the East Coast of North America and crossed to Europe and dropped to Africa, was one of the principal ways the world regulated its temperature. When the northern ice caps suddenly melted, the rush of frigid water shut down the circulatory cycle. At the same time, holes opened in the ozone layer, holes big enough for the moon to roll through. This created permanently unbalanced temperatures, unbalanced pressure systems, some sections of the globe hardening into permafrost, others furnacing so that anything green began to wither and crumble to dust.

Some people headed north; some people headed for the woods. Some hid in caves, where they gathered their rifles and sleeping bags and filled their backpacks with matches and food and clothes for all seasons. They chose the caves because they were isolated, easily defended, and maybe they chose them, too, because people felt already as though they were slipping back in history, to a simpler time dedicated to the gathering of food, the warding off of danger. They made fires and with the cinders drew upon the basalt walls pictures of bodies lying all about with Xs for eyes, a cipher for future generations to behold and puzzle over.

And some, like the citizens of St. Louis, made their last stand. They used bulldozers and cranes from construction sites to help fortify a perimeter, and then they killed any who approached it. Several National Guard units, outfitted in hazmat suits, disposed with a shot to the head any who exhibited the slightest symptoms. The bodies they hurled daily over the wall became part of their defense, a warning against any who might trespass. Some buildings, such as the hospital, they painstakingly drenched with alcohol and bleach. There were a million ways their plan could have gone wrong, but somehow it went right, and a year later, long after the observable world perished, they continued to thrive, and many believed the Sanctuary sterilized.

They were wrong.

This is why Danica descends the staircase with a lantern held before her. Her blond-white hair matches the cobwebs that cling to the walls and singe in her passing. Spiders scuttle from the light. She curls her lip but does not fear them. Even when they drop onto her arm or dash across her feet, she merely shakes them away. Maybe *like* isn't the right word, but she has always admired spiders, their deadly elegance. As a child she would sometimes pluck gently at their webs, as if they were a harp's strings, to draw their fat black bodies into the light. And she made a game out of hunting grasshoppers to tangle in their webs so that she could watch them feed.

This was once a basement, now a crypt. By law the dead are delivered to the morgue, where their remains are harvested. But the ruling class made an exception for itself, their bodies entombed beneath the Dome. The coffins are wood—it is dry enough that they will never rot—the name and likeness of the deceased carved elaborately into each lid. When they were married, Thomas took her down here and led her among the coffins and asked where she might like to be interred. He seemed taken by the place. She knows he comes down here often to lay his hands upon the coffins.

She is not here to commune with boxes of skeletons. She seeks something else. After Thomas toured her through the rows and rows of coffins, he said, "You'll like this," and led her to a metal door with a combination dial. He spun it one way, then the other, and back again—as she spied over his shoulder and committed the numbers to memory—before dragging open the vault. She was not sure of its original purpose, whether for money or safety, but it had since become a place where the Dome's occupants store valuables, relics. There were stacked pyramids of red wine that long ago had turned to vinegar, canned food that no one had bothered or dared to open, velvet-lined jewelry boxes, stacks of crisp, worthless green paper money, a short-wave radio, a diamond-studded watch, satellite phones, memory drives, slick black tablets with fingerprints still streaked across them, all the useless valuables of another time. Among them she spotted some things that might still serve a purpose: city plans, the blueprints of buildings, vials of medicine with yellowed labels, vaccines that might have gone stale. Everything looked new. Nothing aboveground looked new. She marveled at it all, touching everything, until she came upon a polished black box in the far corner. Thomas grabbed her by the wrist when she reached for it. "No," he said, and when she asked why, he told her.

She stands before it now. It is rectangular, like a miniature coffin, small enough to cup in one hand. She reaches for it, the first time without success, withdrawing her hand as if burned. She checks the doorway behind her. Her hand trembles when she reaches again, when she seizes it, and on the shelf leaves behind a dustless space.

There are many things that can kill a virus. Detergents can melt through their lipid envelopes. High temperatures can cook their proteins. Enzymes can damage their nucleic acids. And time. Most viruses, when exposed to air, will survive no more than forty-eight hours.

But there are ways to keep a virus, too. They are made of DNA or RNA, enclosed by proteins. So long as the proteins are maintained, the virus is preserved. Their small size, simple structure, and lack of water allow this. Scientists have discovered the DNA of Paleolithic men, even of velociraptors and megalodons, crushed into stone or ice. Chemicals can sustain them, as can low temperature, as can air-locked pressure, as can freeze-drying. This basement is full of coffins meant to preserve the remains of the elite—and she holds in her hand a miniature version of the same. The greatest of viruses.

When she asked Thomas why, why keep such a thing, he gave her a small smile and said, for the same reason we keep bears in cages, for the same reason this country stored fatal missiles in underground silos. "Because we like feeling we own death."

She nearly forgets to close the vault behind her on her way out—and, twenty minutes later, at the stables, she nearly cries out when Reed lays a hand on her shoulder. She spins around to find him smiling at her. This is where he said he would meet her. He has hay in his hair and a pitchfork in his hand. He is mucking out the horse stalls with the rest of the sentinels. The air buzzes with flies. A horse with a white diamond on its muzzle whinnies and she flinches from the sound. His smile grows wider—and she feels the simultaneous urge to slap him and bed him.

There are others in the stables, brushing down horses, carting away manure, and her eyes dart to them before settling meaningfully on Reed. "When do you leave?"

"Tomorrow." He keeps his voice low, nearly a whisper. "Will you come?"

She pinches her mouth in a frown. "You know I can't."

He looks like he wants to argue the point further, but she shakes her head.

He closes his eyes and sighs through his nose. "You said you had something for me."

She holds out the box—to show him, not to give him. "I do."

"A gift?"

"Not a gift so much as a defense. A weapon." She beckons him to follow her into an empty stall. "I've been thinking about what you were saying. About starting over. If the group lives—and you will. You *will* live. If the group lives and you make it as planned to Oregon, and if the landscape should appear as promising as you hope, you will come back for me, yes?"

"Of course I will."

"But," she says and taps his chest with a finger. "But." If something goes wrong—if the people there prove hostile—he should find a way to gift this box to them and then ride as fast and as far as he can. It will wipe the area clean, and in another year, maybe two, they can return there and make it their own.

"What's inside it?"

She presses it into his open hands. "The end of one world, the beginning of another."

CHAPTER 8

After Lewis leads Clark into the basement, after he shares with her his store of arms and willingness to accompany them, he shows her the grate in the floor, the black square with a rusted ladder and cold, stale breath puffing from it. "We can use the tunnels to escape," he says. "No one knows about them."

She snorts a laugh and he asks her what's so funny.

"You. You're always convinced you know more than everybody else. Where do you think I sent my brother and the girl? There's more than one unsealed grate in this city."

She tells him the plan then. Now that Lewis is in, there will be six of them altogether. This past week, they've been humping supplies through the tunnels, secreting them in a building more than a mile beyond the wall. Matches, flour, knives, lanterns, needles, thread, bedrolls, hardtack, jerky, dried fruit, but mostly water, canteens and leather sacks sloshed full of water. And now they will add guns. The revolvers and rifles from the museum's hidden arsenal.

The tunnels cannot accommodate their horses, and on foot they will not make it far—even if they escape pursuit. Summer is here. The burning face of the sun seems closer every day. By midmorning it hurts to breathe, like sucking on a pipe lit with dust. They will need horses—at least twelve of them, six for riders, the others to rotate out and carry supplies—and they will need to ride hard, before their water runs out, hopefully finding a more forgiving place.

"We leave tomorrow morning. Be ready."

Lewis packs and unpacks and packs again. He paces his office and rubs his hands together with a dry, papery whisper. He does not know how to occupy himself, how to channel his excitement, near giddiness, such an unfamiliar feeling. So he tinkers. He loves to build things, puzzling together gears, soldering wires, fitting joints, creating something mobile and useful out of the scraps of a broken world. A clock that spins with the cycles of the moon. A sturdy set of glasses, each side hinged with a dozen lenses that fold up and down to magnify or telescope. A repurposed coffeemaker that sucks moisture from the air and pools it into a cup for drinking. For the past week, he has been building what he will never finish. A short-wave radio. He gathers parts, mostly from the bazaar, picking out tubes to clean, wires to thread. Knobs. Diodes. Switches. Capacitors. All of them cracked, decayed. He corded the radio into the outlet the other day and the thing popped and fuzzed with static, then grew suddenly hot, several of the tubes exploding in a glass shower. So he began again.

He imagines spinning the dial, for days, weeks, maybe months, finally coming across a voice. Maybe the voice would speak English, maybe not, someone hoping to be heard, no different from the transmissions fired into space so long ago. He would speak into the microphone, saying, *Hello? Can you hear me?* and the voice would go silent for a moment before calling back to him excitedly, manically.

The unfinished radio sits on his desk now. He fastens the antenna mast to the cabinet just as Ella enters the room without knocking.

"What is that?"

"A radio."

"What use is a radio?"

"What use is anything in this museum?"

"I'm calling it a night. What do you want me to do tomorrow?"

"Tomorrow." He hands her a sheet of paper with a long list of errands, all of them outside. He needs her gone.

"This is going to take forever."

"Yes."

She starts for the door and he calls after her, "Oh, and Ella—"

"What?"

He opens his mouth. There is so much to say. Come tomorrow, he knows she will feel betrayed, and he worries about leaving her— worries what will happen once Thomas learns of his escape—but he cannot leave his life's work unattended. For all her annoying qualities, he recognizes her as a fierce, clever girl. She will care for the museum and, if need be, fight for it should anyone try to shut its doors, salvage its materials.

She folds the sheet and then folds it again before giving up on him, vanishing down the hall. "Good-bye," he calls after her.

———

Every morning, the gates open and a ranging party of eleven sentinels rides into the Dead Lands, the last among them seated on the back end of a Ford F-150 cut in half, retaining only its bed and rear wheels, two horses drawing it forward. They arrange their route in advance, working in a wider and wider radius of the wall since so much has already been scavenged. Sometimes they harvest whatever they happen upon—these are called opportunity strikes—as they work their way methodically through cars, homes, businesses, ripping open drawers, closets, cupboards, taking a hammer to a wall and wrenching out its guts. And sometimes, on targeted missions, the city engineers put in orders for copper, steel, wiring, wood, tires, brick, and when they return to the Sanctuary, the bed of the F-150 is heaped with rattling goods.

But not today.

Reed is already waiting at the gates. Clark nudges her horse forward, drawing up next to him. He will not look at her. His eyes are trained on the gates before them. She can see a forked vein throbbing in his forehead. She can hear the other horses falling into place behind them, the creak of leather, the rusty moan of the truck bed. She wonders if he feels as she does now, her stomach a roiling pit, as if she is at once starved and ready to throw up. There is no going back. They are leaving—they are leaving everything and everyone they know—and they can return only if they want their heads decorating pikes.

A slump-shouldered guard tromps toward them. He fights a yawn, barely awake. His hand rattles a set of keys, the keys for the lock, the lock meant to keep people in more than keep the world out. He fumbles them and the keys fall between his feet, like a brass insect that might scurry away. Clark resists the impulse to loosen her foot from her stirrup and kick him in the head.

"You ready?" she says to Reed.

A thought seems to pass his face. What is it? The way his jaw tightens, the way his eyes flit sideways to briefly acknowledge her, she thinks it might be hesitation. She hopes not. The others will look to him as an example. Any weakness on his part will be contagious. She feels the very opposite of indecision—a wild, desperate propulsion that makes it nearly impossible to steady her horse, keep from charging forward.

The sentry scoops up the keys and shakes them until he finds the one he wants. He scrapes it into the lock, twists it sideways. There is a *click*. He then, with the help of another, hefts the bar bracing the two massive doors. They moan under its weight, staggering to the edge of the doorway, where they drop it with a clang.

The sentry then brings to his lips a bone whistle—and blows—signaling their departure.

She tries to concentrate on anything else. Something tangible. Something to distract her from what they are about to do. The crow's feather caught in her horse's mane. The bluebottle fly that orbits her head. The thin crack of sunlight running down the middle of the gate, splitting open now to accommodate their horses as they spur forward.

Clark chooses a Kwik Trip gas station as their meeting place. The pumps are strangled by brittle brown vines. A skeleton in a leather jacket sits at the wheel of a van parked out front. The trees surrounding it are thickly spiderwebbed, like sick clouds that might rain the bones and shrouded bundles tangled up in them. The convenience store was long ago raided, the shelves empty of anything but dust. The glass doors remain intact, though scoured and filmed by wind.

They stack their supplies in the entryway—weapons and food and clothes—bunched into piles to load onto each horse. Lewis waits with three others. The first, a doctor with a pruned face and long gray curiously knotted hair. She accompanied him through the sewers with a lantern and a brittle map. She pinches a pipe between her lips. In one breast pocket she carries sulfur-tipped matches and in the other tobacco. The pads of her fingers are stained the same yellow as her teeth. Her words carry smoke when she tells Lewis how Clark came to her, just as she came to him, and told her the way it would be. "There's no denying her. She's a force."

"But why you?"

"I suppose we can rule out physical strength, so that leaves me to guess you all might need a little mothering along with your medicine. Far as I can tell, that's what's brought her back to my office again and again these past few years. A little mothering."

"And you're willing to say good-bye to everything you know to serve as our wet nurse?"

"I'm a *doctor*. And you won't be sucking on my tit; that's for sure. There's nothing for me here. Nothing for any of us. Anything is better than nothing."

The second man Lewis knows, but not well. York, the street performer, Clark's half brother. They nod at each other in greeting but don't offer a hand. He sits on the counter with his legs swinging and his mouth crooked into a smile. Lewis has always considered him a fool. This has something to do with his appearance—with his brightly dyed clothes and the triangular sideburns carved onto his cheeks—but more so his behavior, his voice always loud, his manner always theatrical, everything out of his mouth seeming to twist into a joke.

And then there is the girl, Gawea. The mere thought of her seems to weigh down the pocket where Lewis keeps the letter. Since it came into his possession, he has read and reread it. The one addressed, impossibly, to him. He doesn't know how to explain it any better than he can explain the curious energy that sometimes possesses him. Maybe he will begin by describing his own disbelief. How, when he first picked the letter up, he thought he misread its script. He tried to untangle the letters and weave them into other names, but they kept coming back to his own.

To Lewis Meriwether—

That is how the letter opened. He sees its contents everywhere: written in pitted concrete, in beetle-bitten bark. A centipede tracks a sentence in the sand. Smoke from a chimney wisps into words.

> *Your dreams are true. You are not alone. I don't mean there are others alive. There are, of course, but you have always guessed that to be the case. I mean there are others* like you*—gifted, special—including the girl I have sent to you, Gawea. She will guide you in more ways than one. Come west. I insist.*

Aran Burr

He asks where Gawea is and York throws up a hand, his thumb indicating the square of space behind the counter. Lewis slowly approaches. He does not know what to expect from her, what she might look like or how she might greet him. She does not appear in a shaft of sunlight. She does not levitate several feet off the ground. She does not shout out his name. When he rounds the counter, he finds her lying on the floor, curled up in a nest of blankets, asleep. She is just a girl, not much older than Ella. Her skin is tanned and drawn tight over her bones, offset by the white bandages that wrap her wounds. Her black hair falls over her cheek like a tattered wing.

"Leave her alone," York says. "She needs her rest."

At that her eyes snap open. They seem at odds with the daylight. Their blackness reflects his looming figure, as if he were an amorphous pupil floating in them. He takes his hands out of his pockets and then puts them back in and says, at a stutter, "I'm the one you're looking for."

When Clark exercises, jacking out push-ups or lunging to the floor, rather than rushing through fifty reps, she focuses on intervals of five. It cures her of her impatience and makes the overall sum seem more manageable. For this reason she keeps her eyes on the Witness Tree. It is like some giant bony hand escaping the underworld, its bare branches reaching up to claw the sky. She rides toward it, and only it, knowing if she thinks only about the horizon, about the many months and thousands of miles that lie ahead of her, she may go mad with impatience. One step at a time. She will focus on a tree, then a building, then a hill, maybe a mountain, whatever increments might draw her forward.

But first, the Witness Tree. This, she knows, is where she will lose sight of the wall and the wall of her. And now, with one last dig of her heels, she hurries past it, and the dark-eyed buildings pinch around her. She slows her horse, and the others match her speed, clopping over broken bits of asphalt, threading around cars, kicking through tongues of sand, trotting down tree-lined avenues with the branches knit loosely overhead and the sunlight falling through them to brighten the ground like shards of glass.

They make their way through a business district and enter a neighborhood of ruined bungalows corralled by chain-link fences clotted with leaves and needles and rust. Today they are supposed to return with screws and nails and lumber, two-by-fours and two-by-sixes especially. She can hear the cart twenty yards behind her, bouncing along and rattling with hammers and saws and screwdrivers and crowbars. With these tools they check decks and porches for treated cedar or polyethylene, tear open drywall for the studs hidden beneath, coffined all this time, only some of them free from rot by weather or termites. But not today.

To their right, the houses fall away into a park whose lush green lawn long ago gave way to patches of yellowy cheatgrass. A rag-tangled body with a thatch of hair still clinging to its skull lies on a bench and gapes at them. A plastic slide has faded from red to a faint pink, cracked like a dried-up tongue. The jungle gym is hairy with weeds. A flower-patterned bike lies abandoned, half-buried in the dirt.

She leads her horse into the park and the others follow. She knows what she needs to do, but for the moment she can only stare at the jungle gym and imagine this as a place where children once played.

A voice calls behind her. "Is something the matter?" When she doesn't answer, the voice calls out again, "What are we doing?"

She hopes they won't fight back. She wants them to make their way home safely, to tell everyone what has happened, to spread the dream of their mission and the promise of their return—before Thomas can warp Clark into a traitor. She plans to cuff their ankles and wrists, to steal their horses. They are only a little more than a mile from the wall and should be able to hop or crawl home before dark. Unless something—spiders or snakes or worse—finds them.

Clark swings her horse around and nods at Reed. The two of them separate from the nine, their horses slowly retreating. Reed withdraws two revolvers. She does the same. Their hands shake. The nine rangers—two women, the rest of them men—stare at the sunlight gleaming from the gunmetal and then settle their gaze on Reed.

"It's time for us to say good-bye," he says.

Gawea might smile at Lewis, but her face has a woodenness that makes it difficult to read. She stands. She walks toward him and he can't help but take a step back. A bloodied bandage scarves her neck. She motions to it, excusing her lack of voice. He is more than a foot taller than she, but there is something about her that makes them seem the same height.

She reaches out both her hands, one of them bandaged, the wrappings looping her palm and binding her wrist. It takes him a moment to realize he should respond in kind. He is not used to touching others, not to embrace, not to shake hands, not even to brush up against on the street. It's more than the intimacy—it's the sense of getting rubbed away. But in this case, when his hands fall into hers, he does not feel drained so much as he feels charged, fuller. More confident and excited than ever about what might lie ahead.

"It's true? It's really true? You're going to take us—you're going to take me to him?"

She nods.

"Why?"

Again she motions to her neck. Then she brings a finger to the counter and cuts through the thick dust, writing out: U R THE NEXT.

"I am the next? What does that mean?"

Gawea is about to write something more when the doctor says, "Think I hear something." The sun is reaching higher—the windows are beginning to glow—and the doctor leans into the glass with pipe smoke coiled around her, her stare fixed on the road.

Something scuttles by the glass doors. A shadow falls across the floor, just for an instant, as if the sun blinked. Lewis cannot distinguish a shape. It is too fast, moving at a blur, and the doctor is standing in the way of it. "There's something out there," she says, taking several steps back.

A rasping sound comes from the wall, as if something is trying to claw its way inside.

"Arm yourself," Lewis says, and they each snatch up a rifle. The doctor and York hold theirs awkwardly, studying them, rearranging their grips.

Lewis has never fired a weapon, but he has studied them, cleaned them, broken them down and built them back up, and he models for them now: finger off the trigger, palm beneath the forestock, butt against the shoulder.

A long silence gives way to a thundering, the swelling sound of horse hooves headed their way. "They're coming," York says, and all of their attention now swings toward readying their supplies.

They have organized a different pile for every horse, each containing clothes, food, canteens, knives, matches, ammunition, rifles rolled into blankets. Lewis's pile, at the end, rises taller than the others, a tidy pyramid built from a compass, many maps, his owl, three silver canisters packed with his medicine, quills and ink and a blank calfskin journal kept shut by a long bicuspid braided through an eyehole loop.

Clark and Reed appear in a storm of dust and dismount and yell at everyone to hurry, move their asses, and Lewis finds his thoughts twined up and his body startled out of his control. The doors are swinging open and closed, open and closed, with rusty shrieks. Everyone is racing back and forth, scooping up their gear, yelling—yelling at him, he realizes—and only then does he rush forward and stumble and knock his pile in many directions.

Everyone is waiting for him, their horses snorting and spinning in circles. He processes his surroundings in flashes—Reed staring back the way they came; York smiling down at him and saying, "So this is the way it's going to be?"; Clark jabbing her finger at an empty mount and telling him to *move*.

The horse—a roan with a gray muzzle and dark-socked legs— shifts away from him when he tries to fill her saddlebags. He chases her one way, then the other, slowly sorting his gear, wasting more minutes and earning the curses of the other riders. When he tries to foot his weight into a stirrup, he grabs hold of the reins and the horse rears and begins to clop slantingly away from him. "No," he cries. "No. Stop."

He is about to ask for help when he notices Clark go rigid in her saddle. Everyone has fallen silent, their eyes on something behind Lewis.

He knows he will not like what he sees. And he is right. A huddle of spiders slink toward them. A dozen of them. As big as dogs. They scuttle from behind the gas station, over and around the pumps, all of them long legged and big butted and spiked with tiny blond hairs. Their many eyes gleam like gems. Their mandibles dangle from their snouts like deadly mustaches.

They pause at the pumps, ten yards away, rasping their mandibles, stuttering their legs. The horses snort and whinny. They stomp their hooves, fighting the commands of their riders. Then, from around the side of the gas station, comes a spider larger than the rest. First there are only legs. They move with a hypnotic needling, like the whirring of a magician's fingers before revealing some horror. Then its segmented body, a hairy fist of a face. Some of the eyes appear blinded, scarred through with what look like slash marks. It reaches one leg forward and pauses it in the air, as if to point.

The other spiders start toward them.

Reed lifts his revolver and Clark says, "No! The sound will carry to the Sanctuary."

She spurs her horse toward Lewis, and he finds himself frozen in their shadow. She raises a hand. He wonders at first if she is going to strike him. Instead she gathers his reins into her fist, steadying the roan. "What's wrong with you?"

He doesn't like how high his voice sounds when he says, "I'm not used to moving so quickly!"

He can hear the patter of the spiders' many legs closing in on him like a dry rain.

Her eyes flash between him and the spiders and the road ahead. Then she grabs him by the arm and helps him onto her own horse and tells him to lasso his arms around her waist and hold on for his very life.

———

Thomas receives the news in the atrium. This is a vast, high-walled garden built onto the Dome. Flowers spring brightly from pots and hanging baskets. Water drips from them like tears. Paths made from paver stones run between boxed beds crammed with potatoes, onions, corn, squash, beans, sunflowers. Some have, some have not. Thomas is happy to *have*. All those who have—among them the council members—have certain things available to them that others do not, including access to the atrium and a seemingly depthless access to water. Or that's how it feels to Thomas anyway.

The ceiling is netted with wire mesh to contain the dozens of birds that nest in the colored boxes that stand on poles. Three peacocks roam about, their feathers a ghostly white and their eyes so red they do not look like eyes at all but the beaded blood that wells from blinded sockets. When they walk, their claws scratch the paver stones and their necks dodge forward and back. Every now and then they stiffen their bodies and fill the atrium with a banshee cry. Thomas likes to take his meals here, at an ironwork table, with the peacocks strutting and the songbirds whistling and flitting around him.

His wife sits across from him. Her hair is pulled back into a braid, making her face appear even more pointed than usual. Despite the heat, Danica wears a thin, open-throated sweater. Her plate remains full. She never eats much—but at a standard meal she will at least prod at her salad. Her chair is angled away from him. She sits so still that a yellow-breasted bird lands on her plate and pecks at the pile of grasshoppers braised with vinaigrette.

He peels a shriveled orange and eats it in three chunks and spits the seeds onto the ground. "Something is bothering you."

"No."

"You're just not hungry?"

"I'm just not hungry."

"Ah."

The door to the kitchen swings open and Rickett Slade ducks through it and marches toward them without pausing to request an audience. A peacock stands on the path before him. At his approach, it unfurls its tail into a fan with a steely rattle of feathers. Slade does not pause. It appears he will crush it, or kick it aside, but at the last moment it skitters to make way for him.

Thomas dabs a napkin at the corner of his mouth. "What?"

Slade towers over them. The breath whistles from his nose. "Two rangers are unaccounted for, among them their captain."

"Unaccounted for?"

"Gone. Missing."

"Well, what do you think has happened to them?"

"They have left."

His hand crushes the napkin. "The Sanctuary?"

"Yes."

"You mean to tell me that they have left the Sanctuary and *deliberately* not returned?"

"Yes."

"How do you know this?"

"Because the sentinels they held at gunpoint told me."

"Guns? *Gun*point? Who has guns to point? What are you talking about?"

"They do. We assume they are somehow in league with the girl."

Thomas absently wipes his mouth. "This is a little hard to take."

"There's more."

"Of course there is."

"Your *friend*, the curator, Meriwether. He is also unaccounted for."

"Impossible."

The bird remains at his wife's place setting. Its claws scratch the plate. Its head darts and its beak pecks at a grasshopper, punching holes in the body, mangling it beyond recognition. She will not look at him, her face as blank as the pale sky above. She seems to be holding her breath. So does the world. Everything motionless except the bird as it tears patches in the grasshopper.

Thomas clears his throat and straightens his posture and wipes the crumbs from his lap, and in a voice that sounds far too calm to be his own, he tells Slade thank you. He tells him to leave. He tells him to return in an hour. By that time he will have made a decision. In the meantime he needs to think.

Slade's eyes flit to Danica before he departs the atrium.

When the door closes, Thomas lunges across the table and brings his hand down on the bird. Its wings snap open, but he strikes it before it can take flight. It has grown lazy, living in the atrium, imbued with a false sense of safety. He catches and breaks its left wing. The plate shatters. His palm bleeds. The bird calls out, then flutters off the edge of the table and flops on the ground, where he pursues it, stomping once, twice, until its body stills and smears. Blood bursts from its beak.

She will not look at him, not even when he says, "What do you know of this?"

"Nothing."

He grabs her by the arm. The sweater is thick enough that he cannot feel her, one more thing coming between them. "I know you've been fucking him."

"That's how this marriage works, isn't it? We fuck other people."

He yanks her from the chair. It overturns with a clatter and her body spills to the ground. She gives him a baleful stare. Her hair has come loose from its braid in white filaments. Thomas says, "You share a bed with someone, you share secrets. What did he tell you?"

Her eyes shine with tears. "I said I know *nothing*."

He stares at her—and she stares back, her eyes too white around the edges and her teeth bared. He grabs her by the throat with one hand and with the other scoops up the dead bird and mashes it into her mouth. That is how he leaves her, gagging out its broken body, scraping feathers from her tongue.

Lewis clutches Clark and keeps his eyes on the surrounding city, certain that at any second, more spiders will drop from trees, wolves will explode from doorways, snakes will twist from porches and pursue them.

He has read about Chernobyl. He knows, in the years that followed the nuclear meltdown, in the two thousand square miles surrounding the power plant, biodiversity exploded. Radiation can result in a kind of accelerated evolution, mutagenesis. Many of the mutations die out. Some are merely deformed. But others grow stronger, accommodating the harsh conditions. After World War II, mutagenic breeding in plants resulted in strange colors, better taste, tougher hulls, but also in disease- and cold-resistant strains of everything from rice to wheat to sunflowers to cocoa to pears that became a sizable portion of harvested crops. Useful mutants.

He knows that the world has become a furnace. St. Louis was not hit by nukes, but the radiation sloshes through the air and soaks the ground and will linger for centuries, cesium 137 and strontium 90 serving as a different kind of vitamin for animals and insects. This is why wolves are hairless and spiders oversized. This is why some people are misshapen with tumors, born with withered limbs and milky, blind eyes and veins that seem to grow on the outside of their skin. And maybe—*maybe*—this is why he is the way he is. A mutant. Another example of the world moving on. But he is not alone. He has the girl now, Gawea. She did not call him a freak. She called him the next. They are the next.

They ride. Sometimes they gallop and sometimes they canter, but for half a day, they do not stop. They take to the roads when the roads permit, but more often the asphalt is buckled, riven. So they ride through yards and over collapsed fences. They dart through the dried maze of Forest Park. They follow ditches. They chase the shoulders of highways. Stalks of mullein *thwap* and stain the horses' breasts yellow. Dried brush claws at their flanks. Sand and cinders kick up in clouds and muddy their eyelashes. They tie handkerchiefs around their mouths to breathe. In the sand, every hoofprint leaves a clear impression, their granular passage there for any to follow, on occasion zigzagging, but otherwise unfurling west. They cannot hope for rain, but with time the wind should chase away some of their tracks.

Already they have gone farther than Clark has been before. They do not speak. The wind whisks dust off branches and it falls through their translucent shadows. With every clopping step, the air seems to vibrate. At strange noises before and behind them they pause and pet their snorting horses and try to shush them so that they might listen better.

When Clark hesitates, reining her horse one way, then another, confused about their direction, the girl waves them forward and digs in her heels and takes the lead. Clark and Reed make eyes—a question crushed into their stare—and then follow her.

They leave behind the city, the suburbs, and break away from the freeway to follow the cracked clay of the Missouri River. Here, in a silver pocket of shade beneath a bridge, they finally pause for water. Their horses foam with sweat. Their legs tremble and jump. They aren't breathing so much as *heaving*. Lewis feels as though he is riding even after he dismounts from Clark's horse, the ground seeming to rock, as if he is in two worlds at once.

York guzzles at a canteen, and Clark twists her brother's ear and drops him to his knees. "Only a taste, you idiot," she says.

The dry riverbed looks like the passage of an enormous snake, the stones running along its bottom like shed scales. A gabled house sits on a bluff overlooking it. The windows are broken, but curtains still hang from them. Their tattered forms move with the wind, rising and falling, so that it looks like there might be bodies in there still breathing. In a way, this is their great gamble—that out here, in the Dead Lands, there is yet life.

Gawea sits in the shade with her hand pressed to her throat. The doctor approaches her, asking if she's all right, asking to check her bandages, and though the girl tries to wave her off, she eventually relents to the doctor's fussing. The doctor makes a *tsk* sound at the dust-caked wounds beneath and digs around in her satchel for cleansing alcohol and fresh dressing. And she hands out to the rest of them a dented can of ointment and tells them to smear it anywhere they feel blisters rising. "You need to tell me where it hurts," she says. "I'll take care of you."

Lewis leans his weight on one leg, then the other. The insides of his thighs burn. The muscles at the small of his back have gathered into a fist. His center sloshes. He opens his silver tin and fills his fingernail twice, snorting and sneezing and shivering with fresh energy.

He does not complain—but his expression is plain for any to read—because Clark approaches him and speaks with the steady, placating voice you would use on an aggrieved child. "No whining."

"I haven't said a word."

"This is only the beginning."

"I understand that."

"From now on, you ride your own horse."

"But I don't—"

"Come here."

She seizes the reins of the roan he earlier had not been able to mount, and she leads it toward him. Its sweat smells of sweet, scorched paper. Black jelly runs from one of its eyes. Its mane is clumped and wet, its coat spotted with burrs. It breathes with an asthmatic wheeze. "Why did you give me this horse?" he says. "It's obviously a terrible horse."

"It's a fine horse. But it's our oldest. And tamest. Tame seems to suit you."

Clark digs into a satchel and scoops out a handful of dried corn. She indicates that Lewis should take it from her, and he does, with two hands brought together to make a bowl. The horse sniffs. Its lips curl back to reveal teeth that look more like broken shells. Its long pink tongue, filmed over white, works every last crumb from his hands.

When it finishes, it raises its muzzle to sniff him. He raises a hand, too fast, and it flinches. He says, "Sorry, sorry." This time he draws his hand slowly toward its neck, and the horse lets him. There is hair and there is skin and there is muscle, not a trace of cushioning fat. The neck ripples under his hand.

"Does he have a name?"

"He's a she," Clark says. "We call her Donkey."

Minutes later, when they straddle their horses and chase their shadows west, Lewis falls immediately to the rear of the company and chokes on the dust they kick up.

They ride on—into what was once a pasture or a field, now a flat stretch of land remarkable only for the scalloped texture and pink color, a vast nothing. That is how he quantifies these sand flats and bone-dry canyons and skeletal forests and sunken-roofed towns—as nothing. All these years, all those books—he has built kingdoms in his skull. The world within him is full. The world without, empty.

They come upon a town and ride through an amusement park, through the mouth of an enormous clown, through an alley of rotten stuffed animals and a dunk tank full of sand, past the rusted remains of Tilt-A-Whirls and roller coasters and drop towers and Gravitrons, past a carousel whose fiberglass horses have faded and cracked like the wings of dead butterflies.

It is then, as the Ferris wheel looms before them like a mechanical moon, that Lewis believes he sees a man. A man in white. He sits in one of the Ferris wheel cars, near the top, appearing at first a blaze of light, what must be the sun on metal, but no, from the rocking back of the horse, if Lewis concentrates, he can make out pieces of the man—hair blown about his face in smoky tendrils, a silver ring on a hand raised in greeting, a ragged robe like a dove's torn wing. Lewis's lungs constrict and can't find enough air. Every hair on his body goes erect. The air seems to shimmer. He knows the man. He phantoms through Lewis's dreams, always far away, always beckoning. And now the man has a name, Aran Burr.

Then the fairground barns close around Lewis, and he is traveling down a shadowy chute between them, the smell of cattle and hogs somehow still in the air. Every few minutes, the others are in the habit of turning in their saddles to check on him, dawdling their horses to make up for the sometimes thirty, sometimes seventy yards he trails behind. Now he slows more than ever, so enchanted by the sight of the man that he might turn around to assure himself he was real, when Clark drops back to pace him. She wears a neckerchief over her nose. It is damp in the shape of her mouth. He can barely hear her voice over the roaring wind and the pounding hooves. She is asking if he is okay.

"I thought I saw someone."

She pulls down the neckerchief. Loose strands of her hair catch in her mouth and she spits them out. "You didn't see anyone."

"I swear I did."

"You didn't. Now, come on."

They reach the edge of town, but before they head into the open country, they ride through a dozen pyramids, each one a heap of blackened bones, what must be hundreds of bodies, heaved here and splashed with gasoline and lit with a match in the hope that fire might stop the flu.

They ride through cars whose tires have rotted away like black socks. They ride by school buses full of skeletons. They ride past fallen barns bordered by silos that look like the missiles that once fell from the sky. They ride past what were once fields, now sandy barrens interrupted by dead cattle, their ribbed impressions like roots or tubers that failed to take purchase.

There is no trail to follow so they make their own. They ride in fear of what lies before them and what lies behind. They ride in pain, but they know pain already or they would not have come, so they ride through the pain in the hope that it will one day lessen. And when night comes, they ride still, following the stars, trying not to worry about what might await them in the dark. They ride through the night. Lewis wakes with a start when his horse lurches beneath him, sliding down a steep grade, and he wakes again in time to jerk his head away from a branch clawing toward him like

111

a hand. Only when dawn breaks behind them and the sun rolls across the empty blue bowl of the sky and chases the shadows to the corners of the earth and glares furiously down at them do they stop to rest, at last.

———

The police headquarters is a rectangular, gray-stoned building with courtrooms in its upper stories and windowless holding cells in its basement. Thomas pushes through the entry, into a shadowy, squared-off room with the seal of St. Louis on the floor, benches along the walls, and a desk manned by a deputy. Slade leans over the deputy and jabs his finger at a map of the Sanctuary.

Thomas overhears the word *mutiny* and clears his throat and the two men raise their eyes to consider him.

"You told me an hour," Slade says.

"It turns out I didn't need that long."

Everything will be all right. He has every confidence that he can manage a situation only temporarily out of his control. On the walk here he could feel his thoughts sticking, clumping, like dust on a wet eye.

Now Slade tells him, "You should have requested an escort."

"I can't walk around my own city?"

"No, you can't. There are plenty who would like to kill you."

"I want you to take me below."

"Below?"

"I want you to take me to see Jon Colter."

His lips might thin. The skin might tighten around his eyes. Otherwise, Slade's face is as hard and featureless as the stone blocks stacked into walls around them. "I'll get the keys."

There is a wind turbine located on top of the building, and the lights pulse on and off at a steady rhythm, so that after a while you get used to the passing darkness, as if a great eye were opening and closing. Slade does not bother to fetch a lantern, so every few paces they pause and wait for the lights to brighten again.

When Slade keys open the door at the top of the stairs, the smell comes rushing out and nearly knocks Thomas back. It is almost tactile, something that grows hair and pisses and shits, something that can crawl down your throat and claw out your insides. He brings a hand to his nose so suddenly he slaps himself. His eyes film over with tears.

Slade says nothing, but his mouth horns at one corner, the beginning of a smile. He leads Thomas down the stairs. With each step his boots thump and his keys rattle, but over the top of this Thomas can hear something else. The sound of many people breathing, like an uncertain wind. A voice muttering. A moan that goes on so long it becomes a wretched song.

At the bottom of the stairs, before a caged door, the lights fade and black out and they wait there for a few long seconds. The noises grow louder. Thomas can hear feet padding against concrete. Hands gripping bars and rattling them. A stream of urine splattering the bottom of a bucket. Whispers.

The lightbulb above them sizzles to life. Slade unlocks the door and the two of them pass through and it shuts behind them with a clank. To their right reaches a cinder-block wall—and to their left, ten cells, their bars a chipped white. Several of the men are naked. Their hair is long and matted. The ones who are white are as white as grubs from lack of sun. Some of them crouch in a corner; some lie on their cots and observe the visitors with craned necks. Others press their faces between the bars, like this man, who looks like a skull with slimy hair and who hisses and spits until Slade slams a baton against his hand and sends him whimpering to the floor.

There are only two lights socketed into the length of the room. They dim and die just as Thomas and Slade reach the final cell. In the bewildering darkness Thomas tries to remember how close he stands to the bars and wonders how far a man might reach. He can hear someone, in the near distance, breathing. He imagines fingers ghosting through the air, grabbing hold of his neck.

He waits, and he waits, what feels like an interminable length, and just as he is about to call out a question to Slade and ask if something is wrong, a surge of light brightens the air. He blinks until he finds his focus.

The man at first appears like some shadow that clings to the cell. He stands with his back to them. He has been imprisoned here as long as Thomas has been mayor, a year now, but confinement has not softened him. One of his arms is raised and his back and shoulders jump with muscle. He is short but square, built like a blunt weapon. His attention is focused on the wall, which he has sketched over, made into a mural. In his fingers he pinches a piece of metal, maybe a nail, and he uses this to scratch the concrete. There are many-headed beasts battling men with swords, naked bodies twined together in lust or combat, severed heads trailing ropes of blood, skeletons dancing, every inch of wall etched into some curious detail. The floor, too, has been sketched over. And small bits of stone carved into what look like trolls, fauns, beasts.

"Turn around," Thomas says.

The man adds some flourish, a horn on a head. "There." He drops his hands to his hips and turns to face them. The light is faint, making every line on his body stand out with shadow. The muscles rippling across his stomach. The scars, too. There are many of those. He appears like several bodies stitched together, many membranes of skin pulled taut and discolored, the most noticeable of them across his face. The left side of it has been torn away, one eye like a white egg deep in a nest of scars. His ear merely a hole, the hair around it gone and the skin a mottled gray. His teeth reach across his cheek, so that half his face appears always gathered up in a grin.

"You've been busy," Thomas says.

"Have to find a way to pass the time. Otherwise, a man's likely to go crazy." His voice sounds rough-edged, rusted out. "You've come to say you're sorry?" His permanent half smile makes it difficult to tell whether he's joking.

"I've come to offer you your freedom," he says to Colter, first in darkness and then in light, as the lights sizzle off and on. "And ask for your help."

Colter's tongue worms along his bottom lip. "Why would *I* want to help *you?*"

"Because this"—Thomas steps close enough to the cell to knock the bars with an open hand—"is your alternative." The clang of metal shakes the air.

Colter runs a finger along his arm, tracing the purple ridge of a scar. "What about my wolves?"

"Still alive. Still scaring children. We've kept them at the zoo."

"All of us in cages, eh?"

"Not anymore. Not if you bring me back some heads."

The lights crackle off again, and in the dark the men keep their silence. Several seconds later, there is a sputtering hum and the air goes from black to gray to yellow, and Thomas sees that Colter has crept closer, to the very edge of the cell, his fingers curling around the bars to either side of his ruined face when he says, "Let me out then. Let me out and bring me my wolves."

PART II

The Forbidden Zone was once a paradise. Your breed made a desert of it, ages ago.
—Dr. Zaius in *Planet of the Apes*

CHAPTER 9

EWIS WAS SUPPOSED to be her supervisor, her teacher, though often their roles seemed reversed. Ella did as he asked, but with some complaint or revision. They had a set of rules between them. She did as she was told—she looked to him for guidance and instruction—but so did she point out his every failing. He did not like his schedule disrupted. He suffered always from headaches and moodiness. He grew peevish and short when he couldn't find what he was looking for, and on and on. He was a difficult person, she told him often, and he did not deny it.

Together they discovered his dead mother. The way he held her, with his arm behind her back, made her body arch as if she were a torture victim suffering some unimaginable pain. When Ella touched him on the elbow, when she told him to set his mother down, he let out a guttural cry but otherwise said nothing and did as he was told. She then took his clammy hand and dragged him down to her height and kissed his cheek.

She doesn't know he is gone, not for sure, until the deputies come looking for him. He has been missing all day. She has never known him to break his routine, but figures, with the recent death of his mother, he may have earned an excuse. After the deputies rip through his office and bedroom, after they knock down bookshelves and turn over his bed, they drag Ella to a medieval display, a room full of lances and flails and tapestries, where Rickett Slade is waiting for her.

Of course she has seen him before, dropped her eyes when they passed in the street, but they have never spoken. He sits in a massive gold-trimmed throne. He barely fits, the arms of it biting into the sides of his belly. Across his thighs rests a baseball bat—her bat, the only weapon she keeps in her quarters, with the word *Peacemaker* burned by a magnifying glass across its cracked, wooden length. On the floor, tossed aside, lies the sign she wrote in careful calligraphy, *Please do not sit on the display*.

"Can't you read?" she says.

He may smile or he may frown; it is difficult to tell. His face is pocked with acne scars, each of them carrying a small shadow. He motions with the bat, across the room, indicating where she arranged a Judas chair opposite the throne. The same sign rests on its spiked seat. "Please," he says, "let's both be where we're not supposed to be."

A deputy—a woman with her head shaved except for a rat-tail braid—grabs her by the wrist and Ella shakes her off and says, "Don't you touch me." She approaches the chair and lowers herself gently onto it. She has done so before, when no one was looking, and knows the points on the seat and back and arms dull enough to be tolerable for a short period of time. "Now is when I tell you I don't know anything and you choose not to believe me."

This time he does smile, she is almost certain. A hint of teeth beneath his upper lip. "Lewis didn't tell you."

"No, he didn't tell me."

"And how does that make you feel?"

"Mad. I'm mad." And she is. She is trembling with anger. "And though I'm sure these feelings will pass, right now, frankly, I hate him."

"How old are you, girl?"

"I'm sixteen."

"And you're going to take care of this museum all on your own?"

She stiffens then. She knows what she looks like to him, a plain-faced girl with short hair the color of old straw. She looks like someone barely worth talking to, someone your eyes pass right over. She isn't going to let him dismiss her. "There's no one else who can do it, is there? And he didn't leave me much choice, did he? That's typical. He's the most arrogant, inconsiderate man in the whole world." She doesn't realize she is yelling until she finishes.

"We could always burn the place down."

She can feel the seat digging into her now, hot points of pressure. "Go ahead. Enjoy policing the riots that follow. This place is holier than any church. The Sanctuary's only escape."

"Not the only escape. Your friend Lewis found some other way." The sensation of his eyes on her is like two hands pushing her around. "We found a radio in his office. Isn't that what it was? A radio?"

"It doesn't work."

"You aren't using it to communicate with him?"

"It *doesn't* work, so no, I am not."

He shrugs. "Well, I smashed it to pieces anyway." He holds up the bat, swinging it one way, then the other, like a metronome. "This yours?"

"You know it is. You found it in my quarters."

"You keep it because you're scared."

"I'm not scared. I'm a realist. Sometimes you have to hurt other people before they hurt you."

He rolls forward, extracting himself from the throne. It groans in relief. He crosses the room and stands before her until he fills up her entire field of vision. He reaches out a hand. "I'm not supposed to believe you." Her entire head seems to fit into his palm. "But I do."

There is a tug—followed by a sting—behind her ear. When he pulls his hand away, he pinches a clump of her hair between his fingers. He tucks it into his pocket. Then departs the room, flanked by his deputies. He speaks without turning to address her. "If you find anything, if he left anything, you tell me."

"I don't know what good it would do you."

"Let me decide that." He drops the bat when he exits the room, and the rattling echo of it seems to linger in the air a long time.

Later, she finds the note. There was a stack of paper squared neatly on his desk. Now the sheets lie scattered like dead leaves around the office. She traces her fingers along each one and brings them to her nose to smell. Finally she finds what she is looking for, the faint texturing and lemon scent. She lights a candle and holds the paper a few inches above the flame, and within seconds the letters begin to darken and shape into words.

Ella—

By now you know that I am gone. Check my office window nightly for the owl. Of course you will take care of the museum, and I'm certain you will do a fine job. Be sure to destroy this letter and deny ever having received it.

Lewis

No apology. No well wishes. No promise to return for her. No explanation beyond what she heard from the deputies. She lowers the note onto the candle and drops it to the stone floor and watches it flame and blacken upon itself. She walks through the museum then, every room of every floor. She has to see for herself that she is alone. She finally comes to a stop in the rotunda, where she throws back her head and yells at the starry mural above, "You son of a bitch!" The words clap back at her, her voice a dozen times angry. "You son of a bitch, why didn't you take me with you!"

———

Slade lives in the prison. Wood rots. Plastic cracks. Cement crumbles. But stone and iron last. And that is what the prison is made of, stone and iron. It is a place of security, a place he can hide things away.

The door is dented steel with a line of rust running like a tear trail from the lock. It groans when he closes it. The room is windowless. Electricity courses through the walls, drawn from the creaking rotor of a wind turbine on the roof, but he keeps no bulb in the ceiling fixture. He lights a linseed oil lamp instead. He likes the room dark, likes the sun shuttered away. Outside he feels exposed, the sun's eye and *their* eyes always on him. Here he feels safe, nested.

The lamp's light makes the mannequins seem to move. There are five of them, collected from a department store with birds roosting in the rafters. Some are missing arms. Their plastic skin, a cancerous shade of yellow, has cracked through the eyes, the mouth, along the neck and belly, their bodies webbed with fissures, some gaping.

They wear clothes, torn and stained. A leather necklace, weighted with a stone, rounds one of their necks. Earrings dangle from another, unevenly, hooked through the cracks in the plastic. He painted four of their faces. Red smears across their mouths. Blue or green or brown pools in their eye sockets. A black smudge of mole. A dusting of freckles. There is a tooth, a canine, embedded in one of the mannequin mouths. Fingernails. All of them have hair, chunks small and large.

"Hello, pretties," he says.

His bed is pressed up against the wall, a knot of blankets over a metal frame. In the center of the room is a chair, a metal chair with leather straps looping from each of its arms. The seat and the legs and the floor beneath are stained a rusty red, a skirt of dried blood. A table reaches along the wall, and above it a pegboard carrying coils of wire, barbed metal instruments.

He goes there now and grabs a ceramic pot of glue. He approaches the only naked mannequin. To bring their faces together he must crouch. They are similarly ruined, his by acne scars, hers by clefts brought on by heat and time. He breathes out of his mouth. He opens the pot of glue and daubs some across the crown of the mannequin's head. Then he reaches into his pocket and removes the clump of straw-colored hair and mashes it into the glue.

The mannequin wobbles a few seconds before going still.

"You're a fierce one," he says. "I like that."

CHAPTER 10

Weeks Pass, and the six of them chase their way west. There are mountains in the distance, Clark knows. The mountains she has dreamed of all her life. She still cannot see them, but Lewis promises they are there, as they move across Missouri, where the dead forests give way to windbeaten yellowed grass that cooks down to sand.

Her entire life she has spent looking at the same thing—the same ruined buildings, the same defeated faces—and now everything new strikes her as particularly vivid, almost painterly. The heat shimmering in the distance so that the world appears through warped glass. The white snakes of dust that come squiggling out beneath the horses' hooves with every step.

She is impervious to the heat. And though her body aches for water, she is less thirsty every day for a pint or a tumbler. Maybe because she knows there is no tavern around the corner. Or maybe because her body needs so many other things. Or maybe because her mind is so distracted and hopped-up with constant adrenaline. But probably it is because of her brother. He is the real reason.

She has always felt protective of him, never more than now. People talk about her arrogance. People talk about her recklessness. She and York share the same blood and the same qualities, his exacerbated by the teenage belief that his story is more important than any other, that his body is indestructible, that guts matter more than brains, that his cock is the compass point worth following.

She keeps her eyes on him constantly, watching with a mixture of affection and annoyance and obligation. He might look like a man, taller and broader than she, but younger, younger by a decade, an almost unfathomable amount of time, and not to be mistaken for mature. Since he was nine, she has shielded him, nursed him when sick, comforted him when scared, punished any bullies who taunted him, made sure he was properly fed and dressed. For five years, he slept in her bunk while she slept on the floor. Other than drinking spirits, and ranging beyond the wall, he has been her main interest. She doesn't want children—who would want to bring something so delicate into this punitive world?—but she has one. He is hers. In the same manner that parents view a child as their body's extension, the closest they come to reincarnation, she wants his life to be better than hers. That's the promise that waits for him, that waits for them all, on the horizon.

His expression is arranged in a sleepy smile, as if he is living some dream he knew would come true, unaware or uncaring of any danger. This isn't a mission to him; it's an adventure, an entertainment. "Why are you always so serious?" he says to her one day, and she says, "Because everything is at stake, even if you don't realize it." When he fires an arrow into a quail and a feather catches the corner of his mouth, Clark tenderly plucks it from his lips. And when he rides beside Gawea or tries to share a canteen with her or juggles stones to entertain her, Clark worries.

Clark does and does not trust Gawea. In part it is the silence, her throat punctured and infected and slow to heal. When she tries to make words, her voice rasps like a rust-deadened hinge, and when she writes, the words come slowly in a mess of bird-scratch letters. Lewis asks who is Aran Burr and she writes, *Leeder. Teecher.* Lewis asks whom he leads and she says, *Everyone*, and Lewis asks if he is like a mayor or a governor and she hesitates before writing, *Mostly.* Lewis asks if she made the birds fall from the sky, if she made them attack the stadium and aid in her escape, and she writes, *Did not maek.* Her bandaged hand, her dominant hand, clumsily grips the pen and scratches out each letter: *Asked.*

"You asked?"

She underlines the word: *Asked.*

One morning, Clark wakes to find Gawea standing at the edge of their camp, a single moth dancing above her. Clark closes her eyes, eking out another minute of sleep, and when she opens them again finds dozens of moths now swirling around Gawea, dirtying the air. The girl does not often smile but she is smiling then, with her hands outstretched and moths balanced on her fingertips. Clark sits up in her bedroll and says, "Hey," and Gawea drops her smile and her arms and the moths flutter off like a blown cloud of ashes.

She did this alone. That's what Clark has to keep reminding herself. That's what makes the distance seem bridgeable, possible, even when they come to the Nebraska border, where the bluffs drop into plains that roll on and on, the color of aged parchment, like one of Lewis's maps forever unscrolled. The girl came all this way without anyone. The balls on her.

"How much longer?" Clark asks her. "When does this end? You said it would end."

It ends, she writes.

"But when?"

Weeks.

"How many?"

Gawea shrugs.

Their water halves, and halves again, and their mouths go to cotton from rationing. At some farms they find iron pumps tapped into deep wells. Besides ceramics, which have the same basic composition as fossils, nothing has lasted like iron. Gates and pans and pipes like this one. The metal was once red, but except for a few specks, the paint is chipped from it. The handle juts out like a one-armed man trying to keep his balance. They take turns priming the arm, and when they first call up the water, it sometimes carries rust and muck for an hour before running clear.

They follow the girl and she follows the river, the Missouri River. "Do you really trust her?" Reed says, and Clark says, "I trust that she knows how to survive out here, but for now, that's all." They ride through crumbling towns and cities, everything a splintered mess, and they ride through the empty spaces between them. They ride around trees that fell years ago and trees that fell last week, through fences, onto houses and cars, across streets. Trees on top of trees on top of trees. They ride past leaning electrical poles with their snapped and frayed wires. They ride past roads buckled to pieces, crumbled to gravel. They ride past the litter of ripped balloons, shriveled condoms, six-pack rings, diapers, and chip bags and Ziploc bags and grocery bags, plastic bags, so many of them, that flutter from bushes and trees and gutters and fences like ruined egg sacs.

At one point, York says, "God, would you look at all this dead shit." There isn't much more to say than that.

The wind creaks and knocks things over with a crash so that the world seems to be muttering about them in their passing. And everywhere—in windows, doorways, the knots of trees—there is the sense of eyes watching.

Coyotes yip and howl at night. Snakes rattle their tails and startle the horses. They surprise a huddle of javelinas, the big bristly pigs snorting and squealing, rushing toward them and hoofing up a big cloud of dust and swinging their tusks from side to side, and Clark drops two of them with arrows before the drove escapes.

They need to be able to protect themselves, but none of them know how to use the guns they carry. When Reed asks if the ammunition will even fire, Lewis says there is only one way to find out. He says the desert climate is to their advantage, the dryness a preservative. That's why archaeologists, he tells them, pulled scrolls thousands of years old out of Egyptian tombs. "It would take moisture to neutralize the powder or primer," he says, and because the bullets have been stored in ammo boxes—in a relatively cool, intensely dry basement—they should ignite.

The bullets rattle when they finger open the .357 boxes. Their metal has oxidized, giving them a slight green crust, but otherwise they have not visibly degraded. The cartridges for the .30-06 rifles appear much the same. And though some of the shotgun shells are a loss, their plastic cracked and spilling buckshot, most seem serviceable.

That morning, everyone sits in a half circle and Lewis stands before them holding a revolver. The sky, still pinpricked with stars, pinkens behind him. He has to hold the weapon with two hands, its weight too great for his thin arms. He lectures everyone first on the mechanics. He thumbs the safety on and off, swings out the cylinder and spins it. The hammer cocks and releases. He goes on for some time about the double-action mechanism, about safety concerns, about how to break down the weapon, clean it with a brush and rag and oil, when York says, "Shut up already and let me try."

The others whistle and clap when he jumps up and smacks the dust from his rear and snatches the revolver Lewis reaches to him, grip first.

York smiles for his audience. He shoves the gun in his belt, crabs out his arms, then draws and pops an imaginary round at each of them. He spins the gun on his finger—then loses his grip and it thuds to the ground.

"Don't be an idiot," Clark says, "you idiot."

He slides the bullets into their chambers, then slams the cylinder home as if he has done so a thousand times before, his hands moving with a magician's adeptness. "What should I aim at?"

The doctor is smoking her pipe, blowing smoke rings. "The moon," she says.

"Yeah, the moon," Reed says. "Blast it out of the sky."

The sun is rising and the moon is sinking out of sight, its crescent like a clean slash. York spreads his legs and raises his arms and draws a bead on it. He holds his breath, then compresses the trigger. The hammer falls with a sharp click.

Nothing.

He lets out his breath. "Broke." His stance relaxes and the revolver droops to the ground. He snaps the trigger twice more, and then again, and a round blasts from the chamber with a sound and force greater than any of them has experienced before. The dirt kicks up a fist-sized crater beside his foot. The gunshot thunders. He whoops and drops the gun and runs a few paces from it before saying, "Shit! Fuck! Damn!"

Everyone ducks down, their hands clapped over their ears or eyes. Now their shocked expressions give way to laughter. The deep-bellied kind. When York dances over to Gawea and says, "What do you think of that? I shot the moon for you, baby!" even she smiles and brings her hands together twice in mock applause.

It feels strange, almost dangerous, for them to be laughing, and, as if in agreement, they all stop and look over their shoulders as if they might be punished for a moment of levity.

———

Gawea wonders if she will have to kill them.

She could do it without any trouble. One by one, a snake curled in a boot, a centipede coaxed into an ear, a few days or weeks between them so as not to arouse suspicion. Or all at once—slit their throats or call down the birds when they are sleeping—but that would be less than ideal. Lewis would know. He would hate her and distrust her and resist her. She has no doubt she could overcome him. He seems so frail, like a bundle of sticks, but it is easier to lead than to drag. She cannot understand why Burr wants him, cannot understand why he refers to Lewis as "the next." But it is not her job to defy or question. It is her job to deliver, as if he were a parcel. She will deliver Lewis, and then Burr will make good on his promise. Everyone else is expendable.

It hurts to swallow. It hurts to breathe. It hurts to turn her neck one way but not the other. Sometimes she wakes up to a line of ants trundling up her shoulder to taste the wound. It feels like a hot stone is lodged there, as if she could nudge it loose with a cough or a finger. But if she does cough—if she sucks in a lungful of dust or woodsmoke—something bursts and blood or pus fills her hand.

If she really tried, if she kept her voice a whisper, she could probably talk. But she won't. This way—with the doctor treating her for a slight fever and wrapping her scabbed-over wounds with bandages—she remains the victim instead of a threat. She is the one hurt, not the one who would hurt. They have so many questions, but her answers can only be few when scratched out on paper or in the sand, agonizingly slow.

Burr warned her. He said that Gawea might face resistance. He said that Lewis would not come alone. He said that others would want to chase what she promised—water, civilization—and she would do well to treat them not as an impediment but as a tool. They might slow her down, but so might they prove useful, offering protection and even camaraderie, neither of which she felt she needed. She can protect herself, and she prefers to be alone. She has always been alone, even in the company of others. She is alone now, though they do their best to engage her. It's the questions that bother her, the constant questions. Some of them logistical: "How many people live in this town you mention, Astoria?" "How about in Oregon?" "In the Pacific Northwest, in the country?" "How does your money work?" "Does everyone speak the same language?" "Where will we live?" "What do people eat?" And some of them poetic: "Will you tell me about the mountains?" "What songs do people sing?" "What does the ocean smell like?" "What does fish taste like?"

And then there is the boy, York, always goofing for her, trying to catch her eye. He rode past her while doing a handstand on his saddle. He juggled three knives along with a chop carved from a javelina's rump and by the time he finished, it was carved into bite-size pieces that fell neatly on a plate. Sometimes she can't help herself. Sometimes she snorts a laugh. And when she does, he is only encouraged, saying, "Oh! Look, everyone! Of all the unknown wonders in this new America, I am most in awe of this: our girl actually smiled!"

They watch her. They are suspicious of her, she knows, but they are more suspicious of the world. She tries to keep as still and silent as possible, and then their attention is drawn to a groaning wind turbine, a dead forest, strange splay-toed tracks, a deer carcass opened up and scattered into a thirty-foot orbit.

And they are suspicious of each other, too. They seem wary of Lewis. And they seem worried about the doctor, whether she can

keep up. And they seem disturbed by the fact that Reed is fucking Clark. Sometimes this happens quietly, deep in the night, with
sighs, shifting fabric, the moist meeting of mouths, and sometimes
more obviously, during the day, in an outbuilding within earshot
of the group. They are not in love. That is clear. They don't stare at
each other fondly, hold hands, rub each other's shoulders or feet.
The sex seems almost accidentally cathartic, like someone picking
up a stone to exercise with or stumbling across a flower to sniff.
Clark constantly questions and belittles Reed, and he testily re-
sponds that he knows what he is doing and will she lay off already?
But they are united, even if only physically, and that alignment
makes people nervous. A joining of power, a sharing of secrets.

It could be Gawea won't have to kill them. It could be they'll be
killed all on their own, maybe by each other.

Wherever they stay the night, they raid the area for supplies. One
time, inside a steel-roofed log home, they find a table still set for
dinner and pajamas laid out on the beds, but no bodies anywhere,
as though the people who once lived there dissolved into dust.
Another time, they find a television in the corner of the living
room, the glass knocked from it, the electronic guts ripped out and
replaced by dolls and action figures arranged in a still life. Clark
stares at it for a long while, as if expecting them to animate and entertain her, but they remain still, entombed in their dark box, and
she can't help but think maybe this is the world, no matter where
or how far they ride.

"I thought we would have found something by now," Reed says
and kicks the television, and a few of the dolls fall over.

"Like what?" Clark says.

"Something better."

She reaches into the broken television and rearranges the fallen
figures. "We'll find it."

"Will we?"

"I don't want to hear questions like that. Neither does anybody else. Okay? We need hope right now, not doubt."

There is a cocoon of soiled blankets on the floor and the back porch is full of garbage—canned food and cereal boxes with their tops torn open. Lewis asks, "Does someone live here?" and Clark says, "I don't see how that's possible," but then they find a plastic mop bucket splattered with shit that still smells and they go silent for a long minute before Lewis asks if they should press on and stay somewhere else. But they have already unsaddled and brushed down their horses, and the sun has set, and the night is so monstrously dark, its star-sprinkled blackness absent of any moon.

They sleep instead in the cavernous pole barn, which stinks of hydraulic oil, and Clark volunteers to take the first watch. She pinches her thigh, slaps her cheek lightly, takes deep breaths, but their days are so long and she can't keep from falling asleep. She wakes hours later. The moon has risen and its light streams in the window and gives the floor a glow, as if a sheet of fog lowered while they slept. She studies the space around her. A snowmobile with a tarp thrown over it, a four-wheeler with sunken tires still caked with mud, a Farmall tractor, a manure spreader, a planter, a combine the size of a dragon, and finally a grain truck with tires as tall as she.

She knows something must have woken her and she listens to the breathing all around her until she discerns a noise different from the rest, a damp smacking, like a foot working its way out of mud. She unholsters her revolver and approaches the barn door and cracks it open and finds one of their horses dead and a bent-backed wild-haired figure lowered over it, ripping into it, feasting. She fires at him, once, twice, three times, until Reed grabs her and says, "Enough. He's dead."

He lies on his back, staring at the sky. The man who arranged toys in a dead television is the same man driven wild enough by hunger to bring down a horse. His hair is dreaded with grime and his beard clotted with blood, making him look more beast than man. But underneath all that, he is just like them. She wonders how far away they all are from crossing that line.

They were on alert when they first departed the Sanctuary, glancing constantly over their shoulders, keeping their fires small at night, sending the owl into the sky to track what lies before and behind them, but they have grown lazy in their habits. Tonight they slept deeply and foolishly and encountered their first realized danger. And it is her fault. She should have stayed awake. She should have taken better care of them—she is responsible for them—and instead of a horse next time it might be her brother.

They bleed the horse and bottle the blood. They butcher the carcass and cook and salt the meat and ride away from the farm in an arrowhead formation, with Gawea at the point. The air is so hot and brittle, it seems, with every breath, they risk the danger of shattering. The sun rises behind them and their shadows lead the way west, one fewer than before.

CHAPTER 11

EVERYONE CALLS IT the news. The windowless wall, several stories high, next to each of the Sanctuary's wells. It is the obligation of every citizen to check the news daily. Whatever they need to know—about an execution, rationing, construction, whatever—is painted there, over a whitewashed background, in giant dripping black letters. For those who can't read, a town crier wanders the streets at dawn, noon, sundown, to shout the same.

Ella stands in a long line with an empty jug. So long that she reads the news a dozen times or more. NEW CURFEW. HOME BY NIGHTFALL. ENFORCED.

With no explanation as to why. There never is. *Why* is irrelevant, Ella knows, to the servant. Why shine shoes, why wash windows, why sweep floors or polish silver or wind clocks? Because someone more powerful than you demands it, and if they tell you to eat shit or crawl on all fours like a dog, you'll do that too. Because if you don't, they can hurt you or take away what's most precious to you, food, water, home, family.

The people around her mutter their theories and complain about the unfairness and malicious idiocy of it all, but they do so quietly enough that they are not overheard by the deputies who wander up and down the line. Ella grinds her teeth, grinds down what she wants to yell at them all. It's Lewis's fault. If they're looking for a *why*, there it is. Him. Damn him. He is the reason for the curfew. He is the reason Slade nearly tossed her in a cell. He is the reason she alone is responsible for a museum that feels suddenly like a shed chitinous husk. She can't not be angry. She hates everyone, and everything is awful. The sun burns down and the wind gusts and the rotor on the turbine spins and eventually she finds

134

herself at the spigot, filling her jug with water so murky she can't see through it.

She lugs the water, leaning into its weight, shifting it from one hand to the other. She crosses a stone bridge over a mud-slick sewage canal. She waves her free hand at the blue-black flies that swarm there. They get caught in her hair and crawl on her skin and follow her for a block, and their buzzing matches the noise of the crowd gathered near the museum. She curses the flies and she curses the people, all of them in her way, a bother.

Then she sees the man chained to the whipping post, the third in as many weeks, and her annoyance gives way to guilt-tinged sadness. He is bearded, shirtless, the skin of his belly and back a grub white compared to the tanned darkness of his face. Already he is pinkening under the sun, burning. He does not weep, not yet, but looks warily about him. He stands on an elevated platform, his wrists bound by two short chains anchored to a metal post. A voice calls out then, a voice she recognizes. She elbows through the crowd until she can see him. Slade.

He and his deputies, dressed in black, are like walking shadows. He steps onto the edge of the platform and surveys the crowd and tells them about the man. At a bar the other night he sang a song about the mayor. "A profane song. A mocking song. Remember, friends, there is always someone listening. There is always someone watching. You are never alone here. What you tell one person you tell forty thousand. Now this man says he is sorry about his little song. He says he meant it only for fun, not as an act of civil disobedience. And for now he has our mercy."

In Slade's hand, a coiled whip. He opens his grip so that its length unravels. He shakes his wrist one way, then the other, making it dance, its tip a fanged barb. He takes a few steps back, gauging the distance between him and the man. Then draws back his arm and casts the whip forward. It seems to pause a moment in a dark parabola—before sinking, darting in to strike. The crack gets mixed up with the scream. The man falls into the pole, hugging it. A winged flap of skin opens across his back. From it blood sleeves.

The whip lashes again and again and again. Eventually flesh gives way to the white nubs of vertebrae. Slade loops the whip in his hand and once again surveys the crowd. His eyes are lost to piggish folds of flesh that turn down their corners, but Ella feels certain his gaze follows her when she hurries away, back to the museum.

This would be a good time to have parents. Someone to turn to in a bad time, ask for help, a hug, a meal. Though Lewis would never think of himself in this way, he was her guardian, the one who years ago snuck up beside her in the west wing and startled her when he said, "You're under this roof more than anyone but me."

Vagrant children were as common as rats, and she was one of them, living in the Fourth Ward, in the pantry of the kitchen of a brothel. She came to the museum nearly every day—it was her way of forgetting. She could think of nothing to say to Lewis in response except, "I'm sorry."

His hands were behind his back, the posture of a scholar. "You should be," he said, looming over her. "You haven't earned your rent."

She flinched when his hands shot from behind his back—she thought he would strike her. But he held a feather duster. He shoved it into her chest, with a puff of motes, and told her to get to work immediately.

She did, and since then she has never really stopped working. She feared him at first. The thin-lipped expression. The words fired from his mouth like poison-tipped darts. The impossible mechanics of the owl and other inventions he sometimes tested out: a steam-powered bicycle, a lantern that never extinguished, a multi-lens set of glasses that could alternately study the moon or an amoeba. But then she discovered how frail and incompetent he was in human affairs, and in that recognition of weakness she gained power over him.

In most matters she bullies him into getting her way. Lewis has given her a roof, a purpose, an education, but she would never describe him as a giving person, not someone to ever touch her gently on the shoulder or offer a kind word. But in this particular matter he would have helped her, he would have protected her, if only he were here.

She tries not to think about Slade, but even with the door shut, she can't shake the feeling he pursues her. His eyes are like hands that touch her all over. She tries to concentrate instead on the small things. She has to eat. She has to sweep and dust and polish. She has to escort four pods of children through the museum exhibits. She has to finish the display cards for the dinosaur collection. She has to check the windowsill outside Lewis's office to see if his owl might perch there. Sometimes, when she works a rag into a stubborn smear of tarnish, when she stomps a scuttling cockroach—the world crushes down to a steel breastplate, a stone square, a task, and she gratefully forgets where and who she is. Then the quiet comes. The moments she can't fill with anything but her thoughts. Night is the worst. She sleeps at the museum, and when she lies in bed, no matter how hard she tries to concentrate, something shadows her, paces the perimeter of her mind.

Tonight—with prayers on her lips and the image of the whipped man's back redly staining her mind—she spends hours staring at the ceiling and noting the clicks and hums of the museum, wondering what they belong to and whether she ought to investigate. Then she hears something she can't ignore. What sounds like singing.

She keeps the bat—the baseball bat Slade played with—by her bed. She carries it with her to the top of the staircase. She leans over the railing and looks down into the dark, and sure enough, a voice spirals faintly toward her. She descends the stairs.

The various hallways and chambers offer noises that are distant and vague and melt into other sounds, the sounds of the nighttime city. Moonlight streams through the windows, and the shadows crisscross the floor. It isn't until she pads all the way down the stairs, creeping into the basement, that she can make out the words to the song—"Yesterday," the Beatles—belted out, full throated, by some phantom tenor.

She snatches a lantern off a hook and lets out the wick and continues into the dark with a shroud of light to guide her. The voice grows louder and louder—until she enters the storage room, where the voice goes suddenly quiet, as if someone dragged a needle off a record.

She pauses among the heaps of boxes, her ears pricked to pick up every sound. The wick of her lantern sputters. A cobweb seems to breathe. There is a breeze. The air moves down here, drawn to some source. She navigates her way through the shadowed maze until she comes upon a clearing where the ground slopes toward a grate.

Her eyes are immediately drawn there because the grate is glowing, like the door of an oven. She can hear something moving beneath it, breathing and clambering upward. She sets down her lantern in order to grip her bat better.

Then the gate lifts, the rusty maw of it moaning outward, and something is rising from below, what appears to be a glowing ghost. She screams and so does the ghost, their voices pitched high.

She sees then his face—the face of a boy—colored orange and warped by shadows thrown by his own lantern. But only for a moment, as he jerks away from her and loses his purchase and drops back into the hole from which he climbed. The grate clangs behind him, shaking the air and nearly masking the noise of his body thudding, the lantern shattering.

She creeps to the edge of the grate. Fifteen feet below, in the dying light of his lantern, he lies on his side, beetled by a backpack. She calls out to him—"What are you doing sneaking around down here?"—but he doesn't answer, biting back a scream.

Only then does she notice the bone showing whitely through the meat of his forearm.

CHAPTER 12

FOR A LONG TIME, they stand on a bluff looking out at the black-ened fangs of high-rises and broken-backed bridges and the shadows that cling to walls even in full sun. The air smells like burned plastic. They can see two craters, each a half mile wide, from which everything seems to lean.

"This is from a missile?" Lewis says.

Paper is precious, so Gawea writes in the sand with a stick. *Yes.*

"Do you know of many other cities in the same condition?"

Many.

Right then, Clark remembers the bullet her brother shot into the sand and tries to imagine the size and sound of what caused this, tries to imagine the windows shattering and roofs peeling upward, the people who barely had a chance to scream before their hair caught fire and their skin crisped and ashed off their bones. Closing her eyes doesn't help. She still sees the city: the afterimage of the sun shining off mangled metal and molten puddles of glass making blue and white networks on her eyelids.

"Are we in danger?"

Gawea writes: *Maybe. Goblins. Moov on.*

"Goblins? What do you mean by goblins?"

She underlines *Moov on* with the stick.

They lead the horses down the bluff and into a neighborhood where the houses are husks and the trees nothing but charcoaled sticks that smear their flanks blackly when they ride past. They pass a mailbox that has lost all its letters but one, Z.

Something skitters out of the underbrush. Something they see only briefly and cannot identify. York says it looks a little like a human head covered in bristly fur. They see other things too. White ants. A two-headed squirrel. Mutations.

Goblins, Gawea writes again in the sand. Soon after that they pass a trampled circle of grass splashed with blood.

Lewis tells them how radiation will cling to the place for thousands of years, so they give the city wide berth, arcing away from the river for fifty miles or so before returning to it.

That night, around the campfire, everyone is jittery, hollow eyed, ready to curl up in a ball or walk into the woods and offer themselves up to whatever might prey on them. At least then the pain will end. It doesn't help matters when Reed asks, "What do you miss?" He is looking at everyone, his sunburned face peeling so badly that the firelight playing off it makes him appear aflame, burning alive. "About the Sanctuary. I mean, you have to miss something."

Clark says, "I don't know if that's the kind of conversation we should be having."

"Why not? What's wrong with missing something?"

"We don't need to be looking back at a time like this."

He pokes the fire with a stick and a spiral of embers rises in the air. It seems that no one will respond until Lewis says, "I miss my books. My desk. Stillness. Aloneness." He opens his silver tin and scoops out a sniff from it.

"Me," York says, "I miss the ladies and the laughter." He smiles and bobs his eyebrows. "What about you, Reed? Since you asked, what do you miss?"

"Oh, I just miss certain people, I guess."

"Like who?"

Reed glances at Clark and then away. "Just the people who used to fill my days."

York says, "Gawea? You miss anybody back home? Anybody special waiting there for you?"

She shakes her head, no.

"Well, that's good. Because I'm all the man you need."

She does not respond except to stare into the fire.

The doctor smiles warmly at Clark. "I don't miss a thing. Anything is better than that place. I couldn't be happier than where I am right now." A lie, of course. But a good one, a necessary one. They need lies like it to get them through the months ahead.

"Me too," Clark says.

York blows on the fire, makes it bend and snap. "Are we really going back? Like, at the end of all this? We're not really going to hump all the way back, are we?"

"Of course we are," Reed says, and then, with his voice lowered, "Aren't we?"

But no one answers.

Clark wakes to the smell of smoke. She is already hot. And terribly thirsty, her mouth like sandpaper. Her head aches from dehydration and the fuzzy memory of yesterday's long ride. She rolls into a seated position and swigs from her canteen, its water somehow seeming warmer than the air.

They are north of St. Joseph, and though the sun has not yet risen, the sky has lightened enough for Clark to see Reed. They spent the night beneath an open-air shelter in a park, and he sits on a splintery picnic table with a revolver split open. He dampens a rag with oil and drags it through the barrel.

"What are you doing up?" she says.

"I'm thinking."

"You like your new toy?" she says, and he looks at her but does not say anything. Half-moons of fatigue bruise the flesh beneath his eyes. His lips are chapped and cracked. His peeling sunburn makes him look like he's falling apart. He appears old, ugly. They all do, she knows. The doctor has been fretting over them, asking them to take foul-tasting supplements from a dropper. She says it will keep them healthy, strong, but they look and feel the opposite. These days, conversation comes less and less frequently, as if they are rationing their voices, too. When they do speak, the words flash like impatient weapons.

She is as guilty as any of them—especially with her brother, whose every decision she sometimes feels compelled to question.

When he drinks too much water, when he builds too big a fire, when he stands too near a cliff's edge or walks too quickly into an abandoned house, as if there is nothing to fear in the world. She often cuffs him, berates him, can't stop herself from pointing out his idiot mistakes. He fights back, cursing her, raising a hand as if to slap her. "You're making me look like a fool."

"You're making yourself look like a fool."

"Treat me like a man, Clark."

"Act like one." Here she lowered her voice and jutted a chin in the direction of the girl. "And don't get too attached to her."

"What do you mean?"

"I see the way you look at her. Keep your guard up. We still don't know if we can trust her."

Even the horses seem angry. One dropped dead from exhaustion. The others droop their heads and hood their eyes. Some of them limp with split hooves. Yesterday, when Lewis spurred his horse, it swung back its head and bit his calf.

Dawn steals across the sky and suffuses everything with a faint orange light. In the center of the shelter is a short-walled fire pit with a round grate that pipes into a chimney. Smoke eases from the grate, bending with the breeze, twisting toward her, acrid with the smell of rotten wood. She stands upright and presses her hands into her back, nudging her spine until it *click-click-clicks* into place with a sound like dry timber. "I suppose we better get moving."

Reed snaps the revolver together. "Suppose we better. Our big hurry to nowhere awaits us."

"Do you have a problem? Something you want to say?"

He won't meet her stare, so she breaks away and calls out to everyone, telling them to move, get their asses up. A few of them groan and roll over. Ever since Kansas City, everyone has been quiet, slow, as if the lingering poison of the place infected them all. It is harder to believe in humanity surviving, she supposes, when you see how it is capable of destroying itself.

She walks from bedroll to bedroll, kicking Lewis, pulling her brother's hair, saying, "Up, up, up, up"—and they yawn and stretch and rub their hands across their faces. Somebody says, "What's the point?" and when she says, "Who said that?" there is no answer except her nickering horse.

She fills a nose bag and fits it into place, and while the horse eats noisily she studies the brightening sky. At first she doesn't recognize the cloud. It isn't much—seen through the trees, a white wisp hanging in the air like a shed feather—and her eyes initially sweep past it. Then she nearly cries aloud. It has been so long. Seeing the cloud is like sitting in a bar and hearing the band strike up a song she knows but forgot existed.

Reed stands with his gun ready. "What?"

The shelter is located next to a wall of trees at the bottom of the sloping hill she races up now. She can hear panicked voices behind her and ignores them. She trips twice in her rush, but she does not pause, not until she reaches the top, where she turns to take in the view.

For so long she has seen the sun rise into a cloudless sky, it is difficult to imagine it any other way. Cerulean. That's the description Lewis used for it the other day. A word that sounds cruel to her.

"Look," she says. "Everyone, come up here and look."

They stagger from beneath the shelter, up the hill, staring at her and then at the sky. What she initially saw—that white wisp—was only the beginning, the first tentacles of a roiling bank of clouds stacked up on the horizon.

CHAPTER 13

WHEN CLARK ROUSES them from sleep, when she calls them up the hill, when they look to the sky and see the clouds piled up like tangled gray scarves, the others cry out with delight—at the promise of shade, of moisture—but Lewis goes silent because he sees something else. He sees the man. The man in white. Aran Burr. He takes up half the sky. His hair is wild, windblown. His eyes and mouth are lit with balls of lightning. His hands—with torn gray fingers—reach for him, beckoning.

He haunts Lewis. Whether he is asleep or awake, Burr is there, at every turn, summoning him. His skin is so pale Lewis can see the veins marbling greenly beneath it. His knuckles are cubed with arthritis. His mouth is a hole that holds a shadow when he whispers his name, "Lewis." Isn't that what he should expect, with his brain drying like a nut from lack of water, with the heat warping the air and the sun heliographing off broken nests of glass? A mirage? But he doesn't see water and he doesn't see his office, the two things he longs for most. He sees Burr.

Lewis was, in his previous capacity, not a teacher but an educator. A curator of stories meant to help people better understand their lives. The museum might make them feel a little richer or entertained or wistful. Or it might make them feel like an irrelevant bit of debris caught up in the cyclonic rotation of history. He didn't particularly care. He just wanted to be sure they knew this wasn't it—the Sanctuary was not the world and human history was a long gauntlet of troubles and triumphs they might learn from, aspire to.

But that life is far behind him now. He no longer frames his thoughts around nurturing others, but on feeding himself, gobbling up everything he encounters. There is nothing in this new America not worth learning. He is the student. A disciple. He bothers

Gawea whenever he can, but even if she wasn't temporarily mute from her injury, he suspects she would give him only so much. There is a notable reluctance whenever someone approaches her with a question.

"If you can make birds come to your rescue, why can't you ward off a snake or lure in a rabbit?"

Her stick sketches the sand. *ASK. NOT MAKE.*

"You ask. So you're saying not everything answers, not everything wants to listen?"

Y is her shorthand for *yes*.

"Did Burr teach you how to ask?"

Y, she writes, *& N*.

"He said we're the same. Do you think we're the same?"

She looks at him with those depthless eyes, then circles what she has already written, *Y & N*.

And then, when he asks if she can teach him, she makes a circle within the circle, around the letter *N*.

She is the messenger. Burr is the educator. And Lewis is impatient for an education. He felt the same way as a child, pulling down books in the library and asking his father to talk to him about them. *I'm too busy* might have been the phrase his father said to him most often, next to *Quiet*. When he remembers his father, he remembers him from a distance—studying documents at a desk or meeting with advisers in a boardroom or giving speeches on a stage—only occasionally looking up to find Lewis, staring back at his son not with pride or affection but with disappointment.

This man, Aran Burr, who lavishes Lewis with attention, who summons him in dreams and in life, who promises him guidance, appears the same age as his father, his hair and beard wilder, but his appearance otherwise similar, so that they are beginning to merge in his mind. Burr wants him—his father wants him—and he feels as excited by this as he does frightened.

They hurry to gather their belongings, to feed and water and saddle their horses, who seem infected by their energy when they set off, no longer stumbling or ignoring their reins, but riding hard and straight toward the clouds, despite their bloodied hooves, toward the man whose vaporous shape Lewis can still see.

He longs for a sniff from his silver tin but knows he must ration it better. It spikes his mind and numbs his senses. Sometimes his thoughts feel so alive and singular that he could shed his body altogether, peel it off like a wet jacket. And sometimes he imagines the sand as powder, imagines diving off his horse, headfirst into a pillowy pile of it, and he would breathe, breathe, breathe, until he is overcome with pleasure.

They slow to a canter when noon comes and the clouds burn away. By then there are birds—not just the crows and vultures they are accustomed to seeing—but a red-winged blackbird, a yellow tanager, even an owl that hoots at them from a high branch. At one point a murmuration of starlings darkens the sky, like a net cast over them.

They drop down into the Missouri River, their constant guide, leaning back on their horses as they slide and stutter down the sandy banks, and then follow its wide-walled passage. Its bed is clay cracking beneath their hooves. They startle three deer bedded down in the shade of a root-twisted overhang and fire three bullets and two arrows uselessly after them.

The water they don't find for two more days.

Lewis senses something different. The air takes on a greater texture, less thin and dry, more palpable, and so does it ripen with a fecund smell, like the breath of an unwashed mouth. Then he notices the riverbed softening. The sound of the clay shattering, once echoing all around them, hushes and then vanishes as the ground grows spongy and then sticky with muck.

Reed is the one who points it out—shouting, "There!"—a great gray tongue of mud twisting its way down the middle of the riverbed. For a quarter mile they follow it. It grows wider, eventually reaching from bank to bank, before giving way to a brackish puddle with salt formations like small cauliflower growing around it.

York lets out a whoop and shifts out of his saddle and falls to the ground and scrabbles on all fours to the edge of the puddle and splashes a handful into his hair before dunking his face beneath the surface to taste it. He reels back, his face distorted. He heaves several times. A line of bile hangs from his lips when he looks up at them. Gawea nudges her horse and shakes her head and *tsk-tsks* him with her tongue. York laughs, the laugh cut short when Clark spurs her horse between him and the girl and berates him for his damned fool idiotness.

The way is now impassable, too swampy for them to ride, and they clamber up the banks and parallel its winding course for an hour. Algae thickens. Bushes cluster. Reeds spring up. Leaves unfurl from branches. To Lewis's eyes, so accustomed to browns and grays, everything seems obscenely green. There is a whine at his ear, and then a sting at his cheek. He slaps it and studies the bloody smear on his hand.

He hears another slap behind him and the doctor says, "What is that? What are they?"

Lewis wipes his hand on his thigh. "Mosquitoes, I think. They drink blood and carry disease."

The bugs thicken, swarming in hazy clouds, and the slapping and clapping becomes as frequent as applause. York says, "Why couldn't they have been wiped out with everything else?"

"Purely to harass you," Lewis says.

York laughs. They all do, despite the welts rising from their skin, because there is water. There is actual water beside them, oozing along thickly at first, then clearing and broadening, creeping up the banks. And where there is water, there is life. The desert has filled their heads with questions and defiled their spirits. But now all those bad feelings wash away. Gawea was right—there is an end to the desert waste—which means they have been right to follow her. She has led them to life, and they are going to live.

When the sun eases toward the horizon, when the shadows begin to cluster, the doctor walks her horse onto a rocky shoal and stares out over a calm stretch of water dimpling with bugs and says, "Let's stay here. And I don't just mean for the night. Let's rest. We need our rest."

When no one says anything—the water has stolen their words—she says, "I insist on it. This will be good medicine for us all."

Right then a possum with a long pink tail and a mouth full of needlelike teeth clambers down a tree and hisses at them before Reed puts an arrow in its side.

Lewis knows that with prey come predators. North America was once home to big mammals that long ago went extinct. Once humans crossed the land bridge, once they notched out shell-shaped projectile points, once they learned to fire arrows and hurl spears with atlatls, the big animals began to die off. The mammoths, the dire wolves and lipoterns, the saber-toothed lions, the giant ground sloths and giant short-faced bears. All gone, replaced by scrawnier, deadlier humans. Nature fills a void. Now that humans are gone, something big will be clambering its way to the top of the predatory chain. He remembers what Gawea wrote in the sand, *Goblins*, and while they butcher the possum and talk excitedly about what tomorrow might bring, he keeps his eyes on the dark forests that wall the riverbank.

CHAPTER 14

THE MELANOMA RISES from the tip of his ear. It has been bothering Thomas for weeks, a faint itching at first, then a throbbing. It is a raised lump, darkly pigmented, purplish at its center, pink and yellow along the edges. Vincent insists he get it removed.

The mayor is not overly worried. He does not feel weak or nauseous. Removing suspicious lesions is as commonplace as getting a haircut, clipping toenails. Everyone is dotted with moles. Everyone has growths lumping them. Their sunburned skin husks away like the peelings of an onion. The UV exposure, with no ozone layer to filter, cooks them, mutates their cells.

His doctor—a man with an eggishly bald head and a nest of black hair rimming it—seats him in a chair and gives him an opiate that a few minutes later makes everything fuzzy around the edges. "It feels like nothing could ever possibly hurt," Thomas says, and the doctor says, "I'm sorry to contradict you," and slices off the top of his ear with a pair of clippers.

He hears the snip. Blood runs into his ear. The doctor smashes a towel against it and tells Thomas to hold it. The pain takes a moment to arrive. A rising heat. Thomas begins to say, "Ah-ah-ah," and the doctor says, "You'll be all right."

Then he smears glue over the wound and bandages it and tells Thomas to follow up with him if he has any questions.

Thomas is late because of the procedure. But then again, he is always late. People wait for him. And they will continue to wait for him, whether for five or fifty minutes, as long as it takes. When he walks late into a room, any room, people feel both relief and exas-

149

peration. For so many decisions he makes, this is his intention. To make clear his power.

Slade meets him in the hallway. "How are they?" Thomas asks, and Slade says, "They're impatient. Pimpton threatened to leave."

"Perfect."

He opens the tall oak door and together they walk into the high-ceilinged chamber. Slade stands in the corner. A chandelier fitted with candles hangs over a long wooden table around which six councilmen are seated. They stand when he enters, though none of them greet him. Only a few even look at him. Some are men; some are women. Some are young, and some have been serving longer than Thomas has been alive, and they look it, graybeards with hunchbacks taking too long to wobble upright at his entrance.

Thomas takes his seat in a tall leather-backed chair at the head of the table. "I call this meeting to order. The minutes, please."

Councilman Pimpton falls back into his chair and sighs theatrically. He walks with a cane made from a crooked length of wood. His eyebrows are combed up his forehead like white feathers. "I've lost too many minutes already. *Waiting.*" He says this at a mutter just loud enough for everyone to hear.

Last week's minutes—about the creation of a water committee and the proposed construction of a new well—are read and approved. Not that Thomas believes there is more water to be found, but they need to look like they are trying. Rain is the real answer, but they can't make a motion to sequester clouds.

The blinds are closed, the room dark except for the candles sparking above them. Water glasses are staggered around the table, along with two sweating pitchers. Thomas fills his glass to the very top and takes a small sip and pops his lips. "New business for to-day's agenda?"

Pimpton raises a hand. It wavers in the air a long moment before Thomas acknowledges him. "What news is there of Jon Colter?"

"What news?" Thomas says. "What do you mean? What news could there possibly be?"

"I don't really know. That's why I'm inquiring."

"I took him out of one cell and I put him in another. One much vaster. He's probably already dead. Just like they're undoubtedly *all* already dead."

"I'm sorry," Pimpton says and quivers his lips, "help an old man understand. Why did you send Colter at all?"

"Because we needed to do *something*. It was a symbolic act. To make everyone fearful. You run away from me and I'll send a monster after you. There's always the chance he might find them. Maybe. And do me the favor of killing them. Maybe. And bring back their bodies. Again, maybe. In which case, I'd have some lovely ornaments to decorate the city with."

"You would think," Pimpton says, "our mayor would be wise enough to not end a sentence with a preposition."

"Oh, I'm so sorry. Let me try again." He clears his throat. "In which case, I'd have some lovely ornaments to decorate the city with, you walking corpse."

The old man pretends not to hear. "I propose we concentrate on actuals instead of hypotheticals. We need water. Let's figure out how to get our people some water. Let's be the leaders we promised to be."

"I'm being the leader I promised to be. A realist, not a soothsayer."

"I don't understand anything that comes out of your mouth."

"Maybe that's because you're a thousand years old and can't hear."

Pimpton scrunches up his face and waves a hand, dismissing him.

The secretary, a shrew-faced man with an inkpot and a pile of paper, scratches down everything said at the meeting so far. For a moment his writing is the only sound. Thomas says to him, "You don't need to record any of this. I'm just going to talk for a minute. I'm going to say a few things. Is that all right with everyone?" Maybe it is the opiates—the bleary warmth that makes him feel capable of anything—but he doesn't want to hold back today. He doesn't see the point of coddling this alliance of fools.

"I had a friend. He was a good friend, but an idiot father. Married to a woman who turned out to be an idiot mother. They ruined their children. They let them breastfeed until they were nine. They let them share their bed until they were twelve. The children were never spanked or scolded. The parents talked things out. 'Why do you think you hit Sally? Why do you think you pissed on John?' Which only taught the children how to manipulate. And so the children grew up to be weak and precious, unable to function. Children are no different than puppies. They must be broken. They must be taught to heel and to roll over, or they'll spend the rest of their lives gnawing on the furniture and shitting on the rugs and waking you in the night for a treat. I am not a parent. I do not wish to be a parent. But if I was a parent, I know exactly how I would raise my children. Fear and love. Those are the fundamentals of leadership. You need people to fear you and love you."

Thomas takes another drink of water. One of the candles spits. A tongue of melted wax plops to the table and hardens into a white shell.

"Excuse me." A voice, Pimpton's.

"Yes?"

"Who loves you? Who are these people who love you?"

His eyes flit to Slade and then to Pimpton. "You don't love me?"

"I most certainly do not."

"That hurts my feelings."

The old man lifts his beard and neatens it across his chest.

Thomas says, "I wonder..."

"Do you?"

"I wonder if you would love me if I tied you down? If I took a long needle, heated by fire until it glowed orange, and slid it into your urethra? Would you love me then? If I held it there until you said so?"

The old man looks at him with his mouth agape.

"I bet you would." He gives a small smile. "Of course you would."

"A question for the table," Pimpton says. "It has come to my attention you closed down a church?"

"I did."

"Without consulting us."

"I did. The minister was speaking out against me, calling for civil disobedience."

"To close down a church." His tongue moves audibly inside his mouth, clicking and popping. "They're saying it's un-American."

"I don't believe in America. America is a myth."

There is a collective intake of air. Several lean forward and grip the arms of their chairs, as if to stand, then reconsider.

Thomas's ear feels so hot and his tongue feels so loose. The words tumble so easily off it. "People believe in America, but America is a myth. It has been since 1776. People believed in the country's greatness because it promised them greatness. Hold a gold coin just out of reach and say, 'This could be yours.' One percent of the population controls everything. One percent. That's how it is here. That's how it was all over the world. That's how it has always been throughout human history. America sponsored the appearance of freedom. I do not. They say I'm a liar? America was a liar. I'm a truth teller."

"But..." This from a woman named Packer, dressed in purple with an acorn-cap haircut. At his gaze she pinches her mouth.

Thomas fondles the damaged tip of his ear. "I'm making a motion."

Pimpton lays his hands flat on the table. "What now?"

"We're going to reduce the water rations again."

"We can't."

"We will. By a third."

The meeting goes on for another thirty minutes until they adjourn. Thomas was the last to arrive but is the first to leave. On his way out the door, Packer puts a hand on his shoulder and he flinches away from her.

"Are you all right?" she says.

"Of course I'm all right."

"Your ear?"

He touches it and examines his hand. "That's nothing." The glue dirties his fingers. "Just a cancer I had cut away."

His eyes then follow Pimpton as the old man shuffles from the room and down a long hallway that will lead him to the entry that opens into the unforgiving white light.

CHAPTER 15

THEY DON'T WANT to waste their bullets, so they hunt with arrows. The quiver rattles at Clark's back when she sneaks along the game trail, a thin strip of dirt polished down by hooves. She pauses often. To run her hand along the trunk of a birch tree and peel away a strip of its papery bark. To study the starburst of a white flower. To listen to the river bubbling. To watch a bird flit among the reeds crowding the banks. Everything is new. She feels as if she has stepped into one of those books read to her as a child—through the wardrobe, down the rabbit hole, up the twister—a portal that leads to the fantastic. It makes her feel giddy, girlish.

Last night they stripped off their clothes and bathed in the river. Though it was only calf high, they laid down flat in the water and let it pour over their bodies. They spread their arms and legs and twirled like pale stars. They dunked their heads and spit bubbles. They splashed at each other and scrubbed their skin with sand and shot arcs of water from their mouths. When she sat up and looked downstream, she could see the water had grown cloudy with the sweat and grime washing off them. The water softened her, melted her, like hard-packed dirt exposed finally to rain. Her clothes are still damp. They stick to her when she moves. It is an unfamiliar feeling, like a tongue touching her all over, and she likes it.

Her brother follows a few paces behind her. They come upon a clearing spotted with coneflowers and waist-high bunches of big bluestem, and in a crouch they wait near the water's edge. At one point she hears her brother's mouth open, forming a question, and she gives him a wilting stare. "Shh," she says. After a time her legs go numb and her vision wavers—and then a deer untangles itself from the forest. A doe. Maybe twenty yards from them. The big pouches of its ears twitch. Its damp black nose tests the air.

Then it lowers its head to eat. This deer is nothing like the ones she occasionally kills near the Sanctuary, their growth stunted and their bones showing sharply through their mangy hides. She can see its muscles jump with every small step it takes and imagines them peeled from the bone and spitted over the fire, dripping fat into the flames.

She notches an arrow, but before she can rise from her crouch and take aim, she hears the snap of string, the shriek of a broadhead cutting the air. York. There is a sound like a fist smacking a palm. The deer jackknifes and falls and stumbles upright again. It starts toward them, then rears back and darts into the woods. Its back leg drags. An arrow spikes from its hip.

They listen to it crashing off into the distance. Then she turns to York. His face is too long and too thin, and his chin juts at an angle, as if someone stepped on his head when he was a soft-skulled baby. No one has shaved since they left the Sanctuary—their water too precious—and his upper lip is wisped by a mustache and his sideburns have extended into a failure of a beard. He is grinning. She is not.

"I got him!"

"You got *her*."

"Exactly."

"Whether we'll ever find her is another story."

He flinches when she starts toward him. She marks out an invisible square on his chest. "Kill zone," she says and then stabs a finger between his ribs.

"But it was still a pretty good shot, right?"

"It wasn't terrible."

They follow the blood trail for a half mile. A puddle among the pine needles. A smear along a tree trunk. What looks like a poisonous spattering of red berries on a bush. Occasionally the grass crushes down where the deer rests. She tells her brother he must have hit something vital.

Far enough from the river, the world dries up again. The grass yellows. The trees lose their leaves. Dust rises with every step and seems to give off its own light and heat when they breathe it into their lungs. They step out of the trees and onto what was once a driveway. Weeds have pushed their way through the fractured asphalt that runs up a hill to a three-story Victorian perched atop a rise. Its siding is gray, the paint long ago flaked away. A section of its peaked roof has collapsed. The wraparound porch is sunken and shot through with grass. The balusters, split or missing altogether, make the railing appear like a rotten mouth.

They find the deer halfway up the porch, laid out like a sacrifice. The front door is missing altogether. The surrounding trim is splintered away as if clawed apart. Her eyes stay on the door, the black rectangle of it, a space that swallows all light. So she does not notice—not until York says, "What is that?"—the white ball bulging from the deer's flank.

At first she believes it to be a swollen strip of intestine that has somehow escaped the gash. But it is not. It is moving, pulsing, tumorous. Tiny claws hold it in place near the arrow's shaft. There is the faint noise of sucking, lapping.

Too late, she says, "Don't touch it."

York has already reached out a boot—and toes the thing softly. Its mouth peels away from the wound and it raises its head to observe them. An albino bat with blind white eyes. It has the look of a shaved kitten. A beard of blood rims its mouth. She remembers what Lewis said about radiation, about mutational genesis. She remembers what Gawea wrote about goblins.

The bat lowers its head again, but before it can drink, York kicks it. It smacks the railing and issues a sharp cry. When it falls to the ground, they lose sight of it among the weeds but hear it rustling and scrabbling beneath the porch.

Normally she would gut the deer where it lies, but not today. She heaves the deer onto York's back, and then, as he buckles beneath the weight of it, they escape to the woods.

She might be imagining it, but she believes she hears something behind her, a shifting of air, as if the house were drawing in its breath.

CHAPTER 16

PIMPTON LIVES NEAR the Dome in a building called the manor. He shares it with the other council members, along with the chair of the farming bureau, the chair of waste management, the chair of finance, and all other elected or appointed officials. Like the Dome, like the museum, their building stands apart from the rest of the Sanctuary, with its marble floors and high, airy ceilings and dark-wooded wainscoting. Paintings hang from the walls. A swing-shift deputy remains stationed at the entrance.

Pimpton's is a second-story apartment. One flight of stairs is enough to exhaust him. He leans hard on his cane and the handrail. He fumbles with his key, his fingernails long and his knuckles twisted with arthritis. Once he pushes inside, he calls for his wife, but she doesn't answer, maybe out with a friend, shopping the bazaar.

The room is dark except for a square of light. The window is open, allowing in the heat of the day. He mumbles a string of obscenities, caning his way across the room to pull it shut, draw the curtains, bringing a cool shadow to the sitting area.

Then he collapses into his reading chair. Something bulges at his back, a decorative pillow that he spends a minute fussing with, renegotiating onto his lap. He folds his hands over it. His chair faces the window and he stares at the line of sunlight burning between the curtains. It grows narrower as his eyelids sag. He can feel sleep pulling at him, almost there. What never comes to him at night always finds him easily during the day. A sudden, pressing exhaustion. He will take a little nap. He always feels better after a little nap. An escape from the heat. An escape from the troubles the Sanctuary faces and the cruel idiocy of Thomas, who seems less a man and more a boy clutching a wooden sword and pretending his power. He must be punished. He must be put in his place. And he will be, once the next election cycles through, but that is a long ways off, longer than Pimpton may live. His eyes ache. His knees ache. His back aches. A nap will be good medicine for what ails him. Yes, a nap is just what he needs. The darkness takes him like a flung blanket.

He can't be sure how long he sleeps, maybe an hour, maybe a minute, but he feels that disoriented dream-tug when he wakes, the edges of the world slippery. He could so easily close his eyes again, but he knows something must have woken him. He calls out for his wife and receives no answer. She is hard of hearing, so he repeats himself, louder this time. With some difficulty, he rocks forward in his chair and twists around, looking behind him.

The living room is shadowy enough that he at first does not recognize the darkness beside him as a man—as Rickett Slade—until the sheriff says, "This will only take a minute," lifting the decorative pillow from his lap and pressing it to his face.

CHAPTER 17

DANGER SEEMS far away from this bend in the river. Lewis bathes until his toes and fingers wrinkle. He drinks until his stomach aches. The horses splash along the banks and feast on grass, and when Lewis walks past his own mount, she whickers and nuzzles his neck and stares at him with her soft black eyes and he pets her and can't help but smile.

The doctor takes a knife and hacks down some leafy willow branches and hands them out for everyone to swing over their shoulders to warn away the mosquitoes and deerflies. The earth has greened and blued. Water unspools beside them, the river ever widening. Flowers bloom in explosions of color that match the feeling inside them all. Gawea helps them forage, showing them what to look for—strawberries and raspberries and blueberries and gooseberries—until their fingers and lips are stained, the flavors impossibly good. They eat bird eggs, sorrel leaves, basswood leaves, oyster mushrooms, currants, clover, worms, grubs. If things are this good now, their mood seems to say, how much better might they be in Oregon? It is unimaginable.

They dig a hole and surround it with stones and fill it with a pyramid of wood and the fire snaps and pops and sends sparks swirling up to join the stars beginning to burn in the iron-colored sky. They eat the venison cut into chops and steaks. York takes a flask of tequila from his saddlebag and says he wasn't planning on sharing, but what the hell—it feels right—it feels like one of those nights.

"You've been hiding that all this time?" Clark says. Her mouth quavers as if eager to accept the flask.

"There's water in the world, after all," he says. "So let's drink!"

They pass around the flask and shudder and hoot at the taste.

All except Clark. She takes it and stares at it a long time. Her mouth goes damp. Her teeth click together. Her throat feels as though it is widening to accommodate whatever she might pour down it. The coldness of its metal like a gun in her hand.

Then she shakes her head—hard—and hands the flask to Gawea. "Take a taste for me," she says. "A lot of tastes."

The girl no longer wears bandages, her neck healed, scarred an angry red. Still she doesn't talk. Clark bothers her as often as possible, no longer believing in the injury, believing instead that the girl is holding back, hiding something from them. It is more than her silence. It is her distance, the thin thread that binds her to them. She rarely engages, often staring off into the distance as if listening to instructions only she can hear. And her looks—eyes black, face dead—indicate her utter indifference, which seems at odds with her mission. Clark forces the flask on her now and hopes the liquor might loosen her, surprise a word out of her.

But Gawea only takes a nip and then cringes and trembles. She passes the flask to York, who throws back his head and guzzles. York, York, everyone keeps saying his name, *York*. They smack him on the side of his head and thank him for the booze and the meat and he grins around a handful of flank steak.

The flask circles the fire twice and then twice again and York's voice grows louder and louder and soon he wobbles upright and tells them to make way, make room, he wants to show them something. This is his standard over the past few weeks—teasing, joking, storytelling—always trying to distract or surprise them with a laugh. He is known for his mouth. He claims to have bedded more than five hundred women, and every woman seems to have something strange or ridiculous about her. This one had nipples so long and rigid a bird might have roosted on them. Another used her teeth so generously when fellating him—he pronounced it *filleting*—that he rolled out of bed the next morning circumcised.

He brings a hand to his stomach, feigning stomach cramps. His tongue peeks between his lips. He begins to dry heave. Out of his mouth—one, two, three—come yellow agates. He bulges his eyes in mock surprise. He tosses one of the stones up and catches it. Then tosses another, and soon he is juggling them in wider and wider arcs. Two he lets fall into his pants pocket—but the third he launches at his sister.

It whizzes through the air. If her reflexes were not as sharp as they are, the rock would strike her square in the forehead. But her hand rises up to snatch it. There is a *smack*. Everyone goes quiet for a moment. Everyone expects her to scold her brother, maybe hurl the rock back his way.

But the river has mellowed her. She slowly brings the rock to her temple and makes a *doink* sound and crosses her eyes and slumps backward in a mock faint. Everyone applauds.

The flask passes around the fire a few times more, and their words begin to tumble freely, their faces flushed, numbed. A pitch pocket pops. Frogs chirp. The river hushes. A *chittering* comes from the sky—followed by the shaky nickering of a horse. Someone claps a hand and crushes a mosquito. Then York clears his throat and announces that he has to take a leak so bad that the river will rise five feet in the next five minutes.

They hear the *chittering* sound again, what could be mistaken for a high-pitched giggling. York is a few yards from the fire now, and he spins around to say he hopes nobody misses him when he's gone. It is then, with his smile a white crescent and his body ghosting into the dark, that a shadow comes alive behind him. And though everyone laughs at first, thinking that this is another trick of his, thinking that his screams might be an act, this is not the case.

Something has him. Something is dragging him away. What it is, Lewis cannot see, his night vision blurred from all his time staring at the fire. Now the horses are screaming along with York. Lewis can hear their hooves kicking, as they rear back against the harnesses that bind them to the trees.

Lewis has had too much to drink. He cannot process what is happening. He studies Clark's face to see if he ought to be scared. She already has her revolver out. A muscle ripples along her cheek. She is standing—she is running—the gun's metal dancing with orange light thrown by the fire. Reed does the same. So does Gawea. The doctor lifts a rifle to her shoulder and swings in an unsteady circle. No one shoots. They don't know what to shoot at.

There is a piercing scream—inhuman—and York races out of the dark. Claw marks run across his face. In his hand he carries a bloodied knife. He throws aside his packs until he finds his holster and belts it around his waist. "Move," he tells Lewis. "Move, move, move, or you're dead."

Lewis is unarmed. He never keeps a weapon ready, not like the others. But he manages to force his brain into action. There is no moon. They need light. They need to shove back the night. His eyes fall to the nearby pile of wood. He tries to run and trips. He scrambles on hands and knees. The first gunshot sounds. The horses keep screaming—a sound like metal dragged across metal—though their screams seem fewer now. Lewis grabs what wood he can, feeding the fire three split logs, a branch full of dead pine needles. The flames rise with a crackling flash. The shadows retreat between the trees. And in the light cast by the fire he sees the bats.

Their skin is as white as moonlight. Some are the size of boys, some the size of men. One is splayed across the back of a rearing horse, its wings wrapped around its sides like some veined shell. It opens up the horse's neck and nuzzles into the arterial spray. Another horse beside it has fallen and gone still, though its neck remains raised, held in place by the reins knotted around a tree branch. Two bats feed on it.

Reed fires his revolvers until they are empty. He continues to snap the triggers until a bat swoops down and he strikes it in the face and then commences tapping out the spent brass, thumbing fresh bullets into the cylinder.

A sudden wind knocks Lewis sideways. He ducks down and cannot help but scream when he sees what displaces the air. The sky above is swirling with bats, too many to count, their winged shapes like pale mouths blotting out the stars.

York takes a knee and fires a round into the sky. From the barrel comes a yellow shout of light. One of the bats screeches and wheels and drops heavily. He aims again, ready to fire, when a bat swoops down from behind, knocking away his gun and pressing him flat against the ground.

Lewis starts toward him—ready to do what, he doesn't know. But another bat drops from the sky, landing in a crouch before him. Slowly it rises into a standing position, taller than he. Its legs are stunted and the steps it takes small. Its eyes are as large as a baby's skull, white and broken along the edges by bright red capillaries. Its mouth is open, and its teeth, sharply pointed, are the color of bone. White downy hair runs down its chest to its belly. It opens its wings like a cloak. He dodges right and the bat follows him, stepping now in front of the fire, the red glow of it filtering through the skin of its wings and highlighting the thin bones and the filamented veins within. It starts toward him.

Lewis makes his hands into fists, ready to fight, when the bat swings a wing. A wind comes rolling off it that scatters grit and momentarily blinds him. The horses have gone quiet, but gunshots continue to thunder all around him. He swings his hands blindly. Something hooks into his mouth, a claw that reaches down his throat. He gags, but the bile doesn't get a chance to rise before his head is yoked aside, the meat of his neck exposed. He can feel its breath as it draws closer. So hot his hair goes damp.

A gun claps beside him. His right ear goes deaf except for a shrill ring. There comes a spray of blood. Not his own. He opens his eyes in time to see the bat slump to the ground.

Gawea does not give him the chance to say thank you. She shoves a shotgun into his arms. Then she races off in the direction of the horses.

Lewis remembers York and finds him gone—and he calls for Clark and gets no answer. There is nothing left to do but chamber a round and empty it into the belly of the bat that spirals above him.

They do not kill all the bats, though they try. The air shakes with gunfire. And then either enough of them die or enough of them eat their fill, because their shapes become less frequent in the sky.

When the red light of dawn comes, they clean the camp. They drag the bats onto the fire. There is nothing to be done for the horses. Lewis crouches over Donkey and runs a hand through her clotted mane and closes his eyes and apologizes for every time he cursed her obstinacy and slowness.

Clark is gone. They have lost her. Truly lost her, her body nowhere to be found. Whether alive or dead, they don't know for certain, but how can it be any other way than dead?

Lewis does not sit so much as collapse onto the stump of a tree. Out of habit he puts his hands to his sides as if to drag forward his chair to his desk, and for a moment he imagines himself there, in his office, happily creaking open a book to study. But only for a moment. The image begins to dissolve even as it takes form. He is surrounded not by his library but by death. He sits not in his chair but on a stump. Beneath him are hundreds of rings, like the whorls of a thumb pad, some of them fat, some thin, the last of them barely traceable. If someone should happen upon his corpse later, like a dry, gray stick half-buried in sand, he wonders if she might snap it over her knee and find inside a similar story. He has doomed himself, agreeing to this journey, and his last moments, these moments, would be his thinnest, his thirstiest.

He takes a sniff from his silver tin. And then another.

The fire is still burning. It crisps the carcasses stacked upon it. Those of the bats, twenty of them killed altogether. Their hair smokes. Their wings burn like paper. Everyone asks Lewis what they are. Bats. That's what they are. What else is he supposed to say? "Ask her," he says.

Gawea says nothing. The fire dances in her eyes.

"Mutants," Lewis says. "Goblins."

Missiles detonate, power plants melt down, radiation spills from them, the rules change. In the previous world, the bats would be considered abnormal, but who remains in this world to designate what is normal or not? This band of humans might as well be considered the unfamiliar, their so-far survival in this place unnatural. They are the mutants.

His hands shake from exhaustion. The fingernails are rimed with ink or dirt or blood; it's difficult to tell in the half-light. He needs a bath in the river, but for the moment he cannot bring himself to do anything but sit in the shape of a ball and imagine himself away from here.

He hears a voice beside him, York's. "Why didn't you do something?" He stands ten yards away with a shotgun in his hands and tears in his eyes. "Both of you." He gestures the gun at Lewis and Gawea.

"We did what we could."

"Bullshit." The tears track trails through the dirt and blood on his face. "I was there, in the basement, when you hurled my sister against that pillar. I was there, in the stadium, when she called down the vultures."

"That's not how it works."

"Oh, how does it work, then? Tell me."

Lewis looks to Gawea and she gives him nothing back. "I wish I knew."

The horses lie in ruined mounds, with the flies already making a meal of them. Reed stands by the fire with the doctor, both of them slump shouldered and staring at the flames that lick the spaces between the bats heaped there.

"We are fucked, you realize that?" York says, his voice cracking, his tone that of a furious boy. "We are absolutely fucked. What are we going to do without our horses? We can't exactly turn around, go home, say we're sorry, can we? So what do we do? What the hell are we supposed to do?"

Lewis licks his lips as if they are too dry for words. It seems impossible that so many hours before they all felt so hopeful. Just as it seems impossible that York—his face now tight with rage—is the same man who pranced and goofed around the fire last night.

"I'll tell you what we're going to do," York says, and now

his voice quiets. "We're going to find my sister." He tightens his grip on the shotgun. "That's what we're going to do. She saved all of us, and now we're going to save her." His voice breaks in the middle, but he keeps his eyes steady on all of them until they nod.

CHAPTER 18

Ⅰɴ ᴛʜᴇ ʙᴀsᴇᴍᴇɴᴛ of the museum, when Simon slips from the ladder, when he holds out an arm to brace his fall and it snaps beneath him, she climbs down. He can hardly hear or see her, the pain so absorbs him, a hot sword that jags from his wrist to his chest. He can see his own bone—his inside brought outside—and he feels as amazed as he does disgusted, touching the sharp, slick point of it with a finger. Already he has lost so much blood. He does nothing to stop the flow of it. He just stares and matches his heartbeat with its ebb and flow.

Then the girl grabs him by the shirt as if to throttle him, but she only means to rip it, a sharp blade of glass in one hand, the remains of his lantern. She slices away the fabric and tears it off him and knots it around his arm to stanch the wound. She slides him out of his backpack and he cries out with pain and she tells him to quit whining, the worst is yet to come.

Then she hoists him onto her shoulders. She grunts her way up the ladder. And in this way, she escorts him outside, through the nighttime city, to the hospital, where a sleepy-eyed doctor sets the bone and sews the puncture and wraps him into a temporary cast and fits him with a sling. Simon faints more than once from the pain. During his moments of wakefulness she berates him. "You are a world-class moron," she says. "World-class."

Her name is Ella, she finally tells him. Her shoulders are squarer than his. She keeps her straw-colored hair cut in a pageboy. Her forehead is so often wrinkled with suspicion and consternation that even when it goes flat it carries red creases. Her eyes rarely blink, steady in their focus, above a small nose freckled and rounded at the tip.

It is still dark when they leave the hospital. He walks in a wobbling way and she supports him with an arm as if he were drunk. He does not think to question where she is taking him. He is not capable of rational thought. He has lost too much blood and the doctor has doped him with an opiate. His mind is a pleasant fog.

At one point, a deputy steps from the shadows and orders them to stop. They are out past curfew, he says, and that is all he says, because the girl lights into him, saying that there is nowhere else she would rather be right now than *home*, but Simon broke his arm badly, a compound fracture, and if not for her, he probably would have died, but she managed to drag him to the hospital and now she has to drag him back home, and that's where they are headed if the deputy would only get out of their way thank you very much.

The man says nothing—he seems afraid that will only encourage her to keep talking—but steps aside. The streets are shadowed canyons Simon does not recognize in his delirium. They branch and branch again and he wonders if they will ever find their way.

"I could have turned you in, you know," she says. Not only was he trespassing in the museum—that was trouble enough—but can you imagine what the deputies would do, she says, if they knew he was roaming around *beneath* the city? They would make an example of him; that's what they would do. Whip him or hang him or worse. What was he thinking?

Simon shrugs and then flinches at the lightning strike of pain in his arm. He is not sure what to think of this girl who never seems to stop talking. That's what she is, a girl, maybe a year older or younger than him, but she speaks with the domineering voice of an adult. She smells nice. He'll give her that. Grassy.

The sky is beginning to lighten and the first bell is ringing when they arrive at the museum. His backpack, he says as she leads him inside. He needs his backpack.

She asks what's in it and he says a fifty-pound load, some to sell, some to keep.

"A load of what? What could you have possibly taken from the sewer?"

Probably he shouldn't speak so loosely, but she has protected him so far—and right now, with drugs in his veins and a poisonous snake with big fangs seeming to twist through his arm, nothing seems to matter.

"I didn't find anything in the sewer. The sewer is the way in and the way out."

"The way out?"

"The way out of the Sanctuary."

CHAPTER 19

THE FIVE OF THEM stand before the house on the hill. A cloud hangs over it like a messy gray wig. The siding is pocked with holes from birds and bugs. The porch sags and blood stains it, they hope from the deer the day before. Lewis stares at the black doorway, with the wood scarred and splintered all around it.

There was a time, when they were children, when Clark bullied him. Knocked a book from his hands. Yanked down his pants and ran away. Fired a pebble at his cheek with a slingshot. Hog-tied him and hung him from a balcony. But there was a time, too, when they played kindly with each other. And on one occasion, during a game of hide-and-seek in the Dome, he feared her gone forever. He searched for what felt like hours, peering under beds and in closets and behind doors, all the usual places where she couldn't be found. He began to cry out—"I give up! I said I give up!"—and even then she did not appear. She had abandoned him, it turned out. Grown bored. Gone outside. He was reduced to tears and the terror that the building had somehow swallowed her up—until he heard laughter out a window and spied her playing in the streets with a gang of children. He had never felt so irrelevant, betrayed.

He wishes for such a betrayal now. He would laugh with relief if she came wandering up, uninjured, whistling a song, asking what was the matter, clueless to their worry. But this time the game isn't a game. This time, a building really has swallowed her up.

Reed grips two revolvers. He snaps off their safeties and starts up the first step. The wood cries out. A swirl of dust rises around his boot.

Lewis tells him to stop. He reaches into his duster. From a pocket he removes the owl, holding it out before him, cradling it in his long, thin hand. "We need to know what we're walking into." He pets it and its bronze feathers shimmer. The gears inside it whir and click. When he sends it off into the darkness, it flies noisily, its wings creaking.

At first they can hear it churning inside, moving up and down the stairs, looping through the rooms, occasionally thudding against a wall. There follows a long silence. They cock their heads to hear it better. Their eyes, trained on the black doorway, come unstuck, and they study each other with the questions no one need utter because no one can answer—*Where is it? What should we do?*

They don't realize they're holding their breath—not until they hear another thud, followed by a ticking and grinding—and all their chests deflate at once. They can see the owl. Deep in the house, it is a glimmering hint, like a candle cupped in a hand, and then it grows brighter as it wings toward them and bursts into the sunlight.

Lewis holds out an arm and it comes to a creaking stop and roosts there. He walks to the shaded side of the house. The others follow. Daylight makes the projection difficult to see. So does the cracked and warped siding. They squint their eyes and edge closer to make out the wobbling blur of the house. The owl circles rooms and bobbles down halls and nearly knocks into a light fixture dangling from the ceiling by a cord. Pictures have fallen from the walls. A chair lies on its side. The springs have coiled through couch cushions. But there are no birds roosting in the closets, no raccoons beneath the beds. Anything with a pulse knows better.

Then the owl bends around the corner and finds the basement, a dark door leading to a dark place. They can see only dimly. The stairs long ago collapsed like a rotten accordion. The plaster walls are crosshatched with claw marks. It is nearly impossible to see, given the speed and bob of the owl's flight, but the floor is a nest of bones. Knobbed vertebrae. Basketed ribs. Skulls cavitied by black sockets. Among them, what appear to be fresher acquisitions, the empty sack of an opossum, two deer with bloodied necks, and Clark. At first she is a mere flash in the darkness, but the owl circles back to focus on her, a curl of a body, her face half-hidden by her hair. Yes, it is her.

Reed says, "How do we know if she's even alive?"

"We don't," Lewis says, but he feels it. A pull.

It is then that the owl swoops upward and they see the ceiling from which the bats dangle. Their eyes are closed, their bodies hanging tightly together like a cluster of stalactites. How many of them, it is impossible to tell, because the projection is already past them, heading out of the basement, toward the hallway, the light at the end of it where Lewis waits with his arm extended.

The air is dim and hot. The smell, puffing from the basement, tangy and fertile like marrow spooned from a split bone. A bare patch has spread across the floor here, where the hardwood drops off into the darkness, a rough circle a few feet across. He touches the splinters of it and imagines claws scraped across it night after night. A landing pad for them as they climb out and drop into their den. Lewis opens his silver tin and takes a dose of white powder up his nose and feels a little braver for it.

The house creaks in the heat. Flies buzz in and out of the doorway. Otherwise, there is no sound. They do not speak, not even to whisper, when they tie one end of the rope to a heat register and the other to a lantern with a low wick. This they drop into the darkness.

Gawea and the doctor will remain above, their weapons ready, while the rest of them descend. Reed goes first. He tries to slide off the ledge as quietly as he can, but he carries two holstered revolvers and they clunk and scrape the wood. Then York bellies into the darkness. Lewis is last. The doctor gives him an encouraging squeeze on the shoulder and he lays his hand over hers. "You bring her back to us," she says, and he says, "I will."

Then he scoots to the edge and takes the rope and allows his weight to pull him down. He dangles there a moment, and when a fly lands on his face, he slaps himself in his hurry to brush it away—and loses his grip.

It is fifteen feet to the floor, the surface of it strewn with the remains of the staircase. And guano. And bones. They lie scattered in piles still webbed together by ligature and papery skin. Lewis falls into the horrible mush. He is muddied with guano and cut along his hip. But somehow the bats remain unfazed by the noise of his descent.

He stands and wipes himself off as best as he can. Reed told them beforehand not to look at the lantern, and yet that's exactly what Lewis does, his eyes drawn to the only light in the room. He immediately turns away, blinking hard, trying to restore his eyes.

Eventually the shape of the basement takes form, and he can see the two men creeping away from him. He yanks his gun from his holster and follows. Every step is uncertain, the ground pulpy from guano and brittle with bones. They cannot be as quiet as they hope to be. To get to the far side of the room, they must pass beneath the bats, many of them man-size. Their faces are snouted and deeply wrinkled. Their claws latch to the rafters and their wings surround them like a veined chrysalis. The ceiling is tall enough to leave three feet of space beneath them. Lewis ducks down to pass beneath them. He has never felt so vulnerable, with the bats hanging above them, as if they might spear his bent back.

By the time he gets past them, the others are already hunched over Clark. She is not moving except as they shake her. Her clothes are torn, her neck and wrists and thighs gashed. Where her skin isn't bloody, it is alabaster pale. They do not know where to check for a pulse, with her neck and wrists opened, but Lewis leans his face into hers and detects a shallow breath. She lives. The bats have kept her to bleed until emptied.

They move as slowly as they can—Reed getting behind her, looping his arms beneath her shoulders—York gripping her by the knees. Lewis takes the lantern. Bones stir and snap. They pause at every noise, waiting for the bats to wake.

When they duck down—beneath maybe a dozen bats altogether, their hanging forms a mob of all different sizes—Reed and York steal forward in small steps, backs bent by the weight of Clark. Lewis follows in a hunch. He moves more slowly than they do. He toes aside a bone. He slides his boot through a pile of black guano. He can feel a breeze, their breath against his neck. He keeps the lantern low. In his hand it feels like a small sun, its light too bright, no matter how spare the wick.

Reed and York already have Clark at the base of the stairs. Lewis tries to concentrate on them. He tries not to look up. But then he senses some movement in his peripheral vision and cannot help himself. A bat hangs beside him and one of its ears is twitching. Maybe because it hears him. Or maybe because it tracks some prey through the night sky of its sleep, its ears spasming like the legs of a dreaming dog. Its mouth opens and closes with a damp sound. Its eyes shudder beneath wrinkled lids.

Ahead, he can see Clark dragged through the air, over the ledge, the rope cinched beneath her armpits. He can see the rope fall again and Reed hoisting himself up. York looks back and waves impatiently. Lewis wakes from his fearful daze and takes another step forward.

A bone shatters beneath his foot. In the silence of the basement, the sound is tremendous, as though the very darkness has cracked open. He looks down to see it was a femur. He looks up to see the bat's eyes snap open. They are huge and white and gelatinous.

Then comes the *chittering* sound, at first only from its mouth, and then from the others waking all around him.

He hears his name. "Lewis?" Reed is calling for him and he is stumbling toward his voice. "Lewis?" The doorway hangs above, his body a black silhouette against the gray light of it. "Lewis!"

There is a rustling behind him, like a wind sweeping across a desk stacked with paper, and then a shotgun blast from York. The clap and crash of it fills his ears and seems to shake the very foundation of the house. He throws down the lantern and it shatters and he staggers and trips and catches the rope and uses it to right himself. York fires again and says, "Go, go, go, go!"

He clambers up, one hand over the other, the rope pinched between his thighs. In this way he inches toward the doorway. He is weak enough and slow enough that Reed knows to help, dragging him the rest of the way.

The splintery lip of the hardwood scrapes his belly raw. He is out, among their legs. He scrabbles forward, and in that moment, moving from darkness into light, he feels as he did as a child, returning from the toilet at night, leaping into bed, certain that a hand with sharp black fingernails would snatch hold of his ankle.

For a second he can't help but stare at Clark. She lies in the hallway, as still as a corpse. The doctor kneels beside her and hauls her body toward the daylight.

Lewis is roused by the screaming above him—of Reed encouraging York to hurry, hurry goddammit—and the screaming below. Lewis rises from the floor. In the basement, the shotgun fires and he sees in its sunburst the bats crowding around York, and when it fires for the second time he sees a spray of blood. He sees tattered wings and cratered chests.

The rope goes taut. York is climbing. Reed fires his revolvers repeatedly into the darkness with a sound like storms crashing against each other, warring for the sky.

Lewis grabs hold of the rope and heaves and heaves again. First the boy's hands, and then his face, appear at the bottom of the doorway. He is smiling. Blood speckles his face. His feet dangle in a cavernous dark. But he is alive and for this he can't help but smile crookedly.

Just as he stands upright, the doorway behind him fills with the white blur of a bat, and before his smile can die, one of its wings curls around him. It draws him back—drawing him down into the dark—but his hand shoots out and catches the doorway and he holds fast there.

It is then that a voice calls out—a throaty, ash-edged voice none of them recognize—yelling, "No!"

Gawea. Her face seems to have cracked open, revealing for the first time actual feeling, raw panic. "Leave him alone!" She rushes forward and shoves her rifle into the bat's open mouth and fires.

The fire catches easily. It begins with the lantern Lewis dropped. Reed adds to it by sparking a match against a bookcase, a lace curtain, a dried bunch of grass beneath the porch. The flames thrash. The smoke rushes from the windows, streaming upward as fast as water, the streams gathering into the dark lake pooling above. Timbers snap. Nails and screws come loose with pings and pops. Hardly ten minutes pass before the house is overcome by a snapping peak of fire, the orange bones of its timbers barely visible through the flames. He and York and Gawea step back and step back again. The air warps and ripples with the heat. They stare into it, the light so painfully bright, with their guns still at their sides. They might see figures writhing within, but they might not. The fire's dance, like the desert's mirage, sometimes gives you what you want.

Lewis does not notice. All of his attention is focused on Clark. He wipes the blood from her face. Her skin is the yellow-white of dough. Her neck and her wrists and thighs have been torn by fangs, the flesh there swollen into purplish white mounds scabbed at their crowns.

The doctor brought her leather satchel—it is split open beside her now—and she withdraws from it wipes, gauze, a short bottle of sugar, a tall bottle of clear alcohol. The breeze rises to a wind that carries smoke and dust. She sets to work cleaning the wounds and instructs Lewis to prop up Clark's head and spoon some sugar water into her mouth. He barely hears her. "That won't be enough," he says.

"We'll do what we can and that's all we can do."

"She's lost too much blood."

Her voice sounds very far away when she says, "Yes."

He thinks about what York said to him that morning: why didn't he *do* anything when the bats descended on their camp? Raise his arms and let loose a flash of light and make everything better? Lewis didn't have an adequate answer. Because he doesn't like what he doesn't understand, what he can't label and quantify? Because it makes him feel inhuman? Because his father made him afraid of himself?

He feels a heat first mistaken for the fire crackling behind him. But this comes from inside him. His chest feels tornadic, a blistering wind caught behind his ribs. He swells with it until he knows he must find an outlet or else incinerate. Embers swirl at the edge of his vision. There is no stopping it this time.

The doctor's face creases. She takes several steps back, telling Lewis to settle down, holding out her hands as if to block something hurled at her.

He feels too full, as if his skin might break and release a flood of energy, and he knows where to release it, recognizes the gaping emptiness inside Clark that must be filled. He reaches into the doctor's satchel and removes a scalpel. With it he traces his wrist—and then rips into it.

He holds his arm over Clark's. His blood puddles onto her. And then, slowly, it begins to siphon into her wound, the gash trembling at the edges like a grateful mouth. He feels separate from himself when he presses their wrists together. It is a compulsive act, as when the proboscis of a butterfly sinks into a flower. Their bodies know what to do. She draws the blood into her, sucking, sucking, until he feels the last corner of his body emptying. His eyes are closed. He may hear screaming.

At last he pulls away from her and discovers the others standing around them, watching him with fear and revulsion, except for Gawea. She steps forward. "Burr was right," she says. "You are like me."

Clark stirs. Her skin has gone from pale to a flushed pink. Her back arches. Her stomach heaves. She turns her head and something hot surges up her throat, escaping her with an oily black splatter. A fly lands at its edge to taste of it—and immediately expires.

Her eyes tremble open just as his fall shut.

CHAPTER 20

GAWEA IS DIFFERENT. She has always known she was different, like a baby raised among wolves, and this difference came with a lifelong sense of separation, loneliness. Loneliness is what she knows best. She was born into it.

After the men swept a knife across her father's throat and smashed his face into the snow, after the men dragged her mother and midwife into the night and through the whirling storm, after dawn came and revealed the snow-swept ruins of the village, Gawea remained alone in the bed she was born in, alternately squalling and sleeping.

Her cries eventually brought her *oma*. She was injured, her gray hair clotted at the temple where the men had struck her twice. But when she shrank into a corner, they left her there, so old she must have already looked dead enough to them.

Oma stood over the bed, where Gawea rested in a nest of blankets, and wept. She cried for the village, much of it burned to ashes, and she cried for her daughter, dead or kidnapped, and she cried for this grandchild of hers, born with a pair of eyes that matched the night-black world.

Deformities are normal. Some are born with extra fingers and toes, others with diminutive limbs, crooked spines, birthmarks brightly staining their faces. In their village, a child was born without any mouth, only a slitted nose, and without any genitals, just a fleshy mound where there might have been a cleft or shaft. Another child, a boy with gigantism, was cut from his mother's belly after only seven months, because they worried his kicks might shatter her ribs. He was born as big as a toddler. He lived and grew to be twice as tall as any man in the village, with a shelf of a forehead and spiked, uneven shoulders, but died before he was twenty.

Some say his heart couldn't keep up with all that body. And then there was Denver, more than a hundred miles away, nicknamed the Goblin City. A warhead detonated there, mangling the downtown and opening up a crater so big it appeared half the city had been scooped by a giant shovel. The buildings glowed at night, some said, as did the people, all of them with skin like melted wax and hair that grew in patches, their mouths hissing a language no one understood but them.

Gawea was a kind of goblin. When she was two and did not want to go to bed, Oma told her, the lantern shattered and licked the floor with a tongue of fire. When she was three, she could whistle and call a bird fluttering from a branch to her shoulder. When she was four, she began to work in their garden and the vegetables grew oversize and the flowers remained in bloom through the fall. When she was five and wandered away from the cabin alone, Oma spanked her and woke up the next morning covered with hundreds of spider bites.

Oma read stories to her, played games with her, taught her how to sew and knit and cook, how to gut a fish, butcher an elk, and though Gawea could talk—in a tiny, calm voice—she never asked questions, only gave answers. Sometimes it seemed she had another way of communicating with the world, plugged in to a connection unavailable to the rest of them. And more than once Oma found herself fetching a cup of water that Gawea reached for eagerly, though she never asked for it.

Oma kept a picture of her daughter, Juliana, a charcoal sketch, the frame stained darkly along the right side from all the time she spent holding it in her hand. Sometimes she and Gawea went hunting. Not for deer or elk or bear, but for information. About the men who had come in the night. They found other villages scorched and riddled with bones. Sometimes dried-out corpses hung from trees like cocoons, and sometimes spears bristled the ground, their tips topped by skulls. They found survivors, mostly old men and women, who told them about a long parade of wheeled cages crammed with men and women and children.

"Which way did they go?"

"That way," the old man said, pointing north. "Or maybe that way." West.

"Thank you," Oma said, and the old man said, "I wouldn't go that way. I'd stay as far away as you can from there. There's a darkness rising."

Then Oma died. Her glands swelled—in her armpits, below her jaw—into lumps, what they knew must be cancer. She became feverish. Her sweat smelled like sulfur. She lost her appetite and slept most of the day and thinned to a skeleton with loose, papery skin. After Gawea buried her in the backyard, she remained by the hump of dirt for hours, and the sky steadily filled with shrieking birds. The birds always listened.

There was nothing for her here. Her sense of aloneness was so complete, so consuming, that the rest of the world blurred away, and there was only her mother's face sketched in charcoal. Her *oma* believed her alive. So did Gawea. She was sad and scared, but Oma taught her what she needed to know to live, and she was fourteen now, not a woman but the beginning of one.

She hiked across Colorado and into Utah and in her pack she carried the sketch. When she smelled smoke, when she happened upon trails that carried footprints and wheel ruts, when she spotted lamplight flaring through the woods, she watched for a long time before she approached. Sometimes people fired arrows or threw rocks at her. And sometimes they talked, though none seemed eager to offer much of themselves to the black-eyed girl.

Many told stories about the slavers, about the wagon trains driven west, about the drumbeats they sometimes heard that took over their pulse and made them fear the night and what it might bring.

The high-walled valley was a bowl of fissured clay, empty of anything except a single boulder deposited there by a glacier. The boulder was pocked and red and round, its own tiny planet. She rested in the shade of it. The day was so hot her lungs felt scalded. She was in Utah, near Salt Lake City, or so she believed from studying her map. She snacked on beef jerky, smoked fish. She drank from her canteen, then spared a few drops to make mud on her palm to spread on her sunburn. She took off her hat and fanned her face and gave up when she felt no relief.

She curled up, hoping to sleep, to hike again after the sun set. So she did not notice, a long way off, near the neck of the valley, a ribbon of dust dirtying the sky, kicked up by a caravan of oxen and carts. Nor did she notice the trembling in the ground. Their slow progress matched the sun—it was as if they were pacing each other—both of them rolling along for the next hour, the sun centering the sky just as the first of the carts heaved to a stop beside the boulder.

It was too late to hide.

The nightmare parade consisted of twenty cages, some built from wood and barbed wire, many of them repurposed truck beds with cages welded over the top, each dragged by two rib-slatted horses or oxen that foamed with sweat and bled at the yokes. The wheels of their caravan cut deep furrows in the clay. Men and women and children peeked out of the cages. Their lips were cracked and bleeding. Those with white faces were a mess of peeling, reddened skin. A few muttered and sobbed, but most observed her silently.

The boulder offered the only shade in the valley, and burrowed beneath rested a jeweled nest of lizards and snakes. One of them rattled its tail now, and the rest joined in, making a sound like a storm of gravel.

The man in the lead cart wore cracked sunglasses and a round-brimmed hat with what looked like a bite taken out of it. His beard had a white streak waterfalling down its middle. "Well, well."

The rattling faded, snake by snake.

He dropped down stiffly from his perch. His boots shattered the crisp patina and a dust cloud rose and breezed away. He jerked a knife from his belt and stepped toward her, ready for trouble. She trembled. Cast down her eyes.

"She alone?" said one of the other drivers.

"Looks it."

The man smelled unwashed, and she breathed in the thick, oily flavor of him. She wanted to run, but this was what she had been looking for—wasn't it? By finding them she might find her mother. The man nudged up her chin—and it was only then that he noticed her eyes, black and empty, watching him. He took a step back.

"What?" the other driver asked.

"Something wrong with her."

"Not so wrong. Throw her in."

He hesitated only a second before grabbing her by the hair and dragging her to the bed of a Toyota. He unlocked the tailgate and forced her inside. Bars reached over the truck bed like a metal rib cage with a threadbare tarp thrown over for shade. It snapped in the wind and a triangle of sunlight flashed the ten people huddled there. Some of the men and women didn't move, slack faced and staring into a middle distance available only to them. Others tried to comfort her, telling her, "It's all right, dear," though they pulled away hesitantly when they noticed her eyes. One of them pressed a baby to a flattened breast.

The man dug through her pack. He tossed aside what he didn't want. In his hand was the picture of her mother, the framed charcoal sketch. He studied her mother's face a moment before letting the wind carry her away.

Soon the caravan groaned forward again, the wheels cutting through the baked skin of the valley floor, hushing the sand beneath. They continued through the day, into the night, and they entered a rockier territory. The truck bed tipped one way, then the other, knocking them about. There was a jug of water that sloshed violently. Now and then they drank from it, everyone saying, take care, take care, who knows when they'll refresh it. Gawea took three little sips before the jug was yanked from her.

Some of the men and women were bone thin, and some were heavy, with arms that slopped and folded over each other many times. All of them were dust smeared. Mostly they huddled in stunned silence, but occasionally they wondered aloud where they would be taken, what would happen to them. "I heard about them," the woman with the baby said. "Heard they were coming. Man came through and warned us. Said he had seen one of their hives with his own two eyes. That's what he called it. Not a city, not a town. But a hive. As if they weren't people, not in the standard sense, not with hearts and minds. Just a bunch of bugs with pinchers and stingers."

A skeletal man with a broken nose was nodding when she spoke. When she finished, he said he had heard stories too. About men on horseback with whips looped at their belts and rifles holstered at their sides overseeing slaves as they felled trees, graded roads, dug irrigation canals, raised barns, built fences. They were building something, trying to put the world back together again, and treating people like the tools to make it happen. "That's us. That's what we're going to be to them."

"Not me," a heavy woman with a red face said. "I'm nobody's tool."

"I guess we'll see about that."

They kept on with their talking and Gawea found her eyes drawn to the cratered face of the moon and the stars that pricked the sky. She got lost in their depths, as if falling into a pond full of quartz. Somehow, despite their lurching passage, they all eventually drifted to sleep.

The next morning the baby did not wake. The mother wailed for half the day before going quiet. Gawea watched her clutch the baby and felt a renewed hollowness, an inversion of her own pain in the mother's.

A week later, the air changed. She could smell the water from a long way off. The mineral sharpness of it, like the tears of a stone. Where before there was no road, they now followed the pocked and rutted tracks of others, a narrow chute between two ridges. When they passed through the other side of it, big pines clustered, their cones crunching underfoot, their branches scraping metal. The shade pooled. The temperature dropped twenty degrees. Through the pine needles the sunlight filtered green. The men and women, who said nothing for days, now pressed their faces against the bars and chirped with excitement at the green bunches of bear grass, the red splash of Indian paintbrush. The sun, which had pressed down on them for so long, now felt worlds away.

Then the pine resin and sage gave way to the smell of smoke. Cooked meat. Their smiles flattened. They passed a dented green sign whose white lettering read, ASHTON, POPULATION 10,272. Once there was an asphalt road here—buckled and broken and made impassable—but the mess of it had been cleared away into a cinder grade.

They passed a white steepled church, a blacksmith, a mercantile, all of them newly constructed, freshly painted. The trees opened up, making room for the sun. A garden, planted with rows of lettuce and carrots and onions and potatoes, reached a square acre. A man sat on a horse beside it. A rifle rested across his lap. Below him ten boys and four girls leaned on hoes, watching them pass with the same blank expression as the cattle that crowded up against the fence of a slatted pen.

The carts rolled past a man at a pump, jacking the metal arm of it, splashing full a bucket. He shaded his eyes to watch them pass. And here was the open garage of what was once a mechanic, now a carpentry shop. A man stood between two sawhorses and carved a tool along a length of wood, dirtying the floor with yellow shavings, making what appeared to be a door. A boy with a broom swept up the mess, his ankles chained loosely.

In the center of town was a park and through the park purled a river. The spring-fed water ran clear except where it made a white collar along a broad shoal built from melon-size stones. Several women crouched in the water, the water foaming with soap. With brushes, they scrubbed at laundry before hanging it from wooden racks to dry upon the shore. Their ankles were chained too.

The caravan pulled into the roundabout of an old yellow-bricked elementary school, and there he was, waiting for them on the front step—a thin man, bald and goosenecked, with a notebook and pen. He was smiling wanly. He, with the help of the drivers, unloaded every cage and examined every slave. That's what they were now, slaves. The heavy woman tried to pull away and got kicked to the ground and beaten with a cudgel. A boy cried and one of the drivers cuffed him in the ear and he cried all the louder.

The thin man did not answer questions, but he asked them. "Have you had any illnesses? Have you had any children? Do you know any trades? Do you know how to cook? Do you know how to sew? Do you know how to garden?" And he commanded: "Open your mouth. Take off your clothes. Hold out your arms. Turn around in a circle."

To Gawea, he said, "Is there something wrong with you?"

"No."

"I ask, because your eyes... You don't have a tail? Or seizures? Any difficulties with language?"

"No."

"Hmm." He made some notes on his clipboard and said, "Next," and sent her into the black mouth of the schoolhouse behind him.

They branded her on the shoulder, along with the rest, her flesh sizzling, bunching up in a letter, *F*, and a number, 131. They cleaned her, gave her fresh clothes, assigned her a bunk. "You are now part of something bigger," the thin man told them. "You're serving a kind of collective. The rebirth of humanity. The reconstruction of the country. Your work matters. It's important. You're better off here. Forget your old lives. Forget what people used to call you. You're a tool now. You're a shovel, you're a hammer, you're a sickle, you're a trowel."

When the heavy woman tried to protest, the thin man nodded to some guards and they dragged her out back and tied her to a post and lashed her with a whip seven times, and after that nobody said a word when told what to do. Everyone had a task. The job of the gardener was to raise and preserve food. The job of the tailor was to weave and sew and patch. The job of the slaver was to harvest slaves. In this way, town by town, or hive by hive, they multiplied, programming behavior, constructing a new world.

Gawea was assigned to the hospital. When they told her what to do, she did it. It was easier that way. Easier to focus on a task, scraping a broom across the floor and making a pile of dirt. Knocking down cobwebs. Mopping up puddles of blood. At first it even felt welcome, curative. She had a place and function in the world. As long as she kept busy, she didn't have to think. Her head remained empty. Emptiness felt safe.

In this way, several days and then weeks passed. She washed trays of tools—scalpels, forceps—until they gleamed. She stripped the beds of sheets, collected towels and aprons from the floor, soiled with blood and shit and amniotic fluid. "It won't be long," the thin man told her, "before you're ready for a child yourself."

Mostly they left her alone. She had a way about her, a stillness even when moving, that didn't draw the eye. Today she paused at a second-story window to observe a papery gray wasp's nest, half the size of her, dangling from a nearby branch. The black-bodied wasps, each the size of a finger, crawled across its outside, thrumming their wings.

Then she went about tidying a cot, folding a blanket around a thin mattress stuffed with wool. She was in the pregnancy wing, and in the room rested three other women, all wearing shapeless gowns to accommodate their rounded stomachs. Two of them weren't much older than her, young enough to still look longingly at dolls. The other had gray threading her hair.

They rubbed their hands across their bellies, sometimes clutching themselves, as if trying to strangle away the pain contracting there. Gawea answered to the midwives, one of them a slit-mouthed, wide-hipped woman who always pointed a finger when she called out, "*You!*" before assigning some errand.

Gawea paused in the doorway of a room where she found the midwives busy with a birth, drawing a squalling purple-skinned baby from between a mother's legs, wiping it with a towel and laying it on the mother's chest before cutting the cord and sewing a tear and easing out the placenta and stanching the bleeding.

In the next room, a woman paced the floor with her fists balled into the small of her back. Her eyes were closed and her teeth bared. She breathed in a pattern of quick pants and long gusts.

And in the room after she found her mother, Juliana.

Gawea recognized her instantly. It was more than the framed picture her *oma* carried around. Her mother was, after all, more than a decade removed from that charcoal likeness. Hollow eyed. With thinning hair, yellowing skin. All these years and several births and so many years of hard labor later. No, the recognition was deeper. As if blood were magnetized.

A baby suckled at her breast. It was curled like a shrimp into the nook of her arm. Its head was still coned from birth, its skin wrinkled and splotchy. Juliana was smiling, stroking its downy hair and humming a song that stopped short when she spied the girl.

"What do you want?"

"Mama."

"What are you talking about?"

"Mama." Her voice was tiny and delicate, like a teacup rarely used. "It's me. It's your daughter." She hurried to the bed and laid a hand on her mother's. Something happened then. Ever since losing Oma, she felt closed down, locked away, unaware. Now, as she grabbed hold of her mother, it was as if two doors on either side of a house burst open and sent the wind rushing in and out, all of it mixed up with birds and bats and bugs and rain. "Mama."

Juliana's eyes watered and her nostrils flared, as if exposed to a whiff of alcohol that once made her sick. "I don't know who you are. Get away from me. I said get away from me."

A scuff sound. In the doorway stood the slit-mouthed midwife.

She was wiping her hands off with a towel that matched her shirt, patterned with blood.

"Get her away from me," Juliana said. "Get her away from my baby. She was trying to take it from me."

"No," Gawea said. "Mama."

The midwife threw down her bloodied towel and started toward her, one of her hands already raised.

"Ma—" The word was cut short by the fist that struck her. She fell to the floor and brought a hand to the hot swelling at her cheek. She looked up at Juliana with dribbling black eyes only to see her mother's face twisted up in a snarl. The years had done something to her, distanced and polluted her. She had forgotten one family and become part of another.

"Stay away," she said, "you *freak*."

There was a sudden electrical hum. The air trembled, like a wind first finding its breath. The midwife raised her hand again to strike her. But the hand never fell.

A dark stream of wasps poured through the window. One moment the midwife was rearing back to strike Gawea and the next moment she was seething with wings and stingers. They covered her completely, a nettling mass. She crashed into a wall and then the floor. She tore at them, clawed at them, but, like smoke, they parted a moment and then filled the space her hands passed through. Their bodies pulsed, jabbing their stingers again and again into every available surface of skin, and then, when the midwife opened her mouth to scream, they scrabbled down her throat.

She was still thrashing on the floor when Juliana, over the storm of wasps, screamed, "Get away!" She wrapped the baby in a blanket now and clutched it two-handed. "Get away get away get away get away!"

Gawea's expression hardened—as if all the anger and sadness and disappointment she might feel had mineralized—until it appeared someone had chipped her face from a piece of rock. She was about to ask the wasps something more. She was about to ask them to hurt the baby. If she concentrated hard enough, if she bent her desire into a question, she knew they would answer.

But they stopped her. First the midwives, then the doctors. They stormed into the room and held her down and knocked her out and she woke later in a barred cell with a swollen eye and a blackening headache. On the other side of the bars she found the thin man, studying her with his head cocked and his eyebrows arched. "You're awake."

She rolled upright and brought a finger to her temple and it came back tacky with blood.

"What are you going to do to me?"

"Me? Nothing."

"What's going to happen to me?"

"That's not my decision. If it was my decision, I might slice you open and see what makes you tick. You make me very, very curious."

"Whose decision is it, then?"

"Aran Burr's."

"Who's Aran Burr?"

"Who's Aran Burr?" The thin man laughed, a reedy clicking. "If you don't know that, then I better tell you the color of the sky and the name of the planet and the smell of a rose."

"Who is he?"

"You'll know soon enough. He wants to meet you. He wants me to take you to him."

CHAPTER 21

ONCE ELLA LEARNS where Simon lives—in a lean-to in an alley—she insists he stay with her. "We'll head back to the doctor in a few days for a proper cast. In the meantime, we need to keep that wound clean. Judging from your clothes and your habit of crawling through sewers and sleeping with rats and trash, you're obviously incapable of taking care of yourself. You'll die. Or they'll have to cut your arm off and then you'll die." So he will stay with her at the museum. In the room they share, there are two beds, and Ella sleeps in one, Simon the other.

His forearm, now purplish with an angry red gash in the middle of it, has swollen to twice its size. His black sausagey fingers will not respond to his commands. Twice a day she helps clean the wound and doses him up with morphine, but she does not permit him as much rest as he would like. She puts him to work instead—sweeping one-handed, scrubbing the bathroom, boxing up a butterfly display and replacing it with reptiles and amphibians. He is especially taken by a specimen of frog—called the Hairy Frog or Horror Frog—skirted around the waist with fur and capable of breaking the bones in its fingers and toes in order to defend itself, forcing the shards through the skin, creating claws. He remembers the pain of the break and rubs his arm and imagines it as a newly carved weapon. He is a weapon. And if he could revenge his father—if he could hurt someone, slash his arm across a throat—it would be Slade.

About this he spends a lot of time daydreaming, and about other things, too. Hunting dinosaurs with a spear. Blasting off to space in a rocket. Lancing a knight in a duel. Whereas before, he spent all of his time trying to fill his stomach and filch valuables and escape detection, his every comfort is now attended to, and he can afford to indulge. The museum encourages his mind to play. For the first time in many years, he is allowed to be a child.

When he asks for his backpack, Ella says, "Maybe later," and when he complains, she says, "You do what I tell you to do. I've got you by the balls, remember?"

So he does as he's told. There seems to be no other way with her. Even when she uses the word *please*, it comes at a near shout, but so does she make him meals and mend his clothes and cut his hair, the clippings of which collect in a thick nest on the floor when she circles his chair and scissors her way to his scalp and finally stands back and nods approvingly and says, "You look much better now. Very presentable indeed. Except for your stuck-out ears."

He runs a hand across his bristling scalp. Without all that hair he feels naked. She is good at making him feel that way. Stripped, revealed, as if there is no hiding anything from her.

It is then they hear a noise. The thudding of what at first sound like footsteps. She puts a hand to his mouth and says, *Shh*. He shoves the hand away and says, "What?" and she returns the hand, muzzling him. She faces the dark hallway. Her scissors rasp open. And then the thudding comes again and she recognizes the sound. "Someone's at the front entrance."

Simon pushes her hand away again, and this time she lets him talk when he says, "It's night. No one's supposed to be out."

She closes the scissors with a snap.

"Maybe we should ignore it," Simon says.

But the thudding stubbornly continues, trembling the air.

He stands from the chair. Cut curls fall from his shoulders and feather his feet. Ella pushes him back into a seated position. "You stay here." When he opens his mouth to protest, she points the scissors at him and says, "And whatever you do, don't make a sound."

———

Sometimes it happens. Someone comes knocking late at night. Usually the feebleminded. The occasional drunk deep in his cups.

Lewis will hiss and snap at them, burn them with a lantern, push them down the steps, send them hurrying off. But that was in the days before the enforced curfew. And now Lewis is not here to help. There is only her. The boy doesn't count. A broken-armed, thin-necked thief. He is as threatening as a gumming puppy. He is to be protected, not offer protection.

She knows who it is. She wishes she didn't, but she does. She can feel him out there—in the same way the old-timers say they can feel storms—when she grips the scissors tightly and follows the staircase to the first floor and approaches the double doors, which shake in their frames. She waits there a long time, willing the sound to stop, but it won't. Not until she undoes the lock, opens a crack, peers out.

In the darkness, in his black uniform, his face appears like a moon hovering over her. He presses a hand against the door to open it wider, but she presses back, giving him only these few inches, enough for him to see her unyielding expression.

"You took quite a long time to answer the door."

"I was busy."

"Doing what?"

"Sleeping."

"You sleep with the light on? I saw the light on."

"I was getting ready to go to sleep."

"Are you with someone?"

"No."

"I didn't have to knock, you know. I was just being polite."

"What do you want?"

She cannot stop him now, though she tries. He leans into the door and it gives way. Her strength is a child's compared to his.

"You haven't heard from him?"

"Who?"

"Lewis? Who else?"

"No, of course not."

The door clicks closed. "What's behind your back?"

She almost says nothing, but she knows that will only make him angry, will make him step toward her, grip her arm and twist it into view. Slowly she reveals the scissors.

"There's hair on these scissors."

"I was cutting my hair."

"That's not your hair. It's not the same color."

"Then I was trimming the clots off a stuffed ground sloth."

"I thought you said you were getting ready for bed?"

"You ask too many questions."

"Do I? I have so many for you."

He snatches the scissors from her. His fingers, too fat, don't fit into the grips, so he must use two hands when he opens and closes them. "Hold still a moment." He steps close to her and she slides back her feet and he says, "I said hold still." She does as he says but will not allow him to observe her fear. She crosses her arms and stares straight ahead when he circles her, teasing the blades across her shoulders, the back of her neck, down her arms. Finally he chooses a section of sleeve, a moth's wing of fabric, that he snips away, and it disappears into his pocket.

She prides herself on her strength. Not just the muscles that ball in her arms, but her heart, her ability to bully back anyone who might take advantage of her. But she feels weak now. Slade makes her feel weak. She almost cries out for the boy. That will only make the situation worse, she knows, give Slade another target to prod with a blade, another line of questioning to delay his stay and renew his suspicion of her. But the scissors are so sharp and his mouth is so close, his breath mingling with hers.

She is close to kicking at his crotch, when just in time Slade drops the scissors. They clatter on the floor. He walks away. He opens the door and pauses at the threshold to regard her. "I could hurt you, you know. And nobody would stop me."

She has to swallow several times before she can say, "I know."

"Good." He pulls the door behind him, his eye in the crack the last thing she sees of him.

Ella won't speak to Simon, not at first. He asks her what happened. He asks her what's the matter. He asks how can he help. She paces the hallway and then their room, stomping her feet, brushing a hand through her hair, slashing the air with the scissors.

"What?" Simon says, and after a few minutes she starts to talk under her breath and Simon says, "I can't hear you," and her voice grows louder and louder and comes out finally as a shout when she goes over all the things she should have said and done but didn't.

He waits for her to finish and then says, "I hate him too."

This seems to irritate her. As if hatred were water and there was only so much to go around. "You hate him? Why would you hate him? What do you even care? What does this have to do with you?"

When he says Slade killed his father, she tucks the scissors into her belt and says, "Oh."

"I'll kill him for you. I'll kill him for both of us."

"For me?" At first she seems taken by the idea. That he would offer such a thing. Then she is struck more by the absurdity than by the nobility of the gesture. "You can't even climb a ladder without breaking your arm. You can't even tie your own shoe. You'll kill him? I'll kill him. I'll kill him my own damn self."

He sees there is no reasoning with or comforting her, so he tries a method of thieving: distraction and inertia. If you sneak up beside somebody and hold a rotten apple to their face, ask them to buy it, they'll naturally reel back, swing up their hands. With that momentum he'll pop off a bracelet or slide coins from a pocket. He'll follow Ella's lead. "How would you do it? You could stab him. Sneak up behind him and—" Here he slashes at an invisible figure and makes a wet, shredding sound.

"No," she says and wrinkles her face. "That wouldn't work. That wouldn't work at all. You'd have to get close and risk him grabbing hold of you. And he's too big. You'd have to stab him a million times. And you'd have to stab him with something long, like a sword, to even reach anything important."

"Then, what? How would you kill him?"

"I don't know. Maybe I'd push something out a window onto him. Something heavy. An anvil. Knock his brains out."

"Or poison!"

"That wouldn't work either. Same as with the knife. He's too big. How much poison would it take to kill someone like that? A lot. And how do you camouflage a lot of poison? You can't just sprinkle it on a biscuit. You see? You need me. You can't think anything through on your own."

Her tone has mellowed. Her mouth has risen into a smile. He has helped lag her fear. Not enough to get her to sleep, but enough to get her ready for it. They share the same room, their beds separated by a night table. They extinguish their lamps and he lies there for a long time, listening to her breath, waiting for it to settle into the rhythm of sleep. Then she says, "Simon?"

"What?"

"Thanks."

"For what?"

"You know." He waits for her to say more, but she doesn't. Outside the turbines turn and croak their lazy circles and sink them into sleep.

The next morning, it takes him a moment to shake off his dreams, to orient himself in the museum, to recognize Ella spreading the curtains and letting in a slash of sunlight.

He sees then his backpack, stained and patched, made mostly from canvas and bottomed with leather. He has asked for it many times—so many times that she has threatened to throw it away if he asks again—and now here it is. The flap is open, as if it has disgorged all its contents on the floor. There is a blister pack of stainless steel nails, a chisel, a hammer, a faded rubber ducky with the beak hanging off, a rusted coil of wire, three sheets of sandpaper, a corroded butcher knife and metal spatula, three bottles of aspirin and another for springtime allergies.

She sits on the edge of the bed and folds her hands in her lap and asks if he sells these things and he says yes, and she asks if people wonder where he finds them and he says not really. "Because I'm a thief, you know. You don't want to ask too many questions when you're buying from a thief."

"You're not a thief. You're a grave robber."

"No, no. I steal from the living too." He tells her that he can pick any lock, climb any wall, slip through any door or window in the Sanctuary. This he says in a rush of pride and excitement—and then realizes whom he is speaking to and goes quiet and readies for a scolding.

But she only tucks her hair behind her ears, a delicate gesture for her, and says, "What about that one?"

She is talking about a photograph, discolored and bent in half, the picture flaking along the crease. A family on a sand dune. Two parents, three kids, all leaning into each other, their smiles bright and their hair windblown, while sunlight sparkles in a thousand crystalline points off the ocean behind them. "Why would you take this?"

"I don't know." He crawls out of bed and squats to study the photo. "I guess I like the way it makes me feel when I look at it and hold it in my hand. It's like it's got this charge, a little life in it still." The mother appears to be laughing. One of the children, a boy, isn't looking at the camera at all, his eyes on a gull riding the breeze. Simon imagines the bones beneath their faces and wonders where they might be interred. "This whole museum is a bit like that, don't you think?"

Ella studies him for a pregnant moment. Then she goes to the closet and swings open the door and pulls from beneath her clothes an old toy chest with a hinged lid and a rocking horse carved into the side.

She shows him what she has never showed anyone. What she calls her dream box. Inside there are toy ponies, a pink plastic comb, a Renoir magnet, a pack of playing cards, an angel calendar, a yellowed copy of *The Hobbit* with the pages crumbling out of it, and more, much more, including a folder full of photos and clippings. She holds everything with the tips of her fingers, taking care not to bend or dirty them. He doesn't ask her why she has it, this box full of everything. He understands. They are the same, both refusing to acknowledge that they live in a place where fantasies must be discarded.

Here is a vinyl record in a brittle paper sleeve. *Françoise Hardy*, it reads across it. Simon takes it from her. "Have you ever listened to this?"

"No."

"My father had records he used to play."

"Your father." The danger of last night, which seemed so far removed a moment ago, now flashes across her face. She looks as though she might say something, but a tapping sound distracts her. They turn to the window, where Lewis's owl waits patiently beyond the glass.

CHAPTER 22

HIS NAME IS Jon Colter, but for some time he was known as the Black Fist. He might have invented the name. He might have encouraged its use. He liked it. He felt it captured what he was, how he wanted others to consider him. Someone once told him the scariest part of any story was when a character crept forward to investigate a strange sound. Whatever nightmare waited around the corner did not matter, its revelation almost always a disappointment. It was the imagined threat that mattered most. A fist was a threat. A clenched fist raised and ready to swing. In this capacity he served the Sanctuary for many years.

He began as a sentinel, and one day, when ranging the Dead Lands, he walked through the open door of a house that was a wolf's den. They sprung and burrowed their muzzles into him and mauled him nearly to death before the other sentinels fired arrows and sent them limping and yipping off.

Eventually he healed, the scabs and then the scars hardening him back into the shape of a man. His mouth slashed open along the left cheek a permanent half smile. He sought out the wolves, hunting them down in their den, chaining them and whipping them into submission, making two of them his own, so that he would walk the streets leashed to them, first as a deputy, then as sheriff under the late Mayor Meriwether.

Saddled on the back of a black horse called Nightmare and guided by his wolves, he now stalks his way across a parched country, a never-ending valley of the dry bones with no Ezekiel to call them up. He is schooled enough to know that God drove men west—across the ocean, across America. They followed the compass of Manifest Destiny and they claimed the country in God's name. But their God must not have been pleased, because he smote them down and cursed them with the hot wind breathed through his clenched teeth.

The same breath that wakes Colter tonight, on a farm outside of Omaha. He first hears the birds squawking and fluttering in the rafters of a pole shed. And then the hiss that swells into a sound like grain sliding down a metal chute. His horse whickers and his wolves whimper and pant and he hurries outside to see a vast section of the sky absent of stars. They have been eaten up by the black wall of sand moving toward him. He barricades the door and drapes blankets over the broken windows. When the sandstorm hits, the shed lets out a metallic groan as if ready to collapse, but it holds strong as the wind scours the metal and sends dust swirling through every available crack and he and the wolves huddle down with their eyes pinched shut.

He is not afraid. Not of the heat, the emptiness, the radiation, the bone piles and splintery ruins, whatever danger awaits him. He prefers to imagine the world fearing him, as it was before, when he roamed the streets of the Sanctuary, one hand leashed to the wolves, the other teasing the machete sheathed to his thigh. Everyone made way for him, darting down alleys, pressing their backs against buildings, closing their eyes if the wolves paused to sniff them.

He was not a big man, but their fearfulness made him feel that way. Too big. So that he and the mayor began to thrash against each other, their tongues like quarreling daggers. He thought he knew one thing and the old man another. "You are the muscle; I am the brain." That's what the mayor always said, and Colter came to reject it. He knew best which wards needed more or fewer patrols. He knew best what ordinances and punishments worked and didn't. After a heated city council session, after they closed the meeting and took to the hallway, after Meriwether jammed a finger against his chest and told him to stand down, Colter lost his temper, twisted the old man's arm behind his back, and broke it with a damp pop. Not on purpose. By accident. If temper could be considered accidental.

Sometimes the world felt like a game in which everyone vied for power. Those who didn't have power tried to maneuver or rage against those who did. And those who had power pushed to oppress further those who didn't. He played the game well, until he lost it. On the floor, with his arm bent unnaturally, the old man screamed and ordered Colter's own deputies against him. He might have said sorry if given the chance.

But they silenced him by disappearing him into a cell. A few might have died dragging him there. And there he has remained, his anger growing viler and more toxic as time progressed. With chunks of stone and hunks of rusted metal, he sketched out on his cell walls scenes of war and torture, a fantasia of retribution that became his reality, like someone who reads over and over again a novel until its words are rote and its characters flesh.

The old man who put him there is dead. The doctors said it was the result of infection brought on by the surgery, his arm broken in several places. The old man had been in a cast only a few days, wracked by the fever that came from the infection, when he suffered a heart attack. Colter knew the heart attack could have come at any time, when he was giving a speech or humping his wife or knifing into a steak, whether his arm was broken or not. But all the what-ifs and maybes did not change the fact that his death more or less came at Colter's hand.

The mayor's son is alive. Hiding somewhere out in all this waste. Colter has been given a gift. The gift of freedom. They let him go and wished him good hunting. Colter knows how to hunt and he knows how to hurt. With knives and ropes and whips and glass and fire. With his own hands. With his wolves. And now he is supposed to hurt Lewis, the man he still thinks of as a thin-wristed, pale-skinned weakling of a boy, the son of the man who clapped him away and left him to rot after all his years of service.

He follows the dry river, follows the messy stream of hoofprints in the sand, follows the ashen piles of dead campfires, the withered lumps of stool, the castaway supplies the wolves sniff, lick. He squints at the horizon, where the sun sets, a kaleidoscope of bloody colors.

CHAPTER 23

EVERYONE CALLS HER the doctor. She doesn't mind. She knows that once a woman becomes a certain age, people stop seeing her. In the Sanctuary, at the hospital, people made eye contact, asked questions, listened to her answers, because she was of service to them. She was *the doctor*. But on the streets she was no one, invisible. Not the doctor and not her given name, Minda Shields. She was a ghost.

She never married, never had children. No one ever bothered to pursue her. Maybe because of the way she looked, face scrunched, prematurely gray, appearing old long before she ever was. Maybe it was because the right man never seemed so important and the right woman always felt impossible to acquire. Or maybe it was the way she behaved. All business, people said. Which was another way of saying, unkind. She didn't mean to be. It was just her way. If someone came in, whimpering about stomach cramps or heatstroke or whatever ailed them, she would say, "We're here for symptoms, not sympathy." She understood the way the body fit together and came apart, the way it ruined and healed, and she wanted to help a person in the same way a builder might mortar a crumbling foundation or a gardener might pull a weed in an overgrown pot.

As the years passed, she tried to be better. She tried to help more, mother more. She wanted people to turn a needy face toward her in a bad time. She had no one but her patients. That is how she knows Clark, as a patient, treated for alcohol poisoning. She pumped her stomach and brought the cups of sugar water to her lips and held her hair as she vomited into a bucket and monitored her for twenty-four hours. She checked up on her weeks later, finding her at the stables, asking if she needed anything.

"What makes you think I need anything?"

"I'm just checking. That's all. Just seeing if you're all right. Healthy."

"I'm fine." Clark looked at her curiously. "Hey, you want to get a drink?"

A patient treated for alcohol poisoning asking her out for a drink. The doctor almost laughed, but she could tell Clark asked the question without irony. To her drinking was like breathing, like talking, and the doctor decided she would like to share that with her. She wasn't one to visit bars, but she visited one that night. Clark had a way of rallying people, convincing them of what they never realized they wanted. It wasn't one drink or two. It wasn't two weeks or three. It was a long seduction, a slow, secret sharing, before Clark revealed their plans and asked if the doctor might join them. They needed someone like her. To care for them.

To be needed. How good that felt.

The doctor realized then she couldn't remember the last dream she dreamed. She couldn't remember the last patient she saw or the last meal she ate or the last book she read. Those things happened, but they happened in the haze that had become her life. Nothing was worth committing to memory any longer. So she said, "Yes." She would go. She would go anywhere Clark asked.

Clark might be reckless, given to wild mood swings, occasionally crippled by her indulgences, but there was something about her—the way she punched the air to punctuate a sentence, the way she never stopped moving except right before she was about to give an order, the way she threw back her head when she laughed, as if her laughter were a swallowed sword. Her heart was too big. It owned her. And when she was angry or happy or sad, you knew about it, because her heart couldn't be hidden, slamming everyone within fifty yards with its drumbeat. It was hard to doubt someone like that, someone who lived so fully.

The doctor is taken. They all are. They are all there because of Clark. She is their rallying force. Which is why, when the doctor leaned over her cold, pale body, when she dug through her bag and searched for anything that might restore the life to this beautiful, precious person, she felt wounded in a way she never had before. She understood at last what it meant to be the weeping patient.

It was not her care that brought Clark back. It was not anything the doctor pretended to understand, a force beyond any education. But none of that mattered. All that did was Clark's survival. About this the doctor feels, with no other comparison available in her life, joy.

The doctor dotes on her. Tidying her blanket. Cleaning the dressing on her wounds. Telling her to rest, rest, please. Pushing back her hair and kissing her on the forehead. Whatever she needs, the doctor will take care of.

She tells Reed to leave Clark be. "She doesn't need *you*."

And she doesn't. The doctor has never liked him. He is the kind of man women love—with his predatory smile, his stalking walk, his way of standing too close—but he has always struck her as a rank dog eager to hump a leg.

She does not care for Lewis either. For other reasons entirely. She has a grandnephew, a boy of seven who can play the fiddle brilliantly but avoids eye contact and makes strange conversation with himself. There is something similarly unsettling about Lewis, who has always seemed to occupy a different room even when in the company of others and who has abilities beyond any of their understanding. A magician, a miracle worker, an aberration—she's not sure what word best suits him.

The doctor thought he would die. After the transfusion—if that's the right word for it—he remained still for two days. His breathing so shallow his chest barely moved. His pulse so weak she gave up trying to read it, sensing only one impossible heartbeat a minute. The doctor stayed away, but Gawea sat by him.

She could talk now—the doctor suspects she has been able to talk for some time—but rarely speaks, as if rationing her words.

If the doctor asks how he is doing, she says, "The same," and if she asks if Gawea has brought a damp rag to his lips, she says, "Yes." Gradually his color flushed. And his eyes began to shudder beneath their lids. And he began to speak in his sleep, uttering words that were clearly enunciated but in no recognizable language.

Gawea is gone, foraging in the woods, when the doctor approaches him tonight with a rag and a bowl of water. She strips him, bathes his thin, wasted body by roughing the rag across his skin. The campfire crackles nearby. The stars are like a fistful of salt flung across a black blanket. His ribs are too visible, pressing painfully against his skin. His black hair, once so short, is now a messy corona. He smells strangely metallic. "What's going on inside of you?" she asks, not expecting an answer, but when she dips the rag in the bowl and wrings it out and brings it to his face, his eyes spring open.

Before she can cry out, he has seized her by the wrist and shot straight up. "Where is my tin?" he says.

She tries to pull away from him. "Clark threw it in the river."

He blinks a few times, swallows hard. "She *what*?"

"She was right to do it." She explains that there is no better time than now to wean himself, when his body is restive, healing. "She gave up the hooch. Now it's your turn to be strong enough to do the same."

"That bitch." At this point the others have gathered around them. "You bitch!" he screams at Clark.

He blinks hard, as if he remains unsure of his whereabouts. The doctor knows his mind and body must feel gripped by an arthritic fist. He releases her then. His face tightens and he brings a hand to his chest.

"What's wrong?" the doctor says, and he says his heart. It feels like one big wound, like nails have been pumped through his veins and clustered there. He lets his head fall back and struggles to breathe and struggles to keep his eyes open.

He obviously wants to say something more—to curse them, wish

206

them dead—but can't find the breath. Sleep pulls him away like a current. His mouth is moving, but they don't hear what he says, the words seeming filtered through water so that he might as well be sinking past the reaches of moonlight to the stony bottom of the nearby river.

CHAPTER 24

SOMETIMES, WHEN no one else is looking, Reed takes out the box. The one Danica gave him. The wood is black and slick, as long as his hand and as wide as his wrist, and heavy, the weight of a book with many words inside it. He runs a finger along its edges, smears a thumb across its lid.

He imagines tossing it in the fire. He imagines digging a deep hole and burying it and rolling a boulder over the top of the disturbed earth so that no one would ever find it. But he also dreams darkly about turning the knob, flipping the latch, leaning forward to see what springs out.

It would be so much easier to give up, to stop plodding forward, to put an end to the heat and the hunger and the thirst and the fear and the suffering. The others see so much promise in the river, but he knows that the lushness does not extend beyond the green vein of it, the desert still reaching on all sides of them like a sea of yellow ash and the sun so blinding it seems to take up the entire sky. There must have been a time when he believed. Why else would he have come if he had not dreamed of a better life? But that time has passed.

The other day, when kicking their way through a house and salvaging what they could from it, he came upon a body in a brass bed, the mattress rotted down to springs, the corpse shrunken down to mummified skin with the hair still clinging to it. He stared for a long time and thought how nice it must be to be dead, how comfortable to lie down and let darkness take you. You would never have to worry about anything again. The others must feel the same way. Even if they don't say it. The weight of this dead world pressing down on them. Even if they're not, like him, fondling their revolver and considering how a bullet might taste when swallowed, there are so many others ways to surrender.

Lewis sleeps most of the day, but when he is awake, for an hour, sometimes two, he writes in his journal or takes short, wobbling walks along the river using a long white branch as a staff to keep his balance. On occasion he sits around the campfire with a blanket thrown over his shoulders, though no one but Gawea and Clark seem comfortable speaking to him. Reed has always been wary of him but now feels repulsed. Can Lewis even be categorized as human, or is he more a mutation, like some giant white bat or hairless sand wolf, a product of this world and not the last? *Other.*

Soon, when Lewis is strong enough, they will pack their things and press forward. Because Clark demands it. She demands they think of their country and not merely themselves. She demands they consider the implications of what they're doing, their small rebellion against the Sanctuary a gateway to something much larger: national redefinition. Ever since they dragged her from the basement, ever since Lewis brought his wrist to hers, she woke with a renewed life and vigor, and when she speaks of their mission, when she speaks of this new America, she manages to somehow make it feel real, not some ridiculous abstraction.

They listen to her. They believe in her. *She* brought them all this far. Not Reed. He is a totem leader, and not even that, not any longer. She gives them the hope that allows them to be led. Hope is a good and dangerous thing, Reed thinks. Hope is the moment that never comes and life is the shit you wallow through when chasing it.

They have not slept together in weeks. More and more often he has trouble keeping his patience around her. He tries to sit by himself—he tries to lie by himself—but she always finds him. When she asks a question, sometimes he does not respond at all, and when he does, his answers are often clipped, sullen. She wants to know why he is so angry and he tells her he is tired; that's all. He's so tired. Which is and is not the truth.

He has fantasized about her death. A snake will bite her. Her horse will throw her. She will eat a poisonous mushroom. When the bats stole her, he couldn't help but feel a kind of relief. Now we can rest. Now we can stop this race to nowhere. That's what he thought.

Every morning, when Lewis wakes, his hand goes immediately to his pocket, searching for the tin that isn't there. Reed has seen him suffer through his days and nights. He knows about the sweats and cramps and headaches and bad-tempered hallucinations. He understands because he feels much the same without her, Danica.

He misses her like a drug. His nose in her hair. His tongue along her collarbone. Her nipples tightening into points when traced by his fingertip. He hates himself for his weakness but cannot deny it. His need for her. She once, when they were still naked and breathing hard and pressed together damply, said the word *love* into his neck. When he asked her to repeat herself, she said, "It was nothing," and he said, "No, you said something," but she would only dart her tongue from her mouth and trace the shape of his ear.

Whether she actually feels love for him, he doesn't know. But he must for her. What else would have drawn him back to her, again and again, despite the danger? What else could make him feel so bruised inside now that she is out of reach? He hears her breathing in the river. He tastes her in the salt of a pebble he clacks between his teeth. And, for so long, he has imagined her face over Clark's. Sometimes the only thing that keeps him going is the thought of them together in a lush, green space with rain falling softly.

Earlier today, they speared seven trout from the river, and now they crisp and brown over the fire. They offer Lewis some, but he waves it away. His skin appears as pale and brittle as an eggshell. Clark asks how he is feeling and he says his joints burn as if padded by coals and every blink feels like a snuffed candle. She asks when he might be ready to pack up and move on, and he says another day or two. Then he coughs into his fist and says that before they go any farther, this one time and one time only, he plans to send his owl to the skies and deliver a message to the Sanctuary.

Clark asks him why in God's name he would do that.

He hoods the blanket over his head and tightens his grip on it, making a kind of bonnet. His face is lost to shadow except for the sharp white nose peeking out. "To give people hope, of course." He has an acidic way of speaking that shrinks his audience into something so small and insignificant he might flick them away. He explains that the mayor has no doubt claimed they are dead, and who knows what dismissive lies he invented to excuse them away. If they are indeed journeying this far for more than themselves—if they plan to return someday and bring down the wall—then they need to give people a reason to hold out.

York tongues a fish bone from his mouth, pulls it from his lips, and flicks it into the fire. "Going back. Damn. With all the miles we've traveled, with all the miles still waiting ahead of us, *that* is the last thing I want to think about."

Lewis ignores him. He will send the letter to Ella and she will find a way to spread the news to others.

Clark says, "If anyone sees that owl, she'll be dead."

"I'm sure that's a risk she'll be willing to take."

Reed says, "If you're sending a letter, I want to as well." He feels Clark's eyes on him. "I have a— I have some people I'd like to let know I'm all right."

"You said it yourselves. A letter risks lives. The more letters, the more lives. One will speak for us all." Lewis rises and excuses himself. He is tired. He must rest. He toddles to his bed now, twenty yards away from their campsite, a willing exile. He uses his staff to keep his balance and to stir the fire he keeps for himself. He adds two logs to it. With a rusty stiffness he lowers his body to the ground. He wobbles there a moment, fighting sleep, but instead of crushing his head into a pillow, he reaches a hand into his satchel and extracts a piece of paper followed by his quill and inkpot.

Reed follows and watches from a short distance as Lewis begins to write—no doubt composing the very letter he mentioned, wishing to send it off before they can question him further. His pen slashes the paper with a speed unavailable to his legs. This is how he will always be swiftest, on the empty page, not the open plain, in his mind and not his body.

But before he finishes the letter, his chin drops to his chest, his posture curls. Sleep overtakes him. A minute passes. Then he startles awake and folds the letter in half, and then in half again, and again, until it is a tiny white square.

The owl perches on a nearby stump. He crawls over and kneels beside it. The action seems to exhaust him. He slumps against the stump, resting his forehead against it like a man praying at an altar. He wakes when he loses his balance, when his body begins to slide. He reaches for the owl and toys with a lever. Its breast swings open to reveal a small cavity into which he fits the letter. By this time all his energy is spent. He curls his body at the base of the stump and succumbs to sleep.

Reed sneaks a sheet of paper and uses the still-wet quill to compose a message. He pauses twice when Lewis stirs or hitches his breathing. His words splotch and the paper tears in his hurry. Then he folds the letter into a small square and seals it with pitch from a split log and tucks it into the owl's breast for Lewis to send skyward when he wakes.

CHAPTER 25

THE THIN MAN told Gawea he would personally escort her from Utah to Oregon, where Aran Burr awaited her. It was a long road and he would protect her, so long as she obeyed him. He kept her wrists bound and her mind drugged with an opiate, so that she wouldn't escape or attack him. She was so numb she didn't feel his hands on her during the night, and during the day she saw the landscape they traversed in a hallucinogenic blur. They rode through forests that had burned down to blackened lances and others electric with the yellow-and-red music of fall. They rode across glinting fields of obsidian that looked as though the night froze and fell and shattered. They rode through striped canyons with whitewater foaming through their bottoms. They climbed cinder cones and buttes and stared out at the way they had come and the way they might go.

Sometimes animals followed her. A jeweled cloud of bees. A parade of humpbacked foam-mouthed bears trundling in a long line. Marmots poking their heads from their warrens to whistle their greeting. Vultures and eagles and crows drafting air currents, spinning in the sky, surrounding her with rippling shadows. A cluster of antlered deer encasing her like a basket that bore her north and west.

She was followed, too, by dreams she could not shake. In them a man visited her, the man named Aran Burr. She could never see his face—but she could see enough of him to know he was old and bent, his bald head ringed by long white hair that tumbled down his back. He spoke in a whispery, papery voice. He told her she was special. He was special too. They could be special together. If only she would come to him, if only she would listen. Come, he said. Come to me.

She wondered if he was a ghost, like the ones Oma used to tell stories about who would drown you in a lake or lead you deep into the woods until you were lost. Burr made her startle at shadows. He made her nerves feel like twigs snapping. At first she clapped her hands to scare his voice away. Dug in her ear, shook her head as if to scrape out a mosquito. Then she began to listen. He wanted to protect her. He wanted to teach her how special she was.

Then, in the Cascades, the thin man's horse lost its footing. They were crossing a slope of scree at the time. The horse tumbled down the hill and took him with it. The ensuing rockslide mangled him. So did the horse, its body rolling over him, bending his body the wrong way. Gawea waited a long time. Long enough for her head to clear. Then she climbed down the hillside and retrieved the keys to her handcuffs and collected the provisions from his saddlebags and whispered good-bye to the lame horse before braining it with a rock.

At this point, she felt she had no place in the world, so she kept moving, following the voice, the voice of Aran Burr, her only beacon.

She could always sense people long before she encountered them. Trails and roads cut the ground. Stumps sprinkled with saw-dust appeared. They made a mechanical storm of noise with their hammers and saws. They stunk the air with their paint and oil and cooking. Some lived in small clusters—giving her some sense of what life must have been like before her father was killed and her mother taken—walled villages with pigs rooting in pens and smoke rising from chimneys. Sometimes, at night, to antidote her loneliness, she would walk unseen among them. She opened and closed their drawers. She stood over their beds and smelled their stale breath and listened to them make love or murmur their way through dreams. She pretended herself, just for a moment, part of a family.

More than anything, that was what she wanted, family. Burr seemed to offer her that. She feared him. She still fears him. But in him she found a mirror, someone who resembled her. Though his hair was a silvery white, though his bones were warped and his skin spotted, they were the same. When they first met, he took her hands in his and said, "You're like me."

With these words he repaired her loneliness. He made her feel like she belonged somewhere. She remembers the first time they sat together, in leather chairs in a library full of light, and when she squinted at him, unable to see him clearly for the blazing sun, he asked if the light bothered her. "A little," she said, and he held up his hand and the shutters slammed shut and in the darkness that followed he laughed until he coughed and then said, "Now you try."

People loved to use *different* as an insult. A spicy dish was *different*. A challenging book or painting was *different*. Someone who dressed unusually was *different*. She was *different*. Burr told her this prejudice came from fear. The fear of change. She was evidence of change. People found comfort in the boring and ordinary. And she was extraordinary. This was a new country and they were a new people. The *next* people. He would teach her how to use her gift. Just as he would teach Lewis. They would help each other. And they would help the world. They were healers, builders, innovators, and it was up to them to fit together the pieces of a broken country.

She often fingered the scar on her shoulder, the place where they'd branded her, and when one day she said, "I wish I could carve it off," Burr said that wouldn't do. That wouldn't do at all.

"It's your constant reminder," he said, "that you serve me." He was good to her so long as she was good to him. So long as she did what he said. Traveling all this distance, seeking out Lewis, risking her life and his—that was doing what he said—and so long as she was successful, he would reward her. She was in it for the reward, for what he promised her.

That is why she tries to keep quiet, keep her distance, keep from growing too familiar with anyone. Farmers don't coddle or even name the cattle they plan to slaughter; they treat them as they do the corn in the fields, as the product of a job. These people—that's how she likes to think of them, not as York or Clark or Reed or the doctor, but as people, a generalized mass—these people mean nothing to her. They could drown in a river or puke up a bad mushroom or fall on a knife and she wouldn't care. She wouldn't. She won't. You get close to someone, if they get hurt, you get hurt. They are expendable. Every one of them but Lewis. That is what Burr told her and that is what she keeps telling herself.

But she can feel doubt tugging at her. She can feel anxiety tunneling through her like little worms. There was a time when she thought by Burr's side was the only place she could feel some sense of belonging—until now. It's the boy's fault. The boy, York, desires her. Ever since he caught her beneath the gallows, ever since she took his hand and raced across the stadium with the vultures crisscrossing the sky above them, he has been following her.

She knows this and secretly revels in it. The other day, when they sat around the fire, he seasoned a trout fillet with some dill she harvested. He ate it and spoke to her with his mouth open, talking nonsense, telling jokes, wondering what life awaited him in Oregon. He had always dreamed of opening a theater— What did she think of that? Did she think that was a good idea? And hey, what was up with the mark on her shoulder? The one she was rubbing now. The one she was always rubbing.

"It's nothing," she said and dropped her hand.

"It's a tattoo, right? You've seen mine? The jester's mask on my back? What does yours mean?"

Rather than answer, she leaned in and stole a fillet from his plate and took a bite of it. "I'm hungry," she said around a mouthful.

He smiled and watched her eat.

She doesn't *want* to feel this way, her mind fizzy with attraction.

She tries to remind herself to feel jealous. In some fashion betrayed. That's how she felt traveling all this way to retrieve the man who would share Burr's attention. She has tried not to get close. She has tried. She kept her mouth shut as long as she could, kept her distance even when riding alongside someone. But her loneliness—an emptiness that aches like a pulled tooth—is a lifelong disability. And when the bat nearly took York, she felt like it was taking him from her.

They hoist their saddlebags. They sling rifles over their shoulders. Pans clank from their packs and ammunition chimes in their pockets. Gawea eyes up the campsite one last time, a place that felt briefly like home to all of them, before hiking away, following the river, feeling a barb of guilt as she once more leads them closer and closer to a destination they may regret. Lewis, she knows, will be protected by Burr. But what will become of the others?

———

Many things have changed since Lewis brought Clark back from the brink. Including the connection between the two of them. Their eyes often meet, and when they do, he feels a rippling in the air between them, like some electrical charge. When she departs the camp to hunt, he worries for her in a way he never did before, his chest constricting. It is almost as if, with so much of him inside her, she has become an extension of him, a third arm, a second head, her heart beating in time with his, so that they seem allied on a cellular level. "What's happening to you?" she asks him one night, and he says, "I'm trying to understand the same."

By the end of each day Lewis's body feels languid but buzzy. He thinks often of his tin, aches for it, but no longer needs a dose of powder to quicken a connection, speed his tongue and hand. His mind, once walled in, is now free to chase paths never considered.

He packed the journal—mottled calfskin cover, yellowed onion-skin pages—to document. He has spent so much of his life clapped away in the museum, reading other people's words, studying and pinning and labeling the world as if it were a still life. By agreeing to leave, he agreed to activity. He left behind stillness for movement, engagement. If this is a new world, then who better to serve as its chronicler than he, the custodian of the old?

In the beginning, every entry seemed some variation of this: *Woke before dawn, rode hard through the day, made it to X lo-*

cation, small argument broke out over lost provisions, no water, everything dead. At first he felt a failure and the world a failure too, everything a skeleton of what once was.

Then things changed. Now that there is water, now that he has risen from near death, now that he has sweated and shivered off his need for the tin, his mind hastens, faster and faster every day, a progression, like an avalanche of sand. He feels he is expanding, along with the world, both of them surprisingly, gloriously alive. Their purpose in exploring the country grows more and more wrapped up in his self-discovery, as if he were America, the next America, their geographies twinned. He scribbles down thoughts like these, along with a short record of their days and entries about whatever plants, animals, and insects he can observe.

"What are you writing?" York says.

"Nothing."

He leans closer. "The corpse of discovery? What's that?"

"The *corps* of discovery, you idiot. That's us." Lewis hunches protectively over the book until York shrugs and leaves him.

He writes, too, about what is happening to him, about how Gawea is helping him.

For most of his life he has been able to contain or ignore *it*. What his father called vile and freakish, what the rest of them call magic. He refuses the word. Magic, to him, is illusion and fancifulness. Magic is the unexplained. He knows himself as a man of precise habits and logical thinking—and he knows the world as a realm to be sampled and studied and categorized. What is happening to him must be explainable. He asks Gawea to help him, please.

She wouldn't before. At first she allowed him only brief and cryptic responses sketched in the sand. Now she talks, at first with reluctance and then more and more willingly, the words tumbling from her, as if learning to talk is learning to trust. In part this is thanks to York, who walks on his hands and springs a flower from her ear and makes her smile, even laugh. And in part this is thanks to Lewis, who opened up his wrist and risked death and in doing so gained Gawea's trust and proved himself worthy of the journey. Every day, she strikes him as more human, whereas before she came across as a wooden carving that only resembled a young woman. He wonders if she sees a similar change in him.

This is what she tells him. If they have left behind a world where a plastic tablet could store a thousand novels, where high-speed elevators could shoot someone seventy stories high in a matter of seconds, where warheads could lay waste to whole cities, then that means there is room in the world for other kinds of technology, more elemental.

One morning, by the fire, Gawea tells him to watch. She reaches out and draws back her hand and opens her fingers to show a ball of light spinning in her palm. She asks him to do the same. When he leans in, when he snatches at the flames, when he feels the heat still in his hand, he can't help but gasp and swat his palm, the fire falling to the ground. The grass catches and he stamps out the blaze and looks around to make sure no one has seen. She tells him to try it once more. He sits there long enough to take ten deep breaths before grabbing again at the fire. Another ball sizzles to life in his hand, and this time he holds it for many minutes, until it blinks out with a twist of smoke. "Good," she tells him.

His dreams are as vivid as life. In one, Aran Burr holds out his hand. Its palm cups a stone. He drops it. It *thunks* to the ground. Then he looks at Lewis and winks, and the stone returns to his hand, as if drawn there by an invisible string. He drops the stone, and it falls. It falls because of gravity, a force. A force most people associate with the earth, but it is more than that, a force that every object has for every other object. A tree has gravity. A chair has gravity. He has gravity.

He asks Gawea what it means and she tells him what Burr told her. If two people stand on opposite ends of a field, they both emit a small charge of gravity that will draw them toward one another. Something that is supposedly too small to be felt. But we have all known people who turn every head, who catch every eye. People are pulled to them. They emit some force. Yet they are not bigger than anyone else, at least on the outside.

If a rock falls, it falls down, not up. Because a force, the force of gravity, draws it down. It is this same force that keeps an arrow from sizzling through the air for a thousand miles, keeps a horse's hooves on the ground instead of pounding the animal upward in the air. To make a rock fall up instead of down requires another force, a force stronger than gravity.

He thinks of the rockets they used to blast into space. An engine could do it. An engine made by man, metal and plastic, conceived by the mind, constructed by hand. Gawea tells him, "There are forces—there is energy—all around. Not only in gravity, but in air and earth and water and fire." Energy that makes things slow and speed up, cool and burn, grow and shrink, and she is helping him discover this, like a child who finds his shadow and begins to cast his hands into doves, dragons.

Today a shadow ripples across his journal. He looks up to see a flash in the sky, the sun reflecting off metal, the owl. It spirals toward them. The sound of its fast descent is as bright as a boiling kettle.

Lewis holds out an arm and it lands there and he sets it on the log beside the fire. The gears wind to a stop inside it. When he reaches for its breast, he pulls his hand back with a hiss, the metal hot from its flight. He tries again, hurriedly flipping open the compartment door. Sand spills from it. He fishes out the note folded inside. He ignores the others when they request he tell them what it says, until he has read it through twice.

His tongue wets his lips. "It says, 'Dear Lewis, You can imagine my surprise and disappointment when I found you gone. Did I curse your name and wish upon you unimaginable pain? Yes. But I also hoped that you might live to write this note, just as I continue to hope you might live to write another, the next time to tell the rest of us to follow. As you might imagine, things have been unwell since your departure, worse even than before. Hurry. Be safe. And please do not forget about us. I will do as you asked and share the news of your success, but your note ended abruptly and it remains unclear to us what you want us to find in the Dome. Ella.'"

"Us?" Lewis says. "Who's *us*?"

Reed snatches the owl. Its wings flap and its claws rake the air. There is a noise inside it like an alarm clock dropped down the stairs. He peers into its hollow breast. "Is that all?"

"What else would there be? Why would there be anything for you?" Lewis holds out a hand until Reed returns the owl to him. Then he starts for the forest. He does not look over his shoulder when he directs someone to bring a blanket. He knows they will.

They follow him between the trees, into the shade, several degrees short of evening, but gray enough. Lewis indicates a low-hanging branch and Clark throws the blanket over it. They huddle close. Lewis holds up the owl. There is a metallic snap, a motorized buzz. Its eyes glow.

On the blanket, a burst of static solidifies into the image of a hillside strewn with red rock. A dead bush trembles in the wind. For a long minute this is all they see and Reed says, "What's the point of this?" and Lewis holds up a finger to hush him.

At that moment there comes a noise from the other side of the hill, a clopping and clanking, like some piece of machinery grinding into motion. No one moves or says a word, not even to say, *What is that?*, though they all wonder.

A shape trundles into view, slowly cresting the hill—a man, Colter. He rides an armored black horse and wears a wide-rimmed black hat that casts a shadow over his face, but Lewis knows him. He knows him immediately. One hand rests on the saddle horn and the other on the machete strapped to his thigh, the blade catching the sun like a crackling spurt of yellow-orange flame. Two sand wolves appear on either side of him, panting and pricking their ears and testing the air with their noses.

"The man who killed my father," Lewis says, "has come to kill me."

CHAPTER 26

LEWIS MUST WANT her dead. That's what Ella keeps saying to Simon. He must want to see her dragged out of the Sanctuary and shackled to the altar and torn to shreds. Or whipped. Or maybe bludgeoned or speared through the middle. Chopped up into tiny pieces and fed to rats. He couldn't possibly want her to live, not with the charge he has given her in this letter.

Ella—

I need you to do something for me. Spread the news of our expedition's success so far. I am writing this letter from northern Kansas, along the banks of the Missouri River, near South Dakota. It is not a riverbed, but a river, a genuine river, surrounded by thick green foliage. We have not yet encountered any human outpost, but I trust now more than ever that we shall. Where there's life, there's hope. We follow Gawea to a better place and a new country. You must find a way to communicate this to the Sanctuary. I understand that this will be difficult, and I won't presume to know the best way you might go about it, but I'm certain you will do your best.

Additionally, you must expose what is hidden in the Dome. You will—

There the letter ends.

"You will," Simon says. "You will *what*?"

She stands by the open window and reads by the dying red sunset. She crumples the letter into a ball—then hurriedly flattens it again. She should feel thrilled, she knows. He is alive. There is water. There is life. There is, as he says, hope after all. But how on earth she will share this news with others—without arousing suspicion that she is the source—she has no idea. And his impersonal tone, his arrogant presumption, his reckless directive—it's enough to make her want to write *fuck you* on a piece of paper and shove it in the owl and hurl it out the window. He is asking her to risk her life. Is a *thank-you* or a *please* or an *I hope you are well* so much to ask?

"I hate him," she says. "I hate hate hate *hate* him."

Simon wears a fresh plaster cast that cuts off at the elbow. He has drawn on it a picture of a broken bone. The skin beneath itches as if socked by fire ants and he keeps an old wire coat hanger handy to creep inside the cast and scratch those hard-to-reach places. "What about the other one?"

On the bed lies the other letter, the one sealed and addressed to Danica Lancer. They crouch on either side of it, their faces propped in their hands, their cheeks bunched and their mouths fishy from the pressure. "Are we supposed to open it, you think?" he says.

"Is that your name?"

"You think that's going to stop me? I'm a thief, remember?"

Ella tightens her lips into a pink button. "Go on, then."

He fingers open the seal and he unfolds its many creases and reads, in a rush, the words scribbled there. "'My darling Danica!'" His voice comes out as a flamboyant yell, as if he were a street performer. "'With every mile I travel, my pulse seems to weaken, as if I am farther from its source, my heart.'"

She rips the letter from his hand. "Let me see that."

"It's just a stupid love letter."

She reads silently at first, then aloud. "'I didn't realize how much you mattered until I left you. And now I feel sick. I'm fucking sick. I'm fucking sick sick sick. I want to eat rocks and puke blood and stab myself with sticks. I want to open that box you gave me and lick its center and let death come because that would be easier than this. We're all going to die anyway. The world is eating us one by one. So we might as well die now.'"

Simon says, "Wow, I thought it started off bad."

She goes quiet another few seconds before saying, "I can't read anything in the last few lines—his handwriting is a mess—except the words *death* and *love*."

A sound comes from the hallway. What could be a cough or a broom sweep or a boot scuffed across stone. Before Ella can process what has happened, before she can say, *Hide* or *Someone's coming*—Simon has already snatched the letter from her hand, the owl from the bedside table, and darted out the open window, cat quick.

She turns to face the sound just as Slade darkens the doorway.

He leans against the doorframe. The last bit of sun flares from the window, reddening his face, which the very next instant goes to shadow. He is smiling. His teeth are too small for his mouth. "Who were you talking to?"

"You can't just come in here."

"Can't I?" His eyebrows are only a suggestion, two fleshy creases above his eyes, but they raise now. "Who were you talking to?"

"No one." She tries to say this casually but she is not a practiced liar.

"Really? I thought I heard voices."

"Sometimes I like to recite Shakespeare. To pass the time."

His voice takes on an affected timbre when he says, "'And oftentimes, to win us to our harm, the instruments of darkness tell us truths, win us with honest trifles, to betray us in deepest consequence.'" He takes one sliding step into the room. "That was Shakespeare."

"'There's daggers in men's smiles.' That's Shakespeare too."

"Clever girl." He has kept one of his hands behind his back all this time. He lets it show now, a jug of water dangling from a finger crooked like a tusk. He gives it a sloshing shake. "I brought you something."

"Why?"

"I thought you might want it. I thought you might be thirsty. The rations can be difficult for all of us." He takes another step toward her and extends the jug. "Here. Take it."

She considers denying him but knows that will only lead to more trouble. Slowly she raises her arms to accept the jug. What he carries with one finger weighs down both her arms. The jug sweats. She sets it on the floor between her legs and feels the cold coming off it, licking her skin. "Will you go now?"

"What's the hurry? And should I be offended that you haven't thanked me? That you're not asking me to sit down? That you're not bringing two glasses to fill so that I might have a taste?" He circles her twice, his footsteps heavy enough to send a trembling through her body, and then approaches the open window. He rests his hands on the sill and the wood complains. He looks out on the turbines spinning all across the city, their blades cutting the air like weapons wound and spun.

She does not know where Simon hides, maybe on the ledge just beyond the window, so she calls to Slade in a panic, "You're right. Thank you. Thank you very much. You're very kind."

He turns. His body eclipses the window entirely, casting a shadow across the room. "That's more like it."

The jug dampens the floor, wets her ankle, sends a chill up her leg. When Slade approaches her, she does not move, willing her body to remain still. Even when he leans in, as if to plant a kiss on her cheek. His mouth pauses next to her ear. She can smell him: wool, onions. For a moment there is only his breathing. Then it pauses—and he takes a small bite of her. She feels her cheek slurp into his mouth, feels the teeth chew down, feels the flesh clip away. Still she does not move or cry out. She pinches shut her eyes and clenches her fists and waits and waits and waits until his footsteps retreat from her, into the hallway, down the stairs.

She does not dare to open her eyes, not until Simon climbs through the window and touches her cheek, where the flesh is bitten and the blood dries in a tacky trail, and says, "I'll kill him before he touches you again."

CHAPTER 27

For a long time they stand in a silent, wavering circle. No one needs to ask the question. They know their options. They can fight or they can run. They look first to each other—well rested, but bony and slumped, their bodies like a bunch of broken dolls—and then their stares settle on Reed. He keeps his face downcast, studying the ground, kicking a hole in it, as if the answer might be buried beneath him. "What are you all looking at me for?" he finally says and then, "This is on you, Clark."

She does not hesitate. "We run."

They have guns and they outnumber Colter, but they have been trained to fear him. With night as his ally and with wolves as his weapons, some of them will probably die. Lewis guesses him a few days away. They plan to continue forward and keep track of his progress with the owl and hope to lose him or find a more defensible position.

As they press on, the water steadily deepens, the river widens. They can wade past their knees. Houses dot the woods, choked with vines and set back on hillsides, sometimes with the gray, crooked remains of stairways leading to the water, where docks remain like bridges to nowhere. They pass many boats, overturned, spun around, mired in the mud. Birds nest in them. Fish rest in their shade.

Periodically, Lewis sends the owl skyward. Less and less time passes before it returns to them, ten hours, nine hours, eight. A horse cannot gallop as fast as the owl can fly, so Lewis can only guess his distance by studying landmarks in the footage, four days away, then two days away.

Reed wants to drop his gear and sit down and flop his hands apologetically and say, "This is the end." The end of their journey, the end of their dream, the end of their lives. The end of the Sanctuary. And the human world, in whatever clusters it still exists, might not be far behind. He is gnashing his teeth and blinking back tears, ready to say, "Enough!" when they find the canoes.

This is outside Sioux City, at a marina, where skiffs and johnboats and bass boats and Jet Skis lie half-buried, where dock posts rise from cracked clay and the slats they once carried accordion all around them. Their wood is gray, beetle bitten, pocked by woodpeckers.

The shed door hangs at an angle, one hinge stubbornly holding on. When they open it, pigeons the color of storm clouds burst from inside. They wander in to the sun-slatted shadows and find six Alumacrafts, seventeen-foot canoes stacked on a metal frame. They are splattered with bird shit, full of feathers and nests, but when dragged to the water, they float. Even when heaped full of supplies, even when bearing the weight of their exhausted bodies, the canoes float and they begin to furiously paddle their way up the river.

In this way, they travel north and west. Every now and then, the canoes will come to a scraping stop and they will climb out and portage to deeper water. And every now and then, they will look over their shoulders as if they expect to see Colter splashing toward them. They battle the current, but the current isn't strong. The finish flakes off their paddles, and cracks run through them, but they do their job, cutting through the water, drawing them forward.

Lewis's shoulders and elbows ache, but he would happily paddle a thousand years before he took another step. He prefers the canoes even to horses. Their speed might be slower, but their passage is so smooth, unlike the rocking jolt of his saddle that every day threatened to knock his bones from their sockets. Sometimes he cannot help but marvel at the novelty of it all. He is traveling by canoe. There is enough water in the world, more than he ever dreamed he would see, to accommodate a canoe. Water dribbles from his paddle. Water runs between his fingers when he dips a hand into the river and cups it to his mouth. Water dimples and splashes when a frog leaps off a rock or when a trout jumps in a rainbowed flash to seize a dragonfly. If he narrows his eyes until the world fuzzes over, he can almost forget what they have left, where they are going, but then, in the river, he will see Aran Burr. Swimming alongside the canoe. Wearing a flowing white robe and a necklace of black stones. He calls Lewis's name, drawing out the *s* in the swishing pull of his paddle.

Once a day, he sends off the owl, and as its flights grow shorter and shorter, so does time seem to stretch longer. An hour could be a day, a day a year. So different, he thinks, from his time at the Sanctuary, when time slipped like sand between his fingers, one day blurring into the next. There, nothing was new, nothing at stake. Every day, he saw the same people wandering the same streets under the same sun. But out here, in the Dead Lands, everything is new, everything a threat, forcing him to notice—every sun-sparkled wave on the river, every shadow sleeving the shore—and the more you notice, the fuller time becomes, and the fuller time becomes, the more it drags. Even the light seems to fall more slowly between the branches.

When the owl returns to him, only thirty minutes after it departs, he yells out to Clark, telling her Colter is close. The time has come. They must find a place to make a stand.

Clouds boil ahead, grumbling with distant thunder and darkening a third of the sky. Rain trails from them like skirts of gray muslin. Lightning jags. The air shudders when thunder calls.

They paddle toward it in silence, and the gray-black clouds violently expand, as if rooted in a volcano, an eruption carrying ash and fire. This is not a sky for big, hopeful dreams like theirs. This is a sky for nightmares.

A hundred yards ahead, between two rushing threads of water, rises an island. They will go there, Clark says. And as long as they need to wait for Colter, an hour or a day or more, the surrounding river will stand guard, serving as their moat.

The rain begins before they arrive, as hot as the sun's tears. Instantly they are soaked. For a moment they can't help but laugh at the novelty of it. Rain. Not a passing shower, but a deluge, the air so packed with water they might well have upended, sunk into the river. They pause their paddling and hold up their hands and open their mouths until their laughing feels like drowning. They can barely keep their eyes open against the lashing rain, can barely see the island they paddle toward, and by the time they arrive, the canoes have filled with enough rain to slosh around their ankles.

CHAPTER 28

THE ISLAND IS thickly wooded and a half mile long, shaped like an arrowhead, the current sharpening its tip, carrying silt downstream to deposit at its bottom. In some places it is edged by steep clay banks with roots spilling from them. In others, by stony beaches littered with logs.

The storm has paused but not passed. They are temporarily caught in some rift. Rain no longer drums the overturned canoes. The wind, once so powerful that it snapped several trees in half, has hushed. But the sky looks like spilled ink and thunder mutters all around them. Lightning blinks so often they feel caught in some seizure.

They stagger their positions along the western bank of the island, hiding behind trees, their rifles bristling like branches. They don't know where Colter will appear, or if he will appear at all. York says maybe he won't, maybe he'll keep searching the shore for some sign of them, trudging past them in the dark. Why search this island of all places?

Lewis cuts him short with a *no*, and when they look to him for an answer, he says a dog's nose, a wolf's nose, is a hundred thousand times more powerful than man's. "I realize it's hard to imagine, because we can only perceive so much of the world, but try to envision a bright yellow fog streaming from this place. That's how obvious we are to them."

The veil of night overtakes the sky. Fireflies emerge, thousands of them. The air is so dark, palpably so, that they can see the shape of the shore by the insects' winking constellation.

Above Clark, the clouds are high, churning in a black circle, while up the river the clouds seem so low their bellies graze the treetops. Lightning flashes and seems to crack the sky, while to either side of them, the shorelines wink and swirl with the yellow light of fireflies.

One hour becomes two becomes three. They do their best to keep their eyes sharp, but time dulls their focus. If anybody sees anything, they are supposed to whistle—two short high bursts followed by a long low note—but with the night birds beginning to call, everything sounds like a beckoning.

Clark is curled behind a stump with her rifle resting on top. Every few minutes one of her legs goes numb, and she shifts her body until the leg prickles back to life, and by then the other is cramping. She studies the shore, the lightning bugs sparkling there, the tufts of grass and thin-angled maze of branches beneath the green awning of leaves.

Clark can hear the rain coming again, the hiss of it not far off.

She looks to her right and thinks she can make out the silhouette of her brother leaning against a tree—and she looks to her left and sees a spark of red, the lit bowl of the doctor's pipe, pulsing as she takes long drags off it. A soft breeze blows and the trees sway and the leaves shake and her eyes sweep up and down the shore until they settle on something.

It appears like a man, a naked man with a long, pointed face, clambering along on all fours. Another appears beside it, both of them trotting back and forth, dipping and raising their heads to test the air. Sand wolves. She might be able to hear them muttering, a soft, high-throated barking that reveals their excitement.

The rain begins again. Thousands of drops dimple the water, making mouths that seem to open hungrily for them. In that instant all the lightning bugs go dark.

Then comes Colter. Barely visible, on his horse, he moves from the forest to the grassy embankment.

Her veins constrict. Her pulse slams. She has seen the wolves before, on the few occasions she visited the zoo, a fly-filled, horseshoe-shaped collection of cages with games and candy carts at the center. Monkeys meticulously picked fleas from each other and ate them. A snake as wide as a man's thigh coiled in the shade of a rock pile. And the wolves prowled constantly across the heaps of concrete that decorated their cage, every now and then gnawing on a log or shredding a tire with their claws or crashing against the bars and snarling when someone drew too near.

Now lightning flashes and arrests a clear picture of them huddled beneath their master, freed from their cages to bite and slash as they please. She cannot see their eyes, but she feels them, like black stones that weigh upon her own.

Colter digs in his heels and the horse starts down the embankment, into the river, where the water splashes around its haunches as it lurches toward the island. The wolves follow to either side, bobbing in the frothing wake of the horse.

A whistle sounds to her left, then another to her right, then another and another, the whole shoreline sounding the alarm at once, and only then does she bring her lips together and blow, the whistle failing on her dry lips. She chambers a round into the rifle and snaps off the safety and does her best to draw a bead on the wolves and then Colter, not sure what to shoot first, the brain or the muscle it commands. The water is first knee-deep, then rises to the horse's breast; then only its head can be seen, with a white lapel of foam around it.

Their plan had been to gather together, to assemble and strike, but the alarm sounded too late and now it is unclear where Colter might come to shore, so they can only settle behind their stations and ready their weapons.

The rain stings like hurled pebbles. Lightning arrows and thunder mutters. It is followed by a volley of gunshots cracking all around her. At first they fire off hesitantly, then one bullet, one bullet, one bullet, becomes a swarm ripping the air. Colter does not stop. The water suds and pops around him with shots that miss their mark. She would have waited longer—waited until the bullet was sure to find an eye socket or open mouth—but the noise of gunfire is contagious. She pulls the trigger. There is a snap. And nothing more. A dead bullet. She ejects and chambers another. She pulls the trigger, and again, nothing. Colter is no more than twenty yards away and seems to be targeting her, the dark section of shore where no gunfire flashes.

Lightning flares again. She flinches at the thunder that follows. There is a moment of pause, when everyone reloads. It is then she notices her rifle is glowing. Blue light dances along its edges, outlining the shape of it, as if it were inhabited by some spirit. She drops it. The hair all over her body prickles and stands on end. She smells something like melting plastic. She looks to either side of her—ready to call out for help—when she sees Lewis stepping from his hiding place and approaching the river.

She can hear Colter now. He is yelling at them, saying something she can't quite make out, his words lost to thunder.

Lewis now appears almost phosphorescent, haloed in blue crackling light, as if costumed in lightning bugs. He moves as if in a dream. The sky flashes with a speed that matches the pulse inside her—and then coalesces into a stream of lightning. The clouds seem to split open and pour down blue jagged light that takes hold of Lewis. He shudders in his place as the electricity courses through him. Then he swings up his arms as if to hurl something heavy.

A white-hot beam blasts from his hands, dazzling its way across the river's surface. Millions of raindrops catch the light and seem to pause in their descent. The electricity channels into the wolves—and then Colter—and for a moment Clark believes she can see their bones glow beneath their skin.

She opens her mouth to scream, but her voice is stolen away by the eruption of thunder seeming to escape it.

PART III

While there's life there's hope.
                    —J.R.R. Tolkien, *The Hobbit*

CHAPTER 29

NORTH DAKOTA CONTAINS one of the richest oil fields in the world—estimated at one time as 503 billion barrels deep—and there are thousands and thousands of gas and oil wells there among the derricks and refineries and pipelines, the herds of snow-humped trailers and clusters of water trucks, the power transmission towers, the radio towers, the wind turbines, the natural gas pumping stations, the oil-loading train yards full of black tankers.

Once the wells were abandoned, the emergency generators kicked on, but after two weeks they ran out of diesel. High pressures matched against high temperatures resulted in explosions resulted in fires. There was no one to man the water sprayers, no one to cap the wellheads. The relief valves only fed the flames that could not be stopped, that will never stop. North Dakota will burn forever.

The air is thick with carbon, with dioxins and furans and lead and mercury and chromium. There is no night here, the horizon lit by flares, snapping pennants of colors red and white and blue. They flame against a black sky made blacker by the rank, sooty smoke.

This makes for a kind of nuclear winter, Lewis tells them.

The cold begins soon after they cross the state line. The wind skins the leaves from the trees. The river crusts over with ice and they abandon their canoes. The cattails shatter like stems of glass. Icicles hang from the trees, like the claws of dragons that might perch there. Snow falls. Sometimes thickly, sometimes in sputtery bursts. But the snow is not as they imagined, not the bright white frosting they have seen in cracked paintings and faded postcards. It is gray, ashen. It smears muddily against their skin. When they open their mouths and let the flakes fall on their tongues, the taste is as bitter as that of a chewed willow stick.

———•———

Colter lost his left arm at the elbow. The doctor sliced away the charred remains and treated the injury with yarrow leaves and snowberries mashed to a cream. From logs she kicked conk fungus, what look like the plates on a dinosaur's back, and ground them into a powder and stirred them into water and made him drink and fight the possibility of infection.

He smelled like seared meat, burned cinnamon. His hair crisped away in places. His clothes scorched. But he is alive. His horse and the wolves were not so lucky. The lightning soaked into them and funneled through their bones and seized their hearts with an electric fist. Colter does not remember much of that night, only strobe-like flashes, and not much of the days that followed either.

They thought he was here to punish them. To cut off their heads and make a garland of them to bring back to the Sanctuary. They were right. That's what the mayor asked him to do. But he does not serve Thomas Lancer. He serves the Meriwether family. He made a mistake when he broke the old man's arm. The worst mistake of his life, it turns out. And the old man, damn him and bless him, clapped him away in a cell—the same way a father paddles a bottom and sends his son to his room to consider his bad behavior. Colter has had a long time to think about this. If the surgery hadn't given the old man an infection, and if the infection hadn't caused a heart attack, and if the heart attack hadn't killed him, everything would be different, all would be forgiven. Colter has no doubt. He would have been released from his cell, humbled, forgiven, a prodigal son. That is how Colter thinks of himself, as a son, which makes Lewis his weakling brother—but a brother all the same.

For too long he has let hate and hurt take hold of his heart. If there were a word that captured dreams of bodies set aflame, glass smashed into open eyes, blades drawn slowly across genitals, then that would be the name of the demon that so often possessed him. He is here to seek atonement. He is here to serve the son of the one he served before. He shouldn't have come in the night and he shouldn't have come in the storm, but his eagerness for reunion was such that he could not stop himself once close.

"Hold your fire!" That was what he tried to yell to them that night. "I'm here for you." It was hard to say then and harder to say now that his wolves are dead and his arm ruined, but he says it all the same: "I'm here to help."

At first they don't believe him, and at night they tie his wrist to his thigh and his ankle to a tree. Every now and then Clark will wander over and stand beside him with a gun dangling from her hand. She watches him curiously, as he alternates between sweating and shivering. "I could put a bullet in your head and no one would complain."

"Don't."

"Because you want to join us?"

"Yes."

"You're a long way from earning our trust."

"And you're a long fucking way from mine."

"Language like that isn't going to help."

He doesn't hold back. That's not his way. Prison won't stop him, the desert won't stop him, lightning won't stop him, and neither will she, no matter if there's a gun in her hand. "You listen. You listen good. You might think you've got a dick, though you're a woman and one I'd like to lay, and you might think you're stronger than me, but that won't last and I'll be strong again, and you might think you can tell me what to do, but you can't, because I came here for Lewis and not for some red-haired, hatchet-faced bitch to tell me my business when my business is my own. I'm here to help and that's the short and the tall and slow and the fast of it."

She points her revolver at him, twists it one way, then the other, and makes a soft explosion with her lips. Then she drops her arm and says, "I guess we'll see about that, won't we?"

"Guess we will."

At first they carry him in a thick plastic utility sled, maybe two feet deep, once used to haul gear for ice fishing. They take turns dragging him, and Colter uses the front lip as a backrest, so that everybody else looks forward while he looks back.

The doctor bandages his stump. Twice a day, when she unwraps it and cleans it, the blackened flesh sputters and crackles and he cries out for her to help, to make it stop, in a voice he doesn't recognize as his own for its jerky neediness.

Afterward he raises his head to swallow from the canteen she brings to his lips. The water dribbles down his chin as the tears dribble from his eyes. "What the hell did Lewis do to me and how the hell is it possible? I don't understand, and don't tell me you do either."

"We don't."

"You don't know that and you don't know this. You don't know how far we have to travel and you don't know what lies ahead and you don't know why a man can piss lightning. I go away for a year and nobody knows one fucking thing."

"Are you always so angry?"

"Who's angry? I've got no arm and my wolves are dead and it's so cold my dick has curled up inside me so that it looks like I've got a second belly button between my legs. This is me in a good mood."

She gives him a mirthless grin, the best bedside manner she can manage. "I'm going to ask you something and I want you to tell me the truth. Did you come here to hurt us?"

"No." It is the truth. "No, I don't want that at all."

She wraps the bandage tight and offers it a gentle pat. "I believe you."

And maybe she does and maybe she says something to Lewis, because Colter wakes the next morning to find him standing nearby. His long, thin figure towers over him, like one more tree in the dim-lit forest. He has been avoiding Colter, and maybe that has something to do with guilt or maybe that has something to do with fear, since back in the day, on more than one occasion, Colter crushed him against a wall and made him eat dirt and told him to stop being such a book-eating puss.

But now he's here to talk, Colter can tell, give him the eye-to-eye, make it clear where he stands and figure out where Colter stands and see if they can find a balance. He looks different than Colter remembers him. Not a boy, but a man, and maybe not a man at all. His forehead is marked with weary lines. His firm mouth beneath the black beard he has grown seems to suck on something bitter. But it's his eyes—the blue-gray eyes, like cold moons—they glint with some curious power and make Colter shrink back a bit and feel small and chastened, aware of his defeat in a way he had never felt when jailed.

"How do I know," Lewis says, "that this is not all some convenient lie to keep you alive?"

"Swear it."

"On what?"

"Your father's grave."

Something splits open in Lewis's face and just as quickly resolves itself. "You put him there. Swearing on his grave means nothing."

"It means everything. Don't you see? Don't you see why I'm here? The old man is why." He is not one to show any emotion beyond anger. He sometimes jokes that the last time he cried, a pebble fell from his eye. And then a rat came along and tasted the pebble and died. But he feels something now, cracking the edge of his voice and dampening the corners of his eyes. "Don't you see that the old man was like a father and I did him wrong?"

Lewis doesn't say anything for a long time. Snow falls and melts on his face and dribbles down his cheek.

"You could have killed me," Colter says.

"I could have, yes."

"But you didn't. You let me live. A part of you must want to believe in the good. There's some good in me once you get past the shit. A man can change, Lewis. You're living proof of that."

They complain about following the river. If they cannot canoe it, then why bother? Why not bear west more directly? Gawea tells them, more than once, that with the constant clouds, she cannot guide them using the stars, and with the vast gray sameness of the snow-swept plains, their maps are made useless. The river is their known conductor, the channel that will lead them. This is the way she came and this is the way they will go. And the water, even when scrimmed with ice, attracts life. Their best chance in finding game is to follow its course. The water will eventually thaw, and when that time comes, perhaps they will find more canoes and take to paddling again.

Questions. They have so many questions for her. And the way she must answer them, always guarded, always worried she will forget or contradict one of her half lies, exhausts her. No, no one ever goes hungry in Oregon, and yes, there are pastures busy with sheep and cattle, pens with pigs, houses with hens, just as there are fields of corn and oats and barley and soybean and wheat, orchards of apples, tangles of blackberries. Hops for beer, grapes for wine. No, there isn't a wall. There isn't a curfew. There are ever-expanding towns and cities with roads threaded between them, the ligature of a larger organism. In the Sanctuary, they were trapped. Because of this, because they were walled in, they considered time and construction vertically, a layering—but out west, people have a horizontal perspective, spreading their fences and buildings outward. "Everything is bigger there."

This keeps them going. The dream of what awaits them. And sometimes she can't help but believe in it too. That everything will be better when they arrive. They trust her. This pleases her and hurts her. At night, they all cram together for heat. York always manages to tuck in beside her and she often wakes up to find his arm around her. She does not knock it away. The closeness feels good.

Clark asks them to stay strong, to cheer up, look alive. She really believes, in the same way sailors and astronauts must have when launching themselves into an unknown darkness, that they have some higher calling, that their survival and whatever they discover might profoundly affect others, the future. "Gawea did this on her own. We can do this together. We're in this *together*."

That includes Colter, who is now strong enough to hike alongside them, cursing the cold. They will not give him a gun, not yet, not until he's proved himself, and he complains about this too, but with a hand tapping his bandaged stump and a smile cutting his face. "I'm unarmed. You've unarmed me, you fucks. An unarmed man's worth as much as a teatless heifer in thirsty times."

The temperature drops steadily. They have come from the Sanctuary, where the holes rotted through the ozone layer created a land of perpetual summer, to the frozen plains, thick with ashen snow and thundering clouds. The seasons do not turn. The seasons have been imprisoned.

There was a time, in South Dakota, when they could still forage for nuts, blackberries, button mushrooms, bolete mushrooms, and now that time is over. At night Clark sets traps in the woods, and when she checks them in the morning, she finds them empty but spotted with blood, clumped with fur, the snow around them crushed flat. Something is stealing from her. She tries to study the tracks. Sometimes they are lost to the falling snow and sometimes there are many of them trailing off in different directions. She does not recognize them, big footed, with a long stride.

Sometimes they hear noises in the woods. What could be deep-throated laughter.

CHAPTER 30

THIS IS SIMON'S chance to prove himself to Ella. She thinks of him as her ward, a clumsy child. He will show her what he is capable of, his guts and prowess, by breaking into the Dome to deliver the letter and search for whatever Lewis wanted them to find.

He will go there at night, when only a few guards haunt the halls and he can whisper in and out without any trouble. He will fold the letter into Danica's panties, they decide. Not her pillow. There it might be discovered by a servant or her husband. And not a gown hanging in the closet. There it might wait undiscovered for a month or more. "No," Ella says, "only her panties will do. A good every-day pair. Faded, worn, maybe even holey."

"Woman like that would never wear a pair of holey panties."

"Every woman has a pair of holey panties. They're her favorite panties."

Simon is disturbed by the two letters, the very different realities they present. Lewis talks of water and Reed talks of death. When he brings this up to Ella, she dismisses the question. "Lewis doesn't lie. And he loves to complain. So let's trust in his version of things. There's water out there. There's hope. And one day, we're going to leave this place and join him."

We. She uses the word so often these days, as if they are one. He likes the way it sounds.

In the museum, in their room, the windows are dark and a candle burns on the bureau. The flame flutters and sends furtive shadows dancing when Simon holds out his arms and turns in a circle and asks, "Am I ready?"

He wears all brown, except for his cast, which earlier she painted black, so that he might better merge with the shadows. She scans his body, then buttons his back pocket so it won't scrape or catch on anything. She tells him to jump up and down, and when he does, his pockets rattle with some coins and a small ivory carving of a heart he hands over to her. "That's from one of the exhibits," she says, and he says, "Sorry. I just wanted to keep it for a little while."

He jumps again, this time without any noise except the patter of his bare feet.

Ella moves to give him a reassuring pat on the shoulder but it feels more like a punch. "Ready."

First the letter, then whatever Lewis alluded to, some *thing* they might use to their advantage. He has no plan except to sneak room to room, to inventory every drawer and closet. Whatever he seeks, he will hopefully know it when he sees it.

The night is wrapped in many sheets of silence. There is the silence of the night sky—flecked with stars, a glossy granite black—an imposing, powerful silence that makes him feel like eyes might very well be watching his every move. There is the silence of the streets, where by day brooms scrape and people walk and cats scamper and carts rattle, a place so often bustling that its barrenness feels like a skull once wild with hair, like branches stripped of leaves by a winter wind, like death. And then there is the silence inside him—the calm he feels whenever he readies to sneak his hand into a pocket or scramble through an open window—every fiber in his body under his control, awaiting his command.

An iron fence, with bales of barbed wire along the top, surrounds the Dome. Simon patrols its perimeter and finds one deputy on watch. He smokes at the front gate, and when he breathes, a bright red eye seems to throb in the dark. Simon slips off his backpack and holds it in one hand. He has been here before and knows he is just thin enough, if he turns his head, to mash his body through the bars. It takes a little more effort this time, maybe because Ella's cooking has rounded him out.

Once through, he pads to the edge of the building, scraping

through the bushes that grow along it. The windowsills are spiked with metal and glass, to keep birds from nesting and people from climbing. He removes from his backpack a pair of leather gloves, one of them slit along the wrist to accommodate his cast. Though it is past midnight, the metal still throbs with the heat of the day. He can feel it when he curls his hands around the spikes and hoists himself up. He does so crookedly, his left arm mostly useless except to stabilize his body as he draws it upward.

The first floor is barred with iron, but not the next level, the living quarters, where the windows remain open through the day and night to accommodate a breeze. Over the years, he has studied these enough to know where there is movement, where there is light, where he needs to worry about running into someone once inside.

The window above him, he knows, will deposit him directly into a hallway nook with a wingback chair and a round-topped pedestal on which rests a vase of dried flowers. He must climb to get there, nearly ten feet, and the stone is impossibly sleek, with no place to grip a toe or finger. While he balances on the ledge—his toes on, his heels off, his knees pinched around a bar—he removes his backpack and slips out a telescoping antenna that he salvaged from an electronics store. Once extended, it locks in place. He has welded to its tip a V of metal that serves as a kind of claw. At the bottom of his backpack he has stored a coil of climbing rope, each end of it threaded into a hook. He fits one of these hooks into the claw at the antenna's tip.

The bottom windows are divided by three vertical bars and two horizontal. He steps onto the first and then the second bar and stretches until his calves bunch painfully and his vertebrae feel like they might pop, finally reaching the rope to the sill above, the hook gripping one of the pigeon spikes on the sill. To climb, he uses his feet as much as his hands. The rope is knotted every twelve inches or so to accommodate his grip. He dangles beneath the second sill, shrugging off his backpack and tossing it over the spikes, shielding his belly when he drags himself over.

He allows himself only a moment's rest before retrieving the rope and coiling it neatly into the bottom of the backpack. He is tempted to leave the pack here, hidden behind the chair in the hallway, but he has learned not to trust the way in as the way out, depending on what trouble he might encounter—maybe nothing but maybe something.

The hallway is socked with darkness broken by blue beams of moonlight. He keeps his feet flat and brings them down softly, so that he makes no more noise than a cat gliding across a rug, when he sneaks his way three doors down, Danica's.

The knob is made from decorative brass. Maybe a minute passes before he turns it completely, and maybe a minute more before he opens enough of a crack to slip through. Her room smells spicy with perfumes. The bed is hers alone; her husband sleeps down the hall.

She is so thin, he cannot make out her body beneath the sheets, but her hair gives her away, as white-blond as thistledown, whiter even than her bed linens. He tries to detect her breathing but cannot, with the window open and the thrum of the city in the room. She has not drawn her curtains and the air is silvered with moonlight. He takes in his surroundings—its desk and dresser, its paintings of wildflower meadows, of lily-padded ponds, of women in white lace twirling sun umbrellas at garden parties—before starting forward.

His hand reaches first for the top left drawer of her dresser and he finds there the skins of stockings and many slips as thin as paper. In the next drawer he finds her panties, so many of them the drawer catches when he slides it out. He digs around, but every pair seems fresh off the sewing table—not a filthy, holey pair of panties in sight. He can't wait to tell Ella.

He has the letter folded in his pocket. He slips it now into the topmost pair of panties. His fingers tease the fabric. Heat spikes inside him. He felt calm until now, his heartbeat fluttering up to the burning tips of his ears.

There is something about stealing he misses. With Ella, his life has grown comfortable, and the other side of comfort is boredom. He feels more alive now than he has in weeks. When you have no home, you find pleasure in taking from others who do. It is about the money, the value, yes, but it is also about energy. Harvesting from them some object that might be worthless—a photo, a trinket—that must matter to them: that seems somehow electrical, and making it his own, energizing himself.

That is how the panties feel to him. Charged. He cannot help himself. He slips a pair from the drawer and bunches it into his pocket—just as he feels a dagger at his spine and breath on his neck.

"Those are mine," the voice says.

CHAPTER 31

GAWEA SHARES A blanket with Lewis, the two of them bundled together for warmth. She watches him scribble in his
journal. The rest of them stare at the campfire and at each
other. They gather at the leeward base of a hill as tall as four
men stacked upon each other's shoulders. It appears to have
been cut by a great knife, its side is so steep. The sky is black,
with the moon and stars forever bundled in clouds. Everyone
huddles close to the fire. A column of heat and smoke twists upward and the snow vanishes into it, extinguished in little wisps
of steam.

Lewis brought the journal with him to chronicle, author the new
world. Map the landscape. Sketch whatever flora and fauna he observed. Such as this plant, with its thin-jointed, odd-angled stalks
topped by purple flowers in the summer, now wilted to a bony
brown and bristling with frost. He lifts his pen and the ink freezes
and he blows on the tip to warm it.

Every day, he has another set of questions for Gawea, and
though she once found him pestering, she now feels a kinship in
their secret sharing. He tells her he has come to understand that
knowledge is not enough. Observation is not enough. He no longer
wishes to be a scholar, a gatherer, a chronicler, but a creator, too.
The same impulse that drove him to tinker with inventions now
compels him to tinker with the world.

"What are you writing?" Clark says.

"Nothing," he says. "Just playing around with some theories."
Then he notices all their eyes on him. They want to know. They
want something from him in the same way he wants something
from Gawea. He looks to her, as if for permission, and she says,
"Go ahead. You're the teacher now."

The wood pops and the wind hushes and Lewis licks his lips several times before he finds the words he wants. "Did you know that humans used to bite like other primates? Their incisors clipped, edge to edge, the bottom and the top coming together to tear and gnash. Then, somewhere around the late eighteenth century, two things happened. People began to braise and pound and cook their meat. And to slice up their food to pop into their mouths with forks. Almost immediately the European population developed an overbite, their incisors now coming together like scissor blades."

Clark says, "What does that have to do with anything?"

"The body changes. People adapt, sometimes in an instant."

He holds his journal upright for them to see. Next to the sketch of the plant he has written down its common designation—skeleton weed—and then its scientific identity—*Lygodesmia texana*—and then its chemical and cellular structure, and then he *knows* it in a way he never has before, like a lover undressed and drawn to bed, a name whispered in an ear, an accommodating body, submissive to his wants. "Gawea taught me this."

He looks at her and smiles and she smiles back.

"When you know something, really know it, its chemicals, its strings and charges, its clustered atoms, in essence you know its secrets, and when you know someone's secrets, they answer when called."

Clark says, "You ask, they answer."

"Pretty much."

Gawea says, "They don't always answer."

Everyone huddles down into their blankets and no one looks particularly convinced.

"Show them," Gawea says. "Show them with the weed."

In a five-foot ring around the fire, the snow has mostly melted. He holds out a hand to the skeleton weed, as if in offering, his fingertips spotted with ink. He looks at Gawea questioningly and she says, "You can do it."

He closes his eyes. The arm shivers from the cold or the effort.

After what feels like many minutes it listens. Greening. Blistering with a lavender bud.

York's eyes seem to grow wider. The doctor shakes her head and sucks her teeth. Clark's face is impassive, her head crowned by a red nimbus of hair. Colter might be grinning, but it's difficult to tell with his torn cheek. Reed has his head in his hands, lost in some private darkness.

The fire snaps and hisses, the wood wet. The wind rises, scuttling leaves, curling snakes of snow around them. "It's magic," York says.

"No," Gawea says. "Magic is just a word people use for what they can't understand. You should know that better than anyone. You and your tricks."

York flinches, hurt.

Lewis tucks his journal and ink and pen away. "My mother once said that she knew when I was in trouble. If I fell and scraped a knee, or if the other boys picked on me"—here he looks at Clark meaningfully—"or girls. If something happened to me, she always knew. She found me once, you know. That time you hog-tied me and hung me from a balcony? She found me and she cut me down. She didn't carry knives but she had a knife in her pocket that day. As if she knew she would need it. Every parent has a story like this, and I suppose it makes sense. We are them. We are made from them. In this same way, everything is born of something else, everything twinned."

Gawea doesn't know why she's being so generous. Maybe it's the enormity of the night, the way it seems to crush them together, make them one instead of many. She says, "You've heard the saying? We're all made of stardust? We're all made of stardust. We're all made of the same thing."

A few of them look up, as if to consult the sky for an answer, but the night and the clouds muddle whatever they might hope to find.

"In a way it's true," Lewis says. "And once Gawea helped me recognize that, to see how everything is connected, it was a little like growing another eye. Or another hand, another nose. Another level of sense. And with that sense comes the ability to manipulate."

Gawea can't help it. She likes it—she does—when he talks about her admiringly. It makes her feel like she matters inside of someone instead of outside, more than a mere guide leading them through a maze.

For a while there is only the fire snapping; then York says, "I hear you, but it's just a bunch of words."

Everyone is staring at the skeleton weed, now unfurling into a purple bloom, a small shoot of life in the season of dying. The wind is ceaseless, whistling around the edges of the hill and whipping up snow. The fire bends and flattens, struggling to right itself against the gusts.

It is then that the body falls.

There is a crack—as the logs break beneath its weight—followed by a concussion of air filled with embers that sting their exposed faces. They cry out and roll away and try to calm their minds, not knowing at first what has happened, not even knowing where they are, still caught up in the unreality of Lewis's demonstration.

It is a deer, they discover. A buck with a sizable rack of antlers. At first they think it might have, in confusion, in the whirling snow, wandered off the edge of the ledge. Then they hold a flaming log closer and examine its body and see its throat torn away.

There was a time, not so long ago, when Gawea wished them all dead, considered them an annoyance, an impediment. Now she is the first one to reach for a gun, eager to defend them. She remembers what Burr said about how she might discover camaraderie, something to fight her perpetual loneliness, and how resistant she was to that suggestion. They need her—that is clear—but now she feels, with some reluctance, she might need them too. Could she call them friends? Was that the right word? It implied a valued closeness at odds with where and why she led them. If only they could remain everlastingly in motion, if only their journey would never end. Because when it ended, this would end, the fond nervous connection she feels to a huddle of bodies shivering in the night.

She does not sleep and nothing comes out of the snowy dark. But she knows the danger is out there. And she knows if it does not find them, she will eventually lead them to it.

CHAPTER 32

REED'S EYES FOCUS on nothing. He won't speak unless pressed, responding yes or no with the barest whisper. He whimpers when dreaming. He waves people away when they come near. His eyes, when closed, look as black as shadows, as if two holes have been bored into his head—and when open they are no less disturbing, threaded with capillaries. His skin is pale, so sunken and drawn against his skull it appears to have given way to bone. He often reaches a hand into his pack to fondle the tiny coffin he keeps nested there.

One day they find him with a knife in one hand and his braid in the other, the long black coil of it sawed roughly from his head, twined around his knuckles. Clark says, "Why would you do that?" and shakes her head sadly.

She must feel some sympathy for him. Every now and then she places a hand on his shoulder, reminds him to drink, to eat. But a part of her—he can feel it—wishes he would die. He is an emotional liability, a smear of human waste. He should die. But really, they should all die. They're going to die. He can taste it like ashes on his tongue.

———

The treetops—some pine, mostly ash and oak—cut through the low-sailing clouds. The air is so cold it hurts to breathe, as if their lungs are crystallizing and might shatter. Their faces and hands are a raw red, windburned. Their lips crack. So do their knuckles. They can never get warm, not fully, as if their very marrow has hardened into a chalky freeze. "Are you sure this is the way?" they ask Gawea, and she says, "This is the way."

They allow Colter to walk and to sleep without restraints. The world is his prison. He will die if he departs them, and he will die if he attacks them, and everyone seems resigned to this. He stops trying to convince them he's on their side, understanding they need time. He plods along with his head down, occasionally reaching for the place where his arm used to be as if to scratch it.

Whatever hurled the deer on their fire, whatever steals the food from their traps, is following them. In a shed Clark discovers an old trap, big enough to look like the jaws of some mechanical beast. One day, when they have settled on a place to camp, she heats the trap in the coals of the fire and limbers the gears, works free the rust. Then she hikes into the woods and buries it in the snow a few feet from a wire trap, in the open space between two trees, the most likely hallway in this tangle of bushes. She drives the spike deep into the ground.

That night, they add more and more wood to the fire, building up the flames to their standing height, and they turn their backs to it to preserve their vision and face the forest. The heat thrown by the fire is so tremendous that sometimes their skin feels as though it might split and peel, but they dare take only so many steps away from it, the black perimeter of the night as solid and forbidding as a wall.

Colter asks for a rifle, and they give him a club. They keep their hands out of gloves, despite the cold, so that their fingers might be free to pull the trigger, snatch a knife. Their breath ghosts from them. They see eyes glowing like twin candle flames. They see shapes, sometimes low to the ground, sometimes standing upright. They hear broken branches, crunching footsteps, growling and huffing. And, at one point late in the night, a high-pitched cry—an animal unmistakably in pain.

They assign a watch in two-hour shifts—while the rest try to sleep, huddling together for warmth. Gawea cozies next to York and pulls his arms around her like a coat.

The next morning Clark works her way through the woods, following her old footsteps between the ice-frosted trees. The sun is only a hazy light seen through the clouds, like a candle buried in cotton. She clicks off the safety on her rifle when she nears the trap.

The wind rises and briefly lifts the branches like so many skeletal arms beckoning her forward. Through the bushes, she sees blood on snow and an uncertain shape caught in the trap. She picks it up. The chain rattles and clanks.

It is two times the size of her hand—white furred and black padded and yellow clawed—severed at the joint, torn or chewed off.

———

Reed has no words for the others and they have few for him except to occasionally ask how is he feeling, how is he holding up? He does not respond except to stare back the way they came, at the long dark channel crushed into the snow, reaching off into the distance, his link to the Sanctuary.

He longs for the time when he mattered, the place where he mattered. He cannot understand what compelled him to leave. There was his opposition to the mayor, his gnawing worry that his dalliance with Danica would be discovered, and his belief that they had to leave behind the Sanctuary to survive. But all those feelings have turned to dust. And all his memories seem like happy ones, lit with a sunset glow. He remembers the thousands of faces that cherished him. He remembers the wind lifting dust from the streets and rooftops like banners. He remembers the chiming progress of jingle carts dragged by tinkers and pharmacists. The laughter in the bars and the shouted parley at the bazaar. The wind turbines creaking and the electricity sizzling. The sun flashing off thousands of points of metal and glass. Swallows flying in dark murmurations that looked like clouds, the only thing marring the blindingly blue sky. He remembers people despairing their lives, sure, but isn't that always the case, everyone wanting more than what they have, expecting something better on the horizon? If this was it, then they could have it.

So when Clark returns to camp, when she shows them the severed paw, Reed says, "I think we need to face the facts."

Clark throws the paw on the fire, where it spits and bubbles and blackens.

"I think we need to turn back."

"Shut up, Reed," she says.

His voice was calm before, but now he hurries out his words. "This is suicide."

"We trust the girl. She said there was an end to the desert, and there was, and she says there is an end to the snow, and there is."

"There's death. If we keep going, we have nothing to look forward to except death."

"What's happened to you?"

"What's happened to *me*? What's happened to you? You used to love me."

"I used to fuck you."

"There's a difference, isn't there?" He smiles terribly. "So now you hate me?"

"I don't know. I might. I don't respect you; I know that."

"People change, you know? I've changed. You've changed. Lewis has changed. Everyone is changing and the change is not good. Not good at all."

She grabs him by the arm and tries to drag him away from the others. "We need to talk."

"No!" He jerks from her grip. "No. I know they feel the same. I know they do." He makes a sweeping gesture with his arm. "How could you not? This is suicide. Am I right? This is suicide."

Their faces, wrapped against the cold, give nothing back.

"You're wrong," Clark says. "They don't. They believe that we're going to get through this, like we've gotten through everything else, and our lives will be better for it."

His vision shakes. He can't seem to settle his eyes on anyone or anything. "Let's vote, then."

"Don't be weak, Reed."

"Let's put it to a vote."

Her hand tightens around his arm, as if it were a neck to strangle. "Shut up, Reed. Please, please, please shut up."

He reels against her and breaks her grip, but it turns out she was the only thing holding him up and he falls to the ground. "You talk about America. You talk about democracy." He knows he sounds out of breath. "So let's vote. We'll vote. We keep going or we turn back."

Everyone is motionless, studying him. He knows how he must look. Like a crazy person. Kneeling on the ground. His arms outstretched, beseeching them. His hat has fallen off and his hair thorns from his head. He stands and brushes away the snow that clings to him. "Who thinks we should turn back? Who thinks that?" He holds a hand up, as high as it will reach. He tries to smile but can feel the smile failing. He studies each of them in turn. They all look away except for Lewis. "Not even you, freak show? No one?"

"That's right." Clark crosses her arms. "No one. Now, pull yourself together."

The horizon is lit red by the oil fires. A black snow begins to fall and blur the air, filling up their tracks, the way home. He cannot do it alone. The distance traveled and the dangers faced already feel impossible. He will starve or he will freeze or he will bake. He will fall or something will fall on him, a boulder or branch. He will succumb to a snakebite and wander for hours in a fever while one of his limbs purples and swells. He will be torn to pieces, a feast for the beasts and birds and bugs. There will be no marker for his grave except a half-buried pile of sinewy bones riddled with tooth marks. And even if he made it, even if he somehow stumbled out of the desert and into St. Louis, toothless from scurvy, mad with loneliness, what then? Maybe he would knock on the gates and shout, "Let me in, I'm back, so sorry to have worried you, it was all a dreadful mistake!" Or maybe he would sneak in, wait outside the Dome until Danica emerged for a walk, then grab her by the wrist, say, "It's me!" She would pull away from him, he felt sure. She wouldn't recognize him, just as Clark didn't recognize him. He didn't recognize himself anymore. And then Thomas would lop off his head and hang it somewhere for everyone to admire. It is clear now: if he returns, he will fail, and if he keeps going, they will fail. He is a failure. Life is a failure.

"Fine." Reed nods. "Okay. You're right. I can see that you're right." He keeps nodding, even when he withdraws his revolver and puts the muzzle in his mouth and pulls the trigger.

CHAPTER 33

DANICA KEPT THE dagger. The one she found on Resurrection Day, in the stadium, when the girl was marched to the gallows, when her husband applauded, when she snuck away and Reed bent her over the table littered with weapons. He filled her, again and again, until she felt something unraveling inside her, as if every ligament and tendon and muscle fiber and nerve ending were loosening at once—and she reached for something, anything, to stabilize her, before she came undone. It was the dagger her hand curled around then. In a way she never let go.

The blade is six inches long, the hilt four, the guard the same. It is flat, meant to be worn close to the skin. She spears cockroaches with it. She tosses it, end over end, into wood floors for the satisfying thunk it makes. When she holds it up to a band of sunlight or moonlight, it makes a shadow like a cross on the wall. When she draws it across the skin at the inside of her thighs, it traces a thin pink line that wells into red dots. She keeps it sheathed beneath her dresses. She sleeps with it beneath her pillow. There is something reassuring, boosting, about always having its sharpness nearby. Maybe that's how men feel about their cocks.

She had a blade when she was a girl. A belt knife. Her grandfather gave it to her, said it wasn't a toy but a tool, said she should learn it like a limb. She carved her name into stucco, carved dwarves and goblins out of wood, carved up meat and cheese, carved off the ear of an older boy once when he tried to get between her legs.

Her hand is on the dagger and she is awake the moment her door cracks and the boy steals his way into the room. She watches him with her eyes half-lidded. Watches him watch her. Then study his surroundings. He wears a backpack. No shoes. When he whispers toward the dresser, she expects him to reach for the jewelry box atop it, but he does not. He slides open one drawer, then another, her underwear drawer, and reaches in. He is a pervert, then.

She could call out for help. But she has always preferred to take care of matters on her own. So she slides out of bed, slides across the floor, so quietly the air seemingly cannot grip her. She wears a silken slip that makes no noise.

And then the knife bites the boy's back, just above his pack, the place where his neck meets his shoulders.

He spins around. He is such a little thing. Narrow headed and wide-eyed and slim limbed, like a skinned cat. He does not seem capable of lust. And when she takes in the sight of him, his hand gripping a bouquet of panties, she feels somewhere between amused and disgusted.

"What is your name?"

He says nothing until she leans the blade into his chest and then he says, with a whimper, "Simon."

"You've come here to steal my panties, Simon?"

"No."

"That's certainly what it looks like."

His eyes flash between her and his fistful of underwear. "I'll admit, I was going to grab a pair."

"Good. It's good to tell the truth."

"But that's not why I came here."

"Isn't it?"

"No."

"Out with it, then. Before I open you up."

"I came to deliver a letter. He sent you a letter."

"Who did?"

"Reed did. That's who. Reed."

She takes two steps back and lowers her arm, nearly dropping the knife when it swings limply at her side. At first she cannot say anything, cannot make words, all of her attention on the flower of blood blooming at his breast where she nicked him. He reaches to touch it, as if bitten by a bug, and examines his red fingertips.

Then she goes to the hallway and checks to make sure it is empty before closing the door and gathering her breath and saying, "Show me."

———

Ella asked how long Simon would be, how long it would take him to break into the Dome, creep through its many rooms, find whatever it is Lewis meant for them to discover. *You must expose what is hidden in the Dome*, he wrote to them—and there the letter trailed off.

Simon told her he might not find anything at all. And he didn't know how long it would take. He would do his best and doing your best takes time. This sort of thing can't be rushed. The necessary silence of his trade came with stillness, slowness. He might be two hours or he might be four hours.

"Four hours, then," she said. "I'll start to worry after four hours."

"Don't worry. I don't want you worrying and I don't want to feel rushed."

"Four hours. It will be dawn in five, so you've got no choice but four."

She tries to sleep but can't. Of course she wonders what he might find—locked away in some closet or hidden in a drawer—whatever secret might serve them. But that seems secondary to him coming home to her. Home—that's how she thinks of the museum—as belonging to them both. They share a room—with beds opposite each other—just as they share meals and duties and conversation. She might bully him, but with tenderness, every rough shove another opportunity to touch, every hard word a breath between them shared.

She waits in the kitchen—a long room crowded with cupboards and counters—where he will enter through a side door. She paces the floor and then collapses in a chair and rests her head in her hands. She imagines him whipped. She imagines him dead. She imagines him trapped somewhere, hiding beneath a bed or in a closet while people move all around him. She hates to admit it, but she cares about him, feels about him as she would a cherished possession, not wanting to let him out of her sight.

Dawn comes. There is a soft knock. The knob rattles. She hurries from her chair and yanks open the door and hisses, "Where have you been?" Her eyes take a moment to adjust to the light, blinking through a red haze, and then she makes sense of what she sees: Simon standing before a hooded figure.

"What's this?" Ella says, her whole body suddenly numb. "What's happened?"

Simon drops his eyes and lifts his shoulders in a shrug. Ella looks to the figure for answers. The hood holds a shadow, the face lost to it. "I'm supposed to just let you in?" Ella says, and Simon says, "Do it, please," and she steps aside to accommodate them, then checks the alley before closing and bolting the door.

She doesn't know what to do. She alternately wants to smack Simon and smash him into her chest as if to smother him with her heart. But before she can act on either impulse, the figure pulls back her hood, revealing the white-blond hair and sharply cut face of Danica Lancer.

There is a held breath of a moment before Danica says, "Let's sit down, everyone."

They gather at a table in the corner of the kitchen. Simon and Ella sit on one side and Danica on the other. "We certainly have a lot to talk about." She looks at them and talks to them as a mother would her disobedient children. Ella knows that Danica wants them to feel that way, as children, because children do as they are told. Lewis would do the same to Ella and she would not tolerate it then and she will not tolerate it now. She crosses her arms and pinches her mouth into a frown.

Danica says, "No one knows I am here, and no one will know I was here, so long as we all understand each other."

The second bell is ringing. The day is brightening, beginning to heat up. Sweat dots their temples. Danica reaches below the table then and withdraws a black dagger like a nightmarish piece of cutlery. "You must realize how complicated this situation is."

Ella has a biting way of speaking when she says, "I realize that very well, thank you."

"I am grateful to you for delivering the letter, but I am worried about you too." Danica runs the blade along her arm, tracing its bare length, pausing a moment in the pale hollow of her elbow, continuing to the snaked veins of her wrists, across her palm, to the very tip of her middle finger, where she scrapes away some sand embedded beneath the nail. "You know things about me you shouldn't. You know things about me that could get me killed."

"We're even, then," Ella says. "You know things about us could do the same."

Danica's eyes narrow. Ella knows what's going on behind them. Danica believes, as a rule, women want to be her, and because they cannot, they choose to hate her. She knows Ella hates her and hate is a great motivator for foolish behavior. Ella tries to release some of her hate by turning to Simon and saying, "You said you could be quiet as a cat. You said you could sneak in and out of there like a shadow."

He wilts with every word, his posture conveying his apology.

Danica says, "Where do we go from here, children?"

"I don't understand."

"The boy says Lewis asked you to spread news of their success."

Ella stabs Simon with her elbow. "Are you an idiot? Do you want to die? Why did you tell her that?"

He does not respond except to shrink even further into his chair and look at her sidelong.

"He had a blade on him. He didn't have much of a choice." Danica twirls the dagger in her palm, spinning it like a clock dial. She wants them to look at it, to acknowledge the power and the slicing threat of it, but Ella refuses, keeping her gaze steady.

Danica says, "In these desperate times, it's hard to know how people will respond to that kind of information. If they learned that there was water—if they knew the expedition had traveled safely to it—they might do nothing. Or they might do something. Something dramatic. Fiery."

Ella shifts in her seat but keeps her face flat with seeming disinterest. "Fiery?"

"Would you like to start a fire? I think we can help each other start a fire. This city is dry enough that it should burn right up."

"I don't understand."

"What don't you understand, dear?"

"Your husband is the mayor. Why would you want to threaten his power?"

She slams the dagger into the table, where it hums upright like an exclamation mark. "Because I hate him."

CHAPTER 34

IT HAS BEEN a long time since Lewis saw the moon. How long, he doesn't know, because its cratered face is his clock and calendar. Ever since they crossed into North Dakota, ever since the oil-black clouds thickened, they have been cut off from its rhythms, lost in time. The new moon is when it is darkest, when its surface is shadowed. In myth, in folklore, in witchcraft, it is associated with death. Since they are living in a world absent light, they are living in a permanent new moon. They are living with death, Reed's.

The ground is frozen, so they don't bother to bury the body except with a gray mound of snow. No one utters any words—except for Lewis, who says they ought to carry on. He believes they are a half day's hike from Bismarck. "That's something to look forward to, isn't it?" He is not the type to utter hopeful phrases, but Clark has gone silent and he feels the need to serve as her mouthpiece, lift their spirits and pressure them onward.

They trudge on and they can see so little, with the snow ripping up and down, left and right, a swirling vertiginous gray-black blur. And they can hear even less, with the wind gusting and the snow making a constant patter against their hoods and hats.

Finally they decide to stop and build a shelter, an igloo. When they shove and pack the snow, it molds nicely to their liking. They build it up into head-high walls, making a half circle that connects to the downed tree. Enough room for all of them, but barely. They use the branches as rafters. And hack down more to drape over the open sections of ceiling so that they can shingle it with snow.

For ventilation, they punch a hole in the center of the ceiling and six more in the walls, each of them small enough to fit a fist through. The air grows instantly warm from their breathing and the small fire. The walls go blue and slick, melting and freezing into a lacquer. In the dim light, they strip off their hats and mittens and scarves. One by one, they curl up their bodies and shut their eyes, exhausted by the cold. The doctor takes the first watch.

———•———

She leans against the wall and warms up with her pipe. She lights it, and then dozes off, and lights the bowl again. She has seated herself next to one of the ventilation holes. Now and then she rises to her knees and peers out of it but sees only a thick veil of snow.

She plops down and studies Clark. Her eyes shudder and her body twitches. Even when dreaming, she cannot stay still. The doctor wishes she could get closer. Comb her fingers through that red hair, over and over, to clear away the burrs and tangles, to massage her scalp, to help calm her. She is so tense, like a body stiffening with death, and the doctor understands why. Clark is the reason they have made it this far, and if they make it any farther, it will be because of her. She, the dear girl, feels responsible for them all. And that responsibility must be sickening. Maybe she'll do better now that Reed is gone, as if he were an excised tumor, a lanced boil. Maybe they'll all do better now. But for the moment the poor dear is sick with guilt. There was a time when she shared a bed with Reed, and the memory of that connection must be poisoning her now. But she'll get over it. She'll heal.

The doctor lights her pipe again and fills her mouth with smoke. When she exhales, she realizes her smoke is twinned by a cloud of steam above her head. As she breathes out, it breathes in, the gusts storming together near the ventilation hole. By the time she realizes what is happening, it is too late.

To either side of her, arms stab through the walls, arms bristling with coarse white hair. She begins a scream that is cut short when the arms wrap around her chest and drag her back and leave a rough cavity in the wall through which snowflakes quietly tumble.

Clark rises on one elbow, still somewhere between waking and dreaming, still seeing Reed, the hopeless look on his face when the gun kicked and the brains coughed out the back of his skull. By the time she realizes what has happened and screams at everyone to arm themselves, it is too late—the walls of the shelter are already crashing inward.

For a moment a storm of snow obscures the air, buries their bodies. She thrashes her way out in time to see the doctor dragged by the long gray rope of her hair. What has her, Clark cannot say, but there are many of them.

They are huge and white, ghostly in the snow except for their red tongues and red eyes that appear like flames crushed into tiny caves. Bears, she realizes, loping and bounding in all different directions. Humpbacked, spade faced, their fat trembling beneath their shaggy white coats.

One dodges toward them. York digs in the snow, unearths a shotgun, fires from the hip, and sends the bear careening into a tree. It bellows, collapses into a heap.

He empties a shell, loads the breech, fires again, this time in the direction of the doctor. The bear opens its jaws, releases her ponytail, flinching back and whimpering in pain from the wound brightening its shoulder. Then it bolts for the woods. Clark counts four others. Their white hair silvered with snow. Their teeth like the shards of a kicked ice puddle.

One of them approaches York from behind and knocks him facefirst into the snow, and then turns to face Gawea. She tries to fire a shotgun but finds it jammed with snow and uses it instead as a club. Another bear has the doctor by the forearm, its teeth clamped down, its head shaking back and forth as if to tear her arm from its socket. And another slashes and lunges at Lewis and Colter, who have not grabbed their weapons in time and now swing sticks and fists.

And the last, creeping toward them, keeps an arm tucked protectively against its chest. Clark sees it is missing a paw—severed, a red nub not fully healed—and remembers her trap in the woods, the scream in the night.

Now she is the one screaming. Screaming until she doesn't have any breath. Screaming her brother's name. Because he lies there, knocked out, half-sunk in a snowbank. He shudders awake only when the bear mashes its mouth into his belly. He throws back his head in a silent cry and grabs its ears and pulls as if to draw the creature more fully inside him.

Then the bear vises its jaws around his shoulder and lumbers toward the woods, dragging him there and leaving behind a bright red runner of blood.

Her feet cannot kick fast enough as she pursues them.

———

Whether it is a knee or a branch or the stock of a rifle, Lewis doesn't know, but when the shelter collapses and the bears attack, something strikes his temple and slows his mind, muddies his vision. He wobbles when he stands beside Colter. He grips a stick in his hands and swings it wildly when any of the bears draw near. All this seems to happen outside him. His head throbs. His legs feel glass stemmed. Distantly, he hears Clark screaming—and then sees her running for the woods, disappearing between the trees.

He stares after her, lowers his stick, and at that moment a bear darts forward and knocks him flat. Its weight sinks him into the snow, empties his lungs. He cannot draw a breath. Above him black clouds roil, his vision of them eclipsed by the triangular snout of the thing. It leans in, blasts him with its hot, carrion-reeking breath. He can see down the tunnel of its throat, the place he will soon travel, the last of this journey.

He closes his eyes, waiting for the worst. But the worst doesn't come. He hears a guttural roar that heightens into a shriek. Then the bear's head thuds into his breast. Its body slumps onto him. He pokes at it, shoves at it. He can barely breathe. It does not move—not until Lewis arcs his back, painfully, rolls its three hundred pounds off him.

His mind is still struggling to keep up. He didn't hear a gunshot. Colter must have stabbed or struck it dead. However it happened, he is saved for now. He takes a deep, aching breath. Blood flows to places pinched off. He struggles to sit up. "Thank you," he says to Colter and Colter says, "Don't thank me."

That's when Lewis sees—in the slack face of the bear—a fletched arrow buried in its eye with blood jellying around it.

Colter remains stiffly where he stands, as if the wind has frozen him in place, and it is only then Lewis follows his gaze.

The snow has stopped. He can see now what they could not before. They stand on the outskirts of Bismarck. Only thirty yards away, ice-mantled houses cluster together, the beginnings of a lost neighborhood. In the distance he spies two collapsed sections of freeway—and beyond them, still soaring over the river, a rusted bridge.

Strangers surround them. Whether men or women, he cannot tell, not at first. They wear stitched gray furs, maybe made from rabbits, coyotes. Their faces are hidden beneath scarves and goggles. Their hands are the only part of them exposed—in order to better grip their bowstrings.

The bears lie in dead heaps, blotched with blood and quilled by arrows.

Lewis counts ten strangers, standing beside trees and snow-shrouded bushes, crouched next to cars, motionless. For a moment there is no noise except the wind hissing and their bowstrings creaking.

CHAPTER 35

ELLA DOESN'T TRUST Danica, but you can't trust a dagger either. You can use it skillfully, keep its point and edge away from your skin, or you can be harmed by it. So she'll do as Danica requested, as Lewis requested. She'll make some noise.

They leave when darkness cloaks the city, when curfew begins and everyone settles into sleep. They wear black pants, black shirts, mash spit and charcoal into a paste and smear their faces and hands, working together. Ella isn't letting Simon out of her sight, not after what happened last time. She's not as careless as Lewis. She won't abandon those closest to her.

"Worried about me, are you?" Simon says. "I like that."

"I just don't want you to screw things up again."

The streets are dark and dead. They slide from alleyways to doorways, moving as quietly as they can from every pool and wedge of shadow. The moonlight feels like a spotlight. Their skin bristles with fear and excitement. They go still whenever they hear a noise—a rat scurrying, a snore spiraling from an open window— and then move on.

When the city council wishes to share some announcement— about the curfew, rations, a death march—they paint it in black capital letters across the windowless wall that rises beside each of the Sanctuary's wells. Simon and Ella will do the same. They will write the news.

They make the paint out of chalk, linseed oil, glue, beets. They carry it in canteens stashed in backpacks with pans and brushes. They have enough for only one well. And they do not have time to whitewash the current notice, wait for it to dry, before slopping out their own message. The beets stain their paint red: the color of anger, the color of danger, the color of the fire Danica said she wanted to spread. They will slop it over the top of whatever is written there already.

A deputy guards the well. They can see him now, walking in slow circles around the stanchion of the wind turbine. The blades rotate and cast spinning shadows and make a rusty, grinding music. Simon isn't worried about being heard over the top of them, but he is worried about being seen. If they can only get up the ladder, into the shadow of the wall, he thinks they'll remain undetected.

He hurls a rock across the square. It sizzles through the air before finally striking a storefront awning made out of a sheet of metal. The sound startles the guard and he marches toward it with his hand at the grip of his machete. Simon tosses another rock— even farther—guiding the guard down an alley.

They scurry then to the wall, invisible in the shadow of it. There are two rebar ladders built into either side of it. They hurry to glug out their canteens, fill their pans, tuck their brushes into their belts, and climb.

———

At dawn, after the first bell rings, after the sun brightens and warps the horizon like hammered gold, people begin to line up for water. They are thirsty, and they are hungry, too, and they are ready for good news. They are ready for the giant red letters slashed across the wall near the well. LEWIS AND CLARK, the message reads, CANOE RIVERS AND SEND HOPE. A brief, bright message. Some people laugh and point their fingers. Others frown and wonder aloud whether it is true—how could it possibly be true?—and whether they dare believe. They share the words with those who can't read. Some are so excited they depart the line without filling their jugs. By the time the sun lightens the wall, two deputies have climbed the ladders to whitewash over what they call graffiti. But they cannot erase words etched already in the mind, words whispered in the streets like a gathering wind that eventually reaches Thomas's ear.

Slade delivers the news. He hunts his way through the Dome, looking for Thomas, finally pushing through the double oaken doors and discovering him alone in the council chambers. He wears a sky-blue silk shirt with an open neck and gold stitching along the collar. He sits in the dark, at the head of the empty table, his hands flat on the wood as though he were about to take up his silverware and carve a meal. The windows are shuttered, but bars of light fall across him.

Thomas appears to be speaking to himself—moving his lips, whispering to an audience of shadows—cut short by Slade clearing his throat.

Thomas twists in his seat and flickers a smile. "You know I've always liked the sound of my own voice."

"I've been looking for you." Slade enters the room fully.

"Bad news, I assume?"

"No other kind these days."

One side of Thomas's face jerks, as if he is uncertain whether he is suffering a barb, and then says, "Give it to me, then."

Slade presses the door until it clicks, then walks to the opposite side of the long table, drags out the chair, and folds his body into it. "When you asked me to be sheriff, you told me you admired my brutal honesty. You told me you trusted me because of it."

"I trust you." And then, like an asterisk, "I trust your muscle."

"Trust me when I say things are getting perilous."

"Perilous. That's a big word for you, Slade."

"I'm more than muscle."

Thomas gives him an assessing look. "Of course you are. Please. Tell me about how perilous things are."

"The bodies are piling up at the morgue, some dead from the heat, some from illness, some from not enough of everything a body needs. But more and more of them are dead from murder. More and more dying because there's more and more willing to thieve and to kill. People are talking. About how things were so much better under Meriwether. About how you're going to ruin us all. How you're fucking that—"

"Yes, yes, yes. Tell me what I *don't* know."

"I was working my way up to it, giving it adequate introduction." He then explains to Thomas the red splatter of graffiti that appeared like a wound overnight. A message seemingly reported by Lewis and Clark. A message meant to excite and entice rebellion. "Maybe a thousand people saw it before we painted it over."

His voice fires off questions like quills from a blowgun. "Do you think it's true? Could they really be alive? Could there be water? Could they be maintaining communication with someone inside the wall?"

When Slade shrugs, his shoulders seem burdened by more than shadows. "Would it change anything if it was true? People seem to think it is. That's what matters."

"The owl. I bet he sent that ridiculous owl of his. Have you been to the museum? Have you searched it? Where else would he have sent it? He must have sent it there."

"He might not have sent anything. The graffiti might be pure invention meant to cause this very response."

His fingernails are long enough to staccato the tabletop. "What's the answer, then? Enlist more deputies? Promise them food and water and we'll have a wave of volunteers ready to serve and protect."

"Done."

"Punish anyone who so much as whispers anything treasonous?"

"Done."

"Good." Thomas leans back, his face escaping the sun, retreating into shadow. "Then there's only one thing left to do."

CHAPTER 36

Clark FOLLOWS THE tracks in the snow—through the woods, through a ruined neighborhood—until she finds her brother. His body abandoned. Still warm but already dead. She has her revolver drawn, but nothing to fire at. She hears a deep-throated huffing—what sounds like laughter—chasing through this frozen world, seeming to come from everywhere and nowhere in particular. Some of the windows are broken, some shuttered with ice. They stare at her. She blasts a round into one of them for no reason except to unleash some misery.

Silence follows. She drags her brother into a brick house with half its roof collapsed. The walls are cracked and so water damaged they appear molten. She collapses in the living room and somehow day becomes night as she hugs and rocks his body. His skin grows hard to the touch, marbled many colors of purple and blue and white, like a winter sky just after the sun sets. His tears, or maybe her tears, have frosted white trails down his cheeks. And his carved-out stomach is a crystalline red.

It takes her a long time to realize she shivers from cold and not grief. She kicks apart a wooden chair and sparks a fire in the stone hearth that casts an orange glow. She does not move except to feed it more and more rotten wood. Thick gray smoke ghosts the air. Her mussed red hair falls across her face, matching the flames before her, as if she has caught fire.

Whatever she told York to do, he did, and now, because of what she told him to do, he is dead. It was a mistake. It was all a mistake. Her brother is lost and so is her confidence. She doesn't know what has happened to the others. She might care in the morning, but she doesn't care now, not in this cave of light she shares with her brother's body. She feels momentarily numb to them, as she did when she stood over Reed's grave. But York is her blood. York belonged to her. His death is like a diseased limb that has reached its rot into her heart.

She tries to sleep. At least then she can escape making any sort of decision. Or maybe she will wake to find this is all a dream. She clenches her body up like a big fist. But after only an hour or so, the fire has gone dead and she wakes, shivering. Even at this simple task, staying warm, she fails.

Now another storm has swirled over Bismarck. The wind carries sleet in it, whipping and tinkling the house with what sound like glass shards. She stirs the embers and tosses more wood in the hearth. A blast of steam escapes her mouth as a sigh or sob.

In the distance, over the noise of the ice storm, she hears grunting and chuffing, what must be the bear, and she cannot help but feel it is singing a hateful, mocking song for her.

Dawn comes. She stands over her brother's body for a long time. Then she begins smashing chairs, splintering tables, ripping off cupboard doors, gathering whatever wood she can find to crush into the hearth. To this smoldering pile she adds his body.

She tells him she's sorry. She should have taken better care of him. She turns to leave just as the flames catch his clothes.

———

They kneel in the snow, the cold creeping through their pants, with their wrists painfully bound behind their backs. Lewis twists against his restraints, testing their strength, until their guard comes by and kicks him in the back of the head hard enough to send him sprawling forward. He struggles upright, with snow powdering the side of his face.

The guard watches Lewis—as he takes a deep, steadying breath, as if swallowing a barbed string of curses—and then backs away.

Clark is gone. So is York. The doctor is hunched over in exhaustion, her eyes closed and her arm bloodied. Colter crouches beside her, still and watchful. And Gawea has been knocked unconscious.

Wrapped up in their furs, masked by their scarves, their guards have no recognizable builds or faces, so they seem like replications of the same person. They skin and butcher the bears and load the meat onto sleds.

An hour later, as instructed, they rise and trudge against the wind, punching their boots through the snow. Some of their captors walk before them and some behind, keeping them enclosed. They drag sleds, one carrying Gawea, the others stacked high with slabs and ribbons of meat. The sun dips lower, merging with the hellish glow of the oil fires on the horizon. The shadows are gray, the clouds even grayer.

The doctor collapses. Lewis tries to help her, but the guards push him away. They prod her with a bow, then kick her softly, and she says, "All right, all right," and rises, and they continue their march.

Lewis notices first the smoke of many chimney fires rising into the sky, barely distinguishable, thin gray cords of smoke that broaden and dissipate and merge with the low-bellied clouds. And then the building comes into view. The sign is cracked and faded and scraped, but he can still make out the words, KIRKWOOD MALL.

He knows the word *mall*—the Sanctuary had its own airy plaza where the bazaar took place—but this looks to him more like a medieval fortress, virtually windowless, with white patches of paint clinging to the crumbling concrete exterior. It is surrounded by a kind of moat, a sea of snow splashed over asphalt, making it easy to spy any approaching enemy. Tracks dirty the ground, packing down trails, like the one they follow now, its bottom a slick blue-black ice that makes his footing uncertain, though their captors crunch along without any trouble, wearing snowshoes, framed by wood and webbed by tendons and clawed at the bottom.

Two rust-pocked trucks have been shoved in front of the wide entryway. Once there were glass doors here, the space now sheeted with wood and metal. Someone drags an unhinged door aside and they enter the dark.

Lewis's eyes take a moment to adjust. Slowly the mall takes shape. A long, low-ceilinged chamber catacombed with stores repurposed into living quarters, some of them glimmering with lamplight. The air smells of urine and leather and smoke.

At that moment, their escorts rip off their hats and goggles, unwrap their scarves, to reveal messy nests of hair. Women. And girls. More of the latter than the former. Not a man among them.

Lewis hears voices muttering, footsteps chuffing the floor. People are standing from their campsites, walking closer to observe them. They, too, are women. They number around twenty altogether. Some are brown and some are black and some are so pale they appear made from winter, carved and spun from ice, except where their skin has splotched red. All of their eyes and cheekbones are carved out by shadows. They are missing teeth. Some of their fingers are half-blackened with frostbite. They look familiar, as survivors. But their expressions offer no welcome.

A taller woman—with close-cropped gray hair and a commanding voice—speaks to the group of them, saying she knew this day would come, she knew *they* would come. "But we hunted them down before they could hunt us down. We're stronger than them. Didn't I tell you that? That we're stronger than them?"

The girls nod, eager for her words.

"No," Lewis says. "We're not—"

But before he can say anything more, he is shoved, along with the rest of his party, into an empty store with a metal curtain that rattles across the entry and locks them in place.

———

There is not a lot of thought left inside her. Clark hears the click and scrape of her revolver, the hammer thumbed back, released, thumbed back, released. She smells the smoke and the puddle of orange urine she left in the corner. She feels the sleet prickling her skin when she steps into the day. Outside of processing these few sensations, her brain is unbusied, more singular, as if requiring only the stem. All this time she's been battling toward human progress and now it is time to succumb to the world's beginning and the world's end. The rules are simple. The fastest claws and the biggest teeth win.

Millions of ice pellets blur and clatter the air. She slides her feet, skating her way out the door, into the street, and after only a minute, her clothes are stiff, cracking and shattering when she moves.

She tucks her revolver beneath her coat so that it doesn't freeze over. Her pockets rattle with bullets. The sun is beginning to rise—and the storm is beginning to subside. She moves slowly. There is no other way to move, everything glassed over, so slick she must slide her boots and constantly readjust her body to keep her balance. Her eyes water in the wind. Her coat flaps around her knees.

"Where are you?" she says.

Everything appears like something else, sheeted and encased with a gray-white ice. A streetlamp is a gleaming proboscis. A tree's branches appear like dead veins reaching up some milky arm. A skeleton, like a man made of glass, hunches in a doorway. She makes her way past the giant brown slab of the civic center, past bars and hotels and credit unions.

A few more ice pellets patter her face, and then the clouds quit. The wind dies. The city quiets except for the ice muttering and splitting. She stands in a shallow canyon of storefronts, the buildings gray squares and the streets gray stripes.

She bites off her gloves and shoves them in her pockets so that she can better grip the revolver. "Come on," she says, her throat raw and croaking. She coughs and swallows her spit and says, "Come on!" louder this time. The words echo away and come back to her mixed up and chittery, as if spoken over a nervous laugh.

She waits a long minute and then keeps going, dragging her feet, darting her eyes down the side streets, next to Dumpsters, anywhere shadows cluster. With a click, a fang of an icicle detaches from a gutter, falls, and shatters. At the sound—a splintering crack—Clark spins around and loses her balance and falls heavily on her side.

The ground knocks the air from her lungs. When she tries to

breathe, there is nothing, a flattened ache. Then her chest opens and she recovers with a gasp. She is lying there, sprawled out in the center of the road, when she sees the bear. It is nothing more than a white blur that bounds between two distant buildings, but she knows. Her cheek lies flat against the ice, and when she tries to push herself up, it sticks, peeling painfully away, taking some skin with it.

She crouches, then wobbles into a standing position and turns in a slow circle, listening. Trees creak under the weight of ice. Something shatters in the distance, like a lightbulb popped underfoot. Then, she is almost certain, she hears it, a chiming.

The sleet has gathered in its hair, crusted it over, so that when it moves, it tinkles and chimes as if festooned with small silver bells.

She rotates toward the sound—slowly this time, not wanting to fall again—lifting her revolver. Her eye squints, looking for a target, but there is none, only the long, glassy channel of the street. The sound has vanished.

She doesn't have to wait long before it comes again—the chiming, almost a ringing now, more frantic—this time to her left. But when she jerks the gun sideways, she finds only an empty sandwich shop with a tree springing through the roof. The chiming continues to evade her, in and out of range, rising from one alley and dying down another, nowhere, everywhere.

Out of the corner of her eye, a darkness where none existed before. This time she doesn't turn to face it, but flits her eyes and observes the bear. There is a bar and grill with a railed porch that it moves along the edge of, slinking along quietly now, humped low to the ground. She wants to be sure. She wants no more than ten yards between them. She does not move her feet, fearing she will fall, but twists her body. When she lifts the gun, the bear is already scrambling back the way it came.

She fires. She probably shouldn't, but she fires anyway. She doesn't know what happens to the bullet, its report and impact lost in the icicles falling and shattering from eaves and lampposts and signs all up and down the block.

The many streets that surround her offer too many outlets to hide in and dart down and burst from, so she keeps moving, hoping to find a more defensible position, a more open space. The bear paces her. She can hear its chiming progress. She can see its body, just as tall as she but twice as broad, flit out of sight. She fires at it and it flinches away but always returns, always shading her.

She is lost in a crystal world, a labyrinth of ice, its walls several stories high. She wanders its corridors. Some of the eaves are messily roofed with nests—whether for birds or squirrels, she doesn't know—and she thinks she can hear them peeping and scraping inside them, sheathed by ice.

A white shape shimmers across a glassy wall—and she startles away from it and fires and recognizes her reflection just as it shatters. There is a popping sound, followed by a scrape and a chuff as the two feet of snow piled on the angled roof come loose and avalanche toward her. She hurls herself down a narrow chute of an alley just as the icy slab crushes and piles brokenly in the place where she stood.

A crystal dust fills the air. Through it shambles the bear, blasting past her, snapping its jaws, dragging its claw across her arm. Her coat shreds, already red with blood. And then it is gone, out the other end of the alley.

She follows. The alley opens into another, where she finds loading docks, a cluster of Dumpsters, a delivery truck with an empty bed, all frozen. She crunches her way forward. She hears a growling, then a chiming, and spins around but does not know where to aim. Shapes slide across the ice so she cannot tell what is real and what is a reflection, a distortion.

She fires the gun. A wall of ice collapses into a thousand tinkling shards. She fires again, and again, and again, fumbling to reload. The gunshots clap off among the buildings and roam the sky. The splintering collapse of ice makes it sound as if someone has launched a china hutch down a staircase.

After the last shards fall, she is left in silence, alone except for the shard-edged piles glinting all around her. In one direction, she sees more buildings—and in the other, maybe a block away, a grayish expanse of rolling hills dotted with mature and stunted trees. A cemetery surrounded by a wrought-iron fence, as if the dead might rise and escape. She hurries there. Most of the tombstones are camouflaged by snow, ambered by ice, but she can see the larger crosses and a few crypts rising from the drifts. Nothing can sneak up on her here.

Ahead rises a hill topped by a single oak. Its vast branches sag beneath the weight of the ice it carries. Gray slivers fall from it like blighted leaves that glimmer in the cloud-filtered light. She walks as fast as she can, making for the rise. The chiming makes her skid to a stop. It comes from behind her, like a concert of bells. The bear waits in the street, its body porcupined with frost.

She fires, and fires again, and it bounds a few paces away before pausing. When she reaches for her pockets to reload, she finds them empty except for one last bullet. She has either blasted off the rest—or lost some from her pocket when slipping in the streets, careening around corners.

One bullet. She takes her time loading it, chambering the round with a snapping finality. Gun smoke drifts. She breathes in the sweet stink of sulfur. For the moment, she doesn't feel poisoned by grief, she doesn't feel guilty for leading a failed expedition to this icy nowhere, she doesn't feel thirsty for whiskey. Instead she feels her hands curling around the revolver. She feels the cold air piping in and out of her throat. She feels an acidic rage boiling in her guts.

She does not bother running any farther. She crouches down among the graves, with a clear avenue between her and the gates and the street beyond. This is where the bear will enter, and when it does, she will be ready.

The bear teases by the entrance many more times, running in a rocking way, and then, when she doesn't fire, it squats down and studies her. Then the bear—the one with the severed paw, the one who killed her brother—starts toward her at a lope, rounding the fence, passing through the entry; and once there, it rushes forward, more swift and sure-footed than she could ever be. Steam blasts from its snout. Its red eyes do not stray from her. The chiming of its ice-clotted fur is manic, matching the feeling inside her.

"Come on," she says. "Come and get me, you son of a bitch!"

The cold brings tears to her eyes and she blinks them hurriedly away, keeping her focus. At first the bear runs low, ready to duck a bullet, and when the bullet doesn't come, its body opens up, curling in on itself and snapping outward as it sprints. Twenty yards, fifteen yards, ten yards. The rest of the world falls away in a blur, all of her attention crushed down to a tunnel of ice through which the bear hurtles. She waits. She waits until she can be sure, until the bear is nearly upon her, widening its jaws.

Then she fires.

Through the teeth, down the throat, out the back of its neck, right where the spine nests in the skull, the bullet finds its mark. A feathery spray of blood. The bear drops, goes limp. Just like that. Like a flip switched, *off*. The gunshot claps through the cemetery. The body skids and rolls heavily into her, knocking her down. The gun skitters off. The back of her head clunks the ground. Her vision wobbles in and out. She is holding the bear, her arms wrapped around it, when it coughs and shudders and goes still.

CHAPTER 37

LEWIS CALLS her name, "Gawea," and she wakes. Her head wobbles and her eyelids shutter. Her face is swollen and netted with blood that seems to contain her, trap her inside herself. "Please," he says. "Are you all right?"

Gawea is supposed to guide, Clark is supposed to lead—and now he doesn't have either of them. But his decisiveness surprises him when he tells Colter to help him and then the doctor out of their restraints. Once freed, he pulls off his shirt and tears it in half. Part of it he uses to tie off the doctor's bitten arm—she has lost a lot of blood and her skin is cold and her breath comes in shallow gasps—and the other half he presses to the girl's wound. "York," she says, her voice muddled. "What happened to York?"

"Rest," he tells her. "You need your rest."

Lewis can smell their meat cooking now and hear the women speaking, but they are out of sight, around the bend of a shadowy corridor. He shakes the caging at the front of the store and calls for help. "Come here. I want to talk to someone this instant." But no one appears except a toothless woman—older than the others—with a blind white eye and a bright red scar dividing her forehead.

She has a phone pressed to her ear, the curled cord dangling from it and wrapped around a finger. "Yes," she says. "Yes, I see," as if plugged in to some lost conversation. When Lewis asks her to fetch someone else, to tell the others that one of their party is gravely ill, she goes still and cups a hand over the receiver and whispers harshly to the imaginary person on the other end of the line. Her white eye catches the light and brightens.

"Please," he says. "Why are you doing this to us?"

She babbles something then about the bad people.

"I don't understand."

"The bad people. You're the bad people. You come in the night. You steal us away. You make slaves of us."

"No, we do not. We most certainly do not. That's not why we're here. We're here—"

But she is already wandering away, again whispering into the phone, leaving him to wonder what has made these women so angry and fearful.

CHAPTER 38

IF YOU COULD observe the Sanctuary from above, as a vulture riding an updraft, you would see the brown and gray squares of buildings, the dusty complicated swirl of streets between, which all together, from this great height, would look rather like a desiccated brain, within which the dark specks of the deputies appear like clots, spreading, spreading, until their infection is complete, the Sanctuary taken hostage.

Smoke rises—from this building, then another—and stains an otherwise pure blue sky, clouds your vision, so you must return to the streets once more to see the deputies hurling torches through the windows of the Dirty Shame, where someone sang a ballad about Lewis and Clark the night before, a ballad that others are now humming in the streets, singing under their breath. The bartender tries to leave, but they push him back in. The flames make a noise like a thousand fingers snapping in excitement. The roof collapses—the metal sheeting sending up a swirl of sparks—as the clay walls blacken and crack. Where there was once a building, there is now a dark hull, like the disintegrating remains of a beetle.

Anyone caught singing the song—or any song—is hurled to the ground and beaten with cudgels until muscle pulps, bone shatters. Some try to help. A group of six men push the deputies, grab them by the wrists, try to wrestle them away. At first they succeed. Then more deputies come, and more still, and by the end of the day the six men are hanged—from balconies, from the wall, all over the Sanctuary—their bodies twisting in the wind, crows roosting on their shoulders and feasting their faces down to bone.

The wells are shut down for two days. Deputies surround them with fresh skins of water hanging plumply from their belts. For personal use. They guzzle from them theatrically. A barrage of people

286

gathers. Before long it is a mob. They beat the bottoms of their buckets and jugs and make a storm of noise. They yell and their dry lips crack and make their mouths bloody.

Graffiti appears overnight, hurriedly smeared onto alley walls, scratched onto shop windows. THE SANCTUARY = PRISON and DEATH TO LANCER and BRING DOWN THE WALL and WHEN HOPE IS DOWN, THE SOLUTION IS UPRISING. The buildings burn. No matter if the people inside are not responsible for the graffiti.

When Oman arrives at his apothecary, the keys jangling in his hand, ready to open for the day, his black-toothed mouth unhinges in a silent scream. Because the shop is burning, crowned with fire that gives off many curious colors—green and purple and pink and gold—as his many powders and potions erupt.

This lasts for a few days, but there are too many buildings to burn now, too much danger in the fire spreading like the anger that reddens their faces and hoarsens their voices.

The deputies retreat, at Lancer's request, still visible but disengaged, walking the streets like black shadows the sun can't erase. The wells open. Long lines form, reaching down alleys, around buildings, no end in sight.

New graffiti appears. TRUST LANCER. And OUR HOME IS A SANCTUARY. Deputies linger nearby and menace anyone who means to scrub it away.

Bodies keep piling up. Two of the sentinels on the wall. A mother and her three children. A drunk in an alley. A tinker at his cart. They are robbed sometimes and sometimes not, killed simply because everyone is burning up with anger.

Then come the bodies reported to be those of the Lewis and Clark expedition. The rangers drag them through the gates one day, piled in a wagon. They are rotted and disfigured beyond recognition. They have been hiding out there this whole time, the rangers say. And now they finally met the end they deserved. Killed by wild animals.

"I don't believe it," some say, but some say they do. Some say the end of the rainbow leads to nothing but a pot of sand and spiders.

CHAPTER 39

IF THE WOMAN on the phone had not gone mad with grief after losing her husband and daughter, if she had lingered to answer Lewis's questions, this is what she would have told him.

The slavers came in the night. Every man who fought back, they killed. Every woman too old and slow to follow their commands, they killed. Every baby, they abandoned or ran through with a knife. Everyone else they kept. They hurled them into wheeled cages—jerry-rigged trailers and truck beds—dragged by horses and oxen. There was a bucket of water, frozen across the top, refreshed daily. And another bucket for waste. And many blankets to share, beneath which they huddled together for warmth.

No matter how they begged or screamed, no matter how desperate and plying their questions, the slavers would not respond except to say, "Hold your tongue. Or we'll cut it out."

They traveled two days across the plains—the snow infrequent here, a mere dusting—with the frozen ground crackling beneath them. They then arrived at a small town of cadaverous houses. Rusted grain elevators reached several stories higher than any other building in town and next to them sat a train station made from red brick with plywood nailed over the windows. Here they came to a creaking stop and the slavers unhitched the oxen and brushed them down and fed them hay while their captives pressed their faces against the bars and asked questions that vanished into vaporous clouds, unanswered.

The slavers retreated inside the train station, and minutes later smoke wormed from its chimney. Only then did the caged men and women notice the trampled snow and grass and the freshly split firewood stacked along one wall of the building with the occasional mouse sprinting in and out of it. The slavers had been here before. But why they chose this building, of all the places they might have taken shelter, their captives could not understand.

Nor did they understand what came a few hours later: the trembling that shook the ground, the banshee wail that split the air. They were already afraid, but now their fear heightened to the borderlands of terror, hysteria. Some of them whimpered and wiped tears from their eyes. Some shook the bars and screamed their throats raw. And some huddled in the corner of the cage and waited for whatever was coming, growing louder by the second.

They could not see it until it was nearly upon them, the black engine car with the pilot grille that looked somewhere between a triangular weapon and a toothy grin. Steam clouded from the smokestack. It continued past them, the crankshaft slowing, the brakes sparking and screeching. It was followed by three coal cars that gave way to a dozen more boxcars and cattle cars and flatcars.

Not all of them knew the word—*train*—but soon they were all uttering it the way some might say *dragon* or *comet*, with a mixture of fear and excitement and otherworldly awe. The train was something out of history, but the train was also now indicative of some strange future, so it made them feel out of time, completely at odds with the present.

There was a long hiss. And a clanking as the metal settled. The slavers exited the station and stood on its porch and watched the train creep to a halt and then set to work.

A metal ramp was drawn from each of the boxcars, and it rattled when the men walked up it. They hauled open the door and a crowd of men and women stood blinking in the gray light. A few tried to escape but were beaten back with the clubs the slavers carried. A joke made, laughter. Buckets of water were replenished. A crate of food was delivered. Waste was collected, along with several stiff, gray-skinned bodies.

And then the slavers came for those in the cages. Some had to be carried or dragged, they were so fearful of the machine. And then, within a few minutes, they were all crowded inside and the door clanged shut behind them. At first, the two groups remained separated, the old and the new, watching each other fearfully in the dim light. Then the train huffed and clanged and lurched and several lost their balance and fell. Their cries broke the silence, and before long everyone was talking, a jibbering flood of words. They hugged just to feel the warmth and support of another.

There was an inch-wide crack along the door, and through it they could see the rolling grasslands punctuated by dead towns. Then the clouds darkened and the snow became ashen and the air tasted acrid and the oil fires bloomed all around them. Every now and then someone would rise to look, but the wind whistled painfully through the crack and their eyes watered over and froze their tears instantly to their cheeks. It was safer to stay in a huddle, beneath the blankets, with their hands tucked into their armpits or crotches for warmth. Some of them could not stop shivering, their teeth chattering along with the wheels clacking the tracks.

Their speed ranged from five to fifteen miles an hour. They stopped often to clear or repair tracks, sometimes progressing only a few miles a day. A man began to cry and would not stop. He had long brown hair but was balding in a way that made his forehead appear tremendous. He was an ugly crier. Not just his appearance, like a red cabbage, but the sound, a phlegmy hiccuping. At first everyone tried to comfort him, but when he would not stop they grew irritated and then furious and struck him with their fists and told him to stop, but this only made him grow louder, wailing now. After six hours, no one could tolerate the sound and several people held him down and strangled him and the long silence that followed was not as comforting as they'd imagined it would be.

It was not long after this that the brakes shrieked and the train shuddered and rattled as it tried to stop too soon, too fast. The cars wobbled when they accordioned their weight. There was a sudden clanking, like the shuffling of a deck of metal cards, followed by an impactful crunch. They did not have time to cry out as they were hurled against the front wall, and then the side wall, and then the ceiling, tumbling one way and then the next, like one massive body that continually broke apart and coalesced, bone and metal, hair and blood. There was no sense of up or down, only a weightlessness interrupted by moments of severe gravity. Gashes opened in the walls. The door rolled open and several people were launched through it. The train was twisting off the tracks, rolling down a snowy berm, throwing up a wave of ice and dirt. The clanging and scraping progress of the crash was so loud it seemed the very world might be rent in half.

And when the last of the metal warped and yawned and settled, when the smoke shushed from the crack in the combustion chamber, when the first of the survivors began to creep from the wreckage, they saw what had caused the crash.

Bison. What appeared to be hundreds of them surrounded the train, but the air was cloaked in sick black fog that made it difficult to see. Shaggy and horned and humpbacked. Their goatees crusted over with ice. Smoke tusking from their snouts. They drifted in and out of sight. A half dozen of them had been struck by the train, their bodies torn apart, strewn across the tracks and berm, limbs that still shivered and red smears that still steamed. The surrounding horde stomped the ground as if impatient to revenge the fallen.

Three slavers crawled from the engine car. One of them bled from both his ears and kept putting his hands over them as if to clap away the ringing there. Another clutched an arm to his chest, an arm whose elbow bent the wrong way. Another seemed unhurt but kept touching himself all over to find the injury that must be hiding somewhere. For a moment they stared dumbly at the train and the captives staggering from it and seemed not to know what to do—but only for a moment.

Their surviving captives were all women, mostly girls. They ganged around the slavers, who held up their hands to defend themselves, but the women pushed through them and knocked their bodies to the ground and beat them with their fists and feet. They did this casually, not rushing, as if they were carrying out some chore. A chest caved. A skull dented.

The girls did not know what to do or where to go, but they felt gifted and cheery and a few of them could not help but hug and cackle nervously before being hushed by the more fearful among them. They checked the wreckage for survivors and found few, one of them a slaver they disposed of with a sharp piece of metal.

By this time the bison had departed and the fog had lifted and in the distance they could see a city, Bismarck.

There are twenty-two of them altogether, mostly teenage girls. They call the mall home. The hundreds of thousands of pounds of steel and concrete feel good. Like armor. As does the charred sky, the icy wind, the oil fires torching the horizon. No one will find them here. No one will harm them ever again. This is what Sasa tells them.

She is one of the oldest among them, certainly the loudest. They look to her as a mother. She is the one who tells them they will live in the mall. She is the one who tells them they must wake from their daze—as they stumble around, trying to get used to the ashen cold, learning how to navigate Bismarck, vacant eyed, hollowed by the loss of their families. She is the one who demands they construct defenses, salvage goods, sew clothes, auger holes in the river to fish, set traps and string bows, feed and arm themselves. In this unfamiliar world, being told what to do is a comfort. They listen to her. They do exactly as she says.

Sasa keeps her graying hair cropped close to the skull in tight curls. She is tall, thin shouldered, long limbed. Her nose and jaw, both strangely pointed, seem like they could come together as a claw. Her skin is the color of old wood and the tip of her nose purpled with frostbite. A long knife hangs at her waist. Her voice is deep and even in standard conversation comes at a shout. Six months ago, she wasn't like this. Six months ago, she saw her husband hanged from a tree and her baby stomped flat. The only way to survive her grief was to harden, shield herself like some crustacean. She has a new family now, these women, and she will defend them from any injury.

Their lives are now a long winter, she says. She will help them endure it.

On this morning, they gather in the atrium, what was once the food court. The floor is cracked tile. The ceiling is a pyramidal skylight cloaked in snow. Three garbage cans crackle and give off waves of heat from the wood burning inside them. Smoke hazes the air. She paces on a short stage and punctuates her sentences with a fist to the palm. Her girls lounge in metal chairs. They nod and mutter their agreement.

Over the past few months they have mentioned the bison. The herd that caused the train wreck, that deposited them at the outskirts of Bismarck. They were saved and they were saved for a reason. The bison were an instrument of God. The world wanted them to live. But to survive, they must be strong. Being strong means making difficult choices. Making difficult choices means hurting back those who mean to hurt them.

"We knew they might come for us. And now they've come for us." She makes a fist that matches her clenched face. "We won't be victims this time."

Her eyes narrow at the sight of the man escorted toward them. He has only one arm, the wrist of it secured to his thigh. He knocks against several chairs, which screech and clatter. He tries to yank away, tries to run, but he trips into a table and falls to the floor. He kicks at the women who huddle around him until they take out their knives and threaten to gut him, and then he goes still and allows them to drag him onstage. He refuses to fall to his knees. Every time they push him down, he struggles to his feet, until Sasa says, "I like this one. He's a fighter. I'm going to give him a fighting chance."

He stares hatefully at her.

Sasa asks for his name and he tells her Jon Colter.

"Why are you smiling, Jon Colter?"

"I'm not," he says. "There's something wrong with my face."

"What's wrong with your face?"

"A wolf bit it." He looks around, as if seeking escape. "Whatever you think we did, we didn't. We didn't do *any*thing to *any* of you."

She raises her eyebrows and tells him with a placid voice, "You killed our parents. You killed our husbands and our sisters and our brothers. You killed our children."

"No." He laughs, but in an ugly way. "No, no, no. I don't know who you are, and I don't care who you are."

"Why else would you come here? A place this cold. A place this sick." When she stands before a crowd, her voice takes on the same rhythms as that of the seer in her village. "Fires burn on the horizon. Ash falls from the sky. No one comes here. This is a place for no one."

"You're here."

"To hide. From you. But you've found us."

He is smiling now. Really smiling, showing all his teeth. "Listen to me. We came from St. Louis. We're passing through—"

She laughs and automatically several of the girls laugh along with her.

The smile dies from half his face. The humor in the situation belongs to her. "What's so funny?"

The fire barrels cough up sparks. Sasa nods and the guard takes a knife to the rope that binds his wrist to his thigh. He flexes his hand and looks around him as if seeking a way out.

She tells him to remove his clothes, and when he refuses, she tells her girls to do it for him, tearing off his boots, his pants, dragging him out of his coat and knifing off his shirt, until he stands naked and trembling before them. His body is a mess of scars that seem to whiten as his skin pinkens in the cold. He would cross his arms if he could, but as is, he can only clutch his middle one-handed.

Sasa studies his body and says, "You look like you've been chewed up and spit out."

"Pretty much."

"Here's how this will work. I'm going to give you a head start of thirty seconds."

"Fuck you."

"And then I'm going to come after you."

"Even if I outrun you, I'll freeze."

"You look like you're accustomed to surviving." She makes a shooing motion with her hands. "One," she says. "Two, three, four, five," and before she can count *six*, he has leapt off the stage, knocked aside tables, padding away.

Sasa continues to count aloud in a calm voice that matches her movements as she steps off the stage and retrieves her bow and quiver and walks down the corridor that leads to the entry.

The women follow her into the half-light of day. The air is bracingly cold. The clouds boil. The horizon burns. An ice storm has coated everything so that it appears as slick as glass. In the distance, almost halfway across the vast open parking lot, Colter races away from them. He keeps his steps short and his good arm outstretched for balance. He falls twice but does not pause, scrambling up to bolt forward again. His buttocks redden. His breath chimneys from his mouth.

She hears a few of her girls say, "Don't" and "Let him go, Sasa," but she doesn't listen. She has to be strong for all of them. She has to expel the hurt stored inside her.

She pinches an arrow from her quiver and notches it into the string and lifts it to her eye and says, "Thirty."

—•—

Simon and Ella expect a visit from Danica, but she doesn't come for several days, and when she does, she is limping, she has a fat lip, and one of her eyes is plum purple, swollen so badly, revealing only a weepy slit. She tries to mask it with makeup. And she tries to walk without wincing.

She comes through the side door, into the kitchen, and Simon pulls out a chair for her at the table and she settles into it with a sigh. She wears a foul, rotten cloak so as not to be recognized, and he helps her out of it and hangs it on a hook and asks her if she needs anything and she says no. When he remains beside her, hovering, leaning into her as if she were a flower, she waves him away.

Ella can't help but feel instantly annoyed. Annoyed by Simon, the way he behaves around her, like a cowed pet. And annoyed by Danica, not for anything she has said or done, just for existing. She cannot help it. She has always found pretty women—the kind who seem to waste time in front of the mirror, who seem to serve no purpose outside of lounging and preening—to be trifling, pathetic, even foul, like dead songbirds with maggots nesting inside their bright breasts. But when Danica rubs her knee, in obvious pain, Ella grudgingly allows her annoyance to give way to concern and asks, "What's happened?"

"He's angry. That's what happened."

"I'm sorry."

"I'm not. I'm glad he's angry. He's angry because he's worried." Her hand rises from her knee to her thigh, where she keeps her dagger beneath her dress. She fingers it and her mouth twitches with a smile. She says she knows what they're wondering. They're wondering, if she hates her husband so much, why not poison him? That is the woman's way, isn't it? Poison. She has considered it. Of course she has considered it. These days, he has grown more and more paranoid, and before he would sip his wine, before he would knife into a steak, he made his chef or server—or sometimes even Danica—taste everything.

Every *s* she utters takes a little too long to get out of her mouth, so that her sentences sound like a spitting fuse. Ella can't tell if it's the swollen lip or some pain-relieving opiate that causes this.

Besides, Danica says, poisoning him, killing him, would accomplish little beyond her temporary satisfaction. She might get away with it or she might get caught. And then? Someone else would take his place of power and similarly abuse it.

Ella cannot help but wonder about her, cannot help but feel this woman is more than she appears. There is something far more sub-stantial and dangerous about her. She is like the blade she carries. A blade is rigid and cold and sharp. A blade is a decoration. A blade is a tool. A blade is a threat.

In a cold voice, carefully enunciating each word, Danica tells them her reason for coming now: she has a plan—and the plan concerns them, and the plan could kill them, if they aren't careful. But if it works, and it just might, then an uprising will come that the deputies will not be able to quell.

"Go ahead, then. What is it?"

"My dear husband," she says, "has decided to throw a ball."

"Who's he going to throw it at?" Simon says.

Ella says, "She means a party, you idiot."

"A party," Danica says. "A costume party no less. With cheeses and meats and sweet liquors and desserts and everything else one might consider far too extravagant for these thin times. And he plans to invite everyone who matters, who has any influence. Just as he believes in terrorizing those who defy him, he believes in spoiling those who would support him." She brings a hand to the corner of her swelled eye. "If there was a time for us to do some-thing, it would be then, wouldn't you agree?"

The first arrow misses, sailing to the left of Colter and embedding itself in the ice. The second arrow, too, skitters past him. The third arrow might have struck its mark if not for Clark.

The crowd of girls did not notice her when they charged out of the mall. Nor did they notice the gone guard, no longer at her post. They were too intent on the naked figure sliding jerkily across the ice-scalloped parking lot.

So when the woman named Sasa falls forward with an arrow nested in the back of her skull, when they spin around to see Clark standing there with another arrow notched, they can only stare dumbly. They are pale and thin and quivering and bent backed.

No longer a mob, just a bunch of lost little girls. Then one of them asks, in the smallest of voices, "What have you done?"

Two of the girls hug each other. One of them—the only old woman among them—whispers into a dead phone. The others look around as if to wait for a command that never comes.

"Anyone else want any trouble?"

The girls shake their heads or study the ground, no threat to her. She lowers her bow and calls out for Colter, tells him to come back.

Then she settles her eyes on the girls and asks them where the rest of her friends are and they point to the mall and she says, "Show me."

CHAPTER 40

FOR DECADES NOW, in the Sanctuary's Fourth Ward, you didn't want to walk around at night unless you were looking for trouble. Something to snort, someone to fuck or fight. Every morning, the first bell rang and the sun chased away the night and revealed the bodies. The bodies of those beaten and stabbed and the bodies of those who choked on their own puke and the bodies of those who decided enough was enough and dove out a window or fell on a knife. In the heat, they bloated and festered, attracted rats and vultures, spread disease. So the Sanctuary authorized a cleanup team. The gatherers, they were called, mostly teenagers without a trade looking for some coin. When she was thirteen years old, Clark joined them. Mornings, a donkey pulled a cart and she hauled the bodies into it, with an apron and elbow-length gloves and a bandana shielding her nose and mouth. She came to associate this color—the ashen color of early morning—with grief. Grief was a color.

And that is the color of this place, North Dakota, and that is the color of her current state of mind.

By the time Lewis finds her, she is already drunk. They have given her what she asked for—a drink, a real drink—a jar of moonshine derived from tree bark. She gulps from it, her thirst returned. This is on the roof of the mall, where her legs dangle over the edge, her body hunched over in the shape of a hook.

Lewis approaches and touches her gently on the back. "I was worried about you."

"Was?"

"Am."

"Yeah? You should worry about yourself." She stiffens and his hand falls off her.

"York?" he says.

She shakes her head and drinks and roughs a sleeve across her mouth.

For a long minute they stare off at the ice-humped city and the furnace glow of the oil fires beyond it. She drinks again from the jar. Her eyes waver in and out of focus. "Hey, have you ever noticed something?" She licks her lips as if her mouth has gone too dry for words. "Have you ever noticed how my head is different shaped? How one side of my face looks different than the other?"

"No."

"It's true. Look." She turns her head one way, then the other, arranging her face into a scowl. Her breath is sour. "See?"

"No."

"It's true. You've just got to look closer. One side is kind of pretty. You're not supposed to say that about yourself, but I'll say it. Okay? I'll say it. I'm pretty. But not the other side! The other side, if you look at it on its own, is ugly." She slaps a hand to her face in order to shade the one side of it. Maybe he can see it now. The drooping cheek. A broader ridge of forehead. The slight bulge of the eye, a little more lid around it. "I'm like two different people."

The wind gusts and carries bits of ice in it. She wobbles on her perch before catching her balance, spilling some of her drink.

"You should come down from there."

"Didn't I say to worry about yourself?"

She looks at him with her red-rimmed eyes. In these long wordless seconds, during which time they stare painfully at each other, he wants to tell her how sorry he is about her brother. He doesn't usually say things like that—*sorry* or *thank you* or *please* or any common pleasantry; it just doesn't occur to him—but he knows he ought to. *Sorry* might be the medicine she needs. He wants to tell her how much he admires her fearlessness and impulsiveness, how he has learned from her, grown into a better man by her example. He wants to tell her he not only worried about her last night—he missed her, too, as if he were a lizard dragged from the sun, so that he felt enervated without her around, sour and cold-blooded. He wants to tell her he *needs* her. They all do. He gathers his breath, but before he can blow out the words, she says, "I'm a killer."

"You—"

"I killed that woman outside. I killed my own brother. I killed Reed. I killed them all. I might kill you next, who knows? This was my idea, coming here. It was a stupid, deadly idea. And we're all worse off for it."

"Stop it. Don't be so self-pitying. It doesn't become you."

"Do you know what I feel like right now?" Her voice comes sliding out of her like sharpened steel. "I feel like eating you."

"Clark—"

"I feel like eating the whole world. Shoving all the metal and concrete and wood and bone and meat into my mouth until there is nothing left."

"You need to rest. You'll feel better once you rest."

"I killed her, Lewis."

"You did what you had to do. She was going to kill Colter."

"I don't mean her."

It takes him a moment to process this. "Then who?"

"Her."

"Her who?"

"Your *mother*, Lewis. I killed her. So that you would come with us."

The world seems to dim. The sky seems to sag. The wind rises and slaps his face. He waits for the anger to come—he knows it is there, inside him, waiting to catch flame—but for the moment there is only a sick feeling, a green-tinged sadness. He opens his mouth, but no words will come.

"Go away, Lewis. Before I hurt you more than I already have."

When he makes no move to leave, she says, "Go!" in what sounds like a half howl.

Now Lewis is running, pounding along as fast as he can, sliding, occasionally falling, but always scrambling to his feet, always moving, away from the world he thought he knew and into the world he does not. Snow kicks up beneath his heels. Though the air is cold, his throat burns with exertion. The mall is behind him, like a great tomb, and he races away from it. He can feel the rage growing, growing, so that his inside feels bigger than his outside. And he is so hot, not just his breathing now, but his head, his skin, the core of him furnaced. He could tear off his clothes, eat snow.

With this comes that familiar feeling—of the sky opening up to watch him. He can sense it homing in on his dodging figure, and he knows he cannot escape it. Above him the clouds begin to twirl, as if spun with a spoon, and he hears the kind of crackling sound that comes from thick wool socks sliding across a rug.

The parking lot reaches on endlessly. No matter how furiously he pumps his legs, the edge of it seems to grow no closer. He sees the vapor of his breath. He sees the ground, thickly floored with ice. He sees the flicker of light gathering in the sky, where the clouds darken and churn and foment, as the anger spills out of him and takes hold of the world.

The air around him seems to sparkle. He listens for thunder but hears only the panicked gusting of his breath. He tries to run faster, but the lightning stops him midstride. It shoots from the sky and spears him, jags through his body like a second spine. Several more bolts join the first, like so many whips lashing at him, their barbs caught in his skin, filling him with painful light.

He wakes naked. His clothes are ashes curled away by the wind. His hair has scorched and brittled, and when he runs his hand across his belly, his eyebrow, his head, it crisps away. He is purely skin, his body as white and rigid as alabaster.

He lies on his back, staring up at a night sky that looks like holes punched through black cloth, the biggest of them the moon. The moon! How he has missed it, as shadowed and pale as a favorite grandfather's face. For a long time this is all he sees, his vision absorbed by the sky, so that he might as well be floating through space.

There is no sound except a distant ring, like the single undying chime of a silver bell. He sits upright and takes in a world he recognizes, but not quite. Here is the parking lot, but it is crowded with cars. Here is the mall, but it is glowing with light. A woman in a red coat approaches, carrying shopping bags weighted with clothes. A man carries a girl on his shoulders. A couple walk arm in arm, laughing at a joke he cannot hear. The woman pauses to cough, and the cough overwhelms her, bending her over and spasming her body, and the man rubs her back to comfort her.

The headlights on a truck flare beside him—and he stands in a hurry, spotlighted.

The truck does not seem to see him, rolling from its spot, and he darts out of the way. He calls out to the woman in the red coat, but she does not look his way, digging into her purse and removing a silvery flash of keys. He grabs her then, presses his thumb deeply into the basin of her elbow, and though she frowns, she does not pause. He releases her as she pulls away.

All around him, he now notices, lights glow, a galaxy of light. Stoplights, streetlamps, headlights, billboards, signage over stores and the windows beneath them. The starlit sky above cannot compare.

Lewis wonders if he is caught in a dream, even as he knows he is not. He is perfectly awake and cannot escape or manipulate what surrounds him, slash a hand through it and make it ripple like water. Yet like a dream, he goes along with whatever presents itself, in this case, a black tunnel toward the edge of the parking lot, the only break he can find in this weird-familiar world. A tunnel of trees, all the trunks leaning inward, arched and raftered with branches silvered with snow.

He moves through its darkness and the darkness moves through him. It is comforting. Familiar. Deep. Timeless. He walks the passage, not cold, not at all, despite his bare feet padding the frosted ground. The sound grows louder, more painful, the farther he travels. Instead of a bell it is now a knife in his ear. It warps and solidifies into a word, his name. A voice calls for him. Burr's. He does not want to go forward but feels pulled there as if down an inhaling throat. A branch scratches his arm. Shadows shift among the trees, pacing him.

At the end of the tunnel a light awaits him—a light that brightens and blackens, brightens and blackens, like a great eye opening and closing. He fears the eye. It makes his breath come faster and yet he can never seem to get enough, as if his chest is leaking, pierced.

And then he is there, at the end, with the eye before him, burning from the top of a lighthouse with the great gray span of the ocean frothing and booming beyond it.

Part IV

Whilst I viewed those mountains, I felt a secret pleasure in finding myself so near the head of the—heretofore conceived—boundless Missouri. But when I reflected on the difficulties which this snowy barrier would most probably throw in my way to the Pacific Ocean, and the sufferings and hardships of myself and the party in them, it in some measure counterbalanced the joy I had felt in the first moments in which I gazed on them. But, as I have always held it little short of criminality to anticipate evils, I will allow it to be a good, comfortable road until I am compelled to believe otherwise.

—*The Journals of Lewis and Clark*

CHAPTER 41

TWO WOMEN. Sisters. The Field sisters. Old enough to thread their hair with gray, but how old exactly, they don't know. They don't keep a calendar. They keep their hair short, a shaggy cut. Their faces and shoulders are broad. One of them has a mole on her upper lip, and the other doesn't, and one of them stands six feet tall, the other a little less, but otherwise they could be the same person. Maybe this is why they don't talk very often. What use are words when you can communicate with a narrow-eyed glance, a pointed finger, a pat on the back.

They go still when asleep. Otherwise, they move quickly and efficiently, when digging clams, when robbing birds' nests of eggs, when cooking and eating, when mending clothes, when scavenging houses and stores. Right now, in a half-moon bay walled in by cliffs, one of them splits logs with a maul while the other digs a wide, shallow crater in the sand. The ax chucks the wood that is piled into the crater and then set aflame. When it burns, they look to the sky, worried who might see the smoke, comforted by the long-hanging clouds. They stir the fire with a length of rebar, then rake it down to coals and let it cool and collect the charcoal.

They already have the rest of what they need. First the potassium nitrate, deposits of bat guano they scraped from caves and attics. They soaked the gray mud of it in water for a day and then collected the crystals. And then the sulfur they salvaged from the cobwebbed shell of an ag store.

They merge and screen and granulate the ingredients and fill up ten ten-gallon drums that weigh several hundred pounds each. The sisters manage to roll them and heft them into the back of a pickup truck that has been welded and patched with sheets of metal so many times that it appears like many vehicles clapped together. The bed sags with the weight. The tires' tubes are full of salt water. The engine runs poorly but runs all the same, rebuilt to process biodiesel, the algae the sisters harvest. The key cranks and the engine bellows and lopes and settles into a steady chug punctuated by the occasional rattling pop.

They keep it in first gear. The speedometer is broken, but their speed couldn't be more than five miles per hour. The pickup breaks down twice on the way to Youngs Bay, and they spend an hour, then another hour, fixing it. One of them hunches over the engine block while the other surveys the road in either direction with a rifle ready.

The road is more an impression than a reality. A place where trees aren't. The asphalt has ground down to gravel. They drive around the occasional fallen limb and rockslide, but mostly the way is clear.

The Warrenton-Astoria Highway reaches across the bay. It is passable but crumbling in sections, the steel caging within visible like bones peeking out of a melting snowdrift. The sisters park and unload the drums and roll them down the bridge and situate them at ten-foot intervals. They are made from a thick plastic that has aged gray. This matches the color of the bridge, camouflages the barrels, makes them appear like short pillars. Their fuses are made from fabric, glue, and oxidizing agents decanted from old weed killer. The sisters run a long web of them that wind together into one thick rope.

They drive the pickup back down the road and next to a tumbledown building and throw clumps of moss on it along with a few sticks. Then they hike back to the bay wearing backpacks and carrying rifles. They lead the thick coil of fuse into the woods and park themselves on a log with a clear view of the bridge. They unzip their backpacks and withdraw binoculars and oil and rags and books and dried fish and berries and nuts and canteens of water. They eat. They wait.

Across the bay, the city of Astoria. A vast hive. Some fifty thousand live there. Chimney smoke dirties the air. If it was night, its hills would glow with lamplight.

Six hours pass. Seagulls screech. Waves lap. Wind hushes. The rain comes steadily here, rarely pausing for more than an hour. And the ocean breathes its salt into the air. Even the buttons on their jackets and jeans rust. So they take good care of their rifles, breaking them apart now to wipe down everything, the receiver, the barrel, the magazine, and then they dampen a rag with oil and wipe the parts down again and fit it all back together. They reload. They lever a round. They set the safety. They lay the rifles beside them in easy reach.

They read in shifts, one of them turning pages while the other peers through binoculars. Then, from across the bay, a caravan starts across the bridge. It is a long train of cows harnessed to empty wheeled cages. Metal clanks. Hooves clop. Leather and rope creak. Their approach will take a good five minutes.

The sisters have paced out the fuse and calculated how quickly it will burn down. One of the sisters holds up a hand, as if to say, *Steady, steady, steady*, while the other readies her matches. Then the hand drops, chopping the air. One match sparks and dies in the wind. Another splinters in half. The third one sputters out against the fuse. The fourth catches.

A long, spitting snake works its way toward the bridge, sizzling its way through underbrush, around trees, across gravel, splitting up and following the ten threads, rising into the barrels. The caravan is nearly upon them and the sisters can see the man at the front of the column standing up in his carriage, pulling back on his reins. But it is too late.

The sisters see the explosion before they hear it. An overlapping series of bright orange flashes surrounded by black roiling smoke run through with chunks of concrete and animal. The bridge drops and rises and expands all at once. The sound thumps the sisters, makes the trees around them shake and drop their leaves. The water in the bay dimples with the debris hailing down.

The sisters remove their hands from their ears. They do not

smile or raise their fists in celebration. They simply watch with composed but satisfied expressions as a burning man crawls a few paces and goes still, as smoke stains the air, as a forty-foot section of the bridge collapses into the bay and sends a wave rolling to the shore.

Then they collect their things and zip their backpacks and shoulder their rifles and hold hands when they hike back to their pickup.

CHAPTER 42

LEWIS MARCHES steadily west through a world laced and spired with ice. The wind never stops and the snow lashes his eyes and scrapes them red. He lost his hair to the lightning. It grew back as white and bristled as the hoarfrost along the riverbanks.

When he first left the Sanctuary, he wondered more than once what the hell he was doing. He buried that question long ago, but it has been replaced by another. How the hell is he going to do it? If he is to survive, if he is to traverse this unforgiving place and avoid threats human and animal and elemental, if he is to arrive in a wondrous American landscape, a new Eden, he will be more than a long way geographically from his old self in St. Louis. He will be a new person entirely. This drives him through the snow. The green promise of a better place, the whispered promise of a better self in the voice of Aran Burr.

Lewis wishes he could simply sweep a hand and knock a hundred pounds of snow this way, another hundred pounds that way, as if he were the wind itself. But whatever powers he possesses are limited, accidental, uncontrolled, as if he were a toddler finding his legs or forming his mouth around a word for the first time. He does not understand what he can do, only yearn and puzzle over whatever happy accidents he produces.

Colter and Gawea hike beside him. They wear snowshoes. Their pants stiffen and fringe white and beneath them their legs feel separate, leaden and thudding with every step, so that sometimes they feel they are clopping along on their hipbones. They do not complain. They do not speak at all.

As far as he can remember, the last time he said anything might have been back in Bismarck, when he told the doctor to rest, and once rested, to watch after Clark. "She's not well. She's going to need you."

He kneeled next to the doctor's cot. She had lost a lot of blood, grown anemic. But she had stubbornly risen back to health, just as Lewis had risen from the smoldering crater in the parking lot, weakened but determined. The silver hair spiraled around her head like roots without purchase. She fumbled for his hand and found it and squeezed it. Her voice came out as if through a filter of sand. "I wasn't so sure before, but I'm certain of it now. You're the best of men."

"Most would call me horrible, I think."

"It's the world that's horrible. But you'll finish what we started?"

"Yes."

She ran a thumb along the ridgeline of his knuckles as if imagining the landscape he must yet navigate. "You're carrying everyone's dreams with you."

Lewis was never one to smile, but he smiled for her then. "We'll see each other down the trail."

"We will indeed."

That seems so long ago, what must be weeks, though he can't be sure, having lost track of time. That is easy to do when everything seems the same. The sky is gray ceilinged, absent of sun and moon and stars, lit by the oil fires that make the air taste like ashes, that make him cough up black slugs every morning.

Sometimes, when he is trudging along, he believes he sees others around him. He believes he is walking with the dead. His mother wisps in and out of sight. Reed coughs up bullets. His horse—rotted down entirely to bone—gallops along with a clatter. A decapitated York juggles three of his heads. And not just them, but others, too, the shades of people driving roads and walking sidewalks and hanging laundry, as if history were a nightmare he can't escape. Their footsteps match his, so that he feels like he is traveling with them, for all of them.

This is not the first time this reach of country has been void of human life. Everything rises and falls, everything cycles, and maybe he will play some small role in the next rotation. He hopes so. How else can he justify pressing on except by imagining himself a seed in the wind, a hero in a song?

They would be lost if not for the river, which grows narrower by the day as they approach its headwaters. Now and then something distinguishes the featureless landscape. A windbreak of trees next to a farm. A cluster of bushes or bunches of wild grass that—frosted with ice—look like white antlers breaking from the ground. A town where they find a house to hunker down, escape the wind.

It is a squat brick home, the gutters wearing glassy fangs of ice. Gawea stomps on a wooden chair to make kindling. Colter shudders with the cold that possesses him. His skin flares pink with white spots. His fingers might be made of wood, stiff and curled, and he shoves them in his armpit to heat.

There was a time when Lewis always felt cold. But now, even when surrounded by snow, he feels warm, as if he carries a torch inside him. He can start a fire with his hands. He grips the wood until it combusts. The process feels a little like blowing out a hard breath until your chest hitches and your lungs have nearly collapsed. This is the only time he feels chilled, when the energy he expels leaves him temporarily empty, husked. He owns fire but fire owns him. They share a dangerous dominion.

Colter holds out his hand to the fire, trying to warm it, and then just as quickly uses it to shield his face as a dark cluster of bats escapes the chimney and fills the room in a twittering rush before breaking apart, escaping to the far corners of the house.

Gawea kicks apart another chair and adds it to the fire, then drags in some wood from outside and adds it, too, and before long the chimney is whistling from the draw. Several bricks fall on the flames and knock embers on the floor. The blankets crack like glass when Colter stomps on them and lays them by the fire to thaw, and they give off wisps of vapor.

"Where are we again?" Colter says.

"Still in North Dakota," Gawea says.

"I wouldn't wish North Dakota on anyone."

In the kitchen Lewis digs through the cupboards and pulls out a dried bundle of noodles, as brittle as straw. He fills a pot with snow to melt. He looks out the window and sees, still hanging from a pole, the tatters of an American flag, nothing but barely colored threads.

At night they are a small cave of light in a never-ending darkness. That is when the noises begin. In uneven waves, the wind howls and moans and mutters, the nightmare sounds of a zoo on fire. Gawea sleeps without any seeming trouble, but Colter wraps a blanket around his head to muffle the sound. Lewis tries to sleep but cannot. The night shrieks. It pleads and threatens and whines.

When he does dream, he dreams of terror. Clark waits for him outside, her face transformed into a wolf's. A lighthouse flares and profiles the figure of Burr standing before it. A lump swells painfully along Lewis's rib cage. He lances it open and finds an eyeball blinking redly at him.

He is awake long before dawn. He watches the fires pluming out in the darkness. He misses the stars he hasn't seen in such a long time. They remain hidden—along with the moon, the sun—behind the suffocating mantle of clouds. He thinks of them now, thinks about how, just out of sight, all that light is streaming down, light that has traveled millions of years, billions of miles—for what? For nothing, all that time and distance sponged away. He worries that is what is happening to them, to the group of people that set out from the Sanctuary, all the energy that made them press across what felt like an interminable nothing, now dissipating, in danger of being lost altogether.

He kneels by the fireplace and unsleeves his journal from the oilcloth that surrounds it. It feels warm in his hands, as if blood courses through it. He fingers through its pages, with a bird-wing flutter. Here is a song York sang around a campfire. Here is a mixture of several herbs the doctor told him would heal an infection.

Here is a sketch of the river alleying through the woods. And another of a mutated squirrel. And another of an unusually large and spotted egg, something waiting to be born.

And another of Clark atop her horse, profiled against the sun. He has left her behind, but in a way he feels he still follows her. He closes the journal with a sense of loss and longing.

They travel farther and farther still, into eastern Montana, where the oil fires cease and the snow thins and gives way to browned grass and sagebrush. In the distance rises the massive spine of the mountains. Their footsteps cut across the grass, the frozen ground, with a shredding sound.

"What were you thinking, Colter?" Lewis says.

"You mean when I was running naked across that field of ice from a group of madwomen who wanted to stick me full of arrows?"

"I actually meant why did you come with me?"

"What was the alternative? Stay behind in the iciest asshole of the world? Besides, you're such good company. I don't know what I'd do without you."

Lewis stops. "Really. I want to know."

"Oh, we're getting all shitty and serious, are we?" Colter pulls down his scarf and reveals his scarred face. He studies Lewis a long time before saying, "I said before, I thought of your father as if he were my own father. I meant that. I guess that makes you a kind of brother. However you want to think about it, we're in common cause. We're both serving something bigger. That's what I used to think about the Sanctuary. That's what I think now. You feel the same, don't you?"

"I do." Lewis trudges forward again and Colter matches his pace. "I wouldn't be able to do it without you."

"Not going to argue with you on that one."

They are so thin the veins stand out from their skin like wires. They kill pheasant, grouse, possum, rabbits, rats, sheep, coyote, deer, antelope, some mutated and some with cancers blooming like mushrooms inside them. Though Lewis has no appetite, every nerve in his body frayed by exhaustion, he forces himself to eat.

Colter believes they are being followed. It is hard to tell, with the wind searing and his eyes welling with tears and blown snow obscuring the air. In a bare passage of land, nothing but bunchgrass, they walk for several miles, making sure there is nothing around they might mistake for a person, and then they spin around. Nothing. "I swear," Colter says. "The hair on the back of my neck swears."

Lewis knows whom it is Colter senses, the same man he feels tugging them forward. The man in white. Aran Burr. In Lewis's dreams, he dropped a stone and the stone fell. And then the stone rose. The stone flew from the ground and snapped into his palm, caged by his fingers, as if he possessed his own gravity. That is how Burr feels to Lewis: gravitational. There was a time in his life when he saw his father everywhere—on a stage before a crowd of people, in a painting in a hallway, at the head of a long table—and even when he didn't see him, he thought of him, anticipating his command or disapproval, *straighten your posture* this and *get your head out of a book* that. And now, no matter how hard he tries, he cannot remember his father's face. It has been replaced by Burr's. He sees him in the snow and in the clouds and in any mirrored surface. Burr visits him when he sleeps. He holds out a hand, beckoning him, and Lewis feels a pull—he feels as the stone must.

"We're being watched," Lewis says. "But there's no one there."

Every day he asks Gawea to tell him more—about Oregon, about Burr—but she no longer wishes to talk. "Just wait and see," she says. Or "It won't be long now." Or sometimes she says nothing at all.

He tries not to feel bothered by this. York's death did something to her. She has regressed, grown guarded and reserved again, as if contained by her own personal wall, not wanting to let anyone get close. Sometimes her eyes look like black puddles that with a blink will go streaming down her cheeks. He hopes time will heal her, bring back the girl they were just getting to know.

CHAPTER 43

SLADE IS TIRED of clearing paths through the whores and beggars on the streets, shoving aside those bone-thin and swollen-bellied and bent-kneed rabble who ask him for money, for food, for water, for a fuck that might come with a favor. He is tired of people speaking to him with voices that range only between pleading and accusatory. He is tired of the blinding sun. He is tired.

So he goes where no one can bother him, to his windowless basement room, where the shadows are as deep and cooling as water. Here he keeps company with his dummies. He walks among them, the mannequins with cracked faces and glued-on hair and torn fingernails and the patchwork ensemble he gathered gradually for all of them. One was Jillian, a baker's daughter, whose hair smelled like flour and whose breasts reminded him of mounds of dough. Another was Becca, the sister of one of his deputies, who liked to whistle when she walked, like a little bird beckoning him. And Manda and Ankeny. And now Ella—so fierce—his favorite so far.

His ears still buzz with the noise of the city—his mind still aches with the brightness of the day—but if he closes his eyes and stands as still as his dummies and breathes deeply through his mouth, he feels like he is drinking in peace, filling himself with a cool, blue calm.

Every day, he enlists more deputies. But he has no illusions about their loyalty. They are devoted only to the food and water that come with the job. And though a man with a weapon and a uniform is worth five without, his police force is outnumbered many times over. The Sanctuary could be overtaken, if only people weren't so afraid. He must keep them that way, as a manager and profiteer of terror.

The other day, when he was walking without an escort through the Fourth Ward—a collection of deteriorating buildings full of cutthroats, gamblers, whores—someone hurled a bag of filth at him. It exploded against his chest and then plopped to the ground. He stood there a moment, incredulously wiping his hands through the oozing smear, before looking around and noticing the streets crammed with crook-mouthed, thin-eyed people who studied him with a collective ferocity that made him feel, for the first time in his life, small. He hurried away, knowing that they might be seconds away from swarming him. For all his administration, Thomas has relied on the enemy beyond the walls, but he must worry now about the enemy within them.

If Thomas knew about Ella, she would be dead. And if Ella were anyone else, Slade would have killed her himself. But so many months ago, when he first questioned her in the museum, he immediately noted her as a favorite, like a special passage earmarked in a book. It was a feeling he knew well—the same spark of recognition he experienced around Jillian and Becca and Manda and Ankeny. His gallery of favorites.

He can harm her. He can harm anyone. He has the power to accuse strangers, beat them senseless, cuff them and noose them, with nothing in the way of consequence except more hatred directed his way. He is omnipotent. And omnipotence comes with boredom. That is why the Greek gods used to assume human form. To play with stakes that at least felt more real. He likes to play. He likes reducing himself to a kind of suitor.

Of course she knew something about Lewis departing the Sanctuary. Of course he would communicate with her by owl. Of course she was responsible for the rabble-rousing graffiti. That was one of the reasons she was a favorite. Because she wasn't a common fool like so many others, but a worthy adversary, a mind sprung with claws. Which made it his job to tame her, cow her.

He follows her sometimes. Through the sun-soaked streets, the cluttered aisles of the bazaar, not because he believes he will learn anything professionally valuable, but simply to make a study of her. He likes the way she marches instead of walks, always square shouldered. He likes the way she bargains with people—pointing a finger and setting her mouth—and the way she touches whatever interests her—a carved door, an overripe melon, a one-armed doll—lets her finger linger as if to taste.

This morning, after she collected her daily ration of water, he followed her back to the museum, trailing her like a shadow. She sensed him only when she keyed open her door, and by then it was too late. She turned in time to see him shove her inside.

Her jug fell and the cap spun off and the water *glug-glug-glugged* across the floor, and for a moment that was the only sound besides their breathing as he rammed her up against the wall with a palm cupping her shoulder, a thumb horning her clavicle.

Then he said, in a calm, quiet voice that hardly paused between words, "You stupid girl. You stupid, stupid girl. You think I don't know about what you've been up to. You think you can go on pretending you're not a part of what's happening. Let me tell you something. Let me give you a little lesson. Some believe love is the most powerful of all emotions. But that's just a nice lie people tell themselves. Terror wins. Terror beats love any day. No emotion can control a crowd, can imprint itself so fully onto the human mind. You run this museum, so you know all about this, don't you? You know about how this country—if you can call it that, a country—has been held hostage by terrorism? The bombing of Pearl Harbor, the assassination of JFK, the terrorist attacks of September eleventh. Yes, I know a thing or two. I'm not as mindless as some people think. Those stories—of long ago and far away—might not seem real. But they happened. And when they happened, they owned everyone. They paralyzed everyone. By the millions. That's what terror can do. That's what I can do. To you. And to this city."

He let her go then and stepped back and the last of her water hiccuped from the jug.

She rubbed her chest where his arm had been. "You're a no-good bully. And you're wrong."

He laughed then. He couldn't help himself. He outweighed her by more than a hundred pounds. He could crush her like a cock-roach. But she would not flinch. She had such fight to her. "Oh, do tell. How am I wrong?"

"It's like this. Terror might make someone kill, but love will make someone die. People die for love. They would give up any-thing for love, even their life. And don't you see, that's a denial of the most basic of all human instincts: survival."

Her eyes wander away from his and seem to zero in on some-thing, but when he turns, there is only an empty doorway. "What were you looking at?"

"Get out of here," she says. "Leave me alone." She tries to push past him. He slaps her and forces her to the floor with an elbow to the throat, and she burbles like a toad at the pressure. "No," she says, but seems again to be looking behind him. "Don't!"

From his pocket he removes a pair of pliers. He fingers open her mouth and shoves the pliers inside and says, "Steady now." With a wrenching crack he removes one of her molars.

He holds up the red-rooted tooth as he departs her. "That's for what you wrote on the wall and all the trouble it's caused me. The next time you do something stupid, I'll come back for the rest of you."

Now, in the basement, in the dark, he holds the molar in his palm. He pops it in his mouth and sucks on it and tongues its grooves and tastes her sour blood. Then he spits it out and dries it on his shirt and retrieves a pot of glue and patiently holds it to the mouth of her dummy as if suffocating it. When he lets his hand fall, the tooth remains, jeweled to the face of the thing.

CHAPTER 44

THE MOUNTAINS grow nearer, gradually dominating the horizon, their peaks cutting into the clouds. In their foothills the snow begins again, whiter now than before. They rest in Billings for several days, and again in Bozeman. Here the downtown is surrounded by a defensive perimeter made from logs with sharpened points. It has been burned and breached. Blackened wood and blackened bones rise out of the snow. The smell of smoke still lingers in the air. The people here have been dead weeks, maybe months.

"Who did this?" Lewis says. He kneels beside a skull, small enough to fit into his hand, a child's. "What happened here?"

"Are you sure we should be going this way?" Colter says.

Gawea shakes her head—maybe she doesn't know or maybe she doesn't care or maybe she doesn't want to tell.

Not so long ago Lewis believed in the end of the rainbow. A shire. An emerald city. Elysian fields. What his childhood storybooks promised. He believed, back when they first set out from the Sanctuary, that something arcadian awaited them. Not anymore. Not now. Not when he sees the bone-riddled ruins of Bozeman. It is not only the landscape that disappoints. It is humankind. Inside and outside the wall, humans remain the same, capable of wonderful things, yes, but more often excelling in ruin. And Burr is human.

He cups a handful of snow over the skull and stands and wipes his hands off. "Is there something you need to tell me, Gawea?"

"No," she says and keeps her head down and continues hiking forward.

At the edge of town they enter a pole shed with rust trails weeping from every bolt. Inside they find a sign, BOZEMAN FOUNDRY, hanging above a desk with a pile of paper squared on it. Lewis picks up a work order for two dozen horseshoes, a sharpened saw, a repaired scythe. There is some dust but not a lot that he runs a finger through. This was a working site, a working community, home to however many thousands.

Gawea shrugs off her pack and lies on the floor and shoves her fists against her eyes. Colter says, "You all right?" and when she doesn't respond, he begins opening and closing drawers, closets, cupboards, not knowing what he might find, something of use, while Lewis walks through the entry office and into the cavernous work space. His boots crunch over metal shavings. Hammers and clamps and files hang from the wall. He wanders past forges, stacks of casings and molds, an induction furnace and an electric arc furnace, a small hill of firewood. The air is dirty with the scorched-nut smell of molten metal. His foot clatters a ladle lying on the floor and the noise brings Colter out of the office.

He's gnawing on something and holds out a handful of it. "Found a stash of jerky. Not bad."

Lewis tours the equipment and then settles his gaze on Colter. "What?"

"I'm sorry I doubted you."

"Only a fool wouldn't have doubted me."

"I want to do something for you."

They spend the rest of the day burning wood, pumping bellows, stirring coals, scraping designs into sand castings. They melt scrap metals and refine the alloy and pour it into the molds and let it cool before tumbling the component from it. They sweat. Their skin blackens with soot. They wield tongs and sledgehammers and scythe hammers and embossing hammers that chirp against the heated metal set upon the bullhorn anvil. Red and yellow sparks fall around their feet. They grind and sand and polish. They fit together hinges, tighten bolts, oil gears, and when they finally finish, Colter slides the stump of his arm into the prosthetic and Lewis tightens the leather straps around his shoulders and buckles them.

In the place of bones there are fitted pipes, and in the place of a hand, three barbed fingers that open into a claw and close into a fist. He experiments with it, bending his elbow, extending his arm for a slash.

"They used to call me the Black Fist, you know?"

"I know." Lewis crumples onto a stool and wipes the soot from his face with a rag. "What do you think?"

Colter bends over and picks up a cinder block. His claw crushes it and a spray of gray gravel dusts the air and dirties the floor. "I think it will do quite nicely."

———

Gawea presses her fists against her eyes and pushes until colors violet and rose red and dandelion yellow explode against the lids. They remind her of flowers, fields of flowers that she might dive into, roll around in, tangled in their stalks, bombed by their perfume. It's so much easier to dream in color than to open her eyes to the gray nothing of the world.

She should have known better. She shouldn't have let herself get close to them. But York wouldn't leave her alone, his face always dodging into her field of vision, his hands always touching her on the shoulder, the waist, the cheek. That day she swiped the trout from his plate and shoved it in her mouth was only the beginning of the tastes shared between them. Now he is gone, just like her parents, like her *oma*, everyone close to her punished and then killed, so that living feels like a rehearsal for dying. She was just so lonely and felt antidoted by his company, warmed by his touch.

She was sent to retrieve Lewis. Not Clark, not Reed, and not the doctor and not Colter. Not York. Just Lewis. But she had no choice. They came as a group. She planned to deliver Lewis, as promised, and then Burr would give her what she requested. Whatever happened to the rest of them, she did not care. Initially, if they got in her way, she might have killed them herself.

They were irrelevant to her. That's what she told herself. That's why she maintained such a cool distance, until she couldn't anymore. They became relevant to her, more than names, but people, friends.

The hard part was supposed to be the journey. The unforgiving temperatures, the cruel landscape, the scarcity of food and water. But it is the mental assault that has been unendurable. Maybe this mission means nothing. On the one side, Burr is a false prophet. On the other side, Lewis strives for irrelevance. There is no human endeavor. No matter how much people clung to family, breeding more children, and to community, building more houses and businesses and roads to bind them, everyone dies alone. Whether from sickness or injury or old age, you die alone, and there is nothing bad or good about death, just as there is nothing redemptive or admirable about being human. It doesn't matter how powerful you are or how far you travel or how many books you read or where you live—that's all one big distraction from the open grave waiting to swallow you in the end. There is no escape for humankind, and there is no escape for her, and none for Lewis either.

But despite all these feelings thrashing inside her, she has continued to put one foot in front of the other, leading them toward Oregon. Trees don't love and they don't mourn, but they strive for sun and for water. They live. That is the one true impulse, she supposes, that everything wants to live. Something waits for her in Oregon that is the equivalent of sun and water. A promise. Burr promised her.

Lewis trusts her. He handed over his life to her. He follows her still, as if they are corded together. He follows her through pillaged and burned communities and the best answer she can give him when he asks what happened is "I don't know." Though she does. The same thing that happened to these villages happened to hers. How can she ignore that? She is betraying herself as much as betraying Lewis. But she guides him and he follows her and she follows the river, and in Three Forks, the river finally dies, a gray wash of seep that they give wide berth, not wanting to get stuck in the slush. They follow the remains of the freeway for three days, before the mountains rise severely before them.

Slabs of stone, like altars and pillars, peek out of the snow with lichen stitched across them like the cipher of some dead race. They pass through Butte and the mountains become a toothy maw that surrounds them. The elevation steepens and the cold makes the air feel thinner than it already is.

In a narrow pass, the road has washed away entirely, replaced by trees and boulders that create a labyrinth of ice. The ground is angled steeply. Its snow-swept corridors cut this way and that way, and it is soon difficult to tell which direction she faces. At one point she looks down, at a slick floor of pure ice that mutters and cracks beneath her weight, and feels certain she is standing hundreds of feet in the air and might plummet through at any second and maybe that would be for the best.

Night comes. When they finally step out of the labyrinth and into the open pass again, a frigid wind roils over her and knocks her back a step before she presses on with her head down and her eyes watering and her tears freezing to her lashes. The road begins again, a white ribbon curling around the mountain, and here she finds a jackknifed semi.

They climb inside and the three of them fall asleep with their arms wrapped around each other, shuddering like old lovers. Her teeth won't stop chattering, a skeleton's song, so she draws closer to Lewis, so close that her mouth is nearly at his ear, and she whispers, "I'm sorry," but he is sleeping and does not hear.

They wake at dawn. The men are weak and sick. They are cold one minute, feverish the next. Every small movement brings a painful pulse to their foreheads. They limp along. They wear snowshoes that sink into the powder, snow collapsing onto them, burdening every footstep. Sometimes they pause for a minute or more to gather their strength before continuing on, making slow progress.

They fall now and then. It takes longer and longer for them to get up each time. And then they don't get up. She does not go to them. She stands over them, wavering in the wind. It would be so easy to leave them there. Then she wouldn't have to see their faces when they realize her betrayal.

CHAPTER 45

ELLA LIES IN BED all day with the curtains drawn, nothing but shadows to keep her company. She tries to empty her mind, but her tongue always finds the swollen cavity at the back of her mouth. Probing it reminds her of Slade, his oniony smell, his pitted cheeks and slitted eyes, when he leaned in to her, smashed her down, ripped out the tooth and held it aloft like a prize.

Lewis once called her belligerently confident. But now she feels so weak and small she wants to crawl in her own pocket and wither into lint.

Not even Simon can help. This morning, when she wouldn't get out of bed, he nudged her and she said, "Leave me alone."

"Is there anything I can do?"

"Yes, leave me alone."

He did, though she isn't sure she wanted him to.

So many hours later, her stomach feels flattened with hunger and her mind warped with loneliness. She ought to feel excited by the knock at her bedroom door, but it's an anxious excitement, wanting and not wanting to be bothered.

In response to the first knock, and the second, she says nothing. Simon cracks the door and light falls across her face and makes her flinch. He is carrying something toward her, setting it on the night table, food maybe. An offering. Without even knowing what it is, she feels both flattered and compelled to reject it.

Then he yanks the curtains and lets in the painful sunlight. She props herself up on an elbow and squints at him. He remains a bit breathless from his climb up the stairs. His thin chest flutters beneath his shirt. He is smiling idiotically. "I brought you something."

"You mean you stole me something."

"Same difference."

She looks at the thing—a dented metal box with a handle and clasp—and says, "What is it?"

"Oh, right." He fumbles with the clasp and swings open the top to reveal a dial and a turntable and an arm with a needle on it. "A portable record player!"

She plops her head back on her pillow and Simon's smile falls with her. "I thought it might cheer you up."

"Why would you think that?"

"Because it's a record player." His mouth gapes and quivers a moment before he finds more words to fill it. "For your record."

She puzzles up her forehead.

"The one you showed me. From your treasure box."

"Dream box."

"That's it." He darts to the closet and digs around and retrieves the vinyl record in a brittle paper sleeve with Françoise Hardy scribbled across it. "I told you, my father used to have one of these." He works the hand crank, grinding it in circles for a good thirty seconds. "That ought to do it." Then he unsleeves the record and sets it two-handed on the turntable and drops the needle, and a rubbery scratch precedes the pop and syrup of the song. "This is called..." He studies the sleeve and shrugs and hands it to her.

Tous les garçons et les filles, it reads. She does her best to pronounce it.

"What does that mean anyway?"

"I don't know, but it's nice."

"It is nice." He bobs his head dreamily along with the music. "Do you want to dance?"

"No." She says it so quickly she must mean it.

"Come on. Can't lie in bed all day. We've got work to do, remember?"

"Then we don't have time to dance."

"Just a quick one. Then we'll knock together our plan. Come on."

"I don't know."

"Won't take no for an answer."

"I mean I don't know how."

"It's easy. You just move your feet." He holds out the hand with the cast still coating it—the very thing that brought him to her, that brought them together. "Here. I'll show you."

Her hand is tucked under the pillow. She withdraws it now and hesitantly allows him to take it. He tugs her to her feet and they stand opposite each other with the husky, hurried voice of Françoise Hardy filling the silence between them.

Then Simon says, "What Slade said to you—he's wrong."

She feels a jolt of pain and her tongue goes automatically to the wound. They haven't spoken of what happened. She wouldn't allow it. She knew he felt angry and disgusted and fearful—just as she did—but impotent, too. He had wanted to do something—she had seen him in the doorway with his pocketknife out and waved him away with a "No!" His knife, no bigger than a finger, would have pricked a man like Slade no more than a bee sting.

Now Simon puts one hand on her waist and holds out the other like an invitation she accepts. He pulls her one way, then another, and she allows him. Her feet feel clumsy, dragging a beat behind, but eventually they fall into a rocking rhythm.

"He was wrong about love, I mean. Love *is* stronger. Love is why we don't give up. Love is the reason we're alive at all."

"We?"

"People, I mean."

She wants to tell him to quit it already—she wants to drop her hands and plop back on the bed—but she doesn't.

He chatters on, saying, "There's a lot of love out there. There's the love a mother feels for her son, which is different than the love a son feels for a mother. There's the love for a dog. There's the love for a painting. There's the love for a warm rain. There's the love for a song like this one."

She doesn't realize she's going to talk until she does. "There's love as infatuation and love that lasts into old age. There's angry love and pitying love."

He nods and shuffles his footing before finding his way again.

She says, "What do you think is the best kind of love?"

He thinks for a time and then says, when he was a child, he woke in the night and came out of his room to see his parents dancing with their eyes closed, turning in small circles. They looked like one person. "That seems like the best kind, I guess."

He clears his throat and she smiles and they continue to twirl around the room until the needle scratches off the record.

CHAPTER 46

L EWIS DREAMS ABOUT the ocean. The waves roll over black and foam red and rattle with bones. The seaweed is made of scalps and the hermit crabs have embedded themselves in skulls that scuttle across dunes. Burr's voice beckons him—but to what? To this? Is this the end that awaits him?

He wakes to the smell of woodsmoke. His eyes snap open, but they might as well remain closed, as it takes him a moment to make sense of what he sees, the ceiling of stone, veined with shadow and firelight, not so different from the underlids of his eyes. His head still pounds with fever. Every thought burns. Then he understands—he is in a cave. He can feel at once the coldness of the air and the heat of the fire beside him, but for the moment, he remains where he lies, dazed and studying the orange light playing across stone.

The cave wall is crowded with faces. Sketched with charcoal and painted with pigment. There are faces that smile and faces that frown. Faces with their mouths rounded in fear or surprise. They seem to move in the firelight. They are crude enough to be anyone and for a few minutes he imagines them as the faces left behind. His mother. Thomas. Clark. His world keeps shrinking, the company he keeps ever fewer. And where would his own face fit on this wall?

It is then he notices another face, bigger than the rest, with horns and pointed ears and forked beard and swirling eyes and a snake's tongue. A face the other faces feared or worshipped, a stranger or a monster to all.

He escapes his fever daze and recalls his circumstances, his last memory of collapsing in the snow, and rolls over.

Colter and Gawea sit huddled beside the fire. She is watching him. He feels unsettled by her gaze, owned by it. The darkness of it darker than he remembers, as if her eyes were black holes, matter with such force, such powerful gravity, not even light can escape them.

"You saved us?" he says.

"That's one way of looking at it."

"What's the other?"

She shrugs.

Colter leans into the fire, his prosthetic arm extended. Its claw grips a cut of meat that cooks near the flames, the fat dripping into the coals with a sizzle.

Lewis feels a sudden hunger and wonders aloud how long he has been asleep.

"Can't say," Colter says. "Been in and out myself."

"Gawea? How long?"

"Days," she says, her voice monotone. "Weeks. I don't know. Does it even matter?"

Lewis shares a look with Colter, who says, "Don't take it personally. She's being a real shit to me, too. I told her she should have left us to freeze and she gave me a look that didn't exactly reassure me."

Gawea tosses Lewis a canteen, tells him to drink, and he does, deeply. She offers him meat next—a venison chop—and he thanks her.

There is a lidless, frightless intensity to her eyes. "Don't thank me."

He doesn't know what to say to this, so he asks where the meat came from, and Colter tells the story about how, a few hours ago, a deer wanders into the cave, stands before her, then kneels and lays aside its neck for her to slit. He makes a knife of his hand, cuts the air. He pulls his own meat out of the fire, blows on it, says, "Why couldn't you stop those bears from attacking us, huh?"

Her voice is surprisingly sharp, almost a yell, beyond the emotional range they've seen in her for some time. "You think I didn't try? You think I wanted that to happen?"

They flinch as her voice echoes around the cave.

"I can only ask," she says through her teeth. Her face grows still again, impassive. Her eyes, glossy black pools, reflect the fire. "I asked the deer. It answered."

"You asked," Lewis says. "And it trusted you. It followed you to slaughter."

She gives him an almost imperceptible nod and then whispers, "Yes."

———

It is soon after this—as they push farther through the mountains and the air begins to warm and the snow thins to gray tatters and green shoots spring from the muddy ground—that Lewis discovers the coffin-shaped box. Reed had the larger backpack, and after he shot himself, Lewis crushed together their supplies into one. There is a zippered interior pocket he has not noticed until this day, when he digs around for a needle and thread to sew a tear in the armpit of his long-sleeve.

The box is the length of his hand. He recognizes it as belonging to Reed. Something he held often, almost like a charm. His thumb flips the lock. The lid swings open. He leans closer to see what waits inside it. Nothing but a shadow, it first appears, but then he tips it toward the sun and sees the vial. A long glass tube. There is a black powdery substance inside, and when he tips it one way, then the other, the shadow comes to life. The label across it reads *Specimen: Live Virus: H3L1*. He understands. The rest of the world blurs and the box seems suddenly to gain weight, to bend his arm.

He imagines the vial opened, the shadow within it escaping, its shape the shape of the wind, ribboning and clouding outward, filling the air around him like a thousand spores of rotten thistle-down.

He claps shut the lid. His first impulse is to bury it, erase it. But something stills his hand. His role as a curator—one who preserves the past, both the awful and the regular—and the memory of the burned-down villages. The heads on sticks, the blackened bones unpuzzled in the snow. Whatever and whoever awaits him at the end of the trail. The lingering worry that humanity isn't worth saving after all and would be better off extinguished.

"What's the matter with you?" Colter says. "You look like you've seen a ghost."

"Nothing," Lewis says and hurries the box back into its secret pocket.

CHAPTER 47

Fitted with backpacks and armed with compasses and clocks and lanterns, Simon and Ella work their way through the sewers. His goal has always been to escape the city as quickly as possible, so he has never gone this way before, down a branching series of tunnels with centuries-old muck scalloping their bottom. They are looking for the basement entry to the Dome, the one Danica told them about. "It was left open as an escape route," she said.

Every minute or so they pause to listen. He wears a belt knife. Ella carries her baseball bat and keeps it constantly raised. Whenever a rat scuttles by or a spider drops on her shoulder, she swallows a scream. And because this is his opportunity to prove himself, to show Ella that he is capable and good on his word as a thief, he pretends himself unafraid, puffing his chest and crushing spiders with his palm and telling her not to worry.

Danica told them to wait until late night, early morning, when everyone slept soundly. That would be safest. Some of the ladders lead to manholes and some to grates, but in the full dark, it is difficult to tell if they are cemented over unless Simon climbs up to them. He loses track of how many he tries until he finds what he believes to be the correct entry, a grate that opens into a dark room.

"I think this is it."

"You think?" Ella says. "What do you mean, *you think*?"

He cracked his cast off that day. It fell away like a shell and he did not recognize the arm within, the stick thinness of it. The skin was yellowish and scraped away beneath his fingernail. His tendons and muscles ache from lack of use and he finds it difficult to hold the lantern now while pushing up the grate with the other arm. The metal scuds across cement. He climbs up and knobs out a longer wick and a room solidifies around him.

"Hmm," he says.

From below, her voice, "Hmm? What does that mean?"

"I don't think we're where we're supposed to be."

There is a chair—that is the first thing he notices—a metal chair with straps dangling from each of its arms. He swings the lantern around him and knocks a chain that jangles and sways. A hook curls the bottom of it. There is a table along the wall and above it a wall of knives and barbed metal instruments he does not recognize.

Then there are the mannequins. With hair and jewelry and whatever else glued to them, they appear like some demented child's attempt to cobble together a person.

He feels breath against his neck and flinches. Ella comes up behind him with her lantern burning in her hand. "Where are we?" she says at a whisper.

"Not the Dome."

They circle the room, working their way through the dummies but not touching them, as if they were strangers asleep. There is a bed against the wall. The blanket is thrown back and Simon puts a hand to the pillow and finds it cold. "Whoever lives here hasn't been home tonight."

"Why wouldn't he be home? With the curfew, where else could he be?"

"Doing something creepy is my guess."

Ella stands before a two-doored closet that takes up most of a wall. They each grab a knob. He steadies his breath and his eyes drop momentarily to his lantern. Because of this, he cannot see as well as he could, his vision smeared with light, so that when they swing open the doors, he believes in the monster. The monster in the closet is real.

It swings out at them, a dark shape, a twisting bunch of shadows. He sees then the hanger that holds it in place, the hollowed arms and legs with leather straps and metal buckles. A deputy's uniform. As massive as a tent.

He runs his fingers along the fabric, and something pricks the pad of his finger. A drop of blood swells and he brings it to his mouth to suck. It tastes like the air of this room, like the air of the morgue. He remembers the pallid face of his mother laid out on a slab. He remembers his father there, too. He remembers the breath of Ella when she sobbed and he clutched her after the tooth ripped from her mouth. He remembers the rage he felt then, and now, when he says, "Slade."

CHAPTER 48

THE DOCTOR HAS a new name now. Mother. That's what the girls call her.

She doesn't know what to think at first. They ask if it's all right, if she minds, and she licks her lips and blows out a breath full of emotion. "If that's what you'd like, I think *mother* will suit me perfectly."

"It would mean a lot to us," they say. "It really would."

"That settles it, then. Mother."

She rather likes the sound of it. And she, after all, calls them her girls, this den of young women she considers a kind of family. They helped her heal, and now she helps them build a life in Bismarck. They construct a greenhouse on the roof. From cellars they harvest mushrooms and lichens and mosses. They dig up roots. They shovel through grain bins and discover preserved cores of corn and soybean to plant and to eat. They mash medicines, vitamins to ruddy their skin and harden their bones and battle the scurvy weakening them. She teaches them everything she knows about anything she knows. For some of them, that means simple reading. For others, basic surgery.

Her injured arm—now scarred over—hangs useless at her side, good only for gripping the walking stick she uses to get about. She lost enough blood to permanently weary her heart. Her body feels shrunken, bent. But she gets by. Her girls keep her busy.

Every morning, they auger fresh holes in the river and bait their hooks with hunks of liver and drop their lines. By the time they snowshoe the banks and woods and fallen neighborhoods to check their traps—collecting into the back of their sleds the rabbits and beaver and otter and mink and porcupine—the tip-ups on the river have flared their fire-bright ribbons. There is no shortage of fish.

The river surges with them, mostly carp, but plenty of catfish and bluegill and trout and smallmouth. Sometimes, on the coldest days, in an effort to stay warm, the fish swirl together beneath the water, coalescing like dark planets, and when this happens the auger holes splutter and the ice begins to thin and crack, and the girls move their tip-ups and find another stretch of river, because they have fallen through before, pulled away by the black current, lost.

They don't see much of Clark. She ranges the outer reaches of Bismarck, the woods, sometimes hunting the plains, where she has shot elk and antelope, once a bison whose herd departed in a thunder that shook the ground.

The doctor is more grandmother than mother to them. They are by and large teenagers, except for Marie. No one knows how old she is, but she has gray in her hair and her blind eye is as white and bulging as a boiled egg. She carries a phone everywhere she goes and mutters into it. The girls treat her kindly, but Clark seems to hate her. "It's that eye. It seems to probe you, see inside you."

One time Marie removed the phone from her ear and held it out to Clark. The cord dangled like a vein. "It's for you," she said.

"Yeah. Who is it?"

"Lewis," she said. "It's Lewis."

Clark knocked the phone from her hand and it went skittering across the floor.

Sometimes the doctor sees Clark staring at the horizon. She doesn't ask, but she knows. She is thinking about Lewis. Something happened between them the doctor does not understand. And something has changed in Clark, turned over inside her like a big black dog, and if the doctor reaches out a hand she knows it will come away bloody. So she waits, hoping Clark will announce her problems when ready.

But she doesn't. The optimism that once brightened her voice—the authority that once straightened her spine—is gone. The Clark she knows is gone. She disappears for days, returning with meat. Or she drinks herself into unconsciousness, seeking that numbing burn that expands inside her, spreading to her toes and fingers, the tips of her ears, fuzzing over any thoughts that might bother her.

Today the doctor finds her kneeling beside the fountain. Here the girls dump buckets of snow that island and melt into gray water for them to drink or wash their dishes and clothes. She splashes her face clean, rubs away what dirties her. She cups handfuls and handfuls to her face. Water was sacred in the Sanctuary, and the old women were always talking about how it cleaned more than your skin, and even wetting your hands, your face, could chase away something that spoiled you. The doctor hopes so. "Do you miss him?" she says.

Clark's face drips. The fountain's surface settles into a rippling mirror. A skylight wavers to life, a silver-shaped diamond that overwhelms her own reflection, her face a mere pale smudge, barely recognizable, barely her. The doctor thinks she sees what Clark sees. A thing. When Clark widens her eyes, the thing widens its eyes. And when she opens her mouth, the thing seems to snarl and spring fangs.

The doctor dashes a hand through the water, and when the image calms this time, it looks a little more like Clark.

"There's a lot of men I miss," Clark says, "but my brother most of all."

"You're not to blame for—"

"Shut up. Just shut up and leave me be. You might think you're their mother, but you're not mine."

CHAPTER 49

IT TAKES ANOTHER hour, but Simon and Ella backtrack and discover where they took a wrong turn and follow the proper sewer channel and crawl into the Dome's basement and discover there the thousands of oak and plastic barrels Danica promised. "Barrels and barrels and barrels," she said. "More than I've ever counted. And far more valuable than any wine. Enough to share. Enough to remedy the Sanctuary's drought for many months. But my *husband* bathes in it instead." This is what Lewis alerted them to in his letter—a vast storeroom of water.

The smell—of mildew—is a new one. Breathing is a little like drinking. Some of the barrels sweat and drip. Simon runs a hand across one and licks his palm. "Son of a bitch."

Ella says they need to hurry. Dawn can't be far off.

They heft one from a stack—wobbling under its weight and nearly dropping it with a crash—and then hitch it with two lengths of rope drawn from his backpack. They curl the ropes around a pillar and stand on the opposite side and keep their grip tight when they hand-over-hand lower the barrel into the dark.

They climb down after it and drag the grate back into place. They do the best they can to secure the entry, threading the grate with a thin length of chain that they then knot around some piping below and anchor with a padlock. "Make sure there is no escape," Danica told them. "The Dome should be watertight."

They untie the barrel and tip it on its side. It sloshes and mutters and Simon imagines taking a knife to it, sucking out a drink to ease his dry mouth. With one hand they hold their lanterns and with the other they roll the barrel awkwardly along the sewer walkway, constantly readjusting their course.

By the time they return to the museum, they are both covered in grime and sweat, bloodied, burned, red-faced. Simon drags the grate back over the sewer entry and then drags a box over the grate and sits down on it and puts his head in his hands and says, "Thank God that's done with."

"Oh no," Ella says.

He looks at her through his fingers. "What?"

He is always the one making mistakes. Falling off the ladder and breaking his arm, allowing Danica to surprise him with the dagger, climbing into the prison instead of the Dome. A small part of him relishes the idea of Ella making an error—until he notices the way she backs away from him with tiny steps and worry creasing her face. "I'm so, so, so sorry."

"What?"

"I forgot my bat. At Slade's."

He lets his hands fall with relief. "I'll steal you another one."

"You don't understand." Her cheeks bunch up. Her eyes glimmer with tears. She explains how Slade toyed with it when he searched the museum, threatened her with it. "He knows it's mine. He'll know I've been there. He'll come for me."

Once again Simon stands in the sewer at the bottom of a ladder. He has not had enough sleep. He has not had any breakfast. He felt excited and driven before, but that has given way to exhausted fearfulness. He studies the tunnels branching all around him. He feels about this place—the Sanctuary—as he feels about the human mind. It seems contained, limited, and yet constantly opens into new corridors and closets, an endless vault, much of it dark.

Ella gives him a nudge. "Are you going or am I going?"

"I'm going."

Slowly he begins to climb. His feet ring against the rungs. His lantern dangles from his bad hand, a clumsy grip, and rust crumbles against the palm of the other as he pulls himself up. He reaches the top and threads his fingers through the grate, ready to shove it aside, when a key sounds in a lock and the door to the room opens.

He keeps his fingers where they are but swings the other arm out, bringing the lantern up against the sewer's ceiling, hoping to shield its light. Slade does not carry a lantern of his own, but the room nonetheless brightens, the residue of the hallway. The footsteps, slow, heavy, grind dust into the concrete. Simon's fingers must be visible, white and rounding the grates like some cellar fungus, and he imagines a boot coming down on them, mashing them into the metal, clipping through bone. He fights the compulsion to pull back.

A foot clunks down on the grate—rust rains down on Simon—and because he turns his face away, he is for a moment unsure whether his fingers remain uninjured. And then the grate shifts again, loosened of weight, and the footsteps continue to the other side of the room.

Simon already knows who it is, but he wants to see. He presses his face up against the grate to study Slade, a massive slab of a man. He wears his black uniform. The back of his head is lined with fleshy rolls. If he spots the bat, wherever it might be, Simon knows it is only a matter of seconds before he checks the grate.

One of his hands rises. It carries a set of metal knuckles, bladed and rimed with blood. He hangs them from a peg like an ornament and there they sway. He spins around and Simon ducks down and cringes as a footstep once more clatters the grate.

All this while his other arm trembles with the weight of the lantern. His wrist feels stabbed through with hornets and he fears he might lose his grip altogether. When the door closes and the bolt turns, he drops his arm and nearly drops the lantern.

Only then does he look for Ella. She has crept back in the tunnel and lowered the wick on her lantern so it gives off only a little light and makes her look small, a hundred miles away.

He waits a long minute and then pushes aside the grate and pokes his head above the floor. The room is empty. For how long, he doesn't know. He can see a crack of light under the door.

The bat remains where it was, unnoticed by Slade, propped against the wall by the closet. He checks the door again, the ribbon of light beneath it, and sees no shadows in the hallway, no indication that anyone might be near. He wills his breathing to quiet, but his lungs cannot fill fast enough to satisfy his body.

Across the room he pads, making no sound. He trades the lantern to his good hand and carries it before him, not wanting to set it down for fear he might forget something else in his haste. His free hand—his bad hand—closes around the bat. His grip is not good enough, ruined by the strain of the past few minutes. He makes it a few steps before the bat slips and falls with a clatter magnified by the concrete floor.

He watches it roll in a long parabola, spinning with the slope of the floor, toward the open grate. It catches briefly at the lip—and then falls through, into the dark square.

A long second of silence passes. Then the bat hits the sewer floor with a dong and rattle. Ella does not scream at him, call him a fool, but he knows she will. He can hear her voice call, "Hurry," can hear the bat scrape when she picks it up. And then he hears something else.

Footsteps. The sound is more than a sound—it is a presence—powerful enough to be felt as well as heard. The very air seems to shake. He knows he cannot escape it. He does not have time to think. If he did, he would not do what he does next. He drags the grate back over the hole and crashes it in place. For a second he stares through the bars at Ella, far below him, her face oranged by her upheld lantern, but before she can question him, he is running for the door, snapping the lock, twisting the knob, yanking it open.

There is only one way to save her. He must steal time, what may very well be his last act as a thief.

When Slade rounds the corner, Simon hurls the lantern at his face and the big man raises an arm to swat it aside, but before he can, Simon has already dropped to the floor in a slide. Slade's legs are wide enough apart to shoot through, and, once past them, the boy bounces up and into a hard run. All this before Slade knocks the lantern against the wall.

The shattering matches the feeling inside Simon. This might be the one building in the Sanctuary he has never visited—the police headquarters—and he can only guess which way he is going as he negotiates a series of dimly lit corridors. He enters a room of barred cells, and several men reach for him and rattle the bars and moan and cheer. One of them nearly snatches him, a raisin-faced man with black snot bubbling from his diseased gash of a nose. Simon makes it through one doorway, then another. He could turn this corner and just as easily find a closet, but his luck holds out. A stone staircase rises before him.

Behind him Slade does not bellow, does not scream or curse or growl. He merely pursues, all his noise invested in his movement, stomping his feet and crashing into walls and shoving through the doors Simon closes on him in his passing.

They race up the stairs and out of the basement and down a tiled hallway framed by dark wood and festooned with old photos of policemen who watch them forbiddingly. Simon has never moved faster in his life. His feet hit the floor so hard pain rifles up his calves. The ceiling bulges upward, into a meeting hall, where the noise of his footsteps and the footsteps pursuing him multiplies.

He races now toward the entry, where two deputies appear. They drop their hands to their machetes. They call out for him to stop. And he does, skidding, nearly falling. He does not bother turning around, knowing Slade can't be far behind, but he spies to his left the staircase that leads to the second level, and he hurries there.

Another deputy appears on the landing, close enough to reach a hand and snatch his collar, but Simon twists from his grip, slipping off his shirt altogether and running bare chested down a long hallway.

He has no plan except to avoid the voices that pursue him. Halfway down the hallway, he pushes through the door of an office. He jumps onto the desk, shoves aside the chair, and worms his way out the window. The sill is spiked with nails and glass, but he does not have time to take care. He slices a finger, spikes his palm, when swinging himself over.

He tries to let go, but his hand won't loosen, his bad hand. It has been run through by a nail. He yanks at it and the pain electrifies him, not from the nail, not yet, but the tendons twisting and snapping in his wrist. His legs dangle in the air, maybe thirty feet between him and the ground.

He feels eyes on him. He hears voices in the street, a gathering crowd.

In his mind, he calls up the vision of Ella—them dancing to the Françoise Hardy record—and wishes her face to be the last thing he sees. But it is not. Another appears above him, like a risen moon. Slade is not smiling or frowning. His slitted eyes study Simon with a predatory fascination. Then he takes hold of his hand and pats it comfortingly before dragging it off the nail—and letting go.

CHAPTER 50

A s often as she can, Clark escapes the mall—its imprisoning walls, its stale air laced with the tangy smell of fish and woodsmoke—and surrounds herself instead with sky. She spends her days hunting, minding the traps and lures. Though she often finds herself distracted. Her eyes look west. Her feet walk west, her body naturally angling in that direction like the point on a compass. She imagines now, as she did when a sentinel on the wall, mountains. White mountains that appear like teeth nested in black gums.

Then she shakes her head or presses her fists to her eyes. If she thinks about the mountains, she thinks about Lewis. If she thinks about Lewis, she thinks about the final look he gave her—made of equal parts hate and sympathy—before escaping this place.

So she works, and when she doesn't work, she drinks. That distracts her mind, numbs it, because when she starts to think, she starts to doubt and hate and grieve. The snow is ash and ash is the color of grief. Everywhere she looks, outside and inside herself, she sees death. There was a time she felt nothing but disgust for Reed, but now she understands. He had it right. There is no such thing as the future. The future is what you longed for. There is nothing left for her to long for, except an end to the pain. Death is an end to the pain. Death is the future. Death is curative, medicinal. In her darkest, drunkest moments, instead of Oregon, she feels beckoned by the grave, a deep black hole where she might find her brother. She thought escaping the wall was freeing, but now death seems the ultimate freedom.

She's sorry she pushed Reed away and she's sorry she couldn't save her brother and she's sorry she betrayed Lewis. She's so goddamn sorry, and though it's too late for the others, maybe it's not too late for him. If she could only find him, if she could only tell him how sorry she was, if she could only get that word out of her, she thinks she might feel better, like coughing up an infection.

Today a warm front moves through, so that fog ghosts between the trees and flows down the river like a second current. The temperature hovers around freezing. Snow sluffs off roofs. The birds are busy, the red flashes of cardinals in the undergrowth, the black nets of crows thrown over trees. More seem to gather by the minute and the air is busy with their muttering.

She prefers to be alone, but the girls call for her this morning and ask her to help, and though she tries to resist them, they beg her and she relents. They are collecting fish from the tip-ups—slitting their bellies and pulling out their guts to use in the shoreline traps—but they can't seem to reel in this one. It's stuck.

"Stuck," she says and tests the line and it hums with tension and when she takes it in her hands it feels like she has taken hold of herself, some central nerve that disappears into a dark place. She rears back—and the line drags—and she waits until it slackens, then reels in until it tightens again, and in this way it takes her a good five minutes before the fish surfaces. She leans over to peer down the hole, more than a foot deep. At the bottom of it, a broad, whiskered, fleshy-lipped mouth gapes. A catfish, a big one, too big, and she orders the girls to their knees to chip and saw away the ice, to accommodate the girth of the massive fish.

Twenty minutes later, her arms ache from fighting the drag, and just in time she hauls out the fish—two-handed, grunting—and it slips and flops and twists on the ice. Snow sticks to it in clumps. It opens and closes its mouth, gaping around the hook. One of the girls gets her arms and legs around it—wrestling it down—and Clark drives a knife into its head and it shudders and goes still. The girls laugh and so does she and the laughter feels strange, exotic, like a language she once knew but forgot.

The fog is beginning to burn away. And the sun seems brighter in the sky, even when filtered by clouds. The crows, thronging in the trees along the river, have been muttering all along, but now they grow wild, *kaak-kaak-kaaaking*.

When they cut open the fish's belly, they find a beaver inside, swallowed whole and socked by yellow jelly, like some malignant birth. Clark sits on the ice, for a moment too tired to care about the cold creeping through her pants, and everyone stands around her, commenting on the big fish and the beaver, saying *gross* and *ick* and nudging each other and still laughing so that their breath clouds.

Then the laughter dies and there is only the *kaak* of the birds. And something else, an undersound she can't quite place. Like a drumming. The drumming of a death parade.

She tells everyone to be quiet and creeps up the riverbank and peeks her head over the berm and sees the men. They are stomping toward Bismarck. They do not roar and brandish their weapons. They come silently, marching in straight lines that match the set of their mouths.

Lewis once called her empathy-proof. Unable to appreciate any desire or despair outside her own. The girls have shared stories—of their village, their families, the nightmare train that brought them here—but Clark hasn't listened, her ears plugged up with her own private pain. She has even seen the train wreck, way out on the plains, but never considered another engine might follow. It isn't until now that she understands. Not only what they face, but what Lewis will face without her.

With that understanding comes fear. Fear for the girls' lives and fear for her own. And if she fears for her life, that means she values her life. If she values her life, that means she's willing to fight for it. Maybe there is such a thing as the future after all.

She counts them, thirty...no, fifty...no, seventy—as more slavers pour out of the fog as if born of it. She turns to the girls then and tells them to hurry and gather their things. They must run for the mall. They must run for their lives.

CHAPTER 51

THE PACIFIC EATS away at dunes and cliffs and the wreckage of towns built too close to the shore. Its waves battle, in a great foaming collar, the current of the long, fat snake of the Columbia River that oozes through the gorge dividing Oregon and Washington. And the rain. An acid rain that yellows leaves and spots skin and falls as many days as it does not.

Water encourages life but so does it promote decay. Birds break windows. Hail breaks windows. Branches break windows. The shingles on even the newest roofs last no more than two decades and then split with ice dams, peel away with the wind, scrape away with branches. Leaves rot in gutters and plants sprout from them, their roots groping their way into the house. Mice and squirrels gnaw their way inside. Termites and beetles, too. Woodpeckers. No matter how it happens, as soon as a hole opens, water penetrates, bringing the mold and rust and rot that dissolve the wood-chip subroofing and drop bricks and crack the foundation and make every building into a slowly collapsing planter box, furred over with moss and spangled with mushrooms.

Fires start. From lightning, from earthquakes cracking gas lines. But because the sewers have clogged, because water mains break, because fire hydrants crack, because basements have filled up like bathtubs, and because so much of the wood is rotten, they extinguish quickly. Winter comes and water freezes, thaws, freezes, thaws, and freezes, and in doing so splits cement, crumbles asphalt, shoves around everything man-made that was once laid or stacked in a straight line.

But not in Bellingham. Not in Walla Walla or Corvallis or Silverton. Not in many places, especially Astoria, Oregon, at the mouth of the Columbia River, where houses stand stubbornly against the attacking rain, where the roads run in clean lines, and where slaves arrive every few weeks.

They cluster in wagons forged from pickup beds and drawn by oxen. They stumble in long lines, weeping and rattling, collared and cuffed by chains. They cram into rust-pocked cattle cars and boxcars dragged by steam engines.

The slaves have numbers and letters branded into their skin, but so do they have names, at least among themselves. They have their own fenced-in shantytowns, their own families. They are tools, but even tools must be treated with some care or they will rust and break. They are told they are part of something bigger, a process of renewal. Some of the slaves work on construction, raising barns, repairing fallen chimneys, hammering together houses. Some of them farm, digging irrigation canals, hoeing and planting and reaping. Some grade roads. Some repair train tracks. Some log trees and some mine for coal in the Powder River Basin. Some birth children. They are, all of them, building something.

Something that extends as far east as Laramie and as far south as Palo Alto. They are growing. And they will continue to grow. Not just as a society, but as a species.

There were sixty-five nuclear power plants in the United States. Their hot innards seeped through cracks and seams. And in Washington, along the Columbia River, there is Hanford, the most contaminated nuclear site in the country, storing two-thirds of America's high-level radioactive waste. Used nuclear fuel—in waste dumps containing rods that give off heat and beta particles and gamma rays—mutates into isotopes of americium and plutonium, making it a million times more radioactive than it was originally. When the facility was abandoned, the cooling ponds boiled over and evaporated. Exposed to the air, the waste ignited, creating a fire that clouds radiation into the air, spills it into the Columbia River, and to this day continues to burn.

The nearby reactors, in a state of meltdown, did not ignite when they overheated. They melted into radioactive lava that consumed the concrete and steel surrounding them, gelling into a massive silvery blob.

Aran Burr calls it the altar. So they call it the altar. Because his word is their word.

Astoria is close enough to the altar, and far enough away from it, kissed but not pummeled by the radiation. Some of them die of cancer. Some die of blood or respiratory disease. And some don't. Some are born with mere deformities. A face that looks melted. A second set of teeth barnacling their shoulder. Cysts bulging and sacs of fluid dangling. Moles so plentiful that a body appears like some fungus found in the forest. But others are special, gifted. Some are born with oversize eyes that can see a mile, see in the dark. Some are born walking on all fours and able to outrun any dog. Some can lift boulders.

It is what makes them so special. Mutational genesis. Become the next. Evolve or face extinction.

That is what he says. And they all do as he says.

CHAPTER 52

G AWEA FINDS a river. The first canoe fills with water. The second floats. Colter takes the stern, Lewis takes the bow, and she nests between two gunwales in the center of the vessel. Sometimes they are walled in by basalt and rushing along whitecapped rapids and sometimes the river broadens and they can see far into hills dotted with sage. The world is not sand and the world is not snow. There are green-leafed trees and green-grassed fields. For the first time, outside of a map, outside of a book, Lewis can see the world the way it was, an inhabitable, living thing.

One night, in eastern Washington, Lewis slicks his cheeks with mud and shaves with a slow scrape of his knife. His beard falls away in white curls spotted with blood. And though the water runs cold, he bathes in it, scraping the grime off his body with handfuls of sand. Afterward, he feels better, tidier than he has in a long time.

He is ready. And they are getting close. New wonders await every bend of the river, but the thrill of discovery has worn off. They have escaped the sand and the ice. They have found the new country promised to them. One goal has been satisfied. Another remains. They can travel to the very edge of the ocean, but Lewis will remain an unfinished map until Aran Burr helps him find his compass.

Birds shuttle through the air and snatch the bugs that fly in clouds above the river. The water glitters with stars. He thinks about all the leftover light, the memory of light, millions of years old. Light streaming from distant stars, soaking now into the river and into his eyes while colliding with light sent forth from the earth thousands of years before, so that in a way that time still exists, the energy of it still present somewhere, and eventually, he knows, because of the shape of space, it will return; the past will intersect with the future. Aran Burr sent off his own message, so many months ago, and now Lewis has come. Now their energies will finally collide.

The river meets up with the wide, fat stream of the Columbia. They pass through a burning plain. The fire has spread for miles and walls them in with high flames and black smoke that makes them cough until they vomit.

They portage the canoe around dams. Some are still solid. Some cracked and seeping. And some split wide, gushing a white-collared rush of water. And then one night, to their north, they pass by the Hanford site, the storage center for nuclear waste, which Gawea calls the altar.

"The altar? Why do you call it the altar?"

"It's just what people call it."

"Why do they call it that?"

"It works invisibly. It brings good things and bad things. It's like a god in that way."

"What good things does it bring?"

She regards him with her nightmare-black eyes. "People like you and me."

The air feels almost palpable, as if you could pack it with your hands and take a bitter bite. And it burns to breathe, smelling like melted plastic. The throbbing glow of it blots out half the stars in the sky. They paddle swiftly, trying to get past this place as soon as they can, and it is then that dark shapes begin to knife past them and riffle the water. Lewis sees a pale set of eyes staring back from the place where he is about to place his paddle.

In the gorge, along the Columbia, the river is dotted with islands, and all around them stacks of basalt rise like dried-out layer cake. Mount Hood looms in the distance, white hatted with snow and glowing at night. The lap lines of the floodwaters of millennia past stitch the canyon walls. Past The Dalles, at Seven Mile Hill, a vast hillside of huge-headed sunflowers wobble in the wind.

They travel through the day and all the next night, knowing the ocean is near, and before dawn they approach not a town but a city. "This is it," Lewis says, "isn't it? This is Astoria."

It is lit with lights, like a net of stars dropped from the sky, lining the banks and rolling into black, humped hills. Lewis leans into his paddle, urging them forward—when Colter says, "Wait."

"Wait?" Lewis says. "Wait what?" He feels a hurried need to get there, as if a sudden wind has risen inside him to hurry him these final few miles.

"I say we do this in the morning."

"Why? We're here."

They raise their paddles and the canoe lists sideways.

"Don't rush into things. I learned that from you. Remember?" He opens and closes his prosthetic claw. "I don't know what to expect and neither do you. She's hiding something from us. That much we know."

"Gawea?" Lewis says.

In the middle of the boat, she is curled into a ball. He says her name again and she says, "I need to think."

"What do you need to think about?"

"We're waiting until morning," Colter says. "This isn't up for debate. Now, paddle."

They keep their canoe to the far side of the Columbia, a safe distance. None of them say anything for fear their voices will carry across the water. Gawea tightens her body, hugs her legs to her chest.

A strange smell fills the air, briny, fishy, like the residue on his fingers in the hours after he guts a trout. Lewis hears something ahead of them, the distant growl of what turns out to be waves curling over, the river spilling into the surf, the ocean, the end.

He stops paddling a moment, made dumb by the realization that after all these miles, all these months, so far and so long, his previous life impossibly distant, he has made it. A sense of accomplishment momentarily overwhelms whatever fears and questions bother him. He is in awe of himself and in awe of the ocean. He stills his paddle, transfixed by the sight of it. The chop rolls over.

The moon is full and its white reflection smears the roiling water. A whole other universe exists beneath its surface. He can't see it, but he knows.

The canoe is beginning to wobble, the current confused. The hills around them slump toward the ocean and fall away completely to reveal a fierce white light—flaring and then going dark, flaring and then going dark—like a great eye blinking in the night.

"There!" he says, yelling over the surf. The vision he dreamed, the lighthouse that beckoned him, now realized.

He feels so excited he might dive into the water and splash toward it. He leans into his paddle and realizes the canoe is turning away, steering them toward another section of shore. "You're going the wrong way." He twists around. "What are you doing?"

"Keeping us alive," Colter says and rips his paddle hard against the current. "You don't need me to tell you what happens to the moth that flies to flame."

CHAPTER 53

THEY MAKE A small fire out of driftwood at the base of a cliff, notched in by high walls of chalky orange clay. From here Lewis cannot see the lighthouse, but it doesn't matter. Even with his eyes closed, the light burns bright in his mind. He hears a whispering, what could be the surf but sounds like his name said softly a thousand times. He feels something almost tidal. Whatever drags the waves to the shore and crashes them against the sand, he feels too.

They try to engage with Gawea, but she refuses to answer their questions, and when Colter grabs her by the wrist, she rips away from him and says, "Don't touch me."

Her tone implies this is more than a command—it is a threat—and Colter takes a few steps back with his prosthetic held before him in defense. But Gawea only stares at him long and hard before saying that she has to pee. Then she turns her back on them, walks from the campsite, from the circle of light thrown by the fire, and lets the dark swallow her up.

They wait five minutes and then ten and then twenty—watching the fire dance on the driftwood and listening to the waves boom—before Colter says, "Well then, I suppose it's time we came up with a plan."

In a few minutes, Colter says, while they retain the advantage of darkness, they will approach the lighthouse. If they find someone there, or more than someone, they will sneak close and then attack. Not to hurt, though that might be necessary, but to detain. To question and better understand what it is they face. "We go to it before it comes for us."

Colter opens and closes his claw when he says they cannot risk an alarm sounded. If they find the lighthouse empty, they will return here before the sun rises and then scout their surroundings.

Normally, at the end of the day, after so many hours of hiking or paddling, Lewis has to force his body to move, as if his joints were calcified and his muscles hardened to wintry stones. But he finds it effortless now. His body does not complain. It does not want to rest. It wants to go where it has been beckoned, as if there awaited the end of pain, a solution to pain.

They belt on their holsters. They walk near the water to camouflage their tracks. The beach rounds a corner and the cliff face falls away into a rocky hillside, the lighthouse speared at the top of it. They push through manzanita clusters and a cedar forest and moss-slick rocks and finally enter a moonlit clearing that anchors the lighthouse.

They wait a moment, studying the structure, white columned, black capped. A cone of light pours from it, swooping in circles, cutting through the night.

Colter lifts an arm and Lewis follows the line of it. He spies movement. A grated catwalk. A figure walking along it. The red glow of a pipe or cigarette. The figure leans against a railing, staring out at the silvered waves. He will not hear them, with the roar of the surf, and he will not see them, so long as he keeps his eyes on the ocean.

The moon makes a long shadow that reaches from the lighthouse to their feet. Colter waves Lewis forward and they duck down and follow it like an avenue, maybe thirty yards, before reaching the base of the structure. They flatten themselves against it. The stone is furred over with moss and slick with moisture that dampens their backs. Colter waits a few seconds, then steps back and cranes his neck, making sure the figure remains where he stood before, a shadow darker than the rest high above them.

There is a black door with a brass knob that they try and find loose. It pushes open with a screech, but the noise is drowned out by the waves crashing below, high tide, full moon.

A metal staircase spirals up and up and up to a square of light, a hinged trapdoor. They unholster their revolvers and begin to climb.

The lighthouse lantern spins and creates a strobe effect, so that they are alternately cast in shadow and light. Colter uses the railing to steady himself, his claw gripping it, clicking and tonging their progress. His revolver is raised beside his face as if he is listening to it. He pops his head through the open trapdoor. "Bunkhouse," he whispers. "Come on."

They enter a low-ceilinged room with a wraparound bench, a squat cupboard, a ticking woodstove, a tiny desk with a map wrinkled across it, a bunk bunched with blankets.

A ladder rises through another trapdoor to the lantern room. Colter scales it, darts his head up, and ducks down again, a second's glance. "I see him."

"Do we wait?"

"We could be waiting until dawn."

"Then what?"

"Up above, one of those glass panels opens as a door. I'll push through it and take him out. The more movement, the greater chance he'll spot us. Stay put for now."

"What are you going to do to him?"

"Hopefully nothing. But maybe something."

He climbs through the trapdoor, and Lewis follows him halfway up the ladder. His head breaches the lantern room at the wrong moment, his eyes seared by the light swinging toward him. Lewis curses and blindly descends the ladder and blinks away the bright cobwebs clinging to his vision.

For this reason he does not see the bunk stir, does not see the blankets pull back, does not see the man squinting confusedly at him. He only hears a voice he does not recognize say, "What are you doing here? Who are you?"

Lewis stiffens.

A gauzy face—with traceries of light glowing around it—floats before him. Gaunt. Bearded. Lewis lifts his revolver, too late. The man knocks his hand aside and the trigger snaps and a gunshot batters the air.

Lewis is not sure what happens next, only that he is on the floor without any breath after a fist or a foot pounds his stomach. His vision is returning, and when he clutches himself and gapes for breath and struggles upright, he sees the man walking to the far side of the bunkhouse and cranking a metal handle attached to the wall. An unearthly wail sounds, rising and falling. A siren.

The man cranks the handle another few seconds. He has a face like a knotted piece of driftwood. He wears a gray sweater with one sleeve coming unstitched. He kneels and collects the revolver from the floor and starts toward Lewis.

His progress halts when a body drops through the trapdoor and knocks him flat.

The lantern above wheels and the bunkhouse alternately glows and dims and Lewis barely has time to process the two bodies tangled on the floor before Colter climbs down the ladder. He lifts his prosthetic claw above his head and brings it down on one man, then the other, stilling and silencing them.

"This isn't going well," Lewis says.

"Time to run."

They pound down the staircase and out the door and into the sea spray. There they see the red line of dawn brightening the horizon and hear the thudding footsteps of the dozen people running toward them.

CHAPTER 54

THOMAS NEVER WEARS black, but he does today. Everything—from his calfskin boots to his cotton pants to his silk shirt with silver buttons that jangle when he walks and embroidery curling like vines along the collar, the shoulders, the sleeves—is a shade of midnight. The hat, too, that perches on his head like a crow. He believes it fitting, given his duty this morning.

He departs his chambers and follows the staircase to the main level, his hand hissing along the railing. Many servants hurry down the marble-floored hallway framed by dark wood and festooned with oil portraits. They bunch flowers into vases. They fill lanterns with linseed oil. They climb ladders to pin streamers from the ceiling. They are getting ready for the ball, the costume party he will throw this evening, the first he has hosted since his inauguration. It will serve as an inoculation, just the dose of goodness they need, with enough liquor and water to drown in. And dressed as they will be—as swans and wolves and dragonflies and devils—they can happily pretend themselves away from their troubles and come together as a community.

The servants do not greet him. Their eyes fall and they stiffen when he moves past.

Vincent approaches and rattles off a series of questions about where he would like to set up the stage for the band, about hors d'oeuvres and drinks and any number of other things that Thomas waves away.

"I can't be bothered with that now." He has other business to attend to.

He finds Slade waiting for him outside. A hot wind stings his eyes and the sun instantly reddens his skin. A single wispy cloud dashes across the face of the sun and for a moment filters the light, making the Sanctuary go from sandy yellow to wintry gray. And then the cloud is gone and all the metal and glass seem to blaze even brighter than before.

Slade holds out the whip, coiled around his hand like something alive. Thomas takes it and his hand drops with the weight. "You're sure this is a good idea?"

"As a show of force, yes."

A pod of deputies escorts him through the Dome's gates and into the streets he has not visited for weeks. People stop to stare. No one says anything, not yet, but he can hear them muttering and can feel their eyes flaying him to the bone.

It is only a short walk to the whipping post. He is relieved to find it shadowed by the museum, some reprieve from the heat. Only a few dozen huddle around it. The news was announced this morning: a terrorist would be punished. No mention was made of Thomas's appearance—they didn't want to tempt a mob—so the crowd buzzes when he takes the platform.

A boy is chained to the whipping post. He kneels before it, his arms and body held upright by restraints, because his legs are swollen, blackened, broken from his fall. Thomas feels a twinge of pity.

Slade addresses them all. He points to the boy chained to the whipping post. The boy caught trespassing in the prison. A terrorist, Slade calls him. A terrorist who intended to release those jailed there. "He will be justly punished—by none other than our mayor."

Thomas feels their eyes on him now. They despise him, he knows. They want him dead, he knows. They want his brains dashed out, his bones broken, his eyes gouged. They would sever his head and tar it to slow the rot and parade it through the streets and cheer when the birds roosted and shat upon it. He is serving himself, of course—there is no other way to justify his baths, his clothes, his meals—but so is he serving them. He is doing the best he can. He does not punish unless someone gets in the way of his vision, the vision for which they elected him into office. Until the rains come, this is the only way they can survive, strictly. Why can't they understand that?

He hears someone call out the name Meriwether and he can't help but think, and not for the first time, this is Meriwether's Dome, this is Meriwether's city, this is Meriwether's place, not mine. He stares up at the museum—Lewis's museum—and thinks he sees a face in the window. As if his old friend has returned to mock him too. He tries to look closer but is quickly blinded by the sun cresting its roof. It spills its light like a splash of magma across the platform where he stands. The temperature spikes.

His discomfort hurries him along, reminds him of his task. With a shake of his wrist, he uncurls the whip. He will do his duty. By whipping the boy, he will whip them all. The sooner he is done with this, the sooner he can escape the heat, the sooner he can return to the Dome, the sooner he can bathe the dust and the blood from his skin, the sooner he can forget about this moment and focus on the next, the party.

The whip is heavy in his hand. Its tip looks like a frayed nerve ending. The boy twists his face to look at him, his face pinched with pain, and Thomas says, "Turn around please."

A fly lands on the boy's face, tasting the corner of his mouth, and he blows it off.

"I said turn around, boy."

"My name's Simon."

"I don't care what your name is. Turn around."

But he won't. The boy won't break eye contact. Neither will the crowd. Nor will Slade. Everyone is watching. Everyone is waiting to see what he is capable of.

———

Ella watches until she can't anymore. When the whip lashes Simon a first, a second, a third time, his body convulsing with every strike, she sinks below the window so she can't see. But she can still hear, the whip cracking, the audience gasping, Simon crying, so she covers her ears and hears then only the blood roaring inside her.

She thought she knew what anger was. She thought she was angry when Lewis left her. She thought she was angry when Slade tore out her tooth. But that wasn't anger. Anger is not yelling. True anger—the deadliest kind of anger—is the white-hot silence that defines her now.

She had someone—Simon was hers, and she his—and they took him away from her and now they will pay their debt in blood. Lewis charged her to maintain the museum. That made her an educator. She is going to exact her revenge through education.

The museum is empty but won't be for long. A crowd gathers outside. They form a line at first, but the bodies soon mash together at the door. The day is heating up. Tower tops seem to glow. The blades of turbines spin with a cutting light. People fan their faces with hats. They suck on stones to water their mouths and they spit on their fingers and dampen their wrists, their necks, anything to cool them down.

It has been a long time since the museum rotated its displays. For the past few days, the sign draped above the entry advertised a new exhibit. Simon helped her hang it there. No one knows the subject. Maybe it's war, the people say. Or maybe anatomy. Maybe electricity. They speculate, but really, they don't care. They're hungry for something new, a diversion they desperately need.

Simon remains chained to the nearby whipping post. On Slade's orders. He will be a reminder to any who think to disobey. His body is crumpled, one cheek crushed against the post. The birds and the flies feast on his body, a seething black drapery. The crowd tries not to look, but the first sweet stirrings of rot offer a constant reminder. It makes them feel as angry as it does depressed, more eager than ever to escape into the museum that will deliver them to a more prosperous, hopeful time.

A man rattles the latch and finds it unlocked. Maybe it has been all along. He creaks open the door and calls out, "Hello?" but Ella is no longer there to hear him, already deep beneath the city and roaming its tunnels with a lantern held before her. His voice echoes back at him like a greeting and he shrugs and steps inside and the rest follow.

In the exhibit hall they find a banner that reads THE RISE AND FALL OF THOMAS LANCER. The room is otherwise empty except for two stages arranged at its center. The barrenness of the space—and the echo chamber of the rotunda—makes their whispers and their footsteps carry into a sound like an army on the march.

On the first stage, which previously housed the bones of a Tyrannosaurus, there is a twenty-gallon plastic barrel set upright. The top has been peeled off to reveal the cool, clear water inside. A ladle hangs beside it. Everyone who walks by dips the ladle and takes a sip and closes their eyes, as if taking communion.

Then they read the sign set on a stand. *Harvested from the basement of the Dome. One of several thousand in storage. This afternoon Thomas Lancer is hosting a lavish party. There will be platters of food and bottles of liquor. And water tapped from barrels like this one. You were not invited.*

On the other stage sits the Judas chair. Thick wooded, with leather straps. Armored with spikes that needle the back and seat and arms of it. Empty except for a note that reads in tidy script: *Reserved for Thomas Lancer.*

Everyone files through the room, some of them silent and awed, some of them already making the noise expected of a mob. There is a third display, though few see it. It hangs from the wall next to the exit. It is labeled *The Uprising.* Beneath today's date reads a story, told in future tense, about the thousands of tired, disenchanted citizens who will take to the streets and who will storm the Dome and who will see Thomas Lancer seated in the throne he deserves before being hanged and dismembered and burned.

The people move through the museum at a slow walk, but they leave at a run.

CHAPTER 55

FOR A FEW LONG hours, Lewis and Colter are locked away in a windowless basement with mildew mucking the floor. There is no light except the gray sliver beneath the door at the top of the stairs. Lewis sits on the bottom step while Colter walks the perimeter of the room, running his hands along the walls, looking for some way out or something to aid them in escaping. "Aren't you going to do anything?"

"What is there to do?" Lewis says. "We are here. We're finally here. And now we need to understand why."

"Why?" Colter says. "I didn't come here for the *why*. I came for the *where*. I came for a place dripping with water and layered with black dirt. That's *why* enough for me."

"I came for those things too."

"And I came for you. Don't you forget that. I came for you and you better not let me down."

"I won't." He glances at the door. He has traveled these many months and thousands of miles for it to open. Aran Burr waits somewhere on the other side. "Let's hope he won't either."

Colter paces back and forth and slashes the air. After so many months of movement, he can't sit still. "They put us in a cell." There is a caged-animal quality to his voice, a desperate growl. "I'm not going to spend any more of my life in a cell."

"Just wait. We've waited this long. What's a few minutes more?" Lewis says, but Colter pushes past him, climbing the stairs, and at their top he swings his prosthetic against the steel door with a clang.

"I wouldn't do that." Lewis backs away from the staircase and says more loudly than before, "Please don't do that. They put us here because we attacked their men."

366

Colter continues to pound the door and punctuates every clang with a word: "I'm—not—going—to—spend—any—"

The door swings open and knocks Colter against the wall. He loses his footing and stumbles down the stairs and falls to the floor, where a moment later he is muscled in place by the five men who come hammering down the steps.

They wrestle with Colter, who does his best to lash his arms, kick his feet, arch his back, bite. One of the men cries out with a gash to the temple, but they soon overpower Colter, knotting his wrists and ankles.

Then one of the men—breathing heavily—turns to Lewis. His arms appear oversize, thicker and longer than legs. Weeping sores fleck his face. "Your name is Lewis Meriwether?"

"Yes."

"He's been waiting for you."

Aran Burr makes his home in the Flavel mansion, a Queen Anne with a hipped roof and a rounded wraparound porch and an iron-work veranda and a peaked three-story tower that looks down the hill and across a bay studded with fishing and crabbing boats. It is in impeccable condition, even its garden, hedged in by white roses so fat they bend their stems. Several men kneel in the garden, dead-heading flowers, ripping out weeds. They have numbers and letters burned brightly along their forearms.

Burr is seated on a patio swing. A wind chime made of wish-bones clinks in the breeze. His mouth hangs open as if he has been waiting to speak for a long time. He waves away Lewis's escort with one hand, knotted with arthritis, and then smiles a yellow-toothed smile and says, "I knew you'd come."

He wears a long white robe and he has long white hair, just as Lewis dreamed, but he otherwise looks different—terribly differ-ent. He is the oldest person Lewis has ever seen, his skin mottled and papery, his joints bent and bulging. His breath sounds like blowing sand. But it is his head that bothers Lewis most. It is twice the size it should be, most of it forehead, with veins worming through it and pulsing visibly beneath his skin. He appears not so much flesh as he does intelligence. "It's nice here."

"Is it?"

"I think you'll like it."

Despite the frailty of Burr's appearance, Lewis feels weak before him. He does his best not to show it, steadying the tremble in his voice. "Where is Gawea?"

"She's fine."

"I said *where* is she?"

"She did what she was supposed to do and got what she wanted."

"What did she want?"

"Never mind that. There are so many other things to discuss."

"Like why I'm here."

"Like why you're here. So many questions. So much to talk about." A black cane lies across his lap. He takes hold of it now and tocks the porch with its tip. Then he leans forward, rocking the swing and using its momentum to help him into a standing position. "Come." He leans heavily on the cane when he struggles across the porch and knobs the front door. "I want to show you something."

Lewis feels drawn to follow as if pulled by a wire. The wood interior gleams, freshly polished. They walk past hand-carved pillars and tiled fireplaces and ceilings busy with plaster medallions and crown molding. There are lamps in every room, with no evident wiring, but they flare when they enter and fade when they leave. The air seems to be humming.

Lewis hears the marbles long before he sees them. Maybe a hundred of them, white and colored and clear, with green and blue and red threads twisting through them, all rolling madly across the wooden floor of the room they enter. They rattle to a stop.

A boy sits in the middle of the floor with his legs folded under him. Maybe five years old. He has a cleft palate and one ear folded over like a shell. Lewis tries to recall everyone he has seen so far, every one of them marred by some deformity. The boy stares at them blankly.

"Go on, Mason." Burr's voice is like a rusted instrument blowing out notes. "Keep playing. Show us how you play."

The boy drops his eyes to the floor and once again the marbles come to life, spinning around him, clacking together. Sometimes they join in streams of color, sometimes in shapes Lewis thinks he might recognize: a bird beatings its wings, a horse galloping through a meadow, a salmon crashing upstream to die.

"Good boy, good boy, good boy." Burr brings his arthritic hands together in a pantomime of applause. He cannot turn his enormous head, so he turns his body to study Lewis. "You see? Do you understand?"

"He's like me."

"He's like you. Yes, yes. He's like Gawea. He's like *us*."

"The next."

"The next people, yes. The next America."

And then Lewis feels invaded, as if something many limbed has crawled into his head to prod at his brain. He hears Burr's voice, but a stronger and younger version, the voice from his dreams. "This country has evolved. Through revolutionary wars and civil wars, wars against terrorism, wars for racial and feminist rights. And now, as a result of the last war, the war to end all wars, it has changed again. And we're changing with it. Fins to limbs, freshwater to air breathing, lobe-finned swimmer to land-dwelling tetrapod. We are the next step."

CHAPTER 56

LEWIS AND BURR sit in two leather chairs in a library walled by books. For the past hour, they have been talking, though Lewis is unsure how much of the conversation has been spoken aloud. His head throbs with the words and images runneling through it. He knows about the altar—the Hanford nuclear site—that feeds the river, that nurtures change, genesis.

He knows, too, about Burr's father. He survived the flu, one of the few immune, but he endured a missile strike on Portland. He was on the Willamette River, out on his boat, his home, the only place he felt safe, anchored far from shore, when half the sky lit up with the trembling white of a gas flame edged blue and red where it battled the night. The concussion arrived seconds later, splitting trees like pencils, melting his skin and crisping his hair and hurling him twenty yards from the deck of his cruiser. He did not know up from down, deep in the swirl of black water, nor did he see what looked like electricity snapping and rippling across the surface— and then suddenly rolling back the way it came—because the blast burned away his vision. His eyes were thereafter sunken hollows, the lids stitched closed. But he could see. He could see things others could not. The radiation changed him, improved him.

"We're both the products of powerful men," Burr says. "My father was the beginning. He taught me and now I teach others."

The mere mention of Lewis's father makes him flinch. Would he be proud of Lewis, having traveled all this way? Or disgusted at the folly of it, putting his faith in a man he had never met, a man he had not made up his mind about, a man who simultaneously terrified and worried and awed him, a man who in many ways resembled his father.

Their conversation is interrupted by a woman appearing in the

370

doorway. She is primitively dressed in a rough brown dress, which seems at odds with the porcelain cups she carries on a silver tray. This she sets on a short table between the two chairs, and when she does, her sleeve pulls back to reveal the scarred numbers beneath.

"Thank you," Lewis says, and Burr says, "You don't need to say thank you."

The cups steam with black coffee roasted from chicory nuts.

"Why not?"

Burr gives a croaking laugh. "Because she's a slave."

The woman bows and leaves them. Lewis sips from his cup and cringes at the bitterness.

Burr holds his with two trembling hands. "Not to your liking?"

"No. It isn't." Lewis sets his cup on its tray, giving up on it. "Gawea had those same markings on her."

"She did." His enormous head shivers more than nods. "She does. I can tell that this bothers you, but if you look back, way back, on the long hoof-marked trail of human history, slaves are the standard of empire. Rome. Egypt. The Macedonians and Ottomans. The Chinese dynasties. These United States. That's how you build something big. You have to abuse some to benefit many. In this case, it's not just about power; it's about survival. We're on the brink. This could be the end. The world will keep spinning without us if we don't stake our claim. I'm the person who is making this happen. You're capable of helping me. Help me." His voice grows kind and weary. "Look at me, Lewis. I won't be around much longer. I need you."

The old Lewis might have believed him. The old Lewis, who held others in disdain, who clapped himself away in his office, who studied the world with a cold remove. But that man is gone, shed like a dark chrysalis, and the new Lewis has traveled to the horizon's rainbow edge, where he has discovered—no better word for it—a magic in himself and others.

His mind turns to Colter then, his demand that Lewis not disappoint him. As a delaying tactic, to get his head in the right place, he nods at the bookshelves and asks, "May I?"

Lewis is a scholar, after all. He is a man who reads in order to figure out how to behave. He rises and walks the length of the shelves and pulls down a book at random and cracks it open and breathes deeply. Parchment, leather, mold. He has missed this, the company of books. And they give him a confidence he lacks when fumbling around on his own. He remembers his own journal. He remembers that he is writing his own book, that *he* is authoring his own story, not this man and not anyone else.

"They're so comforting," Burr says.

"They are."

"Because they feel so fateful. In them people do things for a reason. They are following a predetermined pattern, often one established long ago by another writer, or another hundred writers, or another thousand writers, so that every story might seem unique and particular but is actually recurring, in conversation with others. That's how history works too. That's how life works. We're all characters caught in a cycle of ruin and renewal."

"That's a way of looking at it."

"There's no *way* of looking at it. It's true. We're at the beginning of a time of renewal. And you—you are one of my fateful characters."

"Hmm." Lewis closes the book and fits it back on the shelf.

"Have you read many novels?" Burr says. "I've always liked novels best. The hero comes from humble or disadvantaged circumstances. He suffers a loss or injury that presses him into a fight or quest." His coffee steams. "He gets help. From a *friend*. They push their way through a dark time. They triumph. Everything makes sense. Everything turns out for the best." He slurps loudly. "I can be that friend."

Lewis stares at him a long moment and says, "I tend to prefer nonfiction."

"Of course you do." Except for his head, Burr is so much smaller than expected. Bird boned. As if a hug could crush his ribs. Just looking at him, Lewis doesn't understand his power, his seeming command of this place. "You can read whatever you wish. The library is yours. Consider this home."

Lewis feels the words pulled from his mouth. "I would like that." He brings a hand to his mouth, too late to stop himself.

"You would. Yes, you would. To study under me. To call me your teacher."

Lewis feels something like fingers inside his mouth, his throat, making him gag, making him say, "Yes." He snaps his jaw twice, biting away the word, the sensation. "*No. No, I would not. I con-sider myself a man of science, but what you're doing here seems to go against God.*"

"What God?" Burr croaks out a laugh. "If there was a God, he made cats that play with birds before eating them. Just the same as he made stillborn babies and rapist fathers and brain tumors and viruses that make you cough your lungs inside out. There's no right and no wrong in any of that. Only the survival that comes with strength and a little bit of luck. *We're* God, Lewis. You and I. We're the gods of this time."

Again the fingers in his mouth, pinching his tongue, clawing his throat, drawing something submissive from him. But he fights back with a word, "No."

The lights blaze. Burr seems suddenly to grow larger. Lewis swears he stands, even as he plainly remains seated. "I hoped you wouldn't say that, but I expected you might need some con-vincing."

Footsteps clomp down the hallway. Two figures appear in the doorway. One of them is the man who escorted him here—the one with the arms too big for his body—and the other is a woman with her hands secured and a burlap sack over her head. She struggles against the man's grip and tries to stomp on one of his feet. He brings a fist to her stomach to quiet her. With a moan she bends in half and he rips off the sack to reveal a fiery tangle of hair. Her face is bruised, but Lewis recognizes her all the same.

"Clark!" He tries to move toward her but something invisible grips him, anchors him in place.

"She arrived two days ago by train. I've been very happy to make her acquaintance."

Lewis's face twists in several directions. He can't decide how he feels. First an ebullient giddiness. Then a lingering fury. This mellows when he realizes why she is here, how Burr hopes to use her against him. Lewis feels more and more like a marionette tugged by strings, dragged thousands of miles and now asked to dance, shaken when not compliant.

"You see, don't you?" Burr says gleefully. "You understand? You'll maybe listen a little better now?"

Lewis thinks about lying, about saying she means nothing to him, but he feels as if an eye is rolling through the corridors of his mind and he must dim the lights and close the doors on it. He removes from his mind any thoughts of Clark. In defense, he focuses all his attention instead on the grain of the wood in the floor, how much it looks like the whorl of a fingerprint. For the moment that is all he knows.

"I understand," Lewis says and he feels the eye retreat, releasing him. He realizes only then that he is crumpled on the floor, like a boneless pile of clothes.

He reaches into his pocket—his habit from long ago, when he would seek comfort in his snuffbox—and finds not a silver tin but a wooden case. The coffin-shaped one containing the vial. He transferred it there when they left their bags in the cove. He didn't want to leave it behind, thinking it too valuable and dangerous. How easy it would be to snap its top, shake its contents into the coffee cup beside him. He wonders how much time would pass before Burr began coughing, before his fever spiked. He wonders how long it would take for the infection to work its way through all of Astoria. A viral infection that would wipe away the human infection.

It is then that a thunderclap sounds, though only a few clouds spatter the sky. They all hunker down. A crack runs through the window. A book falls from the shelf. Outside, down the hill, a bloom of fire, a plume of smoke. The aftermath of a bomb. A concrete building crumbles in half, opening its dark, gaping center. The noise of the explosion lengthens as it orbits the town.

Burr has risen from his chair and stands by the window. Lewis can sense his anger, but it is momentarily directed elsewhere. "It's those goddamned women again," he says.

Now. Now would be the time. To crack the container, to twist open the vial, to dose his coffee.

Then he hears a crying. The boy stands in the doorway. The boy with the cleft palate and the marbles. His cheeks are wet with tears. He runs to Burr and clings to his leg and the old man pats him and says, "There, there. Nothing to be afraid of. Just some bugs that need to be squashed."

Boys. Girls. Men and women. The innocent and the terrible alike. If he shook out the specimen and infected Burr, this is what Lewis would be destroying. Then he would indeed be playing God. He will have to find another way.

Outside, with every passing second, the smoke blackens and thickens. Then comes a second explosion, farther away than the first, that jangles the cups on their saucers.

The wrinkles in Burr's face seem to multiply when he turns from the window. "I'm needed elsewhere. Which will give you some time to think about this," he says, with a voice with a lot of teeth in it. "Adapt. Or face extinction."

CHAPTER 57

IT WAS NEVER going to be easy. Gawea knew that. But she thought the trouble would come from hunger and thirst, storms that spit snow, sunlight that scorched, insects that stung and animals that clawed. She thought her flesh would be vulnerable, not her heart.

When they paddled the Columbia, when they followed the final artery of water that would lead them to Astoria, she hoped that she would return in more ways than one—to her home and to her original frame of mind, indifferent to her cargo. She didn't want to care about Lewis anymore. It was too hard.

The current pulled them and their paddles pulled them and Burr pulled them, and at one point she almost yelled at them to stop, turn back, but by then it was too late. The lights of Astoria glowed in the distance. She could call a snake up from its burrow or a bird down from a branch, but she could not control the guilt and the doubt twisting inside her, and on the beach she decided she could not face Lewis any longer. Before she stole off into the night, she told herself that he would be fine. If he gave in and did as he was told, if he became the old man's instrument, he would be rewarded. She would not consider the alternative.

Burr made her a promise. If she delivered Lewis to Astoria, he would give her what she has pined for all these years. Family. Her mother. This, she thought, was what she wanted. This would give her the sense of wholeness that has escaped her all her life.

When dawn comes, when she presents herself to Burr, he pets her hair and thanks her and feeds her and questions her and makes good on his promise and directs her up the bald-sculpted hill where clouds pattern the grass with fast-moving shadows. Here the Astoria column rises, with pioneers and trappers painted in a swirling mural along its length, memorializing all those who braved the way west in the hope of a better life.

Its long shadow points to a gazebo. In it she finds her mother waiting on a bench. She forgets all about Lewis then. Her feet whisper in the grass when she approaches and stands a little off to the side until her mother turns to look at her. The last time Gawea saw her, seven years ago, she clutched a baby to her breast and contorted her face in fear when a storm of wasps came pouring in the window. She looks calm now—sad but calm—acknowledging Gawea and then returning her gaze to the ocean. The salt wind blows and knocks her hair—streaked gray—around her head like tentacles. "I never thought I'd see the ocean," she says. "I've never seen anything like it."

Gawea takes a step closer. "Do you remember me?"

Her mother blinks hard, as if something bothers her eye. "I remember."

Gawea takes another step closer and another still. "They told you why you're here? They've treated you well? You look well."

She does. She is deeply tanned and furrowed with wrinkles—and her hands are so callused they appear hooved—but she is freshly bathed, wearing a pine-green dress that matches her eyes. Which makes it all the more unsettling when she takes a deep breath and asks Gawea in a calm, cool voice, "Why won't you leave me alone?"

It takes her a minute to find any words, and when she does, they're the obvious ones. "Because I want to be with you. I want us to be a family."

"I'm sorry, but I have another family now."

"You were a slave. Now you're free. I made that happen."

"They stole me away once. Now they've stolen me away again. If I'm free, then let me go back. I have children. I have a home."

"I'm your child too."

"Maybe." Her mother's eyes, her green eyes, regard her, so different from Gawea's. She is different. They are different. "But that was a long time ago. And I was another woman. I just want to forget all that. Don't you understand that it's easier to forget? It's harder to remember." She reaches out a hand for Gawea to take. Its fingernails short, its calluses rough. "You must have people who care for you. Go to them."

Her mother was different, but Lewis was like her. Gawea was like him. All this time she kept yearning for her mother, when he was more family to her, a brother beyond blood, fused by their abilities. She needed him, and right now—maybe more than ever— he needed her.

The knob and then the deadbolt lock behind Lewis and Clark, but the footsteps do not retreat. The man waits outside, guarding them, his feet shadowing the light under the door.

This is the tower of the Flavel house, an octagonal sitting room with cushioned benches. At its center, a narrow metal staircase spirals upward into another windowed peak, four stories high. Lewis goes to one of the benches and looks out across the bay, all that open space rolling off to the horizon. No fences, no walls. No fear.

Because these people are the ones to fear. He understands that now.

"I'm sorry," Clark says behind him.

"Are you?"

He has come here looking for an answer. But it is not the answer he is looking for. The present is constructed from the past. The future is predicted by the past. Virgins are hurled into volcanoes. Children are stabbed on altars. Women are burned at the stake. Natives are gifted with blankets smeared with smallpox. Africans are hunted down and chained and stuffed into the bellies of ships. Jews are marched into gas chambers, their bodies wheelbarrowed to furnaces that pump black clouds from tall chimneys. A bomb whistles from the sky and flattens a city. Planes become weapons and rip down buildings. Serbs are killed. Tutsis are killed. Hmong are killed. Homosexuals are killed. Muslims are killed. Christians are killed. The wheel of time turns. People kill people. People enslave people.

Burr is wrong. The world is not evolving. The world stays the same. The circumstances change but not the matter. The world has not destroyed itself. The world has always been destroying itself, a perpetual apocalypse. What hope is there?

He feels suddenly overcome. He has traveled all this way for *this*. He tests the window, toying with the idea of throwing himself out it, but finds it nailed shut.

Clark says, "Back at the Sanctuary, when we were ranging the Dead Lands, we sometimes came across animals. Sand wolves. Bears. Javelinas. Spiders. We were trained to never run. *Never* run. If you run, you give up your power. You face whatever it is that's dangerous. You face it, and if you need to, you fight it." Her voice chokes and she goes quiet a minute. "I forgot that. I ran away from what scared me. But I'm ready to face it now. I'm ready to fight by you again."

She appears beside him. He does not look at her directly, but sidelong, and still he sees her battered face. If she is anything, she is a fighter. She's not going to give up, not on living and not on muscling him over to her side again. "I said I'm sorry and I mean it, Lewis. I'm sorry for everything."

"What happened to the others?"

She tells him. About the hundreds of men who charged out of the fog, who swarmed the mall and overcame their defenses, who beat them and interrogated them and crushed them onto a train. The doctor—here she clears her throat and says, "Minda"—Minda did not make it, a blow to the temple cracking her skull and making her brain swell so that she cried out visions the rest of them could not see before falling into a deep sleep she never woke from.

"I think she might have loved you, you know," Lewis says.

"I know."

Clark reaches for Lewis and at first he flinches from her. Her hand pauses in the air between them and then continues and she runs her fingers across his scalp, his hair now as white and stiff as a horsehair brush. "What happened to you?" she says.

"You. You happened."

She smiles with her whole face, everything bending into an expression of warmth. "Did you ever think you'd see me again?"

"I hoped I would."

"What's going on in that head of yours?"

When he thinks about the Clark he grew up with and the Clark who stands beside him now, he might as well be staring at a mirror with a crack running through it. He sees a similar division in himself. While the Sanctuary brutalized them, the journey has humanized them. He is not the same man; she is not the same woman. To blame her for what she did would be to blame a hard-faced stranger. He would have never been capable of such a gesture before, but he takes her hand now and their fingers knit together.

Lewis blows out a sigh, and, like an echo, another explosion concusses the air.

More and more people appear in the streets. They appear frenzied, lost. They run one way, pause, and then run the next, like ants rushing out of a kicked hill. The sky is dirty with smoke. Maybe they are afraid. Maybe they should be afraid. Maybe they need a wall of their own.

"Somebody is fighting back," he says.

Clark sees him, knows the potential inside him more clearly than Burr ever could. "So are we going to join them or fucking what?"

He feels a small flash of hope once more. "I thought I came here to join something. Now I understand it's to stop something."

"That's the spirit."

He leans against the window, pressing his cheek against the cold glass, fogging it with his breath, trying to see where the latest explosion has come from.

That is when the first gull swings by, a flash of white that startles Lewis back a step. It is followed by another, this one tapping at the glass, chipping it with its beak.

He looks up and sees a flock swarming the sky, so many of them that they make the yard swim with shadows. He sees, then, in the center of the lawn, Gawea staring up at him. The gulls scream and her black eyes shine and she raises a hand to him in greeting or apology. He returns the gesture, his hand flat on the glass.

Behind them, in the hallway, there are voices. Lewis cannot hear the words but recognizes them as pitched high with anger. This is followed by the thunder of a body rolling down the stairs. A second of silence passes. The knob turns and catches and shakes.

There is a bang and the door strains against its hinges. Then another that rains splinters. Then another—and the door crashes inward and Colter steps through the storm of dust and motes of plaster. He waves them forward with his prosthetic. "Come on already. Didn't you hear me knocking?"

CHAPTER 58

THE STREETS ARE buzzing with people, but they are distracted by the explosions and give the four of them no more than a passing glance. Some wear necklaces linked with shells. Some have colored scars and pearls jeweling their noses and ears, forked beards or strange braids stiffened by egg whites. Lewis sees one man with no legs dragging himself along on a wheeled sled. Another with what appears to be a fleshy tail hanging out the back of his pants. So many have physical deformities of one kind or another, and so many more are brightened by sores and lumped with tumors.

Only one man calls out for them to stop. He reaches for the pistol at his belt. But his attention soon turns skyward, where he sees the birds, a white cloud of gulls, all screeching at once. Gawea sends them rushing down. Their white wings make the air appear stormed with windblown paper. Lewis throws up his hands, but none molest him. They concentrate on the man with the pistol, who vanishes into a cyclone of beaks and wings and webbed claws and eyes as black as those of the girl who commands them.

The gulls depart as suddenly as they arrive. They leave behind a damp, musty smell and hundreds of feathers pinwheeling the air and the body of a man with hollowed eyes and bones glimpsed through the many holes in his skin.

They hurry on, down gravel roads, past rows of houses, until they push into the moss-furred woods and then find the bay beyond. Lewis feels suddenly uncollared as he escapes the town, able to breathe better with every step he takes, distancing himself. With the dangerous attraction of Burr so close, he cannot help but think about the black hole at the heart of every galaxy, and how the biggest grow out of elliptical galaxies, where black holes merge

and become one, forming antimatter more powerful and dangerous than any other force in existence. He cannot allow himself to
be taken again.

They splash along the beach until the cliffs fall away, replaced
by sand dunes that roll into a hillside choked with rubber-leaved
salal and bony manzanita. They find a cedar with a kink of roots
hanging over a shallow gully and they settle beneath it to rest.

Lewis looks to Gawea and says, "You came back for me."

"All this time you've been following me. I decided it was time to
follow you."

"We need to find who set off those explosions. Can you help?"

She nods and looks to the sky, where the cloud of gulls spins. At
that instant they break apart and spread in every direction.

———

The sewage-treatment facility is north of Astoria, on a peninsula
that reaches like a mandible across the mouth of the Columbia.
There are massive open-air cauldrons, walled in by concrete, with
metal walkways reaching across them. This is where they find the
sisters, who dip long poles with screened scoops into the sludge beneath them and splat it into one of many five-gallon buckets they
have lined up on the walkway. Their rifles are strapped across their
broad backs, and when Lewis calls out to them, they drop the poles
and quickly arm themselves.

"I'm a friend," he says.

They do not ask him what he wants, but they do not fire either,
when he approaches them with his hands up. The rest of his party
remains below. The seagulls whirl overhead and dapple him with
shadows.

At the museum, in his office, there was a section of his desk
worn smooth and discolored from where he always rested his arm.
It was the best kind of polish, shabbied over time, earned. That is
what their faces remind him of. The women resemble each other,
broad figures, short graying haircuts that look like tweed caps set

on their heads. They both wear denim pants, canvas coats. If he didn't have a rifle pointed at his chest, he might notice more about them, but for now, one is in front, the other in back, and that is what distinguishes them.

"What do you think?" one says.

"Don't know," the other says.

"I don't think he's one of them."

"You one of them?"

"No," Lewis says.

"What about the rest of them. The ones down below?"

"They're good."

"They're good, huh?" The women look at each other. Some sort of unspoken communication seems to pass between them. "I don't know."

"Weird," the other one says. "There's something weird about you."

Lewis lowers his hands and they tense their rifles. "We want to help you," he says.

"Help us?"

"You mean you want to harvest some algae?"

He can't tell if they're joking. Everything they say comes across as a gruff bark. "You set off the explosions earlier today?"

"You bet we did."

"We blew the shit out of them."

"Well," Lewis says. "We want to help. We want to join your army."

The women laugh together, a single mean *ha*. "Army."

"No army. Just us." One of them shoulders her rifle and picks up her pole and returns to skimming the pond, glopping the buckets full.

Lewis says, "There's no one else." His words sound defeated, accusatory. He doesn't know what he imagined, but not this, two women stirring a sewer. He cannot think of anything more to say. He is all out of words. But the second woman, with her rifle now propped on her hip, is staring at him expectantly.

"Why are you harvesting algae?" he says.

"For fuel."

He looks around as though searching for an explanation.

"For our truck." She motions with the rifle. "It's parked right over there."

"You have a truck?"

"Yeah, it's right over there," says the other sister, hoisting up a dripping scoop of sludge.

CHAPTER 59

HIS GUESTS HAVE already arrived, but Thomas remains in the bath. He will make his entrance soon. His costume is a cloak made from the scales of a massive snake speared outside the wall and presented to him by the rangers as a gift. He didn't care for its rubbery meat, but the treated skin shimmers like jeweled chain mail.

For now, though, he splashes in the tub. There is nothing so pleasing as a hot bath. He immerses his head in the water and the sounds of the world muffle to a dribble and plop. The dust soaks from his skin, his every pore opens and eases the stress from him. He takes the water into his mouth, tasting the soap, tasting himself, and spurts it back out. He likes to pretend sometimes he is an infant, floating in his mother's belly, not a care in the world, every need served by the larger body hosting him.

He wants his body like an infant's too, so he asks to be shaved.

Vincent runs the razor along his cheeks, his chest, his belly, his groin. "Make me completely naked," he says.

The windows are shuttered, blinding the sun and softening the noise outside the Dome. People have been gathering outside his gates the last hour. Their chants storm the air. Their feet stomp and shake the ground. They rattle the fence with their hands. A few, he knows, have climbed over it, only to be struck down by deputies, hacked by machetes.

He chanced a look outside earlier. His grounds are a black cluster of deputies—and the gates beyond a seething throng of people. The sun was high enough then to burn every shadow from the city except the blackness held in their open mouths.

The razor scrapes the top of his thigh. The soap and hair ooze from it when Vincent splashes a handful of water. "Can't you just kill them?"

Thomas has his arms draped over the lip of the tub, his head pillowed by the rim. The rest of his body floats, suspended by Vincent's grip. "Who? Who is them? Everyone is them. We can't kill everyone." He stares at the ceiling, where steam swirls, as though an atmosphere is forming, as though this room is a world of its own.

The door knocks open and Slade barges through it and Vincent slips his razor and draws a red line across Thomas's lower belly. "What?" Thomas says at a shriek. "Can't you see we're busy?"

Slade pulls a towel off a hook and stands at the foot of the tub with it bunched in one hand. "Get out."

"I'm not done."

Slade goes to the windows and rips open the shutters and the sunlight shocks the room. The noise outside—the screaming, the chanting—grows fiercer.

Thomas rises from the tub, not yet shaved entirely, one of his legs hairy, the other pink and clean. He pats himself down with the towel and presses it hard against the razor slash, and the blood petals through the threading of the towel.

"Party's over," Slade says. "The gates have been breached."

The guests are racing up the stairs as they race down. One has jewels encrusting her eyebrows. Another wears a dress of white feathers. Another is painted with swirling gold designs, maybe costumed as a sandstorm. They flail their arms and trip their feet, scurrying past, leaving behind tables stacked high with desserts, a stage empty except for its instruments. Broken glass and broken plates glitter the floor. Thomas wears only a robe, no shoes, and he bloodies his feet on a glass shard and cries out and sits down to nurse it, only to be snatched up by Slade and shoved down a hallway. "Hurry up, you fool."

The air shakes with footsteps and screams. Thomas gets a glimpse of the rotunda, a mess of deputies bullied back by the tide of people surging forward, not pausing at the machetes that come down on them. They swing bricks and boards and pipes and fists, whatever they might make into a weapon. A glimpse is all he gets. Slade jostles him through a door, the door to the basement, instructing him to escape through the sewer.

"And then what?" Thomas hates the way his voice sounds, like one more broken glass.

"Then you live."

With that Slade slams the door and leaves him in a darkness broken only by the lantern dangling from a nearby hook. He carries its glow down the stairs, limping with every step, his cut heel leaving behind bursts of blood.

He enters an open room full of coffins, the graves of the ruling class. He stumbles on his sore heel and rams into one and knocks it over and the lid opens and spills out a body with dust puffing from its open mouth. The body of Mayor Meriwether, his predecessor, Lewis's father. His yellowed teeth seem to be grinning at Thomas. "No," Thomas says and hurries away and knocks over three more coffins before he makes it through the doorway opposite him.

He enters the storage room stacked high with water barrels. The flame of his lantern partners the feeling inside him, a flaring of light in the face of impossible darkness. His hair remains wet from his bath and deep beneath the Dome he actually feels chilled.

He searches the room until he finds what he is looking for, the square black grate cut into the floor. He kneels and yanks at it. Then yanks again. And again. It barely moves, rattling in place. At first he believes it rusted shut. Then he spies the chain wrapped around its grating. He yanks and yanks and then a shiver runs through him and he says, "No, no, no."

He can hear thumping above, feet pounding the floor, fists pounding doors. It is only a matter of time before they find him. He stands and feels the sharpness in his heel at the same time that he feels a sharpness at his back.

He spins around. He does not realize how deeply he has been stabbed until he sees the knife, a black blade, bloodied all the way to its hilt. His wife holds it in her hand, and as he turns to face her, she plunges it once more into his chest.

He hardly recognizes her. Her white hair is hidden beneath a wrap. Instead of a silk dress she wears denim pants, a brown shirt made of some coarse fabric. She looks ready for the streets. He almost says something to mock her, but blood gurgles from his mouth in the place of words.

He lurches toward her and she shoves him back and he wilts against a stack of barrels. One of them tips and falls with him to the floor. Its top cracks open. The water *glugs* from it, spilling across the floor, splashing his face. It feels good. It feels cleansing. He closes his eyes. He listens to his heartbeat, so fast at first like the footsteps drumming all through the Dome, and then slower, and then silent.

CHAPTER 60

BURR HAS A good view from the Flavel house. Way up high on a hill, he can see so much of his city and the bay beyond. He stands at an open window in the library. Lewis has escaped him but not for long. He can feel him out there, not far away. He will find him. He will seduce him and humble him and teach him. Once taught, he will be made into something wonderful, a great tool. He, like everyone else, will become an extension of Burr, a million-limbed monster.

This will of course take time. Burr must be gentler—must not present everything in such a forceful rush. He was just so excited, and when Lewis resisted him, Burr could not help but reduce him to a mewling ball. He has dreamed a thousand times what they might accomplish together, so that the future feels like the present, their relationship already under way. It is difficult, courting a person you believe belongs to you. Burr must be patient, must keep in mind his need for Lewis. He has, after all, no sons or daughters. He has tried to cultivate some unnaturally, exposing pregnant slaves to high doses of radiation, hoping for something radiant, not flippered or cleft lipped or turned inside out, but gifted, special, someone who can carry on, inherit what he has built so far. That is immortality. And though he has his students—Gawea among them—none have the same potential as Lewis. He is the next.

Everything will be all right. He is certain of this, even with the smoke rising from the bombed sections of his city. They will re-build, as they have rebuilt before, and they will exterminate those who threaten them, and they will continue to manufacture, to claim, to grow.

There was a time, when he was out on a jetty, the seals and sea lions sunbathing on the rocks or bobbing in the water all around him, when a shark surfaced. Its fin cut the waves. Its eyes rolled over white. It showed its fleshy gums, a smile of a thousand teeth, and then bit down, tearing into a seal, biting again, drawing it deeper inside its mouth. Bubbles frothed white and red when the shark descended. For minutes afterward, Burr shook with fright and awe. There were certain things in the world that could do that to you. You crossed paths with them, even if only for a moment, and they infected you, made your body shake with dark energy.

Objects could have that same power. A nail from the cross. The throne of Charlemagne. The diary of a young Jewish girl. The looped video of the Twin Towers collapsing, replaced by ashen pillars. That is the purpose of a museum—a power plant full of receptacles that can enhance people even glancingly. Lewis has that same power, and Burr has felt it out there for a long time, floating in the dark sea of the world, and it has been borne to him by current, and he would have it, and when he did, others would tremble as he once did, mesmerized by the red wake of the shark. He commands the Northwest now, the country soon. But he is not merely interested in power; he is interested in the larger permanence of humanity. Sometimes a single person comes along and changes history. It is a position that requires more than grand intelligence, but detachment and ruthlessness, the utilitarian ability to hurt others as a way of helping others. He is that person. Lewis will be that person. And their names will become so important that they will never expire so long as humans retain their foothold on the world.

Burr smiles, but his attention is distracted by a bird. He sees it circling above the house and then dropping to his open window, a flash in the air before him. A tiny owl. Its wings creak and its beak twitters. On instinct he holds out his hands to accept it and it lands heavily in the cup of them. Its feathers are cold to the touch, made of metal.

It is then he smells the smoke. It is then he sees the spitting fuse trailing it like a kite's string. Before he can drop it or hurl it aside, the black powder encased in its hollow breast ignites and transforms the library into a white oblivion.

CHAPTER 61

SLADE UNBELTS his machete and swings his way through the throng of rioters, severing a hand, splitting a face, opening up a throat to a geyser of blood, and though he is outnumbered many times over, everyone flinches away from him. In that way, he still owns them, so long as he does not reveal the fear taking wing inside him.

He crashes out of the Dome and through its fallen gates into sunlight so bright he throws up an arm to shade his eyes. For a full minute he runs at a dead sprint, not going anywhere, aiming himself away from the crowds. He trips twice and skins his knees badly but refuses to cry out. Then, in alley empty of anything but shadows, he chokes for breath and orients himself.

The wall cuts into the too-blue sky. Smoke ribbons from burned buildings. A dog pants in the shade of an alley. A jingle cart rolls by. Otherwise the city seems empty. But he can hear a distant roar, the noise many angry voices take on when in chorus.

The man pulling the jingle cart wears a floppy brown hat that looks like it has been torn in half and sewn back together again. He pauses and calls to Slade, "Candies, medicines!" and then he sees the blood-painted machete and lets go of the cart and it rolls a yard before going still.

Slade tracks his way through a city that no longer belongs to him. A low-hanging awning tears his hat from his head. His knees feel wasp stung. He tries not to think about what will happen next, tries to focus only on returning to the place he feels safest.

He finds the police station empty, even the cells beneath. A desk overturned. A door ripped from its hinges. The occasional body slumped in a corner or sprawled on the floor with a knee bent strangely. When he calls out, his voice swirls down the hallways like water down a drain. The noise continues to rage outside, and he hurries to the dark nook in the basement he calls home.

He latches shut the door and leans his forehead against it and feels some sense of peace cooling him. He has separated himself, shuttered away the sun and the noise, in what feels an impenetrable nest. He rattles the dangling chains and makes music of them. He walks among his mannequins, his favorites, reassured by their company. Here he remains powerful. He strokes an arm, grazes a cheek, before finding his bed.

He sits at its edge, crushing the mattress with his weight. The metal frame protests and his sigh sounds similar—when it rises into a shriek. Because of the pain at his ankles. First one, then the other. A sharp slice followed by a hot flood of blood.

He tries to stand but cannot. His legs won't work. He tumbles to the floor and barely throws out his hands in time to catch himself. He crabs his way forward, escaping whatever has injured him. He twists around to see her sliding from beneath the bed and then standing still among his mannequins, shoulder to shoulder with her own.

She is here. She is his at last. His Ella. His fierce, beautiful girl.

She tosses aside the scalpel, one of his own tools, used to slash and sever his tendons.

He smiles—he cannot help himself—but she does not smile back. Her face is grim when she hefts the baseball bat, testing its weight, knotting her fingers around the grip. "Remember what you taught me about terror?" she says. "You were wrong. Love wins."

CHAPTER 62

WHEN THE SISTERS show Lewis their stores of black powder, he knows what to do. He kisses his owl before sending it to the skies one last time.

So many minutes later, he feels something shift. Like a lantern extinguished or a vise released in his mind. And he senses it is done. Burr is dead. He wonders how many others suddenly feel the same, how strong and wide the grip of this one man. Lewis understands that once the queen bee of a hive dies, there is another to take her place, but for now he has done what he can. He has bet on humanity.

This is why he walks to a cliff overlooking the place where the river meets the ocean. He watches the currents mash together, a foamy roiling. Waves boom and turn over endlessly. The wind bites him with sand and dampens him with salt spray. He reaches into his pocket and removes the coffin-shaped box and opens it and fingers out the vial and grips it in his palm. He cannot help but hesitate, debate whether he should open it up, snort its contents, make himself into a human missile and take out the rest of the human population. Destroy what destroys.

Isn't the world better off without people? There is a balance—trees make a mess that fire cleans; rain extinguishes fire and swells green shoots from the ground; a deer eats the grass, then dies and rots into the dirt from which trees grow to make a mess—a balance that everything but man and virus acknowledge.

Then he hears some laughter in the distance, Clark delighting in something small, maybe a joke told or a grasshopper caught in her hair or the sun slanting through the clouds. That is all the convincing he needs. A hard woman giving herself up to joy. For a long time Lewis has felt overwhelmed by immensity—the measurable immensity of time and distance, as he rode and hiked and paddled so many thousands of miles over hundreds of days, and the incalculable immensity that can exist between people who betray or grieve or hate each other. And when he considers all the places he has traveled and dangers surmounted and people encountered and words written over the past few months, he feels overcome, vertiginous, swept away. It is the laughter that brings him back, makes him feel anchored. He is connected to Gawea, just as he is connected to Clark, a kind of family, the beginning of the community and renewal he imagined he might find here all along. There is hope after all. Life might be a catastrophe, but it is a beautiful catastrophe.

He cocks his arm and pitches the vial out. Once exposed to the air, the virus should expire within minutes. Far below, it bursts on some rocks, a glassy dust that sparkles. The river dimples and swallows its remains, one more pollutant.

"What was that?" A voice behind him, Clark's.

"The end of the world."

They walk back together. The sun hangs over the ocean and the moon hangs over the coastal mountains, as if in an uneasy truce. In the cracked parking lot of the sewage-treatment facility, the sisters stand beside their idling truck, the doors of it open. They heft something from the rear cab, what turns out to be a shortwave radio, and plunk it on the front seat and plug it into the cigarette lighter. It sparks out a puff of smoke they wave away.

One of them settles into the seat beside the radio and aims the antenna at the sky and fiddles with the frequency and begins a transmission. "Sam and Olivia Field sending report. Is anyone there? Is anyone there? Is anyone there? Over."

The other leans one arm against the open door, turning when she notices Lewis leaning in to watch them.

"Moon's out," she says. "She's trying for a moon bounce."

"Sam and Olivia Field sending report. Is anyone there? I repeat, is anyone there? Over."

Lewis has been awake for two days. He feels too numb and exhausted to talk, to process what he sees. He can manage a small question, "Which one of you is Olivia?"

She stabs her chest with a thumb. "That's me."

"I'm sorry. I should have asked you that before."

She shrugs.

"It's a pretty name."

Sam speaks into the radio again, waits, hears no response except the pop and buzz of static.

The wind rises and Lewis wavers where he stands. "I don't understand. Who is she speaking to?"

"Boss."

"Who—who do you work for?"

"The government. We work for the government." She says this as though she is talking about what they should expect for weather or what they might cook for dinner.

"What?" Lewis gives a short laugh. "What government?"

"The American government."

He looks at her a moment to see if she is joking. The flat expression on her face tells him she is not.

"You never asked," she says and uncrosses her arms and peels back one of her sleeves to reveal on her biceps a tattoo—an American flag inked in black.

EPILOGUE

WASHINGTON, D.C., is a swamp. The streets are sluggish rivers, the buildings mossy canyons, negotiated by rafts and canoes and johnboats. Mosquitoes dirty the air with their humming swarms. Through the muck walk egrets on stilted legs. Alligators laze on the steps of the Smithsonian. The monument is a broken fang rising from a lake. The rafters and arches of every memorial are busy with the nests of thrashers and waxwings. The dome of the Capitol has cracked open like a hatched egg. Everything smells of crushed earthworms. Night is falling. Balls of blue fire burn, pockets of swamp gas begin to glow. So do the lamplit windows of the White House, though it is hardly white, vined and ridden with algae and bearded with moss. A turbine spins on its roof. Its blades groan up to speed as the wind rises.

Thunder mutters. A storm is coming. A storm is always coming, with hurricanes whirling off the Atlantic every other week. Rain speckles the water, then thickens, lashing at the windows. In one of them, a man looks up, though he can see nothing but his reflection. A black face against a black window. His beard, gouged by a meaty scar, is beginning to gray. He is shirtless and has a bit of a paunch, noticeable only when he is sitting. But his chest and shoulders are round with muscle. Sweat beads on his skin, drips down his back like the rain down the window.

This is a bedroom that doubles as an office. A four-poster bed rises beside the wooden desk where he sits in an orange circle of light thrown by a lamp. There is an inkpot, a pile of paper, books, a shortwave radio. He fiddles with the knobs, scratching through frequencies, settling now and then on voices that sometimes speak English and sometimes languages he does not recognize. He needs no translator to recognize the occasional panic and anger in their words.

There is a knock at the door, and when he does not respond to it, another knock follows, and when he does not respond to this, the door opens. A face peeks through, brown skinned, bald headed. Monroe, his valet. He wears a pocketed vest over a collared shirt. "Mr. President?"

He does not turn. His naked back carries an American flag tattoo across its shoulders. It is inked in black and broken by wormy scars.

"They're waiting for you, sir."

The door closes. He continues to listen for another minute, channeling between silence and voices. Lightning forks the sky outside, and the thunder that follows shakes the windows and fuzzes the radio. He snaps off the volume and rises from his desk and pulls on a shirt and begins to button it.

The room is walled with bookshelves and anchored by a long table made from rough-hewn pine. Around it sits his Cabinet, a small, bug-eyed woman, a man with a tumor bulging redly from his neck, a brown-bearded man missing a thumb, and a black woman with a gray nimbus of hair. They stand when he enters and then tuck their bodies back into their chairs when he motions for them to sit. He takes a chair at the head of the table and it groans beneath his weight.

An enormous map sits at the center of the table. It has been torn into many pieces and fitted together again to create a warped representation of the country. Water stained. Rimed with mold. The Midwest and Southwest are shaded a poisonous yellow. The Plains white. The Northwest green. The South, ranging from Texas to North Carolina, a watery blue. So many sections are surrounded by red circles indicating an uninhabitable blast zone, the biggest of them corralling the entire East Coast.

They motion to the map when they speak, talking about hazards and possibilities, a railroad line reconstructed here, a community built around a coal mine there. There are black Xs and red Xs sketched throughout the West, and there are skulls drawn on several states in the South, and the Cabinet members stab their fingers at these when they talk about rising threats.

All this time, the man they call president says nothing, his posture stiff and his hands balled on the table before him. His eyes flit from speaker to speaker, the only indication he is listening. There is one window with a crack running across it that weeps rain. Every now and then it goes blue-white with lightning. The room shivers with thunder and the lights sputter on and off.

The room goes quiet when something crashes in the hallway. Voices call out. There is a hurried knock at the door that does not wait for an invitation. Monroe enters backward, nearly falling. He is being kicked at by a hooded figure braced by two guards. A voice—a woman's voice—curses them, says she'll stomp their mouths, make a necklace of their teeth. Four more guards follow, clutching two other hooded figures, though these stand quietly and make no move against them.

Monroe brushes off his vest and says, "We found them outside." He begins to say something more, but thunder crashes and steals away his words.

The guards pull off their hoods. The woman, Clark, wears her red hair short around her ears. She looks wildly around the room and tries to rip her arms away from the guards, but they only grip her more tightly. Gawea regards them with black eyes that reflect the astonished expressions of those in the room. Lewis is white haired and clean-shaven, and though he keeps his eyes steady on the president, he tells Clark to settle down and says in a cool voice that they mean no harm and need not be detained.

One of the guards says, "This is what they had on them." He clunks onto the table three holstered belts, each carrying two long-nosed revolvers. Then three more rifles. "And this." A metallic bird, golden and no bigger than an infant, built in the shape of an eagle. He sets it on its side and it does not move, except for an aperture widening in one of its glass eyes.

Monroe stands by the president now. He leans in and speaks at a whisper everyone can hear, "They said you would want to see them. They said they came a long way to speak to you."

The president rises from his chair. He walks slowly, his footsteps thudding, and as he does the windows again blaze with lightning followed instantly by thunder. He does not keep his distance but stops within arm's reach of Lewis, who asks, "Are you President Jefferson?"

His voice is like a rockslide. "What do you want?"

Outside the thunder crashes again. Lewis opens his hands and wires of electricity dance between his fingers. When he speaks, Clark and Gawea speak with him, their voices the same. "We're here to help."

ACKNOWLEDGMENTS

Thanks to my agent, Katherine Fausset, for her wisdom and friendship and muscle and savvy. Thanks, too, to the rest of the gang at Curtis Brown, especially Holly Frederick.

I am eternally grateful to Helen Atsma at Grand Central and Oliver Johnson at Hodder. Due to their editorial vision and encouragement, this novel transformed dramatically from first to final draft. Thank you for riding into battle with me again.

Thanks to Sonya Cheuse, the best publicist in the biz, and everyone else at Hachette (in the US and UK) who make publishing a book so much fun: Brian McLendon, Allyson Rudolph, Jamie Raab, Marissa Sangiacomo, Kerry Hood, Anne Perry.

A short section of this novel originally appeared in *Ploughshares*— thanks for the showcase.

Thanks to William Souder, Dan Hernandez, Jeremy Solin, for their help with environmental research. And I'm indebted to books like Alan Weisman's *The World Without Us* for helping me understand the science of the apocalypse. The Kingkiller Chronicle series by Patrick Rothfuss made me fall in love with fantasy again, and I owe him a debt of gratitude for that and for his intricate magic systems, which influenced my own clumsy attempts at spellbinding.

And finally, thanks to my wife for her unending love and patience and good-heartedness and support.

ABOUT THE AUTHOR

BENJAMIN PERCY has won a Whiting Writers' Award, a Plimpton Prize, two Pushcart Prizes, and a grant from the National Endowment for the Arts. He is a contributing editor at *Esquire* and the author of two other novels, *Red Moon* (also available from Grand Central Publishing) and *The Wilding*, as well as two short story collections, *Refresh, Refresh*, and *The Language of Elk* (available as an e-book from Grand Central Publishing). He lives in Minnesota with his family. For more information, you can visit www.BenjaminPercy.com.

Do you wish this wasn't the end?

Join us at www.hodder.co.uk, or follow us on
Twitter @hodderbooks to be a part of our community
of people who love the very best in books and reading.

Whether you want to discover more about a book
or an author, watch trailers and interviews, have the
chance to win early limited editions, or simply browse
our expert readers' selection of the very best books,
we think you'll find what you're looking for.

And if you don't,
that's the place to tell us what's missing.

We love what we do, and we'd love you to be part of it.

www.hodder.co.uk

@hodderbooks

HodderBooks

HodderBooks